AUTOBIOGRAPHY
and
DELIVERANCE

THE VICTORIAN LIBRARY

AUTOBIOGRAPHY
and
DELIVERANCE

MARK RUTHERFORD

WITH AN INTRODUCTION BY
BASIL WILLEY

NEW YORK: HUMANITIES PRESS
LEICESTER UNIVERSITY PRESS
1969

'Autobiography' first published in 1881
'Deliverance' first published in 1885
Second edition of both works published in 1888
Victorian Library edition (reprinting 1888 text)
published in 1969 by
Leicester University Press

Distributed in North America by
Humanities Press Inc., New York

Printed in Great Britain by
Unwin Brothers Limited, Old Woking, Surrey
Introduction set in Monotype Modern Extended 7

SBN 7185 5000 5

THE VICTORIAN LIBRARY

There is a growing demand for the classics of Victorian literature in many fields, in history, in literature, in sociology and economics, in the natural sciences. Hitherto this demand has been met, in the main, from the second-hand market. But the prices of second-hand books are rising sharply, and the supply of them is very uncertain. It is the object of this series, THE VICTORIAN LIBRARY, to make some of these classics available again, at a reasonable cost. Since most of the volumes in it are reprinted photographically from the first edition, or another chosen because it has some special value, an accurate text is ensured. Each work carries a substantial introduction, by a well-known authority on the author or his subject, and a bibliographical note on the text. The volumes necessarily vary in size, but they appear in a uniform binding.

INTRODUCTION

To reprint Mark Rutherford today is no mere act of scholarly piety or curiosity: it is to bring back into circulation a writer of first-rate and unique excellence whose quality, repeatedly acknowledged by discerning critics, is likely now to be more widely appreciated than ever. William Hale White (1831–1913: his pseudonym "Mark Rutherford", like that of Marian Evans—"George Eliot" —has replaced his own name in popular usage) has been called a "neglected genius"; yet a writer who was highly praised by André Gide, Middleton Murry, Joseph Conrad and D. H. Lawrence cannot be said to have been overlooked. And, apart from such earlier appraisals as those of W. Robertson Nicoll and H. W. Massingham, we have had in more recent years at least three full-length monographs: *The Religion and Art of William Hale White* (Stanford, 1954), by Wilfred Stone; *Mark Rutherford, A Biography* (1955), by Catherine M. Maclean; and *William Hale White, A Critical Study*, with a Foreword by Lionel Trilling (George Allen and Unwin, 1956), by Irvin Stock. No one who has lived with the Mark Rutherford "novels", and with Hale White's Journals and other writings, can doubt that he deserves the attention of such critics and of all serious readers. He belongs to that small central group of writers who leave a permanent mark on all who have confronted them.

I have put inverted commas round the word "novels" because Mark Rutherford's *Autobiography* (1881) and *Deliverance* (1885), though they contain fiction, are only novels in a very special sense. His later books, *The Revolution in Tanner's Lane* (1887), *Miriam's Schooling* (1890), *Catherine Furze* (1893) and *Clara Hopgood* (1896), are undoubtedly novels. Yet all these, together with his short stories, journals and literary criticism, derive their main strength from the same source as the *Autobiography* and *Deliverance*: they are all phases of spiritual autobiography, variations on one theme or a group of related themes, stages in a nineteenth-century Pilgrim's Progress. They are tracts for the times; they teach (in Christopher Smart's phrase) "th'important lesson how to live"—more specifically, how to achieve self-mastery and how to confront the mystery of life in an age of dissolving creeds. Yet they are as far removed as possible from all that is merely dry or didactic; they have no designs upon us. Mark Rutherford is not trying to edify or convert us. Though his books have the force and much more than the usual value of sermons, and though they abound in spiritual commentary, they do not wheedle or attempt to proselytise. Mark Rutherford is no apologist either for orthodoxy or for heresy; he proclaims no gospel. He merely records, in accents whose low pitch and austere restraint only just conceal the underlying passion, some incidents of his own passage through the Slough of Despond and the Valley of Humiliation. His books belong to the confessional tradition; far from being manufactured for literary effect, they have been forced from him by "bitter constraint and sad occasion dear". There is nothing in them that has not been felt, pondered and proved upon the pulses.

The Bunyan allusions I have just made were not brought in at random, for there was real spiritual kinship between these two Bedford men. Hale White was not only a Puritan by birth and upbringing, and a member of the Bunyan Meeting, but he knew at first hand the terrors, despairs and momentary exaltations of Christian's pilgrimage; and many of the vicissitudes described by Bunyan in *Grace Abounding* re-appear, translated into psychological idiom, in Mark Rutherford. What in Bunyan appears as conviction of sin, or despair about his personal election, becomes in Mark Rutherford nervous gloom, depression and self-distrust. The darts of Apollyon are modernised into "the fang of some monomaniacal idea". The chief difference between them is the difference between their centuries; in the middle and later years of the nineteenth century Puritanism had lost its old heroic tone, and east winds, not felt by Bunyan, were blowing across from Germany.

It may seem strange that mid-nineteenth-century Bedford, so untroubled in its puritan respectability, should have become the City of Destruction for a member of its innermost ring of initiates—the Bunyan Meeting. Yet this, as we know, is how the dialectic of history often works; and the young Hale White absolutely had to flee from the Meeting House in order to save his own soul. But not before he had so deeply breathed its spirit, and so carefully marked its outward lineaments, that he

could later become, of all our novelists, the best inter-
preter of the provincial nonconformity of his time. It is
from this world that he derives most of his richest material
as a novelist, and nobody—not even George Eliot or
Arnold Bennett—has etched more sharply some of its
characters or traced more subtly the filaments linking
its various levels, spiritual and social, into an ordered
hierarchy. Some of the best examples of his art are to be
found in the descriptions of "Eastthorpe" in *Catherine
Furze* and "Cowfold" in *The Revolution in Tanner's
Lane* (both recognizably memories of the Bedford of his
youth). In *Catherine Furze,* for example, Mrs Furze
urges her ironmonger husband to begin climbing the
social ladder by removing from his shop (where up to
1840 he, like the other tradesmen, had lived) to the
more respectable "Terrace", to which the doctor, the
brewer and the grocer had already risen:

"Your connection is extending and you want more room.
Now, why should you not move to the Terrace? If we were
to go there, Catherine would be withdrawn from the society
in which she at present mixes. . . . I believe, too, that if we
were in the Terrace Mrs Colston would call on us. As the
wife of the brewer, she cannot do so now. Then there is just
another thing which has been on my mind for a long time.
It is settled that Mr Jennings [Independent Minister] is
to leave, for he has accepted an invitation from the cause at
Ely. I do not think we shall like anybody after Mr Jennings,
and it would be a good opportunity for us to exchange the
chapel for the church. We have attended the chapel regularly, but I have always felt a kind of prejudice there against
us, or at least against myself, and there is no denying that
the people who go to church are vastly more genteel, and
so are the service and everything about it—the vespers—
the bells—somehow there is a respectability in it."

And this is not all; quietly, almost without raising his voice, Hale White can universalise the scene, adding an imaginative dimension which embraces both landscape and history:

The malthouses and their cowls, the wharves and the gaily painted sailing barges alongside, the fringe of slanting willows turning the silver-grey sides of their foliage towards the breeze, . . . the large expanse of sky, the soft clouds distinct in form almost to the far distant horizon, and, looking eastwards, the illimitable distance towards the fens and the sea. . . .

Such was Eastthorpe. For hundreds of years had the shadow of St Mary's swept slowly over the roofs underneath it, and, of all those years, scarcely a line of its history survived, save what was written in the churchyard or in the church registers.

In the *Autobiography* and *Deliverance*, where introspection and reflexion bulk more largely, there is less of the novelist's art to be found. But even here satire and imaginative expansions recur frequently. An example of the first is the ineffable Mr Snale, draper, and deacon at the Water Lane chapel where Mark Rutherford had his first ministry. He it was who warned the minister against reading aloud *The Vicar of Wakefield* at a Dorcas meeting: " 'Because, you know, Mr Rutherford,' he said, with his smirk, 'the company is mixed; there are young leedies present, and *perhaps*, Mr Rutherford, a book with a more requisite tone might be more suitable on such an occasion.' " Later the same hypocrite (a more lifelike character than Chadband) rejects George Fox's Journal as alternative reading, because " 'although Mr Fox might be a very good man, and was a converted character, yet he did not, you know, Mr Rutherford, belong to us.' " Examples of the visionary power are the pictures in *The Deliverance* of London gloom on Sunday afternoons, "more especially about Goodge Street"; of the appalling slum life of Drury Lane; and (in a very different key) of Hastings and the English Channel on a summer's day outing, and of the North Downs in autumn.

Hale White called "Mark Rutherford" a "victim of the century", and in so doing drew attention to his symbolic and representative quality. He stands for the Puritan, who, emancipated by Wordsworth, Carlyle, German biblical criticism and the many other solvents offered by the *zeitgeist*, has thrown off his Hebrew Old Clothes, left the Meeting House, rejected orthodox Christianity, and ventured on a lonely quest for God in the starry heavens or in the moral law within. In all this, though not in every biographical detail, "Mark Rutherford" is Hale White himself. The accounts of Mark's strict upbringing, of his boyhood's exposure to the influences of home and chapel, of his unreal "conversion", and of his attendance at the theological Training College, are all straight autobiography. In this early part of the story he is almost purely destructive; the boy was nearly asphyxiated by the stuffy atmosphere, physical and spiritual, of the Calvinistic Independent Chapel; his "conversion" was a pure formality, and the teaching at the College narrow and unawakened. "It was a time", he says, "in which the world outside was seething with the ferment which had been cast into it by Germany and by those in England whom Germany had influenced, but not a fragment of it had dropped within our walls." The young Hale White was in fact expelled from New College (London), together with two others, for asking questions about the authenticity and "inspiration" of some of the biblical books ("not an open question within these walls"), and for failing to satisfy the College authorities in the ensuing interrogation. In the *Autobiography* Mark Rutherford becomes a minister, whereas Hale White never did—though he preached occasionally in his early manhood at Ditchling Unitarian chapel. The sermons summarised in the *Autobiography* are probably based upon discourses actually given in College days and at Ditchling; they, and the chilling reception they encountered, have the ring of authenticity. After the first of these the President of the College, who had been listening, rebuked him for expecting some exercise of thought from his hearers, and for not having been content with merely repeating " 'the old story of which, Mr Rutherford, you know, we never ought to get weary.' " After a sermon at Water Lane "I went down into the vestry. Nobody came near me but my landlord, the chapel-keeper, who said it was raining, and immediately went away to put out the lights and shut up the building." And after the morning sermon at Ditchling his Unitarian host entertained him in a manner even more dispiriting, offering him potatoes *or* cabbage with his cold mutton, and then going to sleep till the afternoon service. The sermons themselves show clearly how his mind and soul were developing. Convinced that the accepted formulae "had once had a natural origin in the necessities of human nature", he tried to reach through to their original meaning, and thus to connect them with

something he and his hearers had felt and known. "But
it was precisely this reaching after a meaning which
constituted heresy"; as when, in speaking of the Crucifixion, he said that "the innocent had everywhere and
in all time to suffer for the guilty", and that "the atonement, and what it accomplished for man, were therefore
a sublime summing up as it were of what sublime men
have to do for their race". Eventually Mark Rutherford
gave up in despair the attempt to breathe new life into
moribund beliefs and petrified conventicles. Finding that
he could no longer go on using the time-worn phrases in
a sense quite other than that which his hearers would
accept or suppose, he went to London and, after a brief
and traumatic experience as a school-teacher, fell back
on literary hack-work and journalism. This part of
Mark Rutherford's story is again close to Hale White's
own; Wollaston, the publisher of free-thinking books,
represents John Chapman, under whom Hale White
served for a while, and Wollaston's "niece" Theresa
was in fact Marian Evans, who befriended him and won
his heart. This friendship with a truly kindred spirit
might have enriched his life, but he was morbidly
diffident and (as he says in the *Early Life*, written at the
age of 78), "it is a lasting sorrow to me that I allowed my
friendship with her to drop, and that after I left Chapman
I never called on her. She was then unknown, except to
a few friends, but I did know what she was worth."
George Eliot was dead before the Mark Rutherford books
began to appear; had she read them, she would have
recognised their affinity with her own.

The second part of the autobiography is called *The*

Deliverance of Mark Rutherford, but why? Deliverance from what? He was already emancipated from Bedford and its creed before the end of the *Autobiography*, and the second part is not warmed by any sense of final liberation from the ills that dogged him to the end: loneliness, self-distrust, nervous obsessions, speculative doubts, unsatisfied love. "What are the facts?" he wrote towards the end of his life. "Not those in Homer, Shakespeare, or even the Bible. The facts for most of us are a dark street, crowds, hurry, commonplaceness, loneliness, and, worse than all, a terrible doubt which can hardly be named as to the meaning and purpose of the world" (*Last Pages from a Journal*, pp. 289–90). So his "deliverance" remained incomplete to the end. From himself he could never be delivered, though in the very sunset of his life a second marriage brought him nearer to liberation than had ever seemed possible.

To say what Mark Rutherford's "deliverance" meant is to explain the faith by which he came to live, and to which he learnt how to hang on "with claws". First of all it was a belief in God—not the God of the churches, who had "hardened into an idol", but a living spirit variously felt as Wordsworth's "God of the hills"; or as Spinoza's Supreme Being; or as Job's Yahweh who has made Behemoth and Leviathan as well as Orion and the Pleiades. Hale White had pondered all the stock topics and arguments of unbelief; the conversation between Mark Rutherford and Edward Gibbon Mardon (in *The Autobiography*) is a dialogue between two sides of his own mind; and the cheap sneers of the Bradlaugh-type atheist at the "freethinking hall" (in *The Deliverance*)·

show his familiarity with this line of satire. Hale White
was searching for God all his life, and could never have
rested in mere negation. His deliverance, then, was
brought about partly by his learning how to return upon
himself, negating his own former negations in a positive
credo which included the central truth of both sides. Thus,
immediately after recalling his boyhood misery in the
Meeting House, the hypocrisy of the chapel prayers and
the futility of the sermons, he checks himself to record
two priceless lessons taught by his religious upbringing:
regard for truth, and regard for purity of life; the latter
he calls "a simply incalculable gain". He came to see
all religions as expressions of the human need for reconciliation with God, the need for self-conquest, for self-
forgetfulness, for repentance and a loving heart. In the
course of his thinking he reached insights which are
often now, quite absurdly, thought to be "contempo-
rary": "God was obviously not a person in the clouds",
and the whole creation was riven across by contradictions.
"On the one hand was infinite misery; on the other there
were exquisite adaptations producing the highest
pleasure: on the one hand the mystery of life-long
disease, and on the other the equal mystery of the
unspeakable glory of the sunrise on a summer's morning
over a quiet summer sea." Mere "scepticism and insurrection" is a poor and unworthy attitude; "it is
nothing less than a wicked waste of accumulated human
strivings to sneer [the religions] out of existence. . . . The
halt in indifference or in hostility is easy enough and
seductive enough. . . . I say go on: do not stay there . . .
and at last a light, dim it may be, will arise."

Go on where? In the direction, perhaps, of what is now (since Bonhoeffer) called "religionless Christianity" —and this is the second phase of Mark Rutherford's deliverance. He went on in the direction, not of evangelism or religious instruction in the old sense, but of pioneering for the elementary decencies in the appalling slums of Drury Lane. He and his friend M'Kay open a room near Drury Lane, with the object of attracting some of the wretched inhabitants to "come and be saved"— not, of course, in the old sense, but saved from degradation and despair by quiet, cleanliness and nourishment; by human sympathy, and by conversation leading to interest—however slight—in something "universal and impersonal, feeling that in that direction lay healing". There is no evidence that Hale White himself did any slumming of this kind, but his interest in the social work of such men as Cowper Temple, the Rev. C. Anderson (a possible model for M'Kay, as Professor Wilfred Stone has suggested), the Rev. Brooke Lambert and others shows his awareness that Christianity, if it is to survive and spread the spirit of its founder, must come down from the heights of establishment and find its function in humble and costly service to mankind.

Thirdly, the deliverance of Mark Rutherford included the attainment, after several false starts, of conjugal happiness. He adores Theresa from a distance; he proposes to Mary Mardon and is rejected; he finally marries Ellen, his first love, to whom he had long ago been engaged, and who was now a widow with a young daughter. He had broken off this engagement, partly because he thought the girl incapable of sharing his intellectual interests, and partly on the earnest advice of "Miss Arbour" (Mrs Hexton) who warns him, from her own bitter experience, against the miseries of marital incompatibility. Here Mark Rutherford's story again differs widely from Hale White's own. Hale White married his fiancée Harriet Arthur in 1856, when he was twenty-five, and the marriage lasted till his wife's death in 1891. He then remained a widower until 1911, when at the age of 80, he married Dorothy V. Horace Smith. Yet here too there is a link between fact and fiction. The theme of married unhappiness, misunderstanding or incompatibility recurs insistently throughout the Mark Rutherford novels and stories, and in some—e.g. *Miriam's Schooling*, *The Revolution in Tanner's Lane*, *Catherine Furze*, "A Dream of Two Dimensions", "The Sweetness of a Man's Friend", "Mrs Fairfax" etc. —it is central and dominant. Hale White was essentially an autobiographical writer; one who (on his own admission) drew his characters more from memory than from imagination, and found it difficult to create plots and situations. It is therefore hard to avoid the conclusion that he was unhappily married himself. It would however be wrong to interpret this in the usual sense. The real sorrow in Hale White's marriage was that after about five years his wife was stricken with disseminated sclerosis, and that thenceforth for thirty years he and their family had to watch her sinking by slow degrees into worse and worse degrees of paralysis, and passing from the invalid chair to a permanent sick-bed, and finally death. As Zachariah Coleman bitterly exclaims (though, for very different reasons), "his life was blasted, and it might have been different". No doubt he resented this discrimination against him by fate; and there is reason to believe, besides, that Harriet was never the ideal spouse of his youthful dreams. But neither, on the other hand, was she ever a Jane Coleman. Indeed, Ellen Butts (in *The Deliverance*) is probably as close a portrait of her as we have, though her fictional life-story is quite different. And the important point, when speaking of Mark's deliverance, is that he learns the lesson learnt over and over again in the novels—notably by Miriam and Mr Cardew, and by M'Kay—that the undervalued partner may possess stores of unsuspected riches: gifts of heart and spirit, and even powers of intelligence, which are only awaiting the touch of love to be released. The classic situation in Mark Rutherford is for one partner (usually the husband, but not always—cf. Mrs Hexton and Miriam) to be more intellectual than the other, and to languish in self-pity on failing to receive the desired response. However, just as Miriam and Mr Cardew or M'Kay learn to conquer their intellectual pride, and to recognize and love the qualities in their spouse which, though different from their own, are spiritually as fine or even finer, so Mark Rutherford learns the beauty of Ellen's character and faith; and so too, as we know for certain, did Hale White himself conquer his self-pity and learn to reverence Harriet for her saintly endurance of a lifelong agony.

All this self-conquest, all this probing for truth, all this reinterpretation of doctrine, all this search for spiritual reassurance and emotional sympathy, meant that Hale White's life was strenuous and strained, and that joy came to him as a comparatively rare visitant. If he was a victim of his century, he was also the victim of circumstance and his own temperament. The extraordinary happiness and release he experienced in his second marriage (to a woman forty-five years younger than himself), near the end of his life, shows that indeed his story "might have been different". He said himself that if he had married Dorothy in his youth, there would have been no Mark Rutherford novels. As it was, he wrote them partly to discharge his bosom of perilous stuff; to experience the relief of confession; and to demonstrate to himself and to an unknown audience that there was more in him than met the eye. One would not guess from *The Autobiography* and *The Deliverance* that Hale White was in fact a well-paid and efficient Civil Servant living in suburban respectability at Carshalton. But what of that? "Mark Rutherford" was the distillation of his deeper self; and in thus disclosing to us the story of his buried life he has produced work which for honesty, profundity, purity of style and relevance to our own times would be hard to match anywhere else in English literature.

Basil Willey

BIBLIOGRAPHICAL NOTE

The Autobiography of Mark Rutherford, Dissenting Minister was first published in 1881. *Mark Rutherford's Deliverance: Being the Second Part of his Autobiography* followed in 1885. Each volume was described on the title-page as "Edited by his friend, Reuben Shapcott" and was published in London by Trübner & Co.

In 1888 the two works, "corrected and with additions", were published together in a single volume. This second edition has been selected for the present reprint. The edition reproduces with only minor alterations the text of the first edition of each work but adds a new Preface and the short story "A Mysterious Portrait". It omits only the brief Editor's Note which introduced the first edition of *Mark Rutherford's Deliverance*.

Later editions of the works together and individually which were published during William Hale White's life based their texts on the second edition and retained both the Preface included in that edition and "A Mysterious Portrait".

J. L. Madden

AUTOBIOGRAPHY

OF

MARK RUTHERFORD.

THE AUTOBIOGRAPHY OF MARK RUTHERFORD

AND

MARK RUTHERFORD'S DELIVERANCE.

EDITED BY HIS FRIEND,

REUBEN SHAPCOTT.

Second Edition: Corrected and with Additions.

LONDON:

TRÜBNER & CO., LUDGATE HILL.

1888.

Ballantyne Press
BALLANTYNE, HANSON AND CO.
EDINBURGH AND LONDON

CONTENTS.

————◆————

THE AUTOBIOGRAPHY OF MARK RUTHERFORD.

————————

MARK RUTHERFORD'S DELIVERANCE.

CONTENTS.

PREFACE TO THE SECOND EDITION.

THE present edition is a reprint of the first, with corrections of several mistakes which had been overlooked. It also contains in addition a short story "A Mysterious Portrait," which, although it was written by my friend when he was young, seemed to me worth preserving.

There is one observation which I may perhaps be permitted to make on re-reading after some years this autobiography. Rutherford, at any rate in his earlier life, was an example of the danger and the folly of cultivating thoughts and reading books to which he was not equal, and which tend to make a man lonely.

It is all very well that remarkable persons should occupy themselves with exalted subjects, which are out of the ordinary road which ordinary humanity treads; but we who are not remarkable make a very great mistake if we have anything to do with them. If we wish to be happy, and have to live with average men and women, as most of us have to live, we must learn to take an interest in the topics which concern average men and women. We think too much of ourselves. We ought not to sacrifice a single moment's pleasure in our attempt to do something which is too big for us, and as a rule, men and women are always attempting what is too big for them. To ninety-nine young men out of a hundred, or perhaps ninety-nine thousand nine hundred and ninety-nine out of a hundred thousand, the wholesome healthy doctrine is, "Don't bother yourselves with what is beyond you; try to lead a sweet, clean, wholesome life, keep yourselves in health above everything, stick to your work, and when your day is done amuse and refresh yourselves." It is not only a duty to ourselves, but it is a duty to others to take this course. Great men do the world much good, but not without some harm, and we have no business to be troubling ourselves with their dreams if we have duties which lie nearer home amongst persons to whom these dreams are incomprehensible. Many a man goes into his study, shuts himself up with his poetry or his psychology, comes out, half understanding what he has read, is miserable because he cannot find anybody with whom he can talk about it, and misses altogether the far more genuine joy which he could have obtained from a game with his children, or listening to what his wife had to tell him about her neighbours.

"Lor, miss, you haven't looked at your new bonnet to-day," said a servant girl to her young mistress.

"No, why should I?   I did not want to go out."

"Oh, how can you? why, I get mine out and look at it every night."

She was happy for a whole fortnight with a happiness cheap at a very high price.

That same young mistress was very caustic upon the women who block the pavement outside drapers' shops, but surely she was unjust.   They always seem unconscious, to be enjoying themselves intensely and most innocently, more so probably than an audience at a Wagner concert.   Many persons with refined minds are apt to depreciate happiness, especially, if it is of "a low type."   Broadly speaking, it is the one thing worth having, and low or high, if it does no mischief, is better than the most spiritual misery.

Metaphysics, and theology, including all speculations on the why and the wherefore, optimism, pessimism, freedom, necessity, causality, and so forth, are not only for the most part loss of time, but frequently ruinous.   It is no answer to say that these things force themselves upon us, and that to every question we are bound to give or try to give an answer.   It is true, although strange, that there are multitudes of burning questions which we must do our best to ignore, to forget their existence ; and it is not more strange, after all, than many other facts in this wonderfully mysterious and defective existence of ours. One fourth of life is intelligible, the other three fourths is unintelligible darkness; and our earliest duty is to cultivate the habit of not looking round the corner.

"Go thy way, eat thy bread with joy, and drink thy wine with a merry heart; for God hath already accepted thy works. Let thy garments be always white, and let not thy head lack ointment. Live joyfully with the wife whom thou lovest all the days of the life of thy vanity, which He hath given thee under the sun, all the days of thy vanity: for that is thy portion in life."

R. S.

This is the night when I must die,
And great Orion walketh high
In silent glory overhead:
He'll set just after I am dead.

A week this night, I'm in my grave:
Orion walketh o'er the wave:
Down in the dark damp earth I lie,
While he doth march in majesty.

A few weeks hence and spring will come;
The earth will bright array put on
Of daisy and of primrose bright,
And everything which loves the light.

And some one to my child will say,
" You'll soon forget that you could play
Beethoven; let us hear a strain
From that slow movement once again."

And so she'll play that melody,
While I among the worms do lie;
Dead to them all, for ever dead;
The churchyard clay dense overhead.

I once did think there might be mine
One friendship perfect and divine;
Alas! that dream dissolved in tears
Before I'd counted twenty years.

For I was ever commonplace ;
Of genius never had a trace ;
My thoughts the world have never fed,
Mere echoes of the book last read.

Those whom I knew I cannot blame :
If they are cold, I am the same :
How could they ever show to me
More than a common courtesy ?

There is no deed which I have done ;
There is no love which I have won,
To make them for a moment grieve
That I this night their earth must leave.

Thus, moaning at the break of day,
A man upon his deathbed lay ;
A moment more and all was still ;
The Morning Star came o'er the hill.

But when the dawn lay on his face,
It kindled an immortal grace ;
As if in death that Life were shown
Which lives not in the great alone.

Orion sank down in the west
Just as he sank into his rest ;
I closed in solitude his eyes,
And watched him till the sun's uprise.

AUTOBIOGRAPHY

OF

MARK RUTHERFORD.

————◆————

CHAPTER I.

CHILDHOOD.

Now that I have completed my autobiography up to
the present year, I sometimes doubt whether it is right
to publish it. Of what use is it, many persons will
say, to present to the world what is mainly a record
of weaknesses and failures? If I had any triumphs
to tell; if I could show how I had risen superior to
poverty and suffering; if, in short, I were a hero of
any kind whatever, I might perhaps be justified in
communicating my success to mankind, and stimulating them to do as I have done. But mine is the
tale of a commonplace life, perplexed by many
problems I have never solved; disturbed by many
difficulties I have never surmounted; and blotted by
ignoble concessions which are a constant regret. I
have decided, however, to let the manuscript remain.
I will not destroy it, although I will not take the

responsibility of printing it. Somebody may think it worth preserving; and there are two reasons why they may think so, if there are no others. In the first place, it has some little historic value, for I feel increasingly that the race to which I belonged is fast passing away, and that the Dissenting minister of the present day is a different being altogether from the Dissenting minister of forty years ago. In the next place, I have observed that the mere knowing that other people have been tried as we have been tried is a consolation to us, and that we are relieved by the assurance that our sufferings are not special and peculiar, but common to us with many others. Death has always been a terror to me, and at times, nay generally, religion and philosophy have been altogether unavailing to mitigate the terror in any way. But it has been a comfort to me to reflect that whatever death may be, it is the inheritance of the whole human race; that I am not singled out, but shall merely have to pass through what the weakest have had to pass through before me. In the worst of maladies, worst at least to me, those which are hypochondriacal, the healing effect which is produced by the visit of a friend who can simply say, "I have endured all that," is most marked. So it is not impossible that some few whose experience has been like mine may, by my example, be freed from that sense of solitude which they find so depressing.

I was born, just before the Liverpool and Manchester Railway was opened, in a small country town in one of the Midland shires. It is now semi-manufacturing, at the junction of three or four lines of railway, with hardly a trace left of what it was fifty years ago. It then consisted of one long main street, with a few other streets branching from it at right angles. Through this street the mail-coach rattled at night, and the huge waggon rolled through it, drawn by four horses, which twice a week travelled to and from London and brought us what we wanted from the great and unknown city. My father and mother belonged to the ordinary English middle class of well-to-do shopkeepers. My mother's family came from a little distance, but my father's had lived in those parts for centuries. I remember perfectly well how business used to be carried on in those days. There was absolutely no competition, and although nobody in the town who was in trade got rich, except the banker and the brewer, nearly everybody was tolerably well off, and certainly not pressed with care as their successors are now. The draper, who lived a little way above us, was a deacon in our chapel, and every morning, soon after breakfast, he would start off for his walk of about four miles, stopping by the way to talk to his neighbours about the events of the day. At eleven o'clock or thereabouts, he would return and would begin work. Everybody took an hour for dinner —between one and two, and at that time, especially on a hot July afternoon, the High Street was empty from end to end and the profoundest peace reigned.

My life as a child falls into two portions, sharply divided,—week-day and Sunday. During the week-day I went to the public school, where I learned little or nothing that did me much good. The discipline of the school was admirable, and the head-master was penetrated with a most lofty sense of duty, but the methods of teaching were very imperfect. In

Latin we had to learn the Eton Latin Grammar till we knew every word of it by heart, but we did scarcely any retranslation from English into Latin. Much of our time was wasted on the merest trifles, such as learning to write, for example, like copperplate, and, still more extraordinary, in copying the letters of the alphabet as they are used in printing. But we had two half-holidays in the week, which seem to me now to have been the happiest part of my life. A river ran through the town, and on summer Wednesdays and Saturdays we wandered along its banks for miles, alternately fishing and bathing. I remember whole afternoons in June, July, and August, passed half-naked or altogether naked in the solitary meadows and in the water; I remember the tumbling weir with the deep pool at the bottom in which we dived; I remember, too, the place where we used to swim across the river with our clothes on our heads, because there was no bridge near, and the frequent disaster of a slip of the braces in the middle of the water, so that shirt, jacket, and trousers were soaked, and we had to lie on the grass in the broiling sun without a rag on us till everything was dry again. In winter our joys were of a different kind, but none the less delightful. If it was a frost, we had skating; not like the skating on a London pond, but over long reaches, and if the locks had not intervened, we might have gone a day's journey on the ice without a stoppage. If there was no ice we had football, and what was still better, we could get up a steeplechase on foot straight across hedge and ditch. In after-years, when I lived in London, I came to know children who went to school in Gower Street, and travelled backwards and forwards by omnibus, children who had no other recreation than an occasional visit to the Zoological Gardens, or a somewhat sombre walk up to Hampstead to see their aunt; and I have often regretted that they never had any experience of those perfect poetic pleasures which the boy enjoys whose childhood is spent in the country, and whose home is there. A country boarding-school is something altogether different. On the Sundays, however, the compensation came. It was a season of unmixed gloom. My father and mother were rigid Calvinistic Independents, and on that day no newspaper nor any book more secular than the Evangelical Magazine was tolerated. Every preparation for the Sabbath had been made on the Saturday, to avoid as much as possible any work. The meat was cooked beforehand, so that we never had a hot dinner even in the coldest weather; the only thing hot which was permitted was a boiled suet pudding, which cooked itself while we were at chapel, and some potatoes which were prepared after we came home. Not a letter was opened unless it was clearly evident that it was not on business, and for opening these an apology was always offered that it was possible they might contain some announcement of sickness. If on cursory inspection they appeared to be ordinary letters, although they might be from relations or friends, they were put away. After family prayer and breakfast the business of the day began with the Sunday-school at nine o'clock. We were taught our Catechism and Bible there till a quarter past ten. We were then marched across the road into the chapel, a large old-fashioned building dating from the time of Charles II. The floor was covered with high pews. The roof was supported

by three or four tall wooden pillars which ran from
the ground to the ceiling, and the galleries by
shorter pillars. There was a large oak pulpit on
one side against the wall, and down below, immediately under the minister, was the "singing pew,"
where the singers and musicians sat, the musicians
being performers on the clarionet, flute, violin, and
violoncello. Right in front was a long enclosure,
called the communion pew, which was usually occupied
by a number of the poorer members of the congregation. There were three services every Sunday, besides
intermitting prayer-meetings, but these I did not as
yet attend. Each service consisted of a hymn, reading
the Bible, another hymn, a prayer, the sermon, a third
hymn, and a short final prayer. The reading of the
Bible was unaccompanied with any observations or
explanations, and I do not remember that I ever once
heard a mistranslation corrected. The first, or long
prayer, as it was called, was a horrible hypocrisy, and
it was a sore tax on the preacher to get through it.
Anything more totally unlike the model recommended
to us in the New Testament cannot well be imagined.
It generally began with a confession that we were all
sinners, but no individual sins were ever confessed, and
then ensued a kind of dialogue with God, very much
resembling the speeches which in later years I have
heard in the House of Commons from the movers
and seconders of addresses to the Crown at the opening
of Parliament. In all the religion of that day nothing
was falser than the long prayer. Direct appeal to God
can only be justified when it is passionate. To come
maundering into His presence when we have nothing
particular to say is an insult, upon which we should

never presume if we had a petition to offer to any
earthly personage.   We should not venture to take up
his time with commonplaces or platitudes ; but our
minister seemed to consider that the Almighty, who
had the universe to govern, had more leisure at His
command than the idlest lounger at a club.   Nobody
ever listened to this performance.   I was a good child
on the whole, but I am sure I did not ; and if the
chapel were now in existence, there might be traced on
the flap of the pew in which we sat, many curious
designs due to these dreary performances.   The sermon
was not much better.   It generally consisted of a text,
which was a mere peg for a discourse, that was pretty
much the same from January to December.   The minister
invariably began with the fall of man ; propounded the
scheme of redemption, and ended by depicting in the
morning the blessedness of the saints, and in the evening the doom of the lost.   There was a tradition that
in the morning there should be " experience," that is
to say, comfort for the elect, and that the evening
should be appropriated to their less fortunate brethren.
The evening service was the most trying to me of all
these.   I never could keep awake, and knew that to
sleep under the Gospel was a sin.   The chapel was
lighted in winter by immense chandeliers with tiers
of candles all round.   These required perpetual snuff-
ing, and I can see the old man going round the
chandeliers in the middle of the service with a
mighty pair of snuffers which opened and shut with
a loud click.   How I envied him because he had a
semi-secular occupation which prevented that terrible
drowsiness !   How I envied the pew-opener, who was
allowed to stand at the vestry door, and could slip

into the vestry every now and then, or even into the burial-ground if he heard irreverent boys playing there! The atmosphere of the chapel on hot nights was most foul, and this added to my discomfort. Oftentimes in winter, when no doors or windows were open, I have seen the glass panes streaming with wet inside, and women carried out fainting. On rare occasions I was allowed to go with my father when he went into the villages to preach. As a deacon he was also a lay-preacher, and I had the ride in the gig out and home, and tea at a farm-house. Perhaps I shall not have a better opportunity to say that, with all these drawbacks, my religious education did confer upon me some positive advantages. The first was a rigid regard for truthfulness. My parents never would endure a lie or the least equivocation. The second was purity of life, and I look upon this as a simply incalculable gain. Impurity was not an excusable weakness in the society in which I lived; it was a sin for which dreadful punishment was reserved. The reason for my virtue may have been a wrong reason, but anyhow I was saved, and being saved, much more was saved than health and peace of mind. To this day I do not know where to find a weapon strong enough to subdue the tendency to impurity in young men; and although I cannot tell them what I do not believe, I hanker sometimes after the old prohibitions and penalties. Physiological penalties are too remote, and the subtler penalties—the degradation, the growth of callousness to finer pleasures, the loss of sensitiveness to all that is most nobly attractive in woman—are too feeble to withstand temptation when it lies in ambush like a garrotter, and has the reason stunned in a moment. The only thing that can be done is to make the conscience of a boy generally tender, so that he shrinks instinctively from the monstrous injustice of contributing for the sake of his own pleasure to the ruin of another. As soon as manhood dawns, he must also have his attention absorbed on some object which will divert his thoughts intellectually or ideally, and by slight yet constant pressure, exercised not by fits and starts, but day after day, directly and indirectly, his father must form an antipathy in him to brutish selfish sensuality. Above all, there must be no toying with passion, and no books permitted, without condemnation and warning, which are not of a heroic turn. When the boy becomes a man he may read Byron without danger. To a youth he is fatal. Before leaving this subject I may observe, that parents greatly err by not telling their children a good many things which they ought to know. Had I been taught when I was young a few facts about myself, which I only learned accidentally long afterwards, a good deal of misery might have been spared me.

Nothing particular happened to me till I was about fourteen, when I was told it was time I became converted. Conversion, amongst the Independents and other Puritan sects, is supposed to be a kind of miracle wrought in the heart by the influence of the Holy Spirit, by which the man becomes something altogether different to what he was previously. It affects, or should affect, his character; that is to say, he ought after conversion to be better in every way than he was before: but this is not considered as its main consequence. In its essence it is a change

in the emotions and increased vividness of belief.
It is now altogether untrue. Yet it is an undoubted
fact that in earlier days, and, indeed, in rare cases,
as late as the time of my childhood, it was occasionally a reality. It is possible to imagine that under
the preaching of Paul sudden conviction of a life
misspent may have been produced with sudden personal attachment to the Galilean who, until then,
had been despised.   There may have been prompt
release of unsuspected powers, and as prompt an im-
prisonment for ever of meaner weaknesses and tendencies; the result being literally a putting off of the
old, and a putting on of the new man.   Love has always
been potent to produce such a transformation, and the
exact counterpart of conversion, as it was understood by
the apostles, may be seen whenever a man is redeemed
from vice by attachment to some woman whom he
worships, or when a girl is reclaimed from idleness
and vanity by becoming a mother.   But conversion, as
it was understood by me and as it is now understood,
is altogether unmeaning.   I knew that I had to be "a
child of God," and after a time professed myself to be
one, but I cannot call to mind that I was anything
else than I always had been, save that I was perhaps
a little more hypocritical; not in the sense that I
professed to others what I knew I did not believe,
but in the sense that I professed it to myself.   I was
obliged to declare myself convinced of sin; convinced
of the efficacy of the atonement; convinced that I was
forgiven; convinced that the Holy Ghost was shed
abroad in my heart; and convinced of a great many
other things which were the merest phrases.   However,
the end of it was, that I was proposed for acceptance,

and two deacons were deputed, in accordance with the usual custom, to wait upon me and ascertain my fitness for membership. What they said and what I said has now altogether vanished; but I remember with perfect distinctness the day on which I was admitted. It was the custom to demand of each candidate a statement of his or her experience. I had no experience to give; and I was excused on the grounds that I had been the child of pious parents, and consequently had not undergone that convulsion which those, not favoured like myself, necessarily underwent when they were called. I was now expected to attend all those extra services which were specially for the church. I stayed to the late prayer-meeting on Sunday; I went to the prayer-meeting on week-days, and also to private prayer-meetings. These services were not interesting to me for their own sake. I thought they were, but what I really liked was clanship and the satisfaction of belonging to a society marked off from the great world. It must also be added that the evening meetings afforded us many opportunities for walking home with certain young women, who, I am sorry to say, were a more powerful attraction, not to me only but to others, than the prospect of hearing brother Holderness, the travelling draper, confess crimes which, to say the truth, although they were many according to his own account, were never given in that detail which would have made his confession of some value. He never prayed without telling all of us that there was no health in him, and that his soul was a mass of putrefying sores; but everybody thought the better of him for his self-humiliation. One actual indiscretion, however, brought home to him would have been visited by suspension or expulsion.

CHAPTER II.

PREPARATION.

IT was necessary that an occupation should be found for me, and after much deliberation it was settled that I should "go into the ministry." I had joined the church, I had "engaged in prayer" publicly, and although I had not set up for being extraordinarily pious, I was thought to be as good as most of the young men who professed to have a mission to regenerate mankind. Accordingly, after some months of preparation, I was taken to a Dissenting College not very far from where we lived. It was a large old-fashioned house with a newer building annexed, and was surrounded with a garden and with meadows. Each student had a separate room, and all had their meals together in a common hall. Altogether there were about forty of us. The establishment consisted of a President, an elderly gentleman who had an American degree of doctor of divinity, and who taught the various branches of theology. He was assisted by three professors, who imparted to us as much Greek, Latin, and mathematics as it was considered that we ought to know. Behold me, then, beginning a course of training which was to prepare me to meet the doubts of the nineteenth century; to be the guide of men; to advise them in their perplexities; to suppress their tempestuous lusts; to lift them above their petty cares, and to lead them heavenward! About the Greek and Latin and the secular part of the college discipline I will say nothing, except that it was generally inefficient. The theological and biblical teaching was a sham. We had come to the college in the first place to learn the Bible. Our whole existence was in future to be based upon that book; our lives were to be passed in preaching it. I will venture to say that there was no book less understood either by students or professors. The President had a course of lectures, delivered year after year to successive generations of his pupils, upon its authenticity and inspiration. They were altogether remote from the subject; and afterwards, when I came to know what the difficulties of belief really were, I found that these essays, which were supposed to be a triumphant confutation of the sceptic, were a mere sword of lath. They never touched the question, and if any doubts suggested themselves to the audience, nobody dared to give them tongue, lest the expression of them should beget a suspicion of heresy. I remember also some lectures on the proof of the existence of God and on the argument from design; all of which, when my mind was once awakened, were as irrelevant as the chattering of sparrows. When I did not even know who or what this God was, and could not bring my lips to use the word with any mental honesty, of what service was the "watch argument" to me? Very lightly did the President pass over all these initial difficulties of his religion. I see him now, a gentleman with lightish hair, with a most mellifluous voice and a most pastoral manner, reading his prim little tracts to us directed against the "shallow

infidel" who seemed to deny conclusions so obvious
that we were certain he could not be sincere, and those
of us who had never seen an infidel might well be pardoned for supposing that he must always be wickedly
blind. About a dozen of these tracts settled the infidel
and the whole mass of unbelief from the time of Celsus
downwards. The President's task was all the easier
because he knew nothing of German literature; and,
indeed, the word "German" was a term of reproach
signifying something very awful, although nobody knew
exactly what it was. Systematic theology was the next
science to which the President directed us. We used a
sort of Calvinistic manual which began by setting forth
that mankind was absolutely in God's power. He was
our maker, and we had no legal claim whatever to any
consideration from Him. The author then mechanically
built up the Calvinistic creed, step by step, like a house
of cards. Systematic theology was the great business
of our academical life. We had to read sermons to the
President in class, and no sermon was considered complete and proper unless it unfolded what was called
the scheme of redemption from beginning to end. So
it came to pass that about the Bible, as I have already
said, we were in darkness. It was a magazine of texts,
and those portions of it which contributed nothing in
the shape of texts, or formed no part of the scheme,
were neglected. Worse still, not a word was ever
spoken to us telling us in what manner to strengthen
the reason, to subdue the senses, or in what way to
deal with all the varied diseases of that soul of man
which we were to set ourselves to save. All its failings,
infinitely more complicated than those of the body,
were grouped as "sin," and for these there was one

quack remedy. If the patient did not like the remedy, or got no good from it, the fault was his. It is remarkable that the scheme was never of the slightest service to me in repressing one solitary evil inclination; at no point did it come into contact with me. At the time it seemed right and proper that I should learn it, and I had no doubt of its efficacy; but when the stress of temptation was upon me, it never occurred to me, nor when I became a minister did I find it sufficiently powerful to mend the most trifling fault. In after years, but not till I had strayed far away from the President and his creed, the Bible was really opened to me, and became to me, what it now is, the most precious of books.

There were several small chapels scattered in the villages near the college, and these chapels were "supplied," as the phrase is, by the students. Those who were near the end of their course were also employed as substitutes for regular ministers when they were temporarily absent. Sometimes a senior was even sent up to London to take the place, on a sudden emergency, of a great London minister, and when he came back he was an object almost of adoration. The congregation, on the other hand, consisting in some part of country people spending a Sunday in town and anxious to hear a celebrated preacher, were not at all disposed to adore, when, instead of the great man, they saw "only a student." By the time I was nineteen I took my turn in "supplying" the villages, and set forth with the utmost confidence what appeared to me to be the indubitable gospel. No shadow of a suspicion of its truth ever crossed my mind, and yet I had not spent an hour in comprehending, much less in answering, one objection to it. The objections, in fact, had never met me; they were over my horizon altogether. It is wonderful to think how I could take so much for granted; and not merely take it to myself and for myself, but proclaim it as a message to other people. It would be a mistake, however, to suppose that theological youths are the only class who are guilty of such presumption. Our gregarious instinct is so strong that it is the most difficult thing for us to be satisfied with suspended judgment. Men must join a party, and have a cry, and they generally take up their party and their cry from the most indifferent motives. For my own part I cannot be enthusiastic about politics, except on rare occasions when the issue is a very narrow one. There is so much that requires profound examination, and it disgusts me to get upon a platform and dispute with ardent Radicals or Conservatives who know nothing about even the rudiments of history, political economy, or political philosophy, without which it is as absurd to have an opinion upon what are called politics as it would be to have an opinion upon an astronomical problem without having learned Euclid. The more incapable we are of thorough investigation, the wider and deeper are the subjects upon which we busy ourselves, and still more strange, the more bigoted do we become in our conclusions about them; and yet it is not strange, for he who by painful processes has found yes and no alternate for so long that he is not sure which is final, is the last man in the world, if he for the present is resting in yes, to crucify another who can get no further than no. The bigot is he to whom no such painful processes have ever been permitted.

The society amongst the students was very poor.

Not a single friendship formed then has remained with me. They were mostly young men of no education, who had been taken from the counter, and their spiritual life was not very deep. In many of them it did not even exist, and their whole attention was absorbed upon their chances of getting wealthy congregations or of making desirable matches. It was a time in which the world outside was seething with the ferment which had been cast into it by Germany and by those in England whom Germany had influenced, but not a fragment of it had dropped within our walls. I cannot call to mind a single conversation upon any but the most trivial topics, nor did our talk ever turn even upon our religion, so far as it was a thing affecting the soul, but only upon it as something subsidiary to chapels, " causes," deacons, and the like. The emptiness of some of my colleagues, and their worldliness, too, were almost incredible. There was one who was particularly silly. He was a blonde youth with greyish eyes, a mouth not quite shut, and an eternal simper upon his face. He never had an idea in his head, and never read anything except the denominational newspapers and a few well-known aids to sermonising. He was a great man at all tea-meetings, anniversaries, and parties. He was facile in public speaking, and he dwelt much upon the joys of heaven and upon such topics as the possibility of our recognising one another there. I have known him describe for twenty minutes, in a kind of watery rhetoric, the passage of the soul to bliss through death, and its meeting in the next world with those who had gone before. With all his weakness he was close and mean in money matters, and when he left college, the first thing he did was to marry a widow with a fortune.

Before long he became one of the most popular of ministers in a town much visited by sick persons, with whom he was an especial favourite. I disliked him —and specially disliked his unpleasant behaviour to women. If I had been a woman I should have spurned him for his perpetual insult of inane compliments. He was always dawdling after "the sex," which was one of his sweet phrases, and yet he was not passionate. Passion does not dawdle and compliment, nor is it nasty, as this fellow was. Passion may burn like a devouring flame ; and in a few moments, like flame, may bring down a temple to dust and ashes, but it is earnest as flame, and essentially pure.

During the first two years at college my life was entirely external. My heart was altogether untouched by anything I heard, read, or did, although I myself supposed that I took an interest in them. But one day in my third year, a day I remember as well as Paul must have remembered afterwards the day on which he went to Damascus, I happened to find amongst a parcel of books a volume of poems in paper boards. It was called "Lyrical Ballads," and I read first one and then the whole book. It conveyed to me no new doctrine, and yet the change it wrought in me could only be compared with that which is said to have been wrought on Paul himself by the Divine apparition. Looking over the "Lyrical Ballads" again, as I have looked over it a dozen times since then, I can hardly see what it was which stirred me so powerfully, nor do I believe that it communicated much to me which could be put in words. But it excited a movement and a growth which went on till, by degrees, all the systems which enveloped me like a body gradually decayed from me and fell away into nothing. Of more importance, too, than the decay of systems was the birth of a habit of inner reference and a dislike to occupy myself with anything which did not in some way or other touch the soul, or was not the illustration or embodiment of some spiritual law. There is, of course, a definite explanation to be given of one effect produced by the "Lyrical Ballads." God is nowhere formally deposed, and Wordsworth would have been the last man to say that he had lost his faith in the God of his fathers. But his real God is not the God of the Church, but the God of the hills, the abstraction Nature, and to this my reverence was transferred. Instead of an object of worship which was altogether artificial, remote, never coming into genuine contact with me, I had now one which I thought to be real, one in which literally I could live and move and have my being, an actual fact present before my eyes. God was brought from that heaven of the books, and dwelt on the downs in the far-away distances, and in every cloud-shadow which wandered across the valley. Wordsworth unconsciously did for me what every religious reformer has done,— he re-created my Supreme Divinity; substituting a new and living spirit for the old deity, once alive, but gradually hardened into an idol.

What days were those of the next few years before increasing age had presented preciser problems and demanded preciser answers; before all joy was darkened by the shadow of on-coming death, and when life seemed infinite! Those were the days when through the whole long summer's morning I wanted no companion but myself, provided only I was in the country, and when books were read with tears in the eyes. Those were the days when mere life, apart from anything which it brings, was exquisite. In my own college I found no sympathy, but we were in the habit of meeting occasionally the students from other colleges, and amongst them I met with one or two, especially one who had undergone experiences similar to my own. The friendships formed with these young men have lasted till now, and have been the most permanent of all the relationships of my existence. I wish not to judge others, but the persons who to me have proved themselves most attractive, have been those who have passed through such a process as that through which I myself passed; those who have had in some form or other an enthusiastic stage in their history, when the story of Genesis and of the Gospels has been rewritten, when God has visibly walked in the garden, and the Son of God has drawn men away from their daily occupations into the divinest of dreams. I have known men—most interesting men—with far greater powers than any which I have possessed, men who have never been trammelled by a false creed, who have devoted themselves to science and acquired a great reputation, who have somehow never laid hold upon me like the man I have just mentioned. He failed altogether as a minister, and went back to his shop, but the old glow of his youth burns, and will burn for ever. When I am with him our conversation naturally turns on matters which are of profoundest importance: with others it may be instructive, but I leave them unmoved, and I trace the difference distinctly to that visitation, for it was nothing else, which came to him in his youth.

The effect which was produced upon my preaching

and daily conversation by this change was immediate.
It became gradually impossible for me to talk about
subjects which had not some genuine connection with
me, or to desire to hear others talk about them.   The
artificial, the merely miraculous, the event which had
no inner meaning, no matter how large externally it
might be, I did not care for.   A little Greek mytho-
logical story was of more importance to me than a
war which filled the newspapers.   What, then, could
I do with my theological treatises ?   It would be a
mistake, however, to suppose that I immediately became formally heretical.   Nearly every doctrine in
the college creed had once had a natural origin in the
necessities of human nature, and might therefore be
so interpreted as to become a necessity again.   To
reach through to that original necessity; to explain
the atonement as I believed it appeared to Paul, and
the sinfulness of man as it appeared to the prophets,
was my object.   But it was precisely this reaching
after a meaning which constituted heresy.   The dis-
tinctive essence of our orthodoxy was not this or that
dogma, but the acceptance of dogmas as communica-
tions from without, and not as born from within.
Heresy began, and in fact was altogether present,
when I said to myself that a mere statement of the
atonement as taught in class was impossible for me,
and that I must go back to Paul and his century,
place myself in his position, and connect the atonement through him with something which I felt.   I
thus continued to use all the terms which I had
hitherto used ; but an uneasy feeling began to develop
itself about me in the minds of the professors, because
I did not rest in the " simplicity " of the gospel.   To

me this meant its unintelligibility. I remember, for example, discoursing about the death of Christ. There was not a single word which was ordinarily used in the pulpit which I did not use,—satisfaction for sin, penalty, redeeming blood, they were all there,—but I began by saying that in this world there was no redemption for man but by blood; furthermore, the innocent had everywhere and in all time to suffer for the guilty. It had been objected that it was contrary to our notion of an all-loving Being that He should demand such a sacrifice; but, contrary or not, in this world it was true, quite apart from Jesus, that virtue was martyred every day, unknown and unconsoled, in order that the wicked might somehow be saved. This was part of the scheme of the world, and we might dislike it or not, we could not get rid of it. The consequences of my sin, moreover, are rendered less terrible by virtues not my own. I am literally saved from penalties because another pays the penalty for me. The atonement, and what it accomplished for man, were therefore a sublime summing up as it were of what sublime men have to do for their race; an exemplification, rather than a contradiction, of Nature herself, as we know her in our own experience. Now, all this was really intended as a defence of the atonement; but the President heard me that Sunday, and on the Monday he called me into his room. He said that my sermon was marked by considerable ability, but he should have been better satisfied if I had confined myself to setting forth as plainly as I could the "way of salvation" as revealed in Christ Jesus. What I had urged might perhaps have possessed some interest for cultivated people; in fact, he had himself urged pretty much the same thing many years ago, when he was a young man, in a sermon he had preached at the Union meeting; but I must recollect that in all probability my sphere of usefulness would lie amongst humble hearers, perhaps in an agricultural village or a small town, and that he did not think people of this sort would understand me if I talked over their heads as I had done the day before. What they wanted on a Sunday, after all the cares of the week, was not anything to perplex and disturb them; not anything which demanded any exercise of thought; but a repetition of the "old story of which, Mr. Rutherford, you know, we never ought to get weary; an exhibition of our exceeding sinfulness; of our safety in the Rock of Ages, and there only; of the joys of the saints and the sufferings of those who do not believe." His words fell on me like the hand of a corpse, and I went away much depressed. My sermon had excited me, and the man who of all men ought to have welcomed me, had not a word of warmth or encouragement for me, nothing but the coldest indifference, and even repulse.

It occurs to me here to offer an explanation of a failing of which I have been accused in later years, and that is secrecy and reserve. The real truth is, that nobody more than myself could desire self-revelation; but owing to peculiar tendencies in me, and peculiarity of education, I was always prone to say things in conversation which I found produced blank silence in the majority of those who listened to me, and immediate opportunity was taken by my hearers to turn to something trivial. Hence it came to pass that only when tempted by unmistakable sympathy could I be induced to express my real self on any topic of

importance. It is a curious instance of the difficulty
of diagnosing (to use a doctor's word) any spiritual
disease, if disease this shyness may be called. People
would ordinarily set it down to self-reliance, with no
healthy need of intercourse. It was nothing of the
kind. It was an excess of communicativeness, an
eagerness to show what was most at my heart, and to
ascertain what was at the heart of those to whom I
talked, which made me incapable of mere fencing and
trifling, and so often caused me to retreat into myself
when I found absolute absence of response.

I am also reminded here of a dream which I had in
these years of a perfect friendship. I always felt that,
talk with whom I would, I left something unsaid
which was precisely what I most wished to say. I
wanted a friend who would sacrifice himself to me
utterly, and to whom I might offer a similar sacrifice.
I found companions for whom I cared, and who professed to care for me; but I was thirsting for deeper
draughts of love than any which they had to offer;
and I said to myself that if I were to die, not one
of them would remember me for more than a week.
This was not selfishness, for I longed to prove my
devotion as well as to receive that of another. How
this ideal haunted me! It made me restless and
anxious at the sight of every new face, wondering
whether at last I had found that for which I searched
as if for the kingdom of heaven. It is superfluous to
say that a friend of the kind I wanted never appeared,
and disappointment after disappointment at last produced in me a cynicism which repelled people from
me, and brought upon me a good deal of suffering. I
tried men by my standard, and if they did not come

up to it I rejected them; thus I prodigally wasted a good deal of the affection which the world would have given me. Only when I got much older did I discern the duty of accepting life as God has made it, and thankfully receiving any scrap of love offered to me, however imperfect it might be. I don't know any mistake which I have made which has cost me more than this; but at the same time I must record that it was a mistake for which, considering everything, I cannot much blame myself. I hope it is amended now. Now when it is getting late I recognise a higher obligation, brought home to me by a closer study of the New Testament. Sympathy or no sympathy, a man's love should no more fail towards his fellows than that love which spent itself on disciples who altogether misunderstood it, like the rain which falls on just and unjust alike.

CHAPTER III.

WATER LANE.

I HAD now reached the end of my fourth year at college, and it was time for me to leave. I was sent down into the eastern counties to a congregation which had lost its minister, and was there "on probation" for a month. I was naturally a good speaker, and as the "cause" had got very low, the attendance at the chapel increased during the month I was there. The deacons thought they had a prospect of returning prosperity, and in the end I received a nearly unanimous invitation, which, after some hesitation, I accepted. One of the deacons, a Mr. Snale, was against me; he thought I was not "quite sound;" but he was overruled. We shall hear more of him presently. After a short holiday I entered on my new duties. The town was one of those which are not uncommon in that part of the world. It had a population of about seven or eight thousand, and was a sort of condensation of the agricultural country round. There was one main street, consisting principally of very decent, respectable shops. Generally speaking, there were two shops of each trade; one which was patronised by the Church and Tories, and another by the Dissenters and Whigs. The inhabitants were divided into two distinct camps—of the Church and Tory camp the other camp knew nothing. On the other hand, the

knowledge which each member of the Dissenting camp
had of every other member was most intimate. The
Dissenters were further split up into two or three
different sects, but the main sect was that of the Independents. They, in fact, dominated every other. There
was a small Baptist community, and the Wesleyans
had a new red brick chapel in the outskirts; but for
some reason or other the Independents were really the
Dissenters, and until the "cause" had dwindled, as
before observed, all the Dissenters of any note were to
be found on Sunday in their meeting-house in Water
Lane. My predecessor had died in harness at the age
of seventy-five. I never knew him, but from all I
could hear he must have been a man of some power.
As he got older, however, he became feeble; and after
a course of three sermons on a Sunday for fifty years,
what he had to say was so entirely anticipated by his
congregation, that although they all maintained that
the gospel, or, in other words, the doctrine of the fall,
the atonement, and so forth, should continually be presented, and their minister also believed and acted implicitly upon the same theory, they fell away,—some
to the Baptists, some to the neighbouring Independents
about two miles off, and some to the Church, while a
few "went nowhere." When I came I found that the
deacons still remained true. They were the skeleton ;
but the flesh was so woefully emaciated, that on my
first Sunday there were not above fifty persons in a
building which would hold seven hundred. These
deacons were four in number. One was an old farmer
who lived in a village three miles distant. Ever since
he was a boy he had driven over to Water Lane on
Sunday. He and his family brought their dinner with

them, and ate it in the vestry; but they never stopped till the evening, because of the difficulty of getting home on dark nights, and because they all went to bed in winter-time at eight o'clock. Morning and afternoon Mr. Catfield—for that was his name—gave out the hymns. He was a plain, honest man, very kind, very ignorant, never reading any book except the Bible, and barely a newspaper save *Bell's Weekly Messenger*. Even about the Bible he knew little or nothing beyond a few favourite chapters; and I am bound to say that, so far as my experience goes, the character so frequently drawn in romances of intense Bible students in Dissenting congregations is very rare. At the same time Mr. Catfield believed himself to be very orthodox, and in his way was very pious. I could never call him a hypocrite. He was as sincere as he could be, and yet no religious expression of his was ever so sincere as the most ordinary expression of the most trifling pleasure or pain. The second deacon, Mr. Weeley, was, as he described himself, a builder and undertaker; more properly an undertaker and carpenter. He was a thin, tall man, with a tenor voice, and he set the tunes. He was entirely without energy of any kind, and always seemed oppressed by a world which was too much for him. He had depended a good deal for custom upon his chapel connection; and when the attendance at the chapel fell off, his trade fell off likewise, so that he had to compound with his creditors. He was a mere shadow, a man of whom nothing could be said either good or evil. The third deacon was Mr. Snale, the draper. When I first knew him he was about thirty-five. He was slim, small, and small-faced, closely shaven excepting a pair of little curly whiskers, and he was extremely neat. He had a little voice too, rather squeaky, and the marked peculiarity that he hardly ever said anything, no matter how disagreeable it might be, without stretching as if in a smile his thin little lips. He kept the principal draper's shop in the town, and even Church people spent their money with him, because he was so very genteel compared with the other draper, who was a great red man, and hung things outside his window. Mr. Snale was married, had children, and was strictly proper. But his way of talking to women and about them was more odious than the way of a debauchee. He invariably called them "the ladies," or more exactly, "the leedies;" and he hardly ever spoke to a "leedy" without a smirk and some faint attempt at a joke. One of the customs of the chapel was what were called Dorcas meetings. Once a month the wives and daughters drank tea with each other; the evening being ostensibly devoted to making clothes for the poor. The husband of the lady who gave the entertainment for the month had to wait upon the company, and the minister was expected to read to them while they worked. It was my lot to be Mr. Snale's guest two or three times when Mrs. Snale was the Dorcas hostess. We met in the drawing-room, which was over the shop, and looked out into the town market-place. There was a round table in the middle of the room, at which Mrs. Snale sat and made the tea. Abundance of hot buttered toast and muffins were provided, which Mr. Snale and a maid handed round to the party. Four pictures decorated the walls. One hung over the mantelpiece. It was a portrait in oils of Mr. Snale, and opposite to it, on the other side, was a portrait of

Mrs. Snale. Both were daubs, but curiously faithful
in depicting what was most offensive in the character
of both the originals, Mr. Snale's simper being preserved; together with the peculiarly hard, heavy sensuality of the eye in Mrs. Snale, who was large and
full-faced, correct like Mr. Snale, a member of the
church, a woman whom I never saw moved to any
generosity, and cruel, not with the ferocity of the tiger,
but with the dull insensibility of a cart-wheel, which
will roll over a man's neck as easily as over a flint.
The third picture represented the descent of the Holy
Ghost: a number of persons sitting in a chamber, and
each one with the flame of a candle on his head. The
fourth represented the last day. The Son of God was
in a chair surrounded by clouds, and beside Him was
a flying figure blowing a long mail-coach horn. The
dead were coming up out of their graves; some were
half out of the earth, others three-parts out—the whole
of the bottom part of the picture being filled with bodies
emerging from the ground, a few looking happy, but
most of them very wretched; all of them being naked.
The first time I went to Mrs. Snale's Dorcas gathering
Mr. Snale was reader, on the ground that I was a novice;
and I was very glad to resign the task to him. As the
business in hand was week-day and secular, it was not
considered necessary that the selected subjects should be
religious; but as it was distinctly connected with the
chapel, it was also considered that they should have
a religious flavour. Consequently the Bible was excluded, and so were books on topics altogether worldly.
Dorcas meetings were generally, therefore, shut up to
the denominational journal and to magazines. Towards
the end of the evening Mr. Snale read the births, deaths,

and marriages in this journal. It would not have been
thought right to read them from any other newspaper,
but it was agreed, with a fineness of tact which was
very remarkable, that it was quite right to read them
in one which was "serious." During the whole time
that the reading was going on conversation was not
arrested, but was conducted in a kind of half whisper;
and this was another reason why I exceedingly disliked to read, for I could never endure to speak if
people did not listen. At half-past eight the work
was put away, and Mrs. Snale went to the piano and
played a hymn tune, the minister having first of all
selected the hymn. Singing over, he offered a short
prayer, and the company separated. Supper was not
served, as it was found to be too great an expense.
The husbands of the ladies generally came to escort
them home, but did not come upstairs. Some of the
gentlemen waited below in the dining-room, but most
of them preferred the shop, for, although it was shut,
the gas was burning to enable the assistants to put
away the goods which had been got out during the day.
When it first became my turn to read I proposed the
"Vicar of Wakefield;" but although no objection was
raised at the time, Mr. Snale took an opportunity of
telling me, after I had got through a chapter or two,
that he thought it would be better if it were discon-
tinued. "Because, you know, Mr. Rutherford," he said,
with his smirk, "the company is mixed; there are
young leedies present, and *perhaps*, Mr. Rutherford, a
book with a more requisite tone might be more suitable on such an occasion." What he meant I did not
know, and how to find a book with a more requisite
tone I did not know. However, the next time, in my

folly, I tried a selection from George Fox's Journal.
Mr. Snale objected to this too. It was "hardly of a
character adapted for social intercourse," he thought;
and furthermore, "although Mr. Fox might be a very
good man, and was a converted character, yet he did
not, you know, Mr. Rutherford, belong to us." So I
was reduced to that class of literature which of all
others I most abominated, and which always seemed
to me the most profane,—religious and sectarian gossip,
religious novels designed to make religion attractive,
and other slip-slop of this kind. I could not endure
it, and was frequently unwell on Dorcas evenings.

The rest of the small congregation was of no particular note. As I have said before, it had greatly
fallen away, and all who remained clung to the chapel
rather by force of habit than from any other reason.
The only exception was an old maiden lady and her
sister, who lived in a little cottage about a mile out of
the town. They were pious in the purest sense of the
word, suffering much from ill-health, but perfectly
resigned, and with a kind of tempered cheerfulness
always apparent on their faces, like the cheerfulness
of a white sky with a sun veiled by light and lofty
clouds. They were the daughters of a gentleman
farmer, who had left them a small annuity. Their
house was one of the sweetest which I ever entered.
The moment I found myself inside it, I became conscious of perfect repose. Everything was at rest;
books, pictures, furniture, all breathed the same peace.
Nothing in the house was new, but everything had
been preserved with such care that nothing looked old.
Yet the owners were not what is called old-maidish;
that is to say, they were not superstitious worshippers

of order and neatness. I remember Mrs. Snale's children coming in one afternoon when I was there. They were rough and ill-mannered, and left traces of dirty footmarks all over the carpet, which the two ladies noticed at once. But it made no difference to the treatment of the children, who had some cake and currant wine given to them, and were sent away rejoicing. Directly they had gone, the eldest of my friends asked me if I would excuse her; she would gather up the dirt before it was trodden about. So she brought a dust-pan and brush (the little servant was out) and patiently swept the floor. That was the way with them. Did any mischief befall them or those whom they knew; without blaming anybody, they immediately and noiselessly set about repairing it with that silent promptitude of nature which rebels not against a wound, but the very next instant begins her work of protection and recovery. The Misses Arbour (for that was their name) mixed but little in the society of the town. They explained to me that their health would not permit it. They read books—a few—but they were not books about which I knew very much, and they belonged altogether to an age preceding mine. Of the names which had moved me, and of all the thoughts stirring in the time, they had heard nothing. They greatly admired Cowper, a poet who then did not much attract me.

The country near me was rather level, but towards the west it rose into soft swelling hills, between which were pleasant lanes. At about ten miles distant eastward was the sea. A small river ran across the High Street under a stone bridge; for about two miles below us it was locked up for the sake of the mills, but at the end of the two miles it became tidal and flowed between deep and muddy banks through marshes to the ocean. Almost all my walks were by the river-bank down to these marshes, and as far on as possible till the open water was visible. Not that I did not like inland scenery : nobody could like it more, but the sea was a corrective to the littleness all round me. With the ships on it sailing to the other end of the earth it seemed to connect me with the great world outside the parochialism of the society in which I lived.

Such was the town of C——, and such the company amidst which I found myself. After my probation it was arranged that I should begin my new duties at once, and accordingly I took lodgings,—two rooms over the shop of a tailor who acted as chapel-keeper, pew-opener, and sexton. There was a small endowment on the chapel of fifty pounds a year, and the rest of my income was derived from the pew-rents, which at the time I took charge did not exceed another seventy. The first Sunday on which I preached after being accepted was a dull day in November, but there was no dulness in me. The congregation had increased a good deal during the past four weeks, and I was stimulated by the prospect of the new life before me. It seemed to be a fit opportunity to say something generally about Christianity and its special peculiarities. I began by pointing out that each philosophy and religion which had arisen in the world was the answer to a question earnestly asked at the time ; it was a remedy proposed to meet some extreme pressure. Religions and philosophies were not created by idle people who sat down and said, " Let us build up a system of beliefs upon the universe ; what shall we say about immortality,

about sin?" and so on. Unless there had been antecedent necessity there could have been no religion; and
no problem of life or death could be solved except under
the weight of that necessity. The stoical morality
arose out of the condition of Rome when the scholar
and the pious man could do nothing but simply
strengthen his knees and back to bear an inevitable
burden. He was forced to find some counterpoise
for the misery of poverty and persecution, and he
found it in the denial of their power to touch him.
So with Christianity. Jesus was a poor solitary
thinker, confronted by two enormous and overpowering
organisations, the Jewish hierarchy and the Roman
state. He taught the doctrine of the kingdom of
heaven; He trained Himself to have faith in the absolute monarchy of the soul, the absolute monarchy of
His own; He tells us that each man should learn to
find peace in his own thoughts, his own visions. It is
a most difficult thing to do; most difficult to believe
that my highest happiness consists in *my* perception of
whatever is beautiful. If I by myself watch the sun
rise, or the stars come out in the evening, or feel the
love of man or woman, I ought to say to myself, " There
is nothing beyond this." But people will not rest there;
they are not content, and they are for ever chasing
a shadow which flies before them, a something external which never brings what it promises. I said that
Christianity was essentially the religion of the unknown
and of the lonely; of those who are not a success. It
was the religion of the man who goes through life
thinking much, but who makes few friends and sees
nothing come of his thoughts. I said a good deal more
upon the same theme which I have forgotten. After

the service was over I went down into the vestry.
Nobody came near me but my landlord, the chapel-
keeper, who said it was raining, and immediately went
away to put out the lights and shut up the building. I
had no umbrella, and there was nothing to be done but
to walk out in the wet. When I got home I found
that my supper, consisting of bread and cheese with a
pint of beer, was on the table, but apparently it had
been thought unnecessary to light the fire again at that
time of night. I was overwrought, and paced about
for hours in hysterics. All that I had been preaching
seemed the merest vanity when I was brought face to
face with the fact itself ; and I reproached myself bitterly that my own creed would not stand the stress
of an hour's actual trial. Towards morning I got into
bed, but not to sleep ; and when the dull daylight of
Monday came, all support had vanished, and I seemed
to be sinking into a bottomless abyss. I became
gradually worse week by week, and my melancholy
took a fixed form. I got a notion into my head that
my brain was failing, and this was my first acquaintance with that most awful malady hypochondria. I
did not know then what I know now, although I only
half believe it practically, that this fixity of form is a
frequent symptom of the disease, and that the general
weakness manifests itself in a determinate horror, which
gradually fades with returning health. For months—
many months, this dreadful conviction of coming
idiocy or insanity lay upon me like some poisonous
reptile with its fangs driven into my very marrow, so
that I could not shake it off. It went with me wherever I went, it got up with me in the morning, walked
about with me all day, and lay down with me at night.

I managed somehow or other to do my work, but I prayed incessantly for death ; and to such a state was I reduced that I could not even make the commonest appointment for a day beforehand. The mere knowledge that something had to be done agitated me and prevented my doing it. In June next year my holiday came, and I went away home to my father's house. Father and mother were going for the first time in their lives to spend a few days by the seaside together, and I went with them to Ilfracombe. I had been there about a week, when on one memorable morning, on the top of one of those Devonshire hills, I became aware of a kind of flush in the brain and a momentary relief such as I had not known since that November night. I seemed, far away on the horizon, to see just a rim of olive light low down under the edge of the leaden cloud that hung over my head, a prophecy of the restoration of the sun, or at least a witness that somewhere it shone. It was not permanent, and perhaps the gloom was never more profound, nor the agony more intense, than it was for long after my Ilfracombe visit. But the light broadened, and gradually the darkness was mitigated. I have never been thoroughly restored. Often, with no warning, I am plunged in the Valley of the Shadow, and no outlet seems possible ; but I contrive to traverse it, or to wait in calmness for access of strength. When I was at my worst I went to see a doctor. He recommended me stimulants. I had always been rather abstemious, and he thought I was suffering from physical weakness. At first wine gave me relief, and such marked relief that whenever I felt my misery insupportable I turned to the bottle. At no time in my life was I ever the worse for liquor, but I soon found the craving for it was getting the better of me. I resolved never to touch it except at night, and kept my vow; but the consequence was, that I looked forward to the night, and waited for it with such eagerness that the day seemed to exist only for the sake of the evening, when I might hope at least for rest. For the wine as wine I cared nothing; anything that would have dulled my senses would have done just as well. But now a new terror developed itself. I began to be afraid that I was becoming a slave to alcohol; that the passion for it would grow upon me, and that I should disgrace myself, and die the most contemptible of all deaths. To a certain extent my fears were just. The dose which was necessary to procure temporary forgetfulness of my trouble had to be increased, and might have increased dangerously. But one day, feeling more than usual the tyranny of my master, I received strength to make a sudden resolution to cast him off utterly. Whatever be the consequence, I said, I will not be the victim of this shame. If I am to go down to the grave, it shall be as a man, and I will bear what I have to bear honestly and without resort to the base evasion of stupefaction. So that night I went to bed having drunk nothing but water. The struggle was not felt just then. It came later, when the first enthusiasm of a new purpose had faded away, and I had to fall back on mere force of will. I don't think anybody but those who have gone through such a crisis can comprehend what it is. I never understood the maniacal craving which is begotten by ardent spirits, but I understood enough to be convinced that the man who has once rescued himself from the domination even of half a bottle, or three-parts of a bottle of claret daily, may assure himself that there is nothing more in life to be done which he need dread. Two or three remarks begotten of experience in this matter deserve record. One is, that the most powerful inducement to abstinence, in my case, was the interference of wine with liberty, and above all things its interference with what I really loved best, and the transference of desire from what was most desirable to what was sensual and base. The morning, instead of being spent in quiet contemplation and quiet pleasures, was spent in degrading anticipations. What enabled me to conquer, was not so much heroism as a susceptibility to nobler joys, and the difficulty which a man must encounter who is not susceptible to them must be enormous and almost insuperable. Pity, profound pity is his due, and especially if he happen to possess a nervous, emotional organisation. If we want to make men water-drinkers, we must first of all awaken in them a capacity for being tempted by delights which water-drinking intensifies. The mere preaching of self-denial will do little or no good. Another observation is, that there is no danger in stopping at once, and suddenly, the habit of drinking. The prisons and asylums furnish ample evidence upon that point, but there will be many an hour of exhaustion in which this danger will be simulated and wine will appear the proper remedy. No man, or at least very few men, would ever feel any desire for it soon after sleep. This shows the power of repose, and I would advise anybody who may be in earnest in this matter to be specially on guard during moments of physical fatigue, and to try the effect of eating and rest. Do not persist in a blind, obstinate wrestle. Simply take food, drink water, go to bed, and so conquer not by brute strength, but by strategy. Going back to hypochondria and its countless forms of agony, let it be borne in mind that the first thing to be aimed at is patience—not to get excited with fears, not to dread the evil which most probably will never arrive, but to sit down quietly and *wait*. The simpler and less stimulating the diet, the more likely it is that the sufferer will be able to watch through the wakeful hours without delirium, and the less likely is it that the general health will be impaired. Upon this point of health too much stress cannot be laid. It is difficult for the victim to believe that his digestion has anything to do with a disease which seems so purely spiritual, but frequently the misery will break up and yield, if it do not altogether disappear, by a little attention to physiology and by a change of air. As time wears on, too, mere duration will be a relief; for it familiarises with what at first was strange and insupportable, it shows the groundlessness of fears, and it enables us to say with each new paroxysm, that we have surmounted one like it before, and probably a worse.

CHAPTER IV.

EDWARD GIBBON MARDON.

I HAD now been "settled," to use a dissenting phrase, for nearly eighteen months. While I was ill I had no heart in my work, and the sermons I preached were very poor and excited no particular suspicion. But with gradually returning energy my love of reading revived, and questions which had slumbered again presented themselves. I continued for some time to deal with them as I had dealt with the atonement at college. I said that Jesus was the true Paschal Lamb, for that by His death men were saved from their sins, and from the consequences of them; I said that belief in Christ, that is to say, a love for Him, was more powerful to redeem men than the works of the law. All this may have been true, but truth lies in relation. It was not true when I, understanding what I understood by it, taught it to men who professed to believe in the West-minster Confession. The preacher who preaches it uses a vocabulary which has a certain definite mean-ing, and has had this meaning for centuries. He cannot stay to put his own interpretation upon it whenever it is upon his lips, and so his hearers are in a false position, and imagine him to be much more orthodox than he really is. For some time I fell into this snare, until one day I happened to be reading the story of Balaam. Balaam, though most desirous to prophesy smooth things for Balak, had nevertheless a word put into his mouth by God. When he came to Balak he was unable to curse, and could do nothing but bless. Balak, much dissatisfied, thought that a change of position might alter Balaam's temper, and he brought him away from the high places of Baal to the field of Zophim, to the top of Pisgah. But Balaam could do nothing better even on Pisgah. Not even a compromise was possible, and the second blessing was more emphatic than the first. "God," cried the prophet, pressed sorely by his message, "is not a man, that He should lie; neither the son of man, that He should repent : hath He said, and shall He not do it ? or hath He spoken, and shall He not make it good ? Behold, I have received commandment to bless : and He hath blessed; and I cannot reverse it." This was very unsatisfactory, and Balaam was asked, if he could not curse, at least to refrain from benediction. The answer was still the same. "Told not I thee, saying, All that the Lord speaketh, that I must do" ? A third shift was tried, and Balaam went to the top of Peor. This was worse than ever. The Spirit of the Lord came upon him, and he broke out into triumphal anticipation of the future glories of Israel. Balak remonstrated in wrath, but Balaam was altogether inaccessible. "If Balak would give me his house full of silver and gold, I cannot go beyond the commandment of the Lord, to do either good or bad of mine own mind ; but what the Lord saith, that will I speak." This story greatly impressed me, and I date from it a distinct disinclination to tamper with myself, or to deliver what I had to

deliver in phrases which, though they might be con-
ciliatory, were misleading.

About this time there was a movement in the town
to obtain a better supply of water. The soil was
gravelly and full of cesspools, side by side with which
were sunk the wells. A public meeting was held, and
I attended and spoke on behalf of the scheme. There
was much opposition, mainly on the score that the
rates would be increased, and on the Saturday after the
meeting the following letter appeared in the *Sentinel*,
the local paper :—

"Sir,—It is not my desire to enter into the controversy now raging about the water-supply of this
town, but I must say I was much surprised that a
minister of religion should interfere in politics. Sir,
I cannot help thinking that if the said minister would
devote himself to the Water of Life,—

'that gentle fount
Progressing from Immanuel's mount,'—

it would be much more harmonious with his function
as a follower of him who knew nothing save Christ
crucified. Sir, I have no wish to introduce contro-
versial topics upon a subject like religion into your
columns, which are allotted to a different line, but I
must be permitted to observe that I fail to see how a
minister's usefulness can be stimulated if he sets class
against class. Like the widows in affliction of old, he
should keep himself pure and unspotted from the
world. How can many of us accept the glorious
gospel on the Sabbath from a man who will incur spots
during the week by arguing about cesspools like any

other man? Sir, I will say nothing, moreover, about a minister of the gospel assisting to bind burdens—that is to say, rates and taxation—upon the shoulders of men grievous to be borne. Surely, sir, a minister of the Lamb of God, who was shed for the remission of sins, should be *against* burdens.—I am, sir, your obedient servant,   A CHRISTIAN TRADESMAN."

I had not the least doubt as to the authorship of this precious epistle. Mr. Snale's hand was apparent in every word. He was fond of making religious verses, and once we were compelled to hear the Sunday-school children sing a hymn which he had composed. The two lines of poetry were undoubtedly his. Furthermore, although he had been a chapel-goer all his life, he muddled, invariably, passages from the Bible. They had no definite meaning for him, and there was nothing, consequently, to prevent his tacking the end of one verse to the beginning of another. Mr. Snale, too, continually "failed to see." Where he got the phrase I do not know, but he liked it, and was always repeating it. However, I had no external evidence that it was he who was my enemy, and I held my peace. I was supported at the public meeting by a speaker from the body of the hall whom I had never seen before. He spoke remarkably well, was evidently educated, and I was rather curious about him.

It was my custom on Saturdays to go out for the whole of the day by the river, seawards, to prepare for the Sunday. I was coming home rather tired, when I met this same man against a stile. He bade me good-evening, and then proceeded to thank me for my speech, saying many complimentary things about it.

I asked who it was to whom I had the honour of talking, and he told me he was Edward Gibbon Mardon. "It was Edward Gibson Mardon once, sir," he said, smilingly. "Gibson was the name of a rich old aunt who was expected to do something for me, but I disliked her, and never went near her. I did not see why I should be ticketed with her label, and as Edward Gibson was very much like Edward Gibbon, the immortal author of the 'Decline and Fall,' I dropped the 's' and stuck in a 'b.' I am nothing but a compositor on the *Sentinel*, and Saturday afternoon, after the paper is out, is a holiday for me, unless there is any reporting to do, for I have to turn my attention to that occasionally." Mr. Edward Gibbon Mardon, I observed, was slightly built, rather short, and had scanty whiskers which developed into a little thicker tuft on his chin. His eyes were pure blue, like the blue of the speedwell. They were not piercing, but perfectly transparent, indicative of a character which, if it possessed no particular creative power, would not permit self-deception. They were not the eyes of a prophet, but of a man who would not be satisfied with letting a half-known thing alone and saying he believed it. His lips were thin, but not compressed into bitterness; and above everything there was in his face a perfectly legible frankness, contrasting pleasantly with the doubtfulness of most of the faces I knew. I expressed my gratitude to him for his kind opinion, and as we loitered he said—

"Sorry to see that attack upon you in the *Sentinel*. I suppose you are aware it was Snale's. Everybody could tell that who knows the man."

"If it is Mr. Snale's, I am very sorry."

" It is Snale's. He is a contemptible cur ; and yet it is not his fault. He has heard sermons about all sorts of supernatural subjects for thirty years, and he has never once been warned against meanness, so of course he supposes that supernatural subjects are everything and meanness is nothing. But I will not detain you any longer now, for you are busy. Good-night, sir."

This was rather abrupt and disappointing. However, I was much absorbed in the morrow, and passed on.

Although I despised Snale, his letter was the beginning of a great trouble to me. I had now been preaching for many months, and had met with no response whatever. Occasionally a stranger or two visited the chapel, and with what eager eyes did I not watch for them on the next Sunday, but none of them came twice. It was amazing to me that I could pour out myself as I did, poor although I knew that self to be, and yet make so little impression. Not one man or woman seemed any different because of anything I had said or done, and not a soul kindled at any word of mine, no matter with what earnestness it might be charged. How I groaned over my incapacity to stir in my people any participation in my thoughts or care for them ! Looking at the history of those days now from a distance of years, everything assumes its proper proportion. I was at work, it is true, amongst those who were exceptionally hard and worldly, but I was seeking amongst men (to put it in orthodox language) what I ought to have sought with God alone. In other, and perhaps plainer phrase, I was expecting from men a sympathy which proceeds from the Invisible only. Sometimes, indeed, it manifests itself in the long-postponed justice of time, but more frequently it is nothing more and nothing less than a consciousness of approval by the Unseen, a peace unspeakable, which is bestowed on us when self is suppressed. I did not know then how little one man can change another, and what immense and persistent efforts are necessary—efforts which seldom succeed except in childhood—to accomplish anything but the most superficial alteration of character. Stories are told of sudden conversions, and of course if a poor simple creature can be brought to believe that hell-fire awaits him as the certain penalty of his misdeeds, he will cease to do them; but this is no real conversion, for essentially he remains pretty much the same kind of being that he was before.

I remember while this mood was on me, that I was much struck with the absolute loneliness of Jesus, and with His horror of that death upon the cross. He was young and full of enthusiastic hope, but when He died He had found hardly anything but misunderstanding. He had written nothing, so that He could not expect that His life would live after Him. Nevertheless His confidence in His own errand had risen so high, that He had not hesitated to proclaim Himself the Messiah : not the Messiah the Jews were expecting, but still the Messiah. I dreamed over His walks by the lake, over the deeper solitude of His last visit to Jerusalem, and over the gloom of that awful Friday afternoon. The hold which He has upon us is easily explained, apart from the dignity of His recorded sayings and the purity of His life. There is no Saviour for us like the hero who has passed triumphantly through the distress which troubles *us*. Salvation is the spectacle of a victory by another over foes like our own. The story of Jesus is the story of the poor and forgotten. He is not the

Saviour for the rich and prosperous, for they want
no Saviour. The healthy, active, and well-to-do need
Him not, and require nothing more than is given by
their own health and prosperity. But every one who
has walked in sadness because his destiny has not
fitted his aspirations; every one who, having no opportunity to lift himself out of his little narrow town or
village circle of acquaintances, has thirsted for something beyond what they could give him; everybody
who, with nothing but a dull, daily round of mechanical
routine before him, would welcome death, if it were
martyrdom for a cause; every humblest creature, in
the obscurity of great cities or remote hamlets, who
silently does his or her duty without recognition—all
these turn to Jesus, and find themselves in Him. He
died, faithful to the end, with infinitely higher hopes,
purposes, and capacity than mine, and with almost no
promise of anything to come of them.

Something of this kind I preached one Sunday, more
as a relief to myself than for any other reason. Mardon
was there, and with him a girl whom I had not seen
before. My sight is rather short, and I could not very
well tell what she was like. After the service was
over he waited for me, and said he had done so to ask
me if I would pay him a visit on Monday evening. I
promised to do so, and accordingly went. I found him
living in a small brick-built cottage near the outskirts
of the town, the rental of which I should suppose
would be about seven or eight pounds a year. There
was a patch of ground in front and a little garden
behind, a kind of narrow strip about fifty feet long,
separated from the other little strips by iron hurdles.
Mardon had tried to keep his garden in order, and had

succeeded, but his neighbour was disorderly, and had allowed weeds to grow, blacking bottles and old tin cans to accumulate, so that whatever pleasure Mardon's labours might have afforded was somewhat spoiled. He himself came to the door when I knocked, and I was shown into a kind of sitting-room with a round table in the middle and furnished with Windsor chairs, two arm-chairs of the same kind standing on either side the fireplace. Against the window was a smaller table with a green baize tablecloth, and about half-a-dozen plants stood on the window-sill serving as a screen. In the recess on one side of the fireplace was a cupboard, upon the top of which stood a tea-caddy, a workbox, some tumblers, and a decanter full of water; the other side being filled with a bookcase and books. There were two or three pictures on the walls; one was a portrait of Voltaire, another of Lord Bacon, and a third was Albert Dürer's St. Jerome. This latter was an heirloom, and greatly prized I could perceive, as it was hung in the place of honour over the mantel-piece. After some little introductory talk, the same girl whom I had noticed with Mardon at the chapel came in, and I was introduced to her as his only daughter Mary. She began to busy herself at once in getting the tea. She was under the average height for a woman, and delicately built. Her head was small, but the neck was long. Her hair was brown, of a peculiarly lustrous tint, partly due to nature, but also to a looseness of arrangement and a most diligent use of the brush, so that the light fell not upon a dead compact mass, but upon myriads of individual hairs, each of which reflected the light. Her eyes, so far as I could make out, were a kind of greenish grey, but the

eyelashes were long, so that it was difficult exactly to
discover what was underneath them. The hands were
small, and the whole figure exquisitely graceful; the
plain black dress, which she wore fastened right up to
the throat, suiting her to perfection. Her face, as I
first thought, did not seem indicative of strength. The
lips were thin, but not straight, the upper lip showing
a remarkable curve in it. Nor was it a handsome face.
The complexion was not sufficiently transparent, nor
were the features regular. During tea she spoke very
little, but I noticed one peculiarity about her manner
of talking, and that was its perfect simplicity. There
was no sort of effort or strain in anything she said,
no attempt by emphasis of words to make up for weakness of thought, and no compliance with that vulgar
and most disagreeable habit of using intense language
to describe what is not intense in itself. Her yea was
yea, and her no, no. I observed also that she spoke
without disguise, although she was not rude. The
manners of the cultivated classes are sometimes very
charming, and more particularly their courtesy, which
puts the guest so much at his ease, and constrains him
to believe that an almost personal interest is taken in
his affairs, but after a time it becomes wearisome. It
is felt to be nothing but courtesy, the result of a rule
of conduct uniform for all, and verging very closely
upon hypocrisy. We long rather for plainness of
speech, for some intimation of the person with whom
we are talking, and that the mask and gloves may be
laid aside. Tea being over, Miss Mardon cleared away
the tea-things, and presently came back again. She
took one of the arm-chairs by the side of the fireplace,
which her father had reserved for her, and while he

and I were talking, she sat with her head leaning a little sideways on the back of the chair. I could just discern that her feet, which rested on the stool, were very diminutive, like her hands. The talk with Mardon turned upon the chapel. I had begun it by saying that I had noticed him there on the Sunday just mentioned. He then explained why he never went to any place of worship. A purely orthodox preacher it was, of course, impossible for him to hear, but he doubted also the efficacy of preaching. What could be the use of it, supposing the preacher no longer to be a believer in the common creeds? If he turns himself into a mere lecturer on all sorts of topics, he does nothing more than books do, and they do it much better. He must base himself upon the Bible, and above all upon Christ, and how can he base himself upon a myth? We do not know that Christ ever lived, or that if He lived His life was anything like what is attributed to Him. A mere juxtaposition of the Gospels shows how the accounts of His words and deeds differ according to the tradition followed by each of His biographers. I interrupted Mardon at this point by saying that it did not matter whether Christ actually existed or not. What the four evangelists recorded was eternally true, and the Christ-idea was true whether it was ever incarnated or not in a being bearing His name. "Pardon me," said Mardon, "but it does very much matter. It is all the matter whether we are dealing with a dream or with reality. I can dream about a man's dying on the cross in homage to what he believed, but I would not perhaps die there myself; and when I suffer from hesitation whether I ought to sacrifice myself for the truth, it is of immense assistance to me to know that a greater sacrifice has been made before me—that a greater sacrifice is possible. To know that somebody has poetically imagined that it is possible, and has very likely been altogether incapable of its achievement, is no help. Moreover, the commonplaces which even the most freethinking of Unitarians seem to consider as axiomatic, are to me far from certain, and even unthinkable. For example, they are always talking about the omnipotence of God. But power even of the supremest kind necessarily implies an object—that is to say, resistance. Without an object which resists it, it would be a blank, and what then is the meaning of omnipotence? It is not that it is merely inconceivable; it is nonsense, and so are all these abstract, illimitable, self-annihilative attributes of which God is made up."

This negative criticism, in which Mardon greatly excelled, was all new to me, and I had no reply to make. He had a sledgehammer way of expressing himself, while I, on the contrary, always required time to bring into shape what I saw. Just then I saw nothing; I was stunned, bewildered, out of the sphere of my own thoughts, and pained at the roughness with which he treated what I had cherished. I was presently relieved, however, of further reflection by Mardon's asking his daughter whether her face was better. It turned out that all the afternoon and evening she had suffered greatly from neuralgia. She had said nothing about it while I was there, but had behaved with cheerfulness and freedom. Mentally I had accused her of slightness, and inability to talk upon the subjects which interested Mardon and myself; but when I knew she had been in torture all the time, my opinion was

altered. I thought how rash I had been in judging
her as I continually judged other people, without being
aware of everything they had to pass through; and I
thought, too, that if I had a fit of neuralgia, everybody
near me would know it, and be almost as much annoyed
by me as I myself should be by the pain. It is curious,
also, that when thus proclaiming my troubles I often
considered my eloquence meritorious, or, at least, a kind
of talent for which I ought to praise God, contemning
rather my silent friends as something nearer than myself to the expressionless animals. To parade my toothache, describing it with unusual adjectives, making it
felt by all the company in which I might happen to be,
was to me an assertion of my superior nature. But,
looking at Mary, and thinking about her as I walked
home, I perceived that her ability to be quiet, to subdue
herself, to resist the temptation for a whole evening of
drawing attention to herself by telling us what she was
enduring, was heroism, and that my contrary tendency
was pitiful vanity. I perceived that such virtues as
patience and self-denial—which, clad in russet dress, I
had often passed by unnoticed when I had found them
amongst the poor or the humble—were more precious
and more ennobling to their possessor than poetic yearn-
ings, or the power to propound rhetorically to the world
my grievances or agonies.

Miss Mardon's face was getting worse, and as by this
time it was late, I stayed but a little while longer.

CHAPTER V.

MISS ARBOUR.

FOR some months I continued without much change in my monotonous existence. I did not see Mardon often, for I rather dreaded him. I could not resist him, and I shrank from what I saw to be inevitably true when I talked to him. I can hardly say it was cowardice. Those may call it cowardice to whom all associations are nothing, and to whom beliefs are no more than matters of indifferent research; but as for me, Mardon's talk darkened my days and nights. I never could understand the light manner in which people will discuss the gravest questions, such as God, and the immortality of the soul. They gossip about them over their tea, write and read review articles about them, and seem to consider affirmation or negation of no more practical importance than the conformation of a beetle. With me the struggle to retain as much as I could of my creed was tremendous. The dissolution of Jesus into mythologic vapour was nothing less than the death of a friend dearer to me then than any other friend whom I knew. But the worst stroke of all was that which fell upon the doctrine of a life beyond the grave. In theory I had long despised the notion that we should govern our conduct here by hope of reward or fear of punishment hereafter. But under Mardon's

remorseless criticism, when he insisted on asking for
the where and how, and pointed out that all attempts to say where and how ended in nonsense, my
hope began to fail, and I was surprised to find myself
incapable of living with proper serenity if there was
nothing but blank darkness before me at the end of a
few years. As I got older I became aware of the folly
of this perpetual reaching after the future, and of
drawing from to-morrow, and from to-morrow only, a
reason for the joyfulness of to-day. I learned, when,
alas! it was almost too late, to live in each moment as
it passed over my head, believing that the sun as it is
now rising is as good as it will ever be, and blinding
myself as much as possible to what may follow. But
when I was young I was the victim of that illusion,
implanted for some purpose or other in us by Nature,
which causes us, on the brightest morning in June, to
think immediately of a brighter morning which is to
come in July. I say nothing, now, for or against the
doctrine of immortality. All I say is, that men have
been happy without it, even under the pressure of
disaster, and that to make immortality a sole spring
of action here is an exaggeration of the folly which
deludes us all through life with endless expectation,
and leaves us at death without the thorough enjoyment
of a single hour.

So I shrank from Mardon, but none the less did the
process of excavation go on. It often happens that
a man loses faith without knowing it. Silently the
foundation is sapped while the building stands fronting
the sun, as solid to all appearance as when it was first
turned out of the builder's hands, but it last it falls
suddenly with a crash. It was so at this time with

a personal relationship of mine, about which I have hitherto said nothing. Years ago, before I went to college, and when I was a teacher in the Sunday-school, I had fallen in love with one of my fellow-teachers, and we became engaged. She was the daughter of one of the deacons. She had a smiling, pretty, vivacious face; was always somehow foremost in school treats, picnics, and chapel-work, and she had a kind of piquant manner, which to many men is more ensnaring than beauty. She never read anything; she was too restless and fond of outward activity for that, and no questions about orthodoxy or heresy ever troubled her head. We continued our correspondence regularly after my appointment as minister, and her friends, I knew, were looking to me to fix a day for marriage. But although we had been writing to one another as affectionately as usual, a revolution had taken place. I was quite unconscious of it, for we had been be-trothed for so long that I never once considered the possibility of any rupture. One Monday morning, however, I had a letter from her. It was not often that she wrote on Sunday, as she had a religious pre-judice against writing letters on that day. However, this was urgent, for it was to tell me that an aunt of hers who was staying at her father's was just dead, and that her uncle wanted her to go and live with him for some time, to look after the little children who were left behind. She said that her dear aunt died a beau-tiful death, trusting in the merits of the Redeemer. She also added, in a very delicate way, that she would have agreed to go to her uncle's at once, but she had understood that we were to be married soon, and she did not like to leave home for long. She was evidently

anxious for me to tell her what to do. This letter,
as I have said, came to me on Monday, when I was
exhausted by a more than usually desolate Sunday.
I became at once aware that my affection for her, if
it ever really existed, had departed. I saw before me
the long days of wedded life with no sympathy, and I
shuddered when I thought what I should do with such
a wife. How could I take her to Mardon? How could
I ask him to come to me? Strange to say, my pride
suffered most. I could have endured, I believe, even
discord at home, if only I could have had a woman
whom I could present to my friends, and whom they
would admire. I was never unselfish in the way in
which women are, and yet I have always been more
anxious that people should respect my wife than respect me, and at any time would withdraw myself into
the shade if only she might be brought into the
light. This is nothing noble. It is an obscure form
of egotism probably, but anyhow, such always was my
case. It took but a very few hours to excite me to
distraction. I had gone on for years without realising
what I saw now, and although in the situation itself
the change had been only gradual, it instantaneously
became intolerable. Yet I never was more incapable
of acting. What could I do? After such a long
betrothal, to break loose from her would be cruel and
shameful. I could never hold up my head again, and
in the narrow circle of Independency, the whole affair
would be known and my prospects ruined. Then other
and subtler reasons presented themselves. No men
can expect ideal attachments. We must be satisfied
with ordinary humanity. Doubtless my friend with
a lofty imagination would be better matched with

some Antigone who exists somewhere and whom he does not know. But he wisely does not spend his life in vain search after her, but settles down with the first decently sensible woman he finds in his own street, and makes the best of his bargain. Besides, there was the power of use and wont to be considered. Ellen had no vice of temper, no meanness, and it was not improbable that she would be just as good a help-meet for me in time as I had a right to ask. Living together, we should mould one another, and at last like one another. Marrying her, I should be relieved from the insufferable solitude which was depressing me to death, and should have a home. So it has always been with me. When there has been the sternest need of promptitude, I have seen such multitudes of arguments for and against every course that I have despaired. I have at my command any number of maxims, all of them good, but I am powerless to select the one which ought to be applied. A general principle, a fine saying, is nothing but a tool, and the wit of man is shown not in his possession of a well-furnished tool-chest, but in the ability to pick out the proper instrument and use it. I remained in this miserable condition for days, not venturing to answer Ellen's letter, until at last I turned out for a walk. I have often found that motion and change will bring light and resolution when thinking will not. I started off in the morning down by the river, and towards the sea, my favourite stroll. I went on and on under a leaden sky, through the level, solitary, marshy meadows, where the river began to lose itself in the ocean, and I wandered about there, struggling for guidance. In my distress I actually knelt down and prayed, but

the heavens remained impassive as before, and I was
half ashamed of what I had done, as if it were a piece
of hypocrisy. At last, wearied out, I turned home-
ward, and diverging from the direct road, I was led
past the house where the Misses Arbour lived. I was
faint, and some beneficent inspiration prompted me to
call. I went in, and found that the younger of the
two sisters was out. A sudden tendency to hysterics
overcame me, and I asked for a glass of water. Miss
Arbour, having given it to me, sat down by the side of
the fireplace opposite to the one at which I was sitting,
and for a few moments there was silence. I made
some commonplace observation, but instead of answering me she said quietly, "Mr. Rutherford, you have
been upset; I hope you have met with no accident."
How it came about I do not know, but my whole story
rushed to my lips, and I told her all of it with quivering voice. I cannot imagine what possessed me to
make her my confidante. Shy, reserved, and proud, I
would have died rather than have breathed a syllable
of my secret if I had been in my ordinary humour, but
her soft, sweet face altogether overpowered me. As I
proceeded with my tale, the change that came over her
was most remarkable. When I began she was leaning
back placidly in her large chair, with her handkerchief
upon her lap; but gradually her face kindled, she sat
upright, and she was transformed with a completeness
and suddenness which I could not have conceived possible. At last, when I had finished, she put both her
hands to her forehead, and almost shrieked out, "Shall
I tell him ?—O my God, shall I tell him ?—may God
have mercy on him!" I was amazed beyond measure
at the altogether unsuspected depth of passion which

was revealed in her whom I had never before seen
disturbed by more than a ripple of emotion. She drew
her chair nearer to mine, put both her hands on my
knees, looked right into my eyes, and said, " Listen."
She then moved back a little, and spoke as follows :—

"It is forty-five years ago this month since I was
married. You are surprised; you have always known
me under my maiden name, and you thought I had
always been single. It is forty-six years ago this
month since the man who afterwards became my
husband first saw me. He was a partner in a cloth
firm. At that time it was the duty of one member of
a firm to travel, and he came to our town, where my
father was a well-to-do carriage-builder. My father
was an old customer of his house, and the relationship
between the customer and the wholesale merchant was
then very different from what it is now. Consequently,
Mr. Hexton—for that was my husband's name—was
continually asked to stay with us so long as he remained in the town. He was what might be called a
singularly handsome man, that is to say, he was upright,
well-made, with a straight nose, black hair, dark eyes,
and a good complexion. He dressed with perfect
neatness and good taste, and had the reputation of
being a most temperate and most moral man, much
respected amongst the sect to which both of us belonged.
When he first came our way I was about nineteen and
he about three-and-twenty. My father and his had
long been acquainted, and he was of course received
even with cordiality. I was excitable, a lover of poetry,
a reader of all sorts of books, and much given to
enthusiasm. Ah! you do not think so, you do not see
how that can have been, but you do not know how

unaccountable is the development of the soul, and what is the meaning of any given form of character which presents itself to you. You see nothing but the peaceful, long since settled result, but how it came there, what its history has been, you cannot tell. It may always have been there, or have gradually grown so, in gradual progress from seed to flower, or it may be the final repose of tremendous forces. I will show you what I was like at nineteen," and she got up and turned to a desk, from which she took a little ivory miniature. "That," she said, "was given to Mr. Hexton when we were engaged. I thought he would have locked it up, but he used to leave it about, and one day I found it in the dressing-table drawer, with some brushes and combs, and two or three letters of mine. I withdrew it, and burnt the letters. He never asked for it, and here it is." The head was small and set upon the neck like a flower, but not bending pensively. It was rather thrown back with a kind of firmness, and with a peculiarly open air, as if it had nothing to conceal and wished the world to conceal nothing. The body was shown down to the waist, and was slim and graceful. But what was most noteworthy about the picture was its solemn seriousness, a seriousness capable of infinite affection, and of infinite abandonment, not sensuous abandonment — everything was too severe, too much controlled by the arch of the top of the head for that—but of an abandonment to spiritual aims. Miss Arbour continued: " Mr. Hexton after a while gave me to understand that he was my admirer, and before six months of acquaintanceship had passed my mother told me that he had requested formally that he might be considered as my suitor. She put no pressure upon me, nor did my father, excepting that they said that if I would accept Mr. Hexton they would be content, as they knew him to be a very well-conducted young man, a member of the church, and prosperous in his business. My first, and for a time my sovereign, impulse was to reject him, because I thought him mean, and because I felt he lacked sympathy with me. Unhappily I did not trust that impulse. I looked for something more authoritative, but I was mistaken, for the voice of God, to me at least, hardly ever comes in thunder, but I have to listen with perfect stillness to make it out. It spoke to me, told me what to do, but I argued with it and was lost. I was guiltless of any base motive, but I found the wrong name for what displeased me in Mr. Hexton, and so I deluded myself. I reasoned that his meanness was justifiable economy, and that his dissimilarity from me was perhaps the very thing which ought to induce me to marry him, because he would correct my failings. I knew I was too inconsiderate, too rash, too flighty, and I said to myself that his soberness would be a good thing for me. Oh, if I had but the power to write a book which should go to the ends of the world, and warn young men and women not to be led away by any sophistry when choosing their partners for life! It may be asked, How are we to distinguish heavenly instigation from hellish temptation? I say, that neither you nor I, sitting here, can tell how to do it. We can lay down no law by which infallibly to recognise the messenger from God. But what I do say is, that when the moment comes, it is perfectly easy for us to recognise him. Whether we listen to his message or not is another matter. If we do not—if we stop to dispute with him, we are undone, for we shall very soon learn to discredit him. So I was married, and I went to live in a dark manufacturing town, away from all my friends. I awoke to my misery by degrees, but still rapidly. I had my books sent down to me. I unpacked them in Mr. Hexton's presence, and I kindled at the thought of ranging my old favourites in my sitting-room. He saw my delight as I put them on some empty shelves, but the next day he said that he wanted a stuffed dog there, and that he thought my books, especially as they were shabby, had better go upstairs. We had to give some entertainments soon afterwards. The minister and his wife, with some other friends, came to tea, and the conversation turned on parties and the dulness of winter evenings if no amusements were provided. I maintained that rational human beings ought not to be dependent upon childish games, but ought to be able to occupy themselves and interest themselves with talk. Talk, I said,—not gossip, but talk, pleases me better than chess or forfeits; and the lines of Cowper occurred to me—

> 'When one, that holds communion with the skies,
> Has filled his urn where these pure waters rise,
> And once more mingles with us meaner things,
> 'Tis even as if an angel shook his wings ;
> Immortal fragrance fills the circuit wide,
> That tells us whence his treasures are supplied.'

I ventured to repeat this verse, and when I had finished, there was a pause for a moment, which was broken by my husband's saying to the minister's wife, who sat next to him, 'O Mrs. Cook, I quite forgot to express my sympathy with you; I heard that you had lost your cat.' The blow was deliberately administered, and I felt it as an insult. I was wrong, I know. I was ignorant of the ways of the world, and I ought to have been aware of the folly of placing myself above the level of my guests, and of the extreme unwisdom of revealing myself in that unguarded way to strangers. Two or three more experiences of that kind taught me to close myself carefully to all the world, and to beware how I uttered anything more than commonplace. But I was young, and ought to have been pardoned. I felt the sting of self-humiliation far into the night, as I lay and silently cried, while Mr. Hexton slept beside me. I soon found that he was entirely insensible to everything for which I most cared. Before our marriage he had affected a sort of interest in my pursuits, but in reality he was indifferent to them. He was cold, hard, and impenetrable. His habits were precise and methodical, beyond what is natural for a man of his years. I remember one evening—strange that these small events should so burn themselves into me—that some friends were at our house at tea. A tradesman in the town was mentioned, a member of our congregation, who had become bankrupt, and everybody began to abuse him. It was said that he had been extravagant; that he had chosen to send his children to the grammar-school, where the children of gentlefolk went; and finally, that only last year he had let his wife go to the seaside. I knew what the real state of affairs was. He had perhaps been living a little beyond his means, but as to the school, he had rather refined tastes, and he longed to teach his children something more than the ciphering, as it was called, and bookkeeping which they would have learned at the academy at which men in his position usually educated their boys; and as to the seaside, his wife was ill, and he could not bear to see her suffering in the smoky street, when he knew that a little fresh air and change of scene would restore her. So I said that I was sorry to hear the poor man attacked; that he had done wrong, no doubt, but so had the woman who was brought before Jesus; and that with me, charity or a large heart covered a multitude of sins. I added that there was something dreadful in the way in which everybody always seemed to agree in deserting the unfortunate. I was a little moved, and unluckily upset a teacup. No harm was done; and if my husband, who sat next to me, had chosen to take no notice, there need have been no disturbance whatever. But he made a great fuss, crying, ' Oh, my dear, pray mind! Ring the bell instantly, or it will all be through the table-cloth.' In getting up hastily to obey him, I happened to drag the cloth, as it lay on my lap; a plate fell down and was broken; everything was in confusion; I was ashamed and degraded.

"I do not believe there was a single point in Mr. Hexton's character in which he touched the universal; not a single chink, however narrow, through which his soul looked out of itself upon the great world around. If he had kept bees, or collected butterflies or beetles, I could have found some avenue of approach. But he had no taste for anything of the kind. He had his breakfast at eight regularly every morning, and read his letters at breakfast. He came home to dinner at two, looked at the newspaper for a little while after dinner, and then went to sleep. At six he had his tea, and in half-an-hour went back to his counting-house, which he did not leave till eight. Supper at nine, and bed at ten, closed the day. It was a habit of mine to read a little after supper, and occasionally I read aloud to him passages which struck me, but I soon gave it up, for once or twice he said to me, 'Now you've got to the bottom of that page, I think you had better go to bed,' although perhaps the page did not end a sentence. But why weary you with all this? I pass over all the rest of the hateful details which made life insupportable to me. Suffice to say, that one wet Sunday evening, when we could not go to chapel and were in the dining-room alone, the climax was reached. My husband had a religious magazine before him, and I sat still doing nothing. At last, after an hour had passed without a word, I could bear it no longer, and I broke out—

"'James, I am wretched beyond description!'

"He slowly shut the magazine, tearing a piece of paper from a letter and putting it in as a mark, and then said—

"'What is the matter?'

"'You must know. You must know that ever since we have been married you have never cared for one single thing I have done or said; that is to say, you have never cared for me. It is *not* being married.'

"It was an explosive outburst, sudden and almost incoherent, and I cried as if my heart would break.

"'What is the meaning of all this? You must be unwell. Will you not have a glass of wine?'

"I could not regain myself for some minutes, during which he sat perfectly still, without speaking, and without touching me. His coldness nerved me again, congealing all my emotion into a set resolve, and I said—

"'I want no wine. I am not unwell. I do not wish

to have a scene. I will not, by useless words, embitter myself against you, or you against me. You know you do not love me. I know I do not love you. It is all a bitter, cursed mistake, and the sooner we say so and rectify it the better.'

"The colour left his face; his lips quivered, and he looked as if he would have killed me.

"'What monstrous thing is this? What do you mean by your tomfooleries?'

"I did not speak.

"'Speak!' he roared. 'What am I to understand by rectifying your mistake? By the living God, you shall not make me the laughing-stock and gossip of the town! I'll crush you first.'

"I was astonished to see such rage develop itself so suddenly in him, and yet afterwards, when I came to reflect, I saw there was no reason for surprise. Self, self was his god, and the thought of the damage which would be done to him and his reputation was what roused him. I was still silent, and he went on—

"'I suppose you intend to leave me, and you think you'll disgrace me. You'll disgrace yourself. Everybody knows me here, and knows you've had every comfort and everything to make you happy. Everybody will say what everybody will have the right to say about you. Out with it and confess the truth, that one of your snivelling poets has fallen in love with you and you with him.'

"I still held my peace, but I rose and went into the best bedchamber, and sat there in the dark till bedtime. I heard James come upstairs at ten o'clock as usual, go to his own room, and lock himself in. I never hesitated a moment. I could not go home to become the centre

of all the chatter of the little provincial town in which
I was born. My old nurse, who took care of me as a
child, had got a place in London as housekeeper in a
large shop in the Strand. She was always very fond
of me, and to her instantly I determined to go. I
came down, wrote a brief note to James, stating that
after his base and lying sneer he could not expect to
find me in the morning still with him, and telling him
I had left him for ever. I put on my cloak, took some
money which was my own out of my cashbox, and at
half-past twelve heard the mail-coach approaching. I
opened the front door softly—it shut with an oiled
spring bolt; I went out, stopped the coach, and was
presently rolling over the road to the great city. Oh
that night! I was the sole passenger inside, and for
some hours I remained stunned, hardly knowing what
had become of me. Soon the morning began to break,
with such calm and such slow-changing splendour that
it drew me out of myself to look at it, and it seemed
to me a prophecy of the future. No words can tell the
bound of my heart at emancipation. I did not know
what was before me, but I knew from what I had
escaped; I did not believe I should be pursued, and no
sailor returning from shipwreck and years of absence
ever entered the port where wife and children were
with more rapture than I felt journeying through the
rain into which the clouds of the sunrise dissolved, as we
rode over the dim flats of Huntingdonshire southwards.
There is no need for me to weary you any longer, nor
to tell you what happened after I got to London, or
how I came here. I had a little property of my own,
and no child. To avoid questions I resumed my maiden
name. But one thing you must know, because it will

directly tend to enforce what I am going to beseech of
you.   Years afterwards, I might have married a man
who was devoted to me.   But I told him I was married already, and not a word of love must he speak
to me.   He went abroad in despair, and I have never
seen anything more of him.

"You can guess now what I am going to pray of you
to do.   Without hesitation, write to this girl and tell
her the exact truth.   Anything, any obloquy, anything
friends or enemies may say of you must be faced even
joyfully, rather than what I had to endure.   Better
die the death of the Saviour on the cross than live
such a life as mine."

I said: "Miss Arbour, you are doubtless right, but
think what it means.   It means nothing less than
infamy.   It will be said, I broke the poor thing's heart,
and marred her prospects for ever.   What will become
of me, as a minister, when all this is known?"

She caught my hand in hers, and cried with inde-
scribable feeling—

"My good sir, you are parleying with the great
Enemy of Souls.   Oh! if you did but know, if you
could but know, you would be as decisive in your
recoil from him, as you would from hell suddenly
opened at your feet.   Never mind the future.   The
one thing you have to do is the thing that lies next to
you, divinely ordained for you.   What does the 119th
Psalm say?—'Thy word is a lamp unto my feet.'
We have no light promised us to show us our road a
hundred miles away, but we have a light for the next
footstep, and if we take that, we shall have a light
for the one which is to follow.   The inspiration of the
Almighty could not make clearer to me the message

I deliver to you. Forgive me—you are a minister, I know, and perhaps I ought not to speak so to you, but I am an old woman. Never would you have heard my history from me, if I had not thought it would help to save you from something worse than death."

At this moment there came a knock at the door, and Miss Arbour's sister came in. After a few words of greeting I took my leave and walked home. I was confounded. Who could have dreamed that such tragic depths lay behind that serene face, and that her orderly precision was like the grass and flowers upon volcanic soil with Vesuvian fires slumbering below? I had been altogether at fault, and I was taught, what I have since been taught over and over again, that unknown abysses, into which the sun never shines, lie covered with commonplace in men and women, and are revealed only by the rarest opportunity.

But my thoughts turned almost immediately to myself, and I could bring myself to no resolve. I was weak and tired, and the more I thought the less capable was I of coming to any decision. In the morning, after a restless night, I was in still greater straits, and being perfectly unable to do anything, I fled to my usual refuge, the sea. The whole day I swayed to and fro, without the smallest power to arbitrate between the contradictory impulses which drew me in opposite directions. I knew what I ought to do, but Ellen's image was ever before me, mutely appealing against her wrongs, and I pictured her deserted and with her life spoiled. I said to myself that instinct is all very well, but for what purpose is reason given to us if not to reason with it; and reasoning in the main is a correction of what is called instinct, and of hasty first impressions. I knew many cases in which men and women loved one another without similarity of opinions, and, after all, similarity of opinions upon theological criticism is a poor bond of union. But then, no sooner was this pleaded than the other side of the question was propounded with all its distinctness, as Miss Arbour had presented it. I came home thoroughly beaten with fatigue, and went to bed. Fortunately I sank at once to rest, and with the morning was born the clear discernment that whatever I ought to do, it was more manly of me to go than to write to Ellen. Accordingly, I made arrangements for getting somebody to supply my place in the pulpit for a couple of Sundays, and went home.

CHAPTER VI.

ELLEN AND MARY.

I NOW found myself in the strangest position. What was I to do? Was I to go to Ellen at once and say plainly, "I have ceased to care for you"? I did what all weak people do. I wished that destiny would take the matter out of my hands. I would have given the world if I could have heard that Ellen was fonder of somebody else than me, although the moment the thought came to me I saw its baseness. But destiny was determined to try me to the uttermost, and make the task as difficult for me as it could be made. It was Thursday when I arrived, and somehow or other —how I do not know—I found myself on Thursday afternoon at her house. She was very pleased to see me, for many reasons. My last letters had been doubtful, and the time for our marriage, as she at least thought, was at hand. I, on my part, could not but return the usual embrace, but after the first few words were over there was a silence, and she noticed that I did not look well. Anxiously she asked me what was the matter. I said that something had been upon my mind for a long time, which I thought it my duty to tell her. I then went on to say that I felt she ought to know what had happened. When we were first engaged we both professed the same faith. From that faith I had gradually departed, and it seemed to me that it would be wicked if she were not made acquainted before she took a step which was irrevocable. This was true, but it was not quite all the truth, and with a woman's keenness she saw at once everything that was in me. She broke out instantly with a sob—

"O Rough!" a nickname she had given me, "I know what it all means—you want to get rid of me."

God help me, if I ever endure greater anguish than I did then. I could not speak, much less could I weep, and I sat and watched her for some minutes in silence. My first impulse was to retract, to put my arms round her neck, and swear that whatever I might be, Deist or Atheist, nothing should separate me from her. Old associations, the thought of the cruel injustice put upon her, the display of an emotion which I had never seen in her before, almost overmastered me, and why I did not yield I do not know. Again and again have I failed to make out what it is which, in moments of extreme peril, has restrained me from making some deadly mistake, when I have not been aware of the conscious exercise of any authority of my own. At last I said—

"Ellen, what else was I to do? I cannot help my conversion to another creed. Supposing you had found out that you had married a Unitarian and I had never told you!"

"O Rough! you are not a Unitarian, you don't love me," and she sobbed afresh.

I could not plead against hysterics. I was afraid she would get ill. I thought nobody was in the house, and I rushed across the passage to get her some stimulants. When I came back her father was in the room. He was my aversion—a fussy, conceited man, who always prated about "my daughter" to me in a tone which was very repulsive—just as if she were his property, and he were her natural protector against me.

"Mr. Rutherford," he cried, "what is the matter with my daughter? What have you said to her?"

"I don't think, sir, I am bound to tell you. It is a matter between Ellen and myself."

"Mr. Rutherford, I demand an explanation. Ellen is mine. I am her father."

"Excuse me, sir, if I desire not to have a scene here just now. Ellen is unwell. When she recovers she will tell you. I had better leave," and I walked straight out of the house.

Next morning I had a letter from her father to say, that whether I was a Unitarian or not, my behaviour to Ellen showed I was bad enough to be one. Anyhow, he had forbidden her all further intercourse with me. When I had once more settled down in my solitude, and came to think over what had happened, I felt the self-condemnation of a criminal without being able to accuse myself of a crime. I believe with Miss Arbour that it is madness for a young man who finds out he has made a blunder, not to set it right; no matter what the wrench may be. But that Ellen was a victim I do not deny. If any sin, however, was committed against her, it was committed long before our separation. It was nine-tenths mistake and one-tenth something more heinous; and the worst of it is, that while there is nothing which a man does which is of greater consequence than the choice of a woman with whom he is to live, there is nothing he does in which he is more liable to self-deception.

On my return I heard that Mardon was ill, and that probably he would die. During my absence a contested election for the county had taken place, and ur town was one of the polling-places. The lower classes were violently Tory. During the excitement of the contest the mob had set upon Mardon as he was going to his work, and had reviled him as a Republican and an Atheist. By way of proving their theism they had cursed him with many oaths, and had so sorely beaten him that the shock was almost fatal. I went to see him instantly, and found him in much pain, believing that he would not get better, but perfectly peaceful. I knew that he had no faith in immortality, and I was curious beyond measure to see how he would encounter death without such a faith; for the problem of death, and of life after death, was still absorbing me even to the point of monomania. I had been struggling as best I could to protect myself against it, but with little success. I had long since seen the absurdity and impossibility of the ordinary theories of hell and heaven. I could not give up my hope in a continuance of life beyond the grave, but the moment I came to ask myself *how*, I was involved in contradictions. Immortality is not really immortality of the person unless the memory abides and there be a connection of the self of the next world with the self here, and it was incredible to me that there should be any memories or any such connection after the dissolution of the body; moreover, the soul, whatever it may be, is so intimately one with the body, and is affected so seriously by the weaknesses, passions, and prejudices

of the body, that without it my soul would not be
myself, and the fable of the resurrection of the body,
of this same brain and heart, was more than I could
ever swallow in my most orthodox days. But the
greatest difficulty was the inability to believe that
the Almighty intended to preserve all the mass of
human beings, all the countless millions of barbaric
half-bestial forms which, since the appearance of man,
had wandered upon the earth, savage or civilised.
Is it like Nature's way to be so careful about individuals, and is it to be supposed that, having produced,
millions of years ago, a creature scarcely nobler than
the animals he tore with his fingers, she should take
pains to maintain him in existence for evermore? The
law of the universe everywhere is rather the perpetual
rise from the lower to the higher; an immortality of
aspiration after more perfect types; a suppression and
happy forgetfulness of its comparative failures. There
was nevertheless an obstacle to the acceptance of this
negation in a faintness of heart which I could not overcome. Why this ceaseless struggle, if in a few short
years I was to be asleep for ever? The position of
mortal man seemed to me infinitely tragic. He is born
into the world, beholds its grandeur and beauty, is
filled with unquenchable longings, and knows that in
a few inevitable revolutions of the earth he will cease.
More painful still; he loves somebody, man or woman,
with a surpassing devotion; he is so lost in his love
that he cannot endure a moment without it; and when
he sees it pass away in death, he is told that it is extinguished—that that heart and mind absolutely are
not. It was always a weakness with me that certain
thoughts preyed on me. I was always singularly feeble

in laying hold of an idea, and in the ability to compel myself to dwell upon a thing for any lengthened period in continuous exhaustive reflection. But, nevertheless, ideas would frequently lay hold of *me* with such relentless tenacity that I was passive in their grasp. So it was about this time with death and immortality, and I watched eagerly Mardon's behaviour when the end had to be faced. As I have said, he was altogether calm. I did not like to question him while he was so unwell, because I knew that a discussion would arise which I could not control, and it might disturb him, but I would have given anything to understand what was passing in his mind.

During his sickness I was much impressed by Mary's manner of nursing him. She was always entirely wrapped up in her father, so much so, that I had often doubted if she could survive him; but she never revealed any trace of agitation. Under the pressure of the calamity which had befallen her, she showed rather increased steadiness, and even a cheerfulness which surprised me. Nothing went wrong in the house. Everything was perfectly ordered, perfectly quiet, and she rose to a height of which I had never suspected her capable, while her father's stronger nature was allowed to predominate. She was absolutely dependent on him. If he did not get well she would be penniless, and I could not help thinking that with the like chance before me, to say nothing of my love for him and anxiety lest he should die, I should be distracted, and lose my head ; more especially if I had to sit by his bed, and spend sleepless nights such as fell to her lot. But she belonged to that class of natures which, although delicate and fragile, rejoice in difficulty. Her grief for her father was exquisite, but it was controlled by a sense of her responsibility. The greater the peril, the more complete was her self-command.

To the surprise of everybody Mardon got better. His temperate habits befriended him in a manner which amazed his more indulgent neighbours, who were accustomed to hot suppers, and whisky and water after them. Meanwhile I fell into greater difficulties than ever in my ministry. I wonder now that I was not stopped earlier. I was entirely unorthodox, through mere powerlessness to believe, and the catalogue of the articles of faith to which I might be said really to subscribe was very brief. I could no longer preach any of the dogmas which had always been preached in the chapel, and I strove to avoid a direct conflict by taking Scripture characters, amplifying them from the hints in the Bible, and neglecting what was super-natural. That I was allowed to go on for so long was mainly due to the isolation of the town and the igno-rance of my hearers. Mardon and his daughter came frequently to hear me, and this, I believe, finally roused suspicion more than any doctrine expounded from the pulpit. One Saturday morning there appeared the fol-lowing letter in the *Sentinel* :—

"SIR,—Last Sunday evening I happened to stray into a chapel not a hundred miles from Water Lane. Sir, it was a lovely evening, and

> 'The glorious stars on high,
> Set like jewels in the sky,'

were circling their courses, and, with the moon, irre-

sistibly reminded me of that blood which was shed for
the remission of sins. Sir, with my mind attuned in
that direction I entered the chapel. I hoped to hear
something of that Rock of Ages in which, as the poet
sings, we shall wish to hide ourselves in years to come.
But, sir, a young man, evidently a young man, occupied
the pulpit, and great was my grief to find that the
tainted flood of human philosophy had rolled through
the town and was withering the truth as it is in Christ
Jesus. Years ago that pulpit sent forth no uncertain
sound, and the glorious gospel was proclaimed there—
not a *German gospel*, sir—of our depravity and our
salvation through Christ Jesus. Sir, I should like to
know what the dear departed who endowed that chapel,
and are asleep in the Lord in that burying-ground,
would say if they were to rise from their graves and
sit in those pews again and hear what I heard—a
sermon which might have been a week-day lecture.
Sir, as I was passing through the town, I could not feel
that I had done my duty without announcing to you
the fact as above stated, and had not raised a humble
warning from—Sir, yours truly,

" A CHRISTIAN TRAVELLER."

Notwithstanding the transparent artifice of the last
paragraph, there was no doubt that the author of this
precious production was Mr. Snale, and I at once determined to tax him with it. On the Monday morning
I called on him, and found him in his shop.

"Mr. Snale," I said, "I have a word or two to say
to you."

"Certainly, sir. What a lovely day it is! I hope
you are very well, sir. Will you come upstairs?"

But I declined to go upstairs, as it was probable I might meet Mrs. Snale there. So I said that we had better go into the counting-house, a little place boxed off at the end of the shop, but with no door to it. As soon as we got in I began.

"Mr. Snale, I have been much troubled by a letter which has appeared in last week's *Sentinel*. Although disguised, it evidently refers to me, and to be perfectly candid with you, I cannot help thinking you wrote it."

"Dear me, sir, may I ask *why* you think so?"

"The internal evidence, Mr. Snale, is overwhelming; but if you did not write it, perhaps you will be good enough to say so."

Now Mr. Snale was a coward, but with a peculiarity which I have marked in animals of the rat tribe. He would double and evade as long as possible, but if he found there was no escape, he would turn and tear and fight to the last extremity.

"Mr. Rutherford, that is rather—ground of an, of an —what shall I say?—of an assumptive nature on which to make such an accusation, and I am not obliged to deny every charge which you may be pleased to make against me."

"Pardon me, Mr. Snale, do you then consider what I have said is an accusation and a charge? Do you think that it was wrong to write such a letter?"

"Well, sir, I cannot exactly say that it was; but I must say, sir, that I do think it peculiar of you, peculiar of you, sir, to come here and attack one of your friends, who I am sure has always showed you so much kindness—to attack him, sir, with no proof."

Now Mr. Snale had not openly denied his authorship. But the use of the word "friend" was essen-

tially a lie—just one of those lies which, by avoiding
the form of a lie, have such a charm for a mind like
his. I was roused to indignation.

"Mr. Snale, I will give you the proof which you
want, and then you shall judge for yourself. The letter
contains two lines of a hymn which you have mis-
quoted. You made precisely that blunder in talking
to the Sunday-school children on the Sunday before
the letter appeared. You will remember that in accordance with my custom to visit the Sunday school
occasionally, I was there on that Sunday afternoon."

"Well, sir, I've not denied I did write it."

"Denied you did write it!" I exclaimed, with gathering passion; "what do you mean by the subterfuge
about your passing through the town and by your
calling me your friend a minute ago? What would
you have thought if anybody had written anonymously
to the *Sentinel,* and had accused you of selling short
measure? You would have said it was a libel, and
you would also have said that a charge of that kind
ought to be made publicly and not anonymously. You
seem to think, nevertheless, that it is no sin to ruin me
anonymously."

"Mr. Rutherford, I am sure I *am* your friend. I
wish you well, sir, both here"—and Mr. Snale tried
to be very solemn—"and in the world to come. With
regard to the letter, I don't see it as you do, sir. But,
sir, if you are going to talk in this tone, I would advise
you to be careful. We have heard, sir,"—and here Mr.
Snale began to simper and grin with an indescribably
loathsome grimace,—"that some of your acquaintances
in your native town are of opinion that you have not
behaved quite so well as you should have done to a cer-

tain young lady of your acquaintance; and what is more, we have marked with pain here, sir, your familiarity with an atheist and his daughter, and we have noticed their coming to chapel, and we have also noticed a change in your doctrine since these parties attended there."

At the word "daughter" Mr. Snale grinned again, apparently to somebody behind me, and I found that one of his shopwomen had entered the counting-house, unobserved by me, while this conversation was going on, and that she was smirking in reply to Mr. Snale's signals. In a moment the blood rushed to my brain. I was as little able to control myself as if I had been shot suddenly down a precipice.

"Mr. Snale, you are a contemptible scoundrel and a liar."

The effort on him was comical. He cried: "What, sir!—what do you mean, sir?—a minister of the gospel —if you were not, I would—a liar"—and he swung round hastily on the stool on which he was sitting, to get off and grasp a yard-measure which stood against the fireplace. But the stool slipped, and he came down ignominiously. I waited till he got up, but as he rose a carriage stopped at the door, and he recognised one of his best customers. Brushing the dust off his trousers, and smoothing his hair, he rushed out without his hat, and in a moment was standing obsequiously on the pavement bowing to his patron. I passed him in going out, but the oily film of subserviency on his face was not broken for an instant.

When I got home I bitterly regretted what had happened. I never regret anything more than the loss of self-mastery. I had been betrayed, and yet I could not for the life of me see how the betrayal could have been prevented. It was upon me so suddenly, that before a moment had been given me for reflection, the words were out of my mouth. I was distinctly conscious that the *I* had not said those words. They had been spoken by some other power working in me which was beyond my reach. Nor could I foresee how to prevent such a fall for the future. The only advice, even now, which I can give to those who comprehend the bitter pangs of such self-degradation as passion brings, is to watch the first risings of the storm, and to say " Beware; be watchful," at the least indication of a tempest. Yet, after every precaution, we are at the mercy of the elements, and in an instant the sudden doubling of a cape may expose us, under a serene sky, to a blast which, taking us with all sails spread, may overset us and wreck us irretrievably.

My connection with the chapel was now obviously at an end. I had no mind to be dragged before a church meeting, and I determined to resign. After a little delay I wrote a letter to the deacons, explaining that I had felt a growing divergence from the theology taught heretofore in Water Lane, and I wished consequently to give up my connection with them. I received an answer stating that my resignation had been accepted; I preached a farewell sermon; and I found myself one Monday morning with a quarter's salary in my pocket, a few bills to pay, and a blank outlook. What was to be done? My first thought was towards Unitarianism, but when I came to cast up the sum total of what I was assured, it seemed so ridiculously small that I was afraid. The occupation of a merely miscellaneous lecturer had always seemed to me very poor. I could not get up Sunday after Sunday and retail to people little scraps suggested by what I might have been studying during the week; and with regard to the great subjects, for the exposition of which the Christian minister specially exists—how much did I know about them? The position of a minister who has a gospel to proclaim; who can go out and tell men what they are to do to be saved, was intelligible; but not so the position of a man who had no such gospel. What reason for continuance as a preacher could I claim? Why should people hear me rather than read books? I was alarmed to find, on making my reckoning, that the older I got the less I appeared to believe. Nakeder and nakeder had I become with the passage of every year, and I trembled to anticipate the complete emptiness to which before long I should be reduced. What the dogma of immortality was to me I have already described, and with regard to God I was no better. God was obviously not a person in the clouds, and what more was really firm under my feet than this —that the universe is governed by immutable laws? These laws were not what is commonly understood as God. Nor could I discern any ultimate tendency in them. Everything was full of contradiction. On the one hand was infinite misery; on the other there were exquisite adaptations producing the highest pleasure: on the one hand the mystery of life-long disease, and on the other the equal mystery of the unspeakable glory of the sunrise on a summer's morning over a quiet summer sea. I happened to hear once an atheist discoursing on the follies of theism. If he had made the world, he would have made it much better. He would not have racked innocent souls with years of torture, that tyrants might live in splendour. He would not have permitted the earthquake to swallow up thousands of harmless mortals, and so forth. But, putting aside all dependence upon the theory of a coming rectification of such wrongs as these, the atheist's argument was shallow enough. It would have been easy to show that a world such as he imagines is unthinkable directly we are serious with our conception of it. On whatever lines the world may be framed, there must be *distinction*, *difference*, a higher and a lower; and the lower relatively to the higher, must always be an evil. The *scale* upon which the higher and lower both are, makes no difference. The supremest bliss would not be bliss if it were not *definable* bliss, that is to say, in the sense that it has limits, marking it out from something else not so supreme. Perfectly uninterrupted, infinite light, without shadow, is a physical absurdity. I see a thing because it is lighted, but also because of the differences of light, or, in other words, because of shade, and without shade the universe would be objectless, and in fact invisible. The atheist was dreaming of shadowless light, a contradiction in terms. Mankind may be improved, and the improvement may be infinite, and yet good and evil must exist. So with death and life. Life without death is not life, and death without life is equally impossible. But though all this came to me, and was not only a great comfort to me, but prevented any shallow prating like that to which I listened from this lecturer, it could not be said that it was a gospel from which to derive apostolic authority. There remained morals. I could become an instructor of morality. I could warn tradesmen not to cheat, children to honour their parents, and people generally not to lie. The mission was noble, but I could not feel much enthusiasm for it, and more than this, it was a fact that reformations in morals have never been achieved by mere directions to be good, but have always been the result of an enthusiasm for some City of God, or some supereminent person. Besides, the people whom it was most necessary to reach would not be the people who would, unsolicited, visit a Unitarian meeting-house. As for a message of negations, emancipating a number of persons from the dogma of the Trinity or future punishment, and spending my strength in merely demonstrating the nonsense of orthodoxy, my soul sickened at the very thought of it. Wherein would men be helped, and wherein should I be helped? There were only two persons in the town who had ever been of any service to me. One was Miss Arbour, and the other was Mardon. But I shrank from Miss Arbour, because I knew that my troubles had never been hers. She belonged to a past generation, and as to Mardon, I never saw him without being aware of the difficulty of accepting any advice from him. He was perfectly clear, perfectly secular, and was so definitely shaped and settled, that his line of conduct might always be predicted beforehand with certainty. I knew very well what he thought about preaching, and what he would tell me to do, or rather, what he would tell me not to do. Nevertheless, after all, I was a victim to that weakness which impels us to seek the assistance of others when we know that what they offer will be of no avail. Accordingly, I called on him. Both he and Mary were at home, and I was received with more than usual cordiality. He knew already that I had resigned, for the news was all over the town. I said I was in great perplexity.

"The perplexities of most persons arise," said Mardon, "as yours probably arise, from not understanding exactly what you want to do. For one person who stumbles and falls with a perfectly distinct object to be attained, I have known a score whose disasters are to be attributed to their not having made themselves certain what their aim is. You do not know what you believe, consequently you do not know how to act."

"What would you do if you were in my case?"

"Leave the whole business and prefer the meanest handicraft. You have no right to be preaching anything doubtful. You are aware what my creed is. I profess no belief in God, and no belief in what hangs upon it. Try and name now, any earnest conviction you possess, and see whether you have a single one which I have not got."

"I *do* believe in God."

"There is nothing in that statement. What do you believe about Him?—that is the point. You will find that you believe nothing, in truth, which I do not also believe of the laws which govern the universe and man."

"I believe in an intellect of which these laws are the expression."

"Now what kind of an intellect can that be? You can assign to it no character in accordance with its acts. It is an intellect, if it be an intellect at all, which will swallow up a city, and will create the music of Mozart for me when I am weary; an intellect which brings to birth His Majesty King George IV., and the love of an affectionate mother for her child; an intellect which, in the person of a tender girl, shows an exquisite conscience, and in the person of one or two religious creatures whom I have known, shows a conscience almost inverted. I have always striven to prove to my theological friends that their mere affirmation of God is of no consequence. They may be affirming anything or nothing. The question, the all-important question is, *What* can be affirmed about Him?"

"Your side of the argument naturally admits of a more precise statement than mine. I cannot encompass God with a well-marked definition, but for all that, I believe in Him. I know all that may be urged against the belief, but I cannot help thinking that the man who looks upon the stars, or the articulation of a leaf, is irresistibly impelled, unless he has been corrupted by philosophy, to say, There is intellect there. It is the instinct of the child and of the man."

"I don't think so; but grant it, and again I ask, *What* intellect is it?"

"Again I say, I do not know."

"Then why dispute? Why make such a fuss about it?"

"It really seems to me of immense importance whether you see this intellect or not, although you say it is of no importance. It appears to be of less importance than it really is, because I do not think that even you ever empty the universe of intellect. I believe that mind never worships anything but mind, and that you worship it when you admire the level bars of cloud over the setting sun. You think you eject mind, but you do not. I can only half imagine a belief which looks upon the world as a mindless blank, and if I could imagine it, it would be depressing in the last degree to me. I know that I have mind, and to live in a universe in which my mind is answered by no other would be unbearable. Better any sort of intelligence than none at all. But, as I have just said, your case admits of plainer statement than mine. You and I have talked this matter over before, and I have never gained a logical victory over you. Often I have felt thoroughly prostrated by you, and yet when I have left you the old superstition has arisen unsubdued. I do not know how it is, but I always feel that upon this, as upon many other subjects, I never can really speak myself. An unshapen thought presents itself to me, I look at it, and I do all in my power to give it body and expression, but I cannot. I am certain that there is something truer and deeper to be said about the existence of God than anything I have said, and what is more, I am certain of the presence of this something in me, but I cannot lift it to the light."

"Ah, you are now getting into the region of senti- ment, and I am unable to accompany you. When my friends go into the cloud, I never try to follow them."

All this time Mary had been sitting in the arm- chair against the fireplace in her usual attitude, resting her head on her hand and with her feet crossed one over the other on the fender. She had been listening silently and motionless. She now closed her eyes and said—

" Father, father, it is not true."

" What is not true ?"

" I do not mean that what you have said about theology is not true, but you make Mr. Rutherford believe you are what you are not. Mr. Rutherford, father sometimes tells us he has no sentiment, but you must take no notice of him when he talks in that way. I always think of our visit to the seaside two years ago. The railway station was in a disagreeable part of the town, and when we came out we walked along a dismal row of very plain-looking houses. There were cards in the window with 'Lodgings' written on them, and father wanted to go in to ask the terms. I said that I did not wish to stay in such a dull street, but father could not afford to pay for a sea view, and so we went in to inquire. We then found that what we thought were the fronts of the houses were the backs, and that the fronts faced the bay. They had pretty gardens on the other side, and a glorious sunny prospect over the ocean."

Mardon laughed and said—

"Ah, Mary, there is no sea-front here, and no garden."

I took up my hat and said I must go. Both pressed me to stop, but I declined. Mardon urged me again, and at last said—

"I believe you've never once heard Mary sing."

Mary protested, and pleaded that as they had no piano, Mr. Rutherford would not care for her poor voice without any accompaniment. But I, too, protested that I should, and she got out the 'Messiah.' Her father took a tuning-fork out of his pocket, and having struck it, Mary rose and began, 'He was despised.' Her voice was not powerful, but it was pure and clear, and she sang with that perfect taste which is begotten solely of a desire to honour the master. The song always had a profound charm for me. Partly this was due to association. The words and tones, which have been used to embody their emotions by those whom we have loved, are doubly expressive when we use them to embody our own. The

song is potent too, because with utmost musical tenderness and strength, it reveals the secret of the influence
of the story of Jesus. Nobody would be bold enough
to cry, *That too is my case,* and yet the poorest and the
humblest soul has a right to the consolation that Jesus
was a man of sorrows and acquainted with grief. For
some reason or the other, or for many reasons, Mary's
voice wound itself into the very centre of my existence.
I seemed to be listening to the tragedy of all human
worth and genius. The ball rose in my throat, the tears
mounted to my eyes, and I had to suppress myself
rigidly. Presently she ceased. There was silence for
a moment. I looked round, and saw that Mardon's
face was on the table, buried in his hands. I felt that
I had better go, for the presence of a stranger, when
the heart is deeply stirred, is an intrusion. I noiselessly
left the room, and Mary followed. When we got to
the door she said : " I forgot that mother used to sing
that song. I ought to have known better." Her own
eyes were full; I thought the pressure of her hand as
she bade me good-bye was a little firmer than usual,
and as we parted an over-mastering impulse seized me.
I lifted her hand to my lips; without giving her time
to withdraw it, I gave it one burning kiss, and passed
out into the street. It was pouring with rain, and I
had neither overcoat nor umbrella, but I heeded not
the heavens, and not till I got home to my own fireless,
dark, solitary lodgings, did I become aware of any
contrast between the sphere into which I had been
exalted and the earthly commonplace world by which I
was surrounded.

CHAPTER VII.

EMANCIPATION.

THE old Presbyterian chapels throughout the country have many of them become Unitarian, and occasionally, even in an agricultural village, a respectable red brick building may be seen, dating from the time of Queen Anne, in which a few descendants of the eighteenth century heretics still testify against three Gods in one and the deity of Jesus Christ. Generally speaking, the attendance in these chapels is very meagre, but they are often endowed, and so they are kept open. There was one in the large straggling half-village, half-town of D——, within about ten miles of me, and the pulpit was then vacant. The income was about £100 a year. The principal man there was a small general dealer, who kept a shop in the middle of the village street, and I had come to know him slightly, because I had undertaken to give his boy a few lessons to prepare him for admission to a boarding-school. The money in my pocket was coming to an end, and as I did not suppose that any dishonesty would be imposed on me, and although the prospect was not cheering, I expressed my willingness to be considered as a candidate. In the course of a week or two I was therefore invited to preach. I was so reduced that I was obliged to walk the whole distance on the Sunday morning, and as I

was asked to no house, I went straight to the chapel,
and loitered about in the graveyard till a woman came
and opened a door at the back. I explained who I
was, and sat down in a Windsor chair against a small
kitchen table in the vestry. It was cold, but there
was no fire, nor were any preparations made for one.
On the mantel-shelf were a bottle of water and a glass,
but as the water had evidently been there for some
time, it was not very tempting. I waited in silence
for about twenty minutes, and my friend the dealer
then came in, and having shaken hands and remarked
that it was chilly, asked me for the hymns. These I
gave him and went into the pulpit. I found myself
in a plain-looking building designed to hold about
two hundred people. There was a gallery opposite
me, and the floor was occupied with high, dark,
brown pews, one or two immediately on my right and
left being surrounded with faded green curtains. I
counted my hearers, and discovered that there were
exactly seventeen, including two very old labourers,
who sat on a form near the door. The gallery was
quite empty, except a little organ or seraphine, I
think it was called, which was played by a young
woman. The dealer gave out the hymns, and accompanied the seraphine in a bass voice, singing the air.
A weak whisper might be perceived from the rest of
the congregation, but nothing more. I was somewhat
taken aback at finding in the Bible a discourse which
had been left by one of my predecessors. It was a
funeral sermon, neatly written, and had evidently done
duty on several occasions, although the allusions in it
might be considered personal. The piety and good
works of the departed were praised with emphasis, but

the masculine pronouns originally used were altered above the lines all throughout to feminine pronouns, and the word "brother" to "sister," so that no difficulty might arise in reading it for either sex. I was faint, benumbed, and with no heart for anything. I talked for about half-an-hour about what I considered to be the real meaning of the death of Christ, thinking that this was a subject which might prove as attractive as any other. After the service the assembly of seventeen departed, save one thin elderly gentleman, who came into the vestry, and having made a slight bow, said: "Mr. Rutherford, will you come with me, if you please?" I accordingly followed him, almost in silence, through the village till we reached his house, where his wife, who had gone on before, received us. They had formerly kept the shop which the dealer now had, but had retired. They might both be about sixty-five, and were of about the same temperament, pale, thin, and ineffectual, as if they had been fed on gruel. We had dinner in a large room with an old-fashioned grate in it, in which was stuck a basket stove. I remember perfectly well what we had for dinner. There was a neck of mutton (cold), potatoes, cabbage, a suet pudding, and some of the strangest-looking ale I ever saw— about the colour of lemon juice, but what it was really like I do not know, as I did not drink beer. I was somewhat surprised at being asked whether I would take potatoes *or* cabbage, but thinking it was the custom of the country not to indulge in both at once, and remembering that I was on probation, I said "cabbage." Very little was spoken during dinner-time by anybody, and scarcely a word by my hostess. After dinner she cleared the things away, and did not again appear. My host drew near the basket stove, and having remarked that it was beginning to rain, fell into a slumber. At twenty minutes to two we sallied out for the afternoon service, and found the seventeen again in their places, excepting the two labourers, who were probably prevented by the wet from attending. The service was a repetition of that in the morning, and when I came down my host again came forward and presented me with nineteen shillings. The fee was a guinea, but from that two shillings were abated for my entertainment. He informed me at the same time that a farmer, who had been hearing me and who lived five miles on my road, would give me a lift. He was a very large, stout man, with a rosy countenance, which was somewhat of a relief after the gruel face of my former friend. We went round to a stable-yard, and I got into a four-wheeled chaise. His wife sat with him in front, and a biggish boy sat with me behind. When we came to the guide-post which pointed down his lane, I got out, and was dismissed in the dark with the observation— uttered good-naturedly and jovially, but not very helpfully—that he was "afraid I should have a wettish walk." The walk certainly was wettish, and as I had had nothing to eat or drink since my midday meal, I was miserable and desponding. But just before I reached home the clouds rolled off with the south-west wind into detached, fleecy masses, separated by liquid blue gulfs, in which were sowed the stars, and the effect upon me was what that sight, thank God, always has been—a sense of the infinite, extinguishing all mean cares.

I expected to hear no more from my Unitarian acquaintances, and was therefore greatly surprised when,

a week after my visit, I received an invitation to
" settle " amongst them. The usual month's trial was
thought unnecessary, as I was not altogether a stranger
to some of them. I hardly knew what to do. I could
not feel any enthusiasm at the prospect of the engagement, but, on the other hand, there was nothing else
before me. There is no more helpless person in this
world than a minister who is thrown out of work. At
any rate, I should be doing no harm if I went. I
pondered over the matter a good deal, and then reflected
that in a case where every opening is barred save one,
it is our duty not to plunge at an impassable barrier,
but to take that one opening, however unpromising it
may be. Accordingly I accepted. My income was to
be a hundred a year, and it was proposed that I should
lodge with my friend the retired dealer, who had the
only two rooms in the village which were available. I went to bid Mardon and Mary good-bye. I
had not seen either of them since the night of the
song. To my surprise I found them both away. The
blinds were down and the door locked. A neighbour,
who heard me knocking, came out and told me the
news. Mardon had had a dispute with his employer,
and had gone to London to look for work. Mary had
gone to see a relative at some distance, and would
remain there until her father had determined what was
to be done. I obtained the addresses of both of them,
and wrote to Mardon, telling him what my destiny for
the present was to be. To Mary I wrote also and to
her I offered my heart. Looking backward, I have
sometimes wondered that I felt so little hesitation ;
not that I have ever doubted since, that what I did
then was the one perfectly right thing which I have

done in my life, but because it was my habit so to
confuse myself with meditative indecision. I had
doubted before. I remember once being so near engaging myself to a girl that the desk was open and the
paper under my hand. But I held back, could not
make up my mind, and happily was stayed. Had I
not been restrained, I should for ever have been miserable. The remembrance of this escape, and the certain
knowledge that of all beings whom I knew I was most
likely to be mistaken in an emergency, always produced in me a torturing tendency to inaction. There
was no such tendency now. I thought I chose Mary,
but there was no choice. The feeblest steel filing
which is drawn to a magnet, would think, if it had
consciousness, that it went to the magnet of its own free
will. My soul rushed to hers as if dragged by the
force of a loadstone. But she was not to be mine. I
had a note from her, a sweet note, thanking me with
much tenderness for my affectionate regard for her,
but saying that her mind had long since been made
up. She was an only child of a mother whom her
father had loved above everything in life, and she
could never leave him nor suffer any affection to
interfere with that which she felt for him and which
he felt for her. I might well misinterpret him, and
think it strange that he should be so much bound up
in her. Few people knew him as she did.

The shock to me at first was overpowering, and I
fell under the influence of that horrible monomania
from which I had been free for so long. For weeks I
was prostrate, with no power of resistance ; the evil
being intensified by my solitude. Of all the dreadful
trials which human nature has the capacity to bear

unshattered, the worst—as, indeed, I have already said
—is the fang of some monomaniacal idea which cannot
be wrenched out. A main part of the misery, as I
have also said, lies in the belief that suffering of this
kind is peculiar to ourselves. We are afraid to speak
of it, and not knowing, therefore, how common it is,
we are distracted with the fear that it is our own
special disease. I managed to get through my duties,
but how I cannot tell. Fortunately our calamities are
not what they appear to be when they lie in perspective
behind us or before us, for they actually consist of
distinct moments, each of which is overcome by itself.
I was helped by remembering my recovery before, and
I was able now, as a reward of long-continued abstinence from wine, to lie much stiller, and wait with
more patience till the cloud should lift. Mardon
having gone to London, I was more alone than ever,
but my love for Mary increased in intensity, and had a
good deal to do with my restoration to health. It was
a hopeless love, but to be in love hopelessly is more
akin to sanity than careless, melancholy indifference
to the world. I was relieved from myself by the
anchorage of all my thoughts elsewhere. The pain of
loss was great, but the main curse of my existence has
not been pain or loss, but gloom ; blind wandering in
a world of black fog, haunted by apparitions. I am
not going to expand upon the history of my silent
relationship to Mary during that time. How can I ?
All that I felt has been described better by others ; and
if it had not been, I have no mind to attempt a description myself, which would answer no purpose. I continued to correspond with Mardon, but with Mary I
interchanged no word. After her denial of me I should

have dreaded the charge of selfishness if I had opened my lips again. I could not place myself in her affection before her father.

My work at the chapel was of the most lifeless kind. My people really consisted of five families—those of the retired dealer, the farmer who took me home the first day I preached, and a man who kept a shop in the village for the sale of all descriptions of goods, including ready-made clothing and provisions. He had a wife and one child. Then there was a super-annuated brassfounder, who had a large house near, and who nominally was a Unitarian, having professed himself a Unitarian in the town in which he was formerly in business, where Unitarianism was flourish-ing. He had come down here to cultivate, for amuse-ment, a few acres of ground, and play the squire at a cheap rate. Released from active employment, he had given himself over to eating and drinking, particularly the drinking of port wine. His wife was dead, his sons were in business for themselves, and his daughters all went to church. His connection with the chapel was merely nominal, and I was very glad it was so. I was hardly ever brought into contact with him, except as trustee, and once I was asked to his house to dinner; but the attempt to make me feel my inferiority was so painful, and the rudeness of his children was so marked, that I never went again. There was also a schoolmaster, who kept a low-priced boarding-school with a Unitarian connection. He lived, however, at such a distance that his visits were very unfrequent. Sometimes on a fine summer's Sunday morning the boys would walk over—about twenty of them alto-gether, but this only happened perhaps half-a-dozen times in a year. Although my congregation had a freethought lineage, I do not think that I ever had anything to do with a more petrified set. With one exception, they were meagre in the extreme. They were perfectly orthodox, except that they denied a few orthodox doctrines. Their method was as strict as that of the most rigid Calvinist. They plumed themselves, however, greatly on their intellectual superiority over the Wesleyans and Baptists round them; and so far as I could make out, the only topics they delighted in, were demonstrations of the unity of God from texts in the Bible, and polemics against tri-theism. Sympathy with the great problems then beginning to agitate men, they had none. Socially they were cold, and the entertainment at their houses was pale and penurious. They never considered themselves bound to contribute a shilling to my support. There was an endowment of a hundred a year, and they were relieved from all further anxiety. They had no enthusiasm for their chapel, and came or stayed away on the Sunday just as it suited them, and without caring to assign any reason. The one exception was the wife of the shopkeeper. She was a contrast to her husband and all the rest. I do not think she was a Unitarian born and bred. She talked but little about theology, but she was devoted to her Bible, and had a fine sense for all the passages in it which had an experience in them. She was generous, spiritual, and possessed of an unswerving instinct for what was right. Oftentimes her prompt decisions were a scandal to her more sedate friends, who did not believe in any way of arriving at the truth except by rationalising, but she hardly ever failed to hit the mark. It was in questions of relationship between persons, of behaviour, and of morals, that her guidance was the surest. In such cases her force seemed to keep her straight, while the weakness of those around made it impossible for them not to wander, first on one side and then on the other. She was unflinching in her expressions, and at any sacrifice did her duty. It was her severity in obeying her conscience which not only gave authority to her admonitions, but was the source of her inspirations. She was not much of a reader, but she read strange things. She had some old volumes of a magazine, a " Repository " of some kind—I have forgotten what, and she picked out from them some translations of German verses which she greatly admired. She was not a well-educated woman in the school sense of the word, and of several of our greatest names in literature had heard nothing. I do not think she knew anything about Shakespeare, and she never entered into the meaning of dramatic poetry. At all points her path was her own, intersecting at every conceivable angle the paths of her acquaintances, and never straying along them, except just so far as they might happen to be hers. While I was in the village an event happened which caused much commotion. Her son was serving in the shop, and there was in the house at the time a nice-looking, clean servant-girl. Mrs. Lane, for that was my friend's name, had meditated discharging her, for, with her usual quickness, she thought she saw something in the behaviour of her son to the girl which was peculiar. One morning, however, both her son and the girl were absent, and there was a letter upon the table announcing that they were in a town about twenty miles off and were married.

The shock was great, and a tumult of voices arose, confusing counsel. Mrs. Lane said but little, but never wavered an instant. Leaving her husband to " consider what was best to be done," she got out the gig, drove herself over to her son's lodging, and presented herself to her amazed daughter-in-law, who fell upon her knees and prayed for pity. " My dear," said Mrs. Lane, " get up this instant; you are my daughter. Not another word. I've come to see what you want." And she kissed her tenderly. The girl was at heart a good girl. She was so bound to her late mistress and her new mother by this behaviour, that the very depths in her opened, and she loved Mrs. Lane ever afterwards with almost religious fervour. She was taught a little up to her son's level, and a happier marriage I never knew. Mrs. Lane told me what she had done, but she had no theory about it. She merely said that she knew it to be the right thing to do. She was very fond of getting up early in the morning and going out, and in such a village this was an eccentricity bordering almost on lunacy. At five o'clock she was often wandering about in her large garden. She was a great lover of order in the house, and kept it well under control, but I do not think I ever surprised her when she was so busy that she would not easily, and without any apparent sacrifice, leave what she was doing to come and talk with me. As I have said, the world of books in which I lived was almost altogether shut to her, but yet she was the only person in the village whose conversation was lifted out of the petty and personal into the region of the universal. I have been thus particular in describing her—I fear without raising any image of her—because she was of incalculable service

to me. I languished from lack of life, and her mere
presence, so exuberant in its full vivacity, was like
mountain air. Furthermore, she was not troubled much
with my philosophical difficulties. They had not come
in her path. Her world was the world of men and
women—more particularly of those she knew, and it
was a world in which it did me good to dwell. She
was all the more important to me, because outside our
own little circle there was no society whatever. The
Church and the other dissenting bodies considered us
as non-Christian. I often wondered that Mr. Lane
retained his business, and, indeed, he would have lost
it if he had not established a reputation for honesty,
which drew customers to him, who, notwithstanding
the denunciations of the parson, preferred tea with
some taste in it from a Unitarian to the insipid wood-
flavoured stuff which was sold by the grocer who
believed in the Trinity.

CHAPTER VIII.

PROGRESS IN EMANCIPATION.

I WAS with my Unitarian congregation for about a twelvemonth. My life during that time, save so far as my intercourse with Mrs. Lane, and one other friend presently to be mentioned, was concerned, was as sunless and joyless as it had ever been. Imagine me living by myself, roaming about the fields, and absorbed mostly upon insoluble problems with which I never made any progress, and which tended to draw me away from what enjoyment of life there was which I might have had. One day I was walking along under the south side of a hill, which was a great place for butterflies, and I saw a man, apparently about fifty years old, coming along with a butterfly net. He did not see me, for he looked about for a convenient piece of turf, and presently sat down, taking out a sandwich box, from which he produced his lunch. His occupation did not particularly attract me, but in those days, if I encountered a new person who was not repulsive, I was always as eager to make his acquaintance as if he perchance might solve a secret for me, the answer to which I burned to know. I have been disappointed so many times, and have found that nobody has much more to tell me, that my curiosity has somewhat abated, but even now, the news that anybody who has the reputation for intelligence has come near me, makes me restless to see him. I accordingly saluted the butterfly catcher, who returned the salutation kindly, and we began to talk. He told me that he had come seven miles that morning to that spot, because he knew that it was haunted by one particular species of butterfly which he wished to get; and as it was a still, bright day, he hoped to find a specimen. He had been unsuccessful for some years. Presupposing that I knew all about his science, he began to discourse upon it with great freedom, and he ended by saying that he would be happy to show me his collection, which was one of the finest in the country.

"But I forget," said he, "as I always forget in such cases, perhaps you don't care for butterflies."

"I take much interest in them. I admire exceedingly the beauty of their colours."

"Ah, yes, but you don't care for them scientifically, or for collecting them."

"No, not particularly. I cannot say I ever saw much pleasure in the mere classification of insects."

"Perhaps you are devoted to some other science?"

"No, I am not."

"Well, I daresay it looks absurd for a man at my years to be running after a moth. I used to think it was absurd, but I am wiser now. However, I cannot stop to talk; I shall lose the sunshine. The first time you are anywhere near me, come and have a look. You will alter your opinion."

Some weeks afterwards I happened to be in the neighbourhood of the butterfly catcher's house, and I called. He was at home, and welcomed me cordially. The first thing he did was to show me his little museum.

It was really a wonderful exhibition, and as I saw the creatures in lines, and noted the amazing variations of the single type, I was filled with astonishment. Seeing the butterflies systematically arranged was a totally different thing from seeing a butterfly here and there, and gave rise to altogether new thoughts. My friend knew his subject from end to end, and I envied him his mastery of it. I had often craved the mastery of some one particular province, be it ever so minute. I half or a quarter knew a multitude of things, but no one thing thoroughly, and was never sure, just when I most wanted to be sure. We got into conversation, and I was urged to stay to dinner. I consented, and found that my friend's household consisted of himself alone. After dinner, as we became a little more communicative, I asked him when and how he took to this pursuit.

"It will be twenty-six years ago next Christmas," said he, "since I suffered a great calamity. You will forgive my saying anything about it, as I have no assurance that the wound which looks healed may not break out again. Suffice to say, that for some ten years or more my thoughts were almost entirely occupied with death and our future state. There is a strange fascination about these topics to many people, because they are topics which permit a great deal of dreaming, but very little thinking: in fact, true thinking, in the proper sense of the word, is impossible in dealing with them. There is no rigorous advance from one position to another, which is really all that makes thinking worth the name. Every man can imagine or say cloudy things about death and the future, and feel himself here, at least, on a level with the ablest brain which he knows. I went on gazing gloomily into dark emptiness, till all life became nothing for me. I did not care to live, because there was no assurance of existence beyond. By the strangest of processes, I neglected the world, because I had so short a time to be in it. It is with absolute horror now that I look back upon those days, when I lay as if alive in a coffin of lead. All passions and pursuits were nullified by the ever-abiding sense of mortality. For years this mood endured, and I was near being brought down to the very dust. At last, by the greatest piece of good fortune, I was obliged to go abroad. The change, and the obligation to occupy myself about many affairs, was an incalculable blessing to me. While travelling I was struck with the remarkable and tropical beauty of the insects, and especially of the butterflies. I captured a few, and brought them home. On showing them to a friend, learned in such matters, I discovered that they were rare, and I had a little cabinet made for them. I looked into the books, found what it was which I had got, and what I had not got. Next year it was my duty to go abroad again, and I went with some feeling akin to pleasure, for I wished to add to my store. I increased it considerably, and by the time I returned I had as fine a show as any private person might wish to possess. A good deal of my satisfaction, perhaps, was unaccountable, and no rational explanation can be given of it. But men should not be too curious in analysing and condemning any means which nature devises to save them from themselves, whether it be coins, old books, curiosities, butterflies, or fossils. And yet my newly-acquired passion was not altogether inexplicable. I was the owner of something which other persons did not own, and in a little while, in my own limited domain I was supreme. No man either can study any particular science thoroughly without transcending it; and it is an utter mistake to suppose, that because a student sticks to any one branch, he necessarily becomes contracted. However, I am not going to philosophise; I do not like it. All I can say is, that I shun all those metaphysical specu- lations of former years as I would a path which leads to madness. Other people may be able to occupy themselves with them and be happy; I cannot. I find quite enough in my butterflies to exercise my wonder, and yet, on the other hand, my study is not a mere vacant, profitless stare. When you saw me that morn- ing, I was trying to obtain an example which I have long wanted to fill up a gap. I have looked for it for years, but have missed it. But I know it has been seen lately where we met, and I shall triumph at last."

A good deal of all this was to me incomprehensible. It seemed mere solemn trifling compared with the in- vestigation of those great questions with which I had been occupied, but I could not resist the contagion of my friend's enthusiasm when he took me to his little library, and identified his treasures with pride, pointing out at the same time those in which he was deficient. He was specially exultant over one minute creature which he had caught himself, which he had not as yet seen figured, and he proposed going to the British Museum almost on purpose to see if he could find it there.

When I got home I made inquiries into the history of my entomologist. I found that years ago he had married a delicate girl, of whom he was devotedly fond.

She died in childbirth, leaving him completely broken. Her offspring, a boy, survived, but he was a cripple, and grew up deformed. As he neared manhood he developed a satyr-like lustfulness, which was almost uncontrollable, and made it difficult to keep him at home without constraint. He seemed to have no natural affection for his father, nor for anybody else, but was cunning with the base beastly cunning of the ape. The father's horror was infinite. This thing was his only child, and the child of the woman whom he worshipped. He was excluded from all intercourse with friends; for, as the boy could not be said to be mad, he could not be shut up. After years of inconceivable misery, however, lust did deepen into absolute lunacy, and the crooked, misshapen monster was carried off to an asylum, where he died, and the father well-nigh went there too.

Before I had been six months amongst the Unitarians, I found life even more intolerable with them than it had been with the Independents. The difference of a little less belief was nothing. The question of Unitarianism was altogether dead to me; and although there was a phase of the doctrine of God's unity which would now and then give me an opportunity for a few words which I felt, it was not a phase for which my hearers in the least cared or which they understood. Here, as amongst the Independents, there was the same lack of personal affection, or even of a capability of it —excepting always Mrs. Lane—and, in fact, it was more distressing amongst the Unitarians than amongst the orthodox. The desire for something like sympathy and love absolutely devoured me. I dwelt on all the instances in poetry and history in which one human being had been bound to another human being, and I

reflected that my existence was of no earthly importance to anybody.   I could not altogether lay the blame
on myself.   God knows that I would have stood against
a wall and have been shot for any man or woman whom
I loved, as cheerfully as I would have gone to bed, but
nobody seemed to wish for such a love, or to know
what to do with it.   Oh the humiliations under which
this weakness has bent me!   Often and often I have
thought that I have discovered somebody who could
really comprehend the value of a passion which could
tell everything and venture everything.   I have over-
stepped all bounds of etiquette in obtruding myself on
him, and have opened my heart even to shame.   I have
then found that it was all on my side.   For every
dozen times I went to his house, he came to mine once,
and only when pressed: I have languished in sickness
for a month without his finding it out; and if I were to
drop into the grave, he would perhaps never give me
another thought.   If I had been born a hundred years
earlier, I should have transferred this burning longing to
the unseen God and have become a devotee.   But I was
a hundred years too late, and I felt that it was mere
cheating of myself and a mockery to think about love
for the only God whom I knew, the forces which maintained the universe.   I am now getting old, and have
altered in many things.   The hunger and thirst of those
years have abated, or rather, the fire has had ashes
heaped on it, so that it is well-nigh extinguished.   I
have been repulsed into self-reliance and reserve,
having learned wisdom by experience; but still I know
that the desire has not died, as so many other desires
have died, by the natural evolution of age.   It has been
forcibly suppressed, and that is all.   If anybody who

reads these words of mine should be offered by any young dreamer such a devotion as I once had to offer, and had to take back again refused so often, let him in the name of all that is sacred accept it. It is simply the most precious thing in existence. Had I found anybody who would have thought so, my life would have been redeemed into something which I have often imagined, but now shall never know.

I determined to leave, but what to do I could not tell. I was fit for nothing, and yet I could not make up my mind to accept a life which was simply living. It must be a life through which some benefit was conferred upon my fellow-creatures. This was mainly delusion. I had not then learned to correct this natural instinct to be of some service to mankind by the thought of the boundlessness of infinity and of nature's profuseness. I had not come to reflect that, taking into account her eternities, and absolute exhaustless-ness, it was folly in me to fret and fume, and I there-fore clung to the hope that I might employ myself in some way which, however feebly, would help mankind a little to the realisation of an ideal. But I was not the man for such a mission. I lacked altogether that concentration which binds up the scattered powers into one resistless energy, and I lacked faith. All I could do was to play the vagrant in literature, picking up here and there an idea which attracted me, and pre-senting it to my flock on the Sunday ; the net result being next to nothing. However, existence like that which I had been leading was intolerable, and change it I must. I accordingly resigned, and with ten pounds in my pocket, which was all that remained after paying my bills, I came to London, thinking that until I could

settle what to do, I would try and teach in a school.
I called on an agent somewhere near the Strand, and
after a little negotiation, was engaged by a gentleman
who kept a private establishment at Stoke Newington.
Thither I accordingly went one Monday afternoon in
January, about two days before the term commenced.
When I got there, I was shown into a long schoolroom,
which had been built out from the main building. It
was dark, save for one candle, and was warmed by a
stove. The walls were partly covered with maps, and
at one end of the room hung a diagram representing a
globe, on which an immense amount of wasted ingenuity
had been spent to produce the illusion of solidity. The
master, I was told, was out, and in this room with one
candle I remained till nine o'clock. At that time a
servant brought me some bread and cheese on a small
tray, with half-a-pint of beer. I asked for water, which
was given me, and she then retired. The tray was set
down on the master's raised desk, and sitting there I
ate my supper in silence, looking down upon the dimly-
lighted forms, and forward into the almost absolute
gloom. At ten o'clock a man, who seemed as if he
were the knife and boot cleaner, came and said he
would show me where I was to sleep. We passed
through the schoolroom into a kind of court, where
there was a ladder standing against a trap-door. He
told me that my bedroom was up there, and that when
I got up I could leave the ladder down, or pull it up
after me, just as I pleased. I ascended and found a
little chamber, duly furnished with a chest of drawers,
bed, and washhand stand. It was tolerably clean and
decent; but who shall describe what I felt. I went
to the window and looked out. There were scattered

lights here and there marking roads, but as they crossed
one another, and now and then stopped where building
had ceased, the effect they produced was that of bewil-
derment with no clue to it. Further off was the great
light of London, like some unnatural dawn, or the
illumination from a fire which could not itself be seen.
I was overcome with the most dreadful sense of loneliness. I suppose it is the very essence of passion, using
the word in its literal sense, that no account can be
given of it by the reason. Reflecting on what I suffered
then, I cannot find any solid ground for it, and yet
there are not half-a-dozen days or nights of my life
which remain with me like that one. · I was beside
myself with a kind of terror, which I cannot further
explain. It is possible for another person to understand
grief for the death of a friend, bodily suffering, or any
emotion which has a distinct cause, but how shall he
understand the worst of all calamities, the nameless
dread, the efflux of all vitality, the ghostly haunting
horror which is so nearly akin to madness? It is many
years ago since that evening, but while I write I am at
the window still, and the yellow flare of the city is still
in my eyes. I remember the thought of all the happy
homes which lay around me, in which dwelt men who
had found a position, an occupation, and, above all
things, affection. I know the causelessness of a good
deal of all those panic fears, and all that suffering, but
I tremble to think how thin is the floor on which we
stand which separates us from the bottomless abyss.

The next morning I went down into the schoolroom,
and after I had been there for some little time, the
proprietor of the school made his appearance. He was
not a bad man, nor even unkind in his way, but he

was utterly uninteresting, and as commonplace as
might be expected after having for many years done
nothing but fight a very uphill battle in boarding the
sons of tradesfolk, and teaching them, at very moderate
rates, the elements of Latin, and the various branches
of learning which constitute what is called a commercial
education. He said that he expected some of the boys
back that day ; that when they came, he should wish
me to take my meals with them, but that meanwhile
he would be glad if I would breakfast with him and
his wife. This accordingly I did. What his wife was
like I have almost entirely forgotten, and I only saw
her once again. After breakfast he said I could go
for a walk, and for a walk I went; wandering about
the dreary intermingled chaos of fields with damaged
hedges, and new roads divided into building plots.

Meanwhile one or two of the boys had made their
appearance, and I therefore had my dinner with them.
After dinner, as there was nothing particular to do, I
was again dismissed with them for a walk just as the
light of the winter afternoon was fading. My companions were dejected, and so was I. The wind was
south-easterly, cold and raw, and the smoke came up
from the region about the river and shrouded all the
building plots in fog. I was now something more than
depressed. It was absolutely impossible to endure such
a state of things any longer, and I determined that,
come what might, I would not stop. I considered
whether I should leave without saying a word, that is
to say, whether I should escape, but I feared pursuit
and some unknown legal proceedings. When I got
home, therefore, I sought the principal, and informed
him that I felt so unwell that I was afraid I must

throw up my engagement at once. He naturally observed that this was a serious business for him; that my decision was very hasty—what was the matter with me? I might get better; but he concluded, after my reiterated asseverations that I must go, with a permission to resign, only on one condition, that I should obtain an equally efficient substitute at the same salary. I was more agitated than ever. With my natural tendency to believe the worst, I had not the least expectation of finding anybody who would release me. The next morning I departed on my errand. I knew a poor student who had been at college with me, and who had nothing to do, and to him I betook myself. I strove—as even now I firmly believe—not to make the situation seem any better than it was, and he consented to take it. I have no clear recollection of anything that happened till the following day, excepting that I remember with all the vividness of actual and present sensuous perception, lugging my box down the ladder and sending for a cab. I was in a fever lest anything should arrest me, but the cab came, and I departed. When I had got fairly clear of the gates, I literally cried tears of joy—the first and the last of my life. I am constrained now, however, to admit that my trouble was but a bubble blown of air, and I doubt whether I have done any good by dwelling upon it.

CHAPTER IX.

OXFORD STREET.

UNTIL I had actually left, I hardly knew where I was going, but at last I made up my mind I would go to Reuben Shapcott, another fellow-student, whom I knew to be living in lodgings in one of the streets just then beginning to creep over the unoccupied ground between Camden Town and Haverstock Hill, near the Chalk Farm turnpike gate. To his address I betook myself, and found him not at home. He, like me, had been unsuccessful as a minister, and wrote a London letter for two country papers, making up about £100 or £120 a year by preaching occasionally in small Unitarian chapels in the country. I waited till his return, and told him my story. He advised me to take a bed in the house where he was staying, and to consider what could be done. At first I thought I would consult Mardon, but I could not bring myself to go near him. How was I to behave in Mary's presence ? During the last few months she had been so continually before me, that it would have been absolutely impossible for me to treat her with assumed indifference. I could not have trusted myself to attempt it. When I had been lying alone and awake at night, I had thought of all the endless miles of hill and valley that lay outside my window, separating me from the one house in which I could be at peace; and at times I scarcely prevented myself from getting up and taking the mail train and presenting myself at Mardon's door, braving all consequences. With the morning light, however, would come cooler thoughts, and a dull sense of impossibility. This, I know, was not pure love for her; it was a selfish passion for relief. But then I have never known what is meant by a perfectly pure love. When Christian was in the Valley of the Shadow of Death, and, being brought to the mouth of hell, was forced to put up his sword, and could do no other than cry, *O Lord, I beseech Thee, deliver my soul,* he heard a voice going before him and saying, *Though I walk through the Valley of the Shadow of Death, I will fear none ill, for Thou art with me.* And by and by the day broke. "Then," said Christian, "He hath turned the Shadow of Death into morning. Whereupon Christian sang—

> " Oh world of wonders ! (I can say no less)
> That I should be preserved in that distress
> That I have met with here ! Oh, blessed be
> That hand that from it hath delivered me ! "

This was Christian's love for God, and for God as his helper. Was that perfectly pure ? However, this is a digression. I determined to help myself in my own way, and thought I would try the publishers. One morning I walked from Camden Town to Paternoster Row. I went straightway into two or three shops and asked whether they wanted anybody. I was ready to do the ordinary work of a publisher's assistant, and aspired no higher. I met with several refusals, some of them not over polite, and the degradation—for so I felt it—of wandering through the streets and suing for employment cut me keenly. I remember one man in particular, who spoke to me with the mechanical brutality with which probably he replied to a score of similar applications every week. He sat in a little glass box at the end of a long dark room lighted with gas. It was a bitterly cold room, with no contrivance for warming it, but in his box there was a fire burning for his own special benefit. He surveyed all his clerks unceasingly, and woe betide the unhappy wretch who was caught idling. He and his slaves reminded me of the thrashing machine which is worked by horses walking round in a ring, the driver being perched on a high stool in the middle and armed with a long whip. While I was waiting his pleasure, he came out and spoke to one or two of his miserable subordinates words of directest and sharpest rebuke, without anger or the least loss of self-possession, and yet without the least attempt to mitigate their severity. I meditated much upon him. If ever I had occasion to rebuke anybody, I always did it apologetically, unless I happened to be in a flaming passion—and this was my habit, not from any respectable motive of consideration for the person rebuked, but partly because I am timid, and partly because I shrink from giving pain. This man said with perfect ease what I could not have said unless I had been wrought up to white heat. With all my dislike to him, I envied him: I envied his complete certainty; for although his language was harsh in the extreme, he was always sure of his ground, and the victim upon whom his lash descended could never say that he had given absolutely no reason for the chastisement, and that it was altogether a mistake. I envied also his ability to make himself disagreeable and care nothing about it; his power to walk in his own path, and his resolve to succeed, no matter what the cost might be. As I left him, it occurred to me that I might be more successful perhaps with a publisher of whom I had heard, who published and sold books of a sceptical turn. To him I accordingly went, and although I had no introductions or recommendatory letters, I was received, if not with a cordiality, at least with an interest which surprised me. He took me into a little back shop, and after hearing patiently what I wanted, he asked me somewhat abruptly what I thought of the miracles in the Bible. This was a curious question if he wished to understand my character; but his mind so constantly revolved in one circle, and existed so completely by hostility to the prevailing orthodoxy, that belief or disbelief in it was the standard by which he judged men. It was a very absurd standard doubtless, but no more absurd than many others, and not so absurd then as it would be now, when heresy is becoming more fashionable. I explained to him as well as I could what my position was; that I did not suppose that the miracles actually happened as they are recorded, but that, generally speaking, the miracle was a very intense statement of a divine truth; in fact, a truth which was felt with a more than common intensity seemed to take naturally a miraculous expression. Hence, so far from neglecting the miraculous stories of the Bible as simply outside me, I rejoiced in them, more, perhaps, than in the plain historical or didactic prose. He seemed content, although hardly to comprehend, and the result was that he asked me if I would help him in his business. In order to do this, it would be more economical if I would live in his house, which was too big for him. He promised to give me £40 a year, in addition to board and lodging. I joyously assented, and the bargain was struck. The next day I came to my new quarters. I found that he was a bachelor, with a niece, apparently about four or five and twenty years old, acting as a housekeeper, who assisted him in literary work. My own room was at the top of the house, warm, quiet, and comfortable, although the view was nothing but a wide reaching assemblage of chimney pots. My hours were long—from nine in the morning till seven in the evening; but this I did not mind. I felt that if I was not happy, I was at least protected, and that I was with a man who cared for me, and for whom I cared. The first day I went there, he said that I could have a fire in my bedroom whenever I chose, so that I could always retreat to it when I wished to be by myself. As for my duties, I was to sell his books, keep his accounts, read proofs, run errands, and, in short, do just what he did himself. After my first morning's work we went upstairs to dinner, and I was introduced to "my niece Theresa." I was rather surprised that I should have been admitted to a house in which there lived a young woman with no mother nor aunt, but this surprise ceased when I came to know more of Theresa and her uncle. She had yellowish hair which was naturally waved, a big arched head, greyish blue eyes, so far as I could make out, and a mouth which, although it had curves in it, was compressed and indicative of great force of character. She was rather short, with square shoulders, and she had a singularly vigorous firm walk. She had a way, when

she was not eating or drinking, of sitting back in her
chair at table and looking straight at the person with
whom she was talking.   Her uncle, whom, by the way,
I had forgotten to name—his name was Wollaston—
happened to know some popular preacher whom I
knew, and I said that I wondered so many people
went to hear him, for I believed him to be a hypocrite,
and hypocrisy was one of the easiest of crimes to discover.   Theresa, who had hitherto been silent, and
was reclining in her usual attitude, instantly broke
out with an emphasis and directness which quite
startled me.

"The easiest to discover, do you think, Mr. Rutherford ; I think it is the most difficult, at least for
ordinary persons; and when they do discover it, I
believe they like it, especially if it is successful.   They
like the sanction it gives to their own hypocrisy.   They
like a man to come to them who will say to them, ' We
are all hypocrites together,' and who will put his finger
to his nose and comfort them.   Don't you think so
yourself ? "

In conversation I was always a bad hand at assum-
ing a position contrary to the one assumed by the
person to whom I might be talking; nor could I per-
sistently maintain my own position if it happened to be
opposed.   I always rather tried to see as my opponent
saw, and to discover how much there was in him with
which I could sympathise.   I therefore assented weakly
to Theresa, and she seemed disappointed.   Dinner was
just over; she got up and rang the bell and went out
of the room.

I found my work very hard, and some of it even
loathsome.   Particularly loathsome was that part of

it which brought me into contact with the trade. I
had to sell books to the booksellers' assistants, and I
had to collect books myself. These duties are usually
undertaken in large establishments by men specially
trained, who receive a low rate of wages, and who are
rather a rough set. It was totally different work to
anything I had ever had to do before, and I suffered
as a man with soft hands would suffer, who was suddenly called to be a blacksmith or a dock-labourer.
Specially, too, did I miss the country. London lay
round me like a mausoleum. I got into the habit of
rising very early in the morning and walking out to
Kensington Gardens and back before breakfast, varying
my route occasionally so as even to reach Battersea
Bridge, which was always a favourite spot with me.
Kensington Gardens and Battersea Bridge were poor
substitutes for the downs, and for the level stretch by
the river towards the sea where I first saw Mardon,
but we make too much of circumstances, and the very
pressure of London produced a sensibility to whatever
loveliness could be apprehended there, which was absent
when loveliness was always around me. The stars seen
in Oxford Street late one night; a sunset one summer
evening from Lambeth pier; and above everything,
Piccadilly very early one summer morning, abide with
me still, when much that was more romantic has been
forgotten. On the whole, I was not unhappy. The
constant outward occupation prevented any eating of
the heart or undue brooding over problems which were
insoluble, at least for my intellect, and on that very
account fascinated me the more. I do not think that
Wollaston cared much for me personally. He was a
curious compound, materialistic yet impulsive, and for

ever drawn to some new thing; without any love for
anybody particularly, as far as I could see, and yet with
much more general kindness and philanthropy than
many a man possessing much stronger sympathies and
antipathies. There was no holy of holies in him, into
which one or two of the elect could occasionally be
admitted and feel God to be there. He was no temple,
but rather a comfortable hospitable house open to all
friends, well furnished with books and pictures, and
free to every guest from garret to cellar. He had
"liberal" notions about the relationship between the
sexes. Not that he was a libertine, but he disbelieved
in marriage, excepting for so long as husband and wife
are a necessity to one another. If one should find the
other uninteresting, or somebody else more interesting
he thought there ought to be a separation. All this I
soon learned from him, for he was communicative without any reserve. His treatment of his niece was peculiar. He would talk on all kinds of subjects before her,
for he had a theory that she ought to receive precisely
the same social training as men, and should know just
what men knew. He was never coarse, but on the
other hand he would say things to her in my presence,
which brought a flame into my face. What the evil
consequences of this might be, I could not at once
foresee, but one good result obviously was, that in his
house there was nothing of that execrable practice of
talking down to women; there was no change of level
when women were present. One day he began to speak
about a novel which everybody was reading then, and
I happened to say that I wished people who wrote
novels would not write as if love were the very centre
and sum of human existence. A man's life was made

up of so much besides love, and yet novelists were never weary of repeating the same story, telling it over and over again in a hundred different forms.

"I do not agree with you," said Theresa. "I disagree with you utterly. I dislike foolish inane sentiment— it makes me sick; but I do believe, in the first place, that no man was ever good for anything who has not been devoured, I was going to say, by a great devotion to a woman. The lives of your great men are as much the history of women whom they adored as of themselves. Dante, Byron, Shelley, it is the same with all of them, and there is no mistake about it; it is the great fact of life. What would Shakespeare be without it? and Shakespeare *is* life. A man, worthy to be named a man, will find the fact of love perpetually confronting him till he reaches old age, and if he be not ruined by worldliness or dissipation, will be troubled by it when he is fifty as much as when he was twenty-five. It is the subject of all subjects. People abuse love, and think it the cause of half the mischief in the world. It is the one thing that keeps the world straight, and if it were not for that overpowering instinct, human nature would fall asunder; would be the prey of inconceivable selfishness and vices, and finally, there would be universal suicide. I did not intend to be eloquent: I hate being eloquent. But you did not mean what you said; you spoke from the head or teeth merely."

Theresa's little speech was delivered not with any heat of the blood. There was no excitement in her grey eyes, nor did her cheek burn. Her brain seemed to rule everything. This was an idea she had, and she kindled over it because it was an idea. It was impossible, of course, that she should say what she did without some movement of the organ in her breast, but how much share this organ had in her utterances, I never could make out. How much was due to the interest which she as a looker-on felt in men and women, and how much was due to herself as a woman, was always a mystery to me. She was fond of music, and occasionally I asked her to play to me. She had a great contempt for bungling, and not being a professional player, she never would try a piece in my presence of which she was not perfectly master. She particularly liked to play Mozart, and on my asking her once to play a piece of Beethoven, she turned round upon me and said: "You like Beethoven best. I knew you would. He encourages a luxurious revelling in the incomprehensible and indefinably sublime. He is not good for you."

My work was so hard, and the hours were so long, that I had little or no time for reading, nor for thinking either, except so far as Wollaston and Theresa made me think. Wollaston himself took rather to science, although he was not scientific, and made a good deal of what he called psychology. He was not very profound, but he had picked up a few phrases, or if this word is too harsh, a few ideas about metaphysical matters from authors who contemned metaphysics, and with these he was perfectly satisfied. A stranger listening to him would at first consider him well read, but would soon be undeceived, and would find that these ideas were acquired long ago; that he had never gone behind or below them, and that they had never fructified in him, but were like hard stones, which he rattled in his pocket. He was totally unlike Mardon. Mardon, although he would have agreed with many of

Wollaston's results, differed entirely from him in the processes by which they had been brought about; and a mental comparison of the two often told me what I had been told over and over again, that what we believe is not of so much importance as the path by which we travel to it. Theresa too, like her uncle, eschewed metaphysics, but she was a woman, and a woman's impulses supplied in her the lack of those deeper questionings, and at times prompted them. She was far more original than he was, and was impatient of the narrowness of the circle in which he moved. Her love of music, for example, was a thing incomprehensible to him, and I do not remember that he ever sat for a quarter of an hour really listening to it. He would read the newspaper or do anything while she was playing. She never resented his inattention, except when he made a noise, and then, without any rebuke, she would break off and go away. This mode of treatment was the outcome of one of her theories. She disbelieved altogether in punishment, except when it was likely to do good, either to the person punished or to others. "A good deal of punishment," she used to say, "is mere useless pain."

Both Theresa and her uncle were kind and human, and I endeavoured to my utmost to repay them by working my hardest. My few hours of leisure were sweet, and when I spent them with Wollaston and Theresa, were interesting. I often asked myself why I found this mode of existence more tolerable than any other I had hitherto enjoyed. I had, it is true, an hour or two's unspeakable peace in the early morning, but, as I have said, at nine my toil commenced, and, with a very brief interval for meals, lasted till seven. After seven I was too tired to do anything by myself, and could only keep awake if I happened to be in company. One reason certainly why I was content, was Theresa herself. She was a constant study to me, and I could not for a long time obtain any consistent idea of her. She was not a this or a that or the other. She could not be summarily dismissed into any ordinary classification. At first I was sure she was hard, but I found by the merest accident that nearly all her earnings were given with utmost secrecy to support a couple of poor relatives. Then I thought her self-conscious, but this, when I came to think upon it, seemed a mere word. She was one of those women, and very rare they are, who deal in ideas, and reflectiveness must be self-conscious. At times she appeared passionless, so completely did her intellect dominate, and so superior was she to all the little arts and weaknesses of women; but this was a criticism she contradicted continually. There was very little society at the Wollastons', but occasionally a few friends called. One evening there was a little party, and the conversation flagged. Theresa said that it was a great mistake to bring people together with nothing special to do but talk. Nothing is more tedious than to be in a company assembled for no particular reason, and every host, if he asks more than two persons at the outside, ought to provide some entertainment. Talking is worth nothing unless it is perfectly spontaneous, and it cannot be spontaneous if there are sudden and blank silences, and nobody can think of a fresh departure. The master of the house is bound to do something. He ought to hire a Punch and Judy show, or get up a dance. This spice of bitterness and flavour of rudeness was altogether characteristic of

Theresa, and somebody resented it by reminding her
that *she* was the hostess. "Of course," she replied,
"that is why I said it: what shall I do?" One of her
gifts was memory, and her friends cried out at once
that she should recite something. She hesitated a
little, and then throwing herself back in her chair,
began "*The Lass of Lochroyan.*" At first she was
rather diffident, but she gathered strength as she went
on. There is a passage in the middle of the poem, in
which Lord Gregory's cruel mother pretends she is
Lord Gregory, and refuses to recognise his former love,
Annie of Lochroyan, as she stands outside his tower.
The mother calls to Annie from the inside

> "Gin thou be Annie of Lochroyan
> (As I trow thou binna she),
> Now tell me some of the love tokèns
> That passed between thee and me."

> "Oh dinna ye mind, Lord Gregory,
> As we sat at the wine,
> We changed the rings frae our fingers,
> And I can show thee thine?

> "Oh yours was gude, and gude enough,
> But aye the best was mine;
> For yours was o' the gude red gowd,
> *But mine o' the diamond fine.*"

The last verse is as noble as anything in any ballad
in the English language, and I thought that when
Theresa was half way through it her voice shook a
good deal. There was a glass of flowers standing near
her, and just as she came to an end her arm moved
and the glass was in a moment on the floor, shivered
into twenty pieces. I happened to be watching her,

and felt perfectly sure that the movement of her arm
was not accidental, and that her intention was to conceal, by the apparent mishap, an emotion which was
increasing and becoming inconvenient. At any rate,
if that was her object it was perfectly accomplished,
for the recitation was abruptly terminated, there was
general commiseration over the shattered vase, and
when the pieces were picked up and order was restored,
it was nearly time to separate.

  Two of my chief failings were forgetfulness and a
want of thoroughness in investigation. What misery
have I not suffered from insufficient presentation of a
case to myself, and from prompt conviction of insuffi-
ciency and inaccuracy by the person to whom I in turn
presented it ! What misery have I not suffered from
the discovery that explicit directions to me had been
overlooked or only half understood ! One day in particular, I had to take round a book to be " subscribed "
which Wollaston had just published, that is to say, I
had to take a copy to each of the leading booksellers
to see how many they would purchase. Some books
are sold " thirteen as twelve," the thirteenth book being
given to the purchaser of twelve, and some are sold
" twenty-five as twenty-four." This book was to be sold
" twenty-five as twenty-four " according to Wollaston's
orders. I subscribed it thirteen as twelve. Wollaston
was annoyed, as I could see, for I had to go over all
my work again, but in accordance with his fixed principles, he was not out of temper. It so happened that
that same day he gave me some business correspondence
which I was to look through; and having looked through
it, I was to answer the last letter in the sense which he
indicated. I read the correspondence and wrote the

letter for his signature. As soon as he saw it, he pointed out to me that I had only half mastered the facts, and that my letter was all wrong. This greatly disturbed me, not only because I had vexed him and disappointed him, but because it was renewed evidence of my weakness. I thought that if I was incapable of getting to the bottom of such a very shallow complication as this, of what value were any of my thinkings on more difficult subjects, and I fell a prey to self-contempt and scepticism. Contempt from those about us is hard to bear, but God help the poor wretch who contemns himself. How well I recollect the early walk on the following morning in Kensington Gardens, the feeling of my own utter worthlessness, and the longing for death as the cancellation of the blunder of my existence ! I went home, and after breakfast some proofs came from the printer of a pamphlet which Wollaston had in hand. Without unfastening them, he gave them to me, and said that as he had no time to read them himself, I must·go upstairs to Theresa's study and read them off with her. Accordingly I went and began to read. She took the manuscript and I took the proof. She read about a page, and then she suddenly stopped. " O Mr. Rutherford," she said, " what have you done ? I heard my uncle distinctly tell you to mark on the manuscript, when it went to the printer, that it was to be printed in demy octavo, and you have marked it twelvemo." I had had little sleep that night, I was exhausted with my early walk, and suddenly the room seemed to fade from me and I fainted. When I came to myself, I found that Theresa had not sought for any help; she had done all that ought to be done. She had unfastened my collar and had sponged my face with cold water.

The first thing I saw as I gradually recovered myself, was her eyes looking steadily at me as she stood over me, and I felt her hand upon my head. When she was sure I was coming to myself, she held off and sat down in her chair. I was a little hysterical, and after the fit was over I broke loose. With a storm of tears, I laid open all my heart. I told her how nothing I had ever attempted had succeeded; that I had never even been able to attain that degree of satisfaction with myself and my own conclusions, without which a man cannot live; and that now I found I was useless, even to the best friends I had ever known, and that the meanest clerk in the city would serve them better than I did. I was beside myself, and I threw myself on my knees, burying my face in Theresa's lap and sobbing convulsively. She did not repel me, but she gently passed her fingers through my hair. Oh the transport of that touch! It was as if water had been poured on a burnt hand, or some miraculous Messiah had soothed the delirium of a fever-stricken sufferer, and replaced his visions of torment with dreams of Paradise. She gently lifted me up, and as I rose I saw her eyes too were wet. "My poor friend," she said, "I cannot talk to you now. You are not strong enough, and for that matter, nor am I, but let me say this to you, that you are altogether mistaken about yourself. The meanest clerk in the city could not take your place here." There was just a slight emphasis I thought upon the word "here." "Now," she said, "you had better go. I will see about the pamphlet." I went out mechanically, and I anticipate my story so far as to say that, two days after, another proof came in the proper form. I went to the printer to offer to pay for

setting it up afresh, and was told that Miss Wollaston
had been there and had paid herself for the rectification
of the mistake, giving special injunctions that no notice
of it was to be given to her uncle.   I should like to add
one more beatitude to those of the gospels and to say,
Blessed are they who heal us of self-despisings.   Of
all services which can be done to man, I know of none
more precious.

When I went back to my work I worshipped Theresa,
and was entirely overcome with unhesitating absorbing
love for her.   I saw nothing more of her that day nor
the next day.   Her uncle told me that she had gone
into the country, and that probably she would not
return for some time, as she had purposed paying a
lengthened visit to a friend at a distance.   I had a
mind to write to her; but I felt as I have often felt
before in great crises, a restraint which was gentle and
incomprehensible, but nevertheless unmistakable.   I
suppose it is not what would be called conscience, as
conscience is supposed to decide solely between right
and wrong, but it was none the less peremptory, although
its voice was so soft and low that it might easily have
been overlooked.   Over and over again, when I have
purposed doing a thing, have I been impeded or arrested
by this same silent monitor, and never have I known
its warnings to be the mere false alarms of fancy.

After a time, the thought of Mary recurred to me.
I was distressed to find that, in the very height of my
love for Theresa, my love for Mary continued unabated.
Had it been otherwise, had my affection for Mary
grown dim, I should not have been so much perplexed,
but it did not.   It may be ignominious to confess it, but
so it was; I simply record the fact.   I had not seen

Mardon since that last memorable evening at his house, but one day, as I was sitting in the shop, who should walk in but Mary herself. The meeting, although strange, was easily explained. Her father was ill, and could do nothing but read. Wollaston published free-thinking books, and Mardon had noticed in an advertisement the name of a book which he particularly wished to see. Accordingly he sent Mary for it. She pressed me very much to call on him. He had talked about me a good deal, and had written to me at the last address he knew, but the letter had been returned through the dead letter office. It was a week before I could go, and when I did go, I found him much worse than I had imagined him to be. There was no virulent disease of any particular organ, but he was slowly wasting away from atrophy, and he knew, or thought he knew, he should not recover. But he was perfectly self-possessed. "With regard to immortality," he said, " I never know what men mean by it. *What* self is it which is to be immortal? Is it really desired by anybody that he should continue to exist for ever with his present limitations and failings? Yet if these are not continued, the man does not continue, but something else, a totally different person. I believe in the survival of life and thought. People think that is not enough. They say they want the survival of their personality. It is very difficult to express any conjecture upon the matter, especially now when I am weak, and I have no system —nothing but surmises. One thing I am sure of, that a man ought to rid himself as much as possible of the miserable egotism which is so anxious about self, and should be more and more anxious about the Universal." Mardon grew slowly worse. The winter was coming on, and as the temperature fell, and the days grew darker, he declined. With all his heroism and hardness he had a weakness or two, and one was, that he did not want to die in London or be buried there. So we got him down to Sandgate near Hythe, and procured lodging for him close to the sea, so that he could lie in bed and watch the sun and moon rise over the water. Mary, of course, remained with him, and I returned to London. Towards the end of November I got a letter, to tell me that if I wished to see him alive again, I must go down at once. I went that day, and I found that the doctor had been, and had said that before the morning the end must come. Mardon was perfectly conscious, in no pain, and quite calm. He was just able to speak. When I went into his bedroom, he smiled, and without any preface or introduction he said : " Learn not to be over-anxious about meeting troubles and solving diffi- culties which time will meet and solve for you." Excepting to ask for water, I don't think he spoke again. All that night Mary. and I watched in that topmost garret looking out over the ocean. It was a night entirely unclouded, and the moon was at the full. Towards daybreak her father moaned a little, then became quite quiet, and just as the dawn was chang- ing to sunrise, he passed away. What a sunrise it was ! For about half-an-hour before the sun actually appeared, the perfectly smooth water was one mass of gently heaving opaline lustre. Not a sound was to be heard, and over in the south-east hung the planet Venus. Death was in the chamber, but the surpassing splendour of the pageant outside arrested us, and we sat awed and silent. Not till the first burning point of the great orb itself emerged above the horizon, not till the day awoke with its brightness and brought with it the sounds of the day and its cares, did we give way to our grief. It was impossible for me to stay. It was not that I was obliged to get back to my work in London, but I felt that Mary would far rather be alone, and that it would not be proper for me to remain. The woman of the house, in which the lodgings were, was very kind, and promised to do all that was necessary. It was arranged that I should come down again to the funeral. So I went back to London. Before I had got twenty miles on my journey the glory of a few hours before had turned into autumn storm. The rain came down in torrents, and the wind rushed across the country in great blasts, stripping the trees, and driving over the sky with hurricane speed great masses of continuous cloud, which mingled earth and heaven. I thought of all the ships which were on the sea in the night, sailing under the serene stars which I had seen rise and set; I thought of Mardon lying dead, and I thought of Mary. The simultaneous passage through great emotions welds souls, and begets the strongest of all forms of love. Those who have sobbed together over a dead friend, who have held one another's hands in that dread hour, feel a bond of sympathy, pure and sacred, which nothing can dissolve. I went to the funeral as appointed. There was some little difficulty about it, for Mary, who knew her father so well, was unconquerably reluctant that an inconsistency should crown the career of one who, all through life, had been so completely self-accordant. She could not bear that he should be buried with a ceremony which he despised, and she was altogether free from that weakness which induces a compliance with the rites of the Church from persons who avow themselves sceptics. At last a burying-ground was found, belonging to a little half-forsaken Unitarian chapel; and there Mardon was laid. A few friends came from London, one of whom had been a Unitarian minister, and he "conducted the service," such as it was. It was of the simplest kind. The body was taken to the side of the grave, and before it was lowered a few words were said, calling to mind all the virtues of him whom we had lost. These the speaker presented to us with much power and sympathy. He did not merely catalogue a disconnected string of excellences, but he seemed to plant himself in the central point of Mardon's nature, and to see from what it radiated. He then passed on to say that about immortality, as usually understood, he knew nothing; but that Mardon would live as every force in nature lives—for ever; transmuted into a thousand different forms; the original form utterly forgotten, but never perishing. The cloud breaks up and comes down upon the earth in showers which cease, but the clouds and the showers are really undying. This may be true, but, after all, I can only accept the fact of death in silence, as we accept the loss of youth and all other calamities. We are able to see that the arrangements which we should make, if we had the control of the universe, would be more absurd than those which prevail now. We are able to see that an eternity of life in one particular form, with one particular set of relationships, would be misery to many and mischievous to everybody; however sweet those relationships may be to some of us. At times we are reconciled to death as the great regenerator, and we

pine for escape from the surroundings of which we have
grown weary; but we can say no more, and the hour of
illumination has not yet come.　Whether it ever will
come to a more nobly developed race, we cannot tell.

———————

Thus far goes the manuscript which I have in my
possession.　I know that there is more of it, but all
my search for it has been in vain.　Possibly some
day I may be able to recover it.　My friend discon-
tinued his notes for some years, and consequently the
concluding portion of them was entirely separate from
the earlier portion, and this is the reason, I suppose,
why it is missing.　Miss Mardon soon followed her
father.　She caught cold at his funeral; the seeds of
consumption developed themselves with remarkable
rapidity, and in less than a month she had gone.　Her
father's peculiar habits had greatly isolated him, and
Miss Mardon had scarcely any friends.　Rutherford
went to see her continually, and during the last few
nights sat up with her, incurring not a little scandal
and gossip, to which he was entirely insensible.　For
a time he was utterly broken-hearted; and not only
broken-hearted, but broken-spirited, and incapable of
attacking the least difficulty.　All the springs of his
nature were softened, so that if anything was cast upon
him, there it remained without hope, and without any
effort being made to remove it.　He only began to
recover when he was forced to give up work altogether
and take a long holiday.　To do this he was obliged to
leave Mr. Wollaston, and the means of obtaining his

much-needed rest were afforded him, partly by what
he had saved, and partly by the kindness of one or two
whom he had known. I thought that Miss Mardon's
death would permanently increase my friend's intellectual despondency, but it did not. On the contrary,
he gradually grew out of it. A crisis seemed to take a
turn just then, and he became less involved in his old
speculations, and more devoted to other pursuits. I
fancy that something happened; there was some word
revealed to him, or there was some recoil, some healthy
horror of eclipse in this self-created gloom which drove
him out of it. He accidentally renewed his acquaintance with the butterfly catcher, who was obliged to
leave the country and come up to London. He, however, did not give up his old hobby, and the two friends
used every Sunday in summer time to sally forth some
distance from town and spend the whole live-long day
upon the downs and in the green lanes of Surrey.
Both of them had to work hard during the week.
Rutherford, who had learned shorthand when he was
young, got employment upon a newspaper, and ultimately a seat in the gallery of the House of Commons. He never took to collecting insects like his companion, nor indeed to any scientific pursuits, but he
certainly changed. I find it very difficult to describe
exactly what the change was, because it was into
nothing positive; into no sect, party, nor special
mode. He did not, for example, go off into absolute
denial. I remember his telling me, that to suppress
speculation would be a violence done to our nature as
unnatural as if we were to prohibit ourselves from
looking up to the blue depths between the stars at
night; as if we were to determine that nature required

correcting in this respect, and that we ought to be so constructed as not to be able to see anything but the earth and what lies on it. Still, these things in a measure ceased to worry him, and the long conflict died away gradually into a peace not formally concluded, and with no specific stipulations, but nevertheless definite. He was content to rest and wait. Better health and time, which does so much for us, brought this about. The passage of years gradually relaxed his anxiety about death by loosening his anxiety for life without loosening his love of life. But I would rather not go into any further details, because I still cherish the hope that some day or the other I may recover the contents of the diary. I am afraid that up to this point he has misrepresented himself, and that those who read his story will think him nothing but a mere egoist, selfish and self-absorbed. Morbid he may have been, but selfish he was not. A more perfect friend I never knew, nor one more capable of complete abandonment to a person for whom he had any real regard, and I can only hope that it may be my good fortune to find the materials which will enable me to represent him autobiographically in a somewhat different light to that in which he appears now.

MARK RUTHERFORD'S DELIVERANCE.

"Ego doceo sine strepitu verborum, sine confusione opinionum, sine fastu honoris, sine impugnatione argumentorum."

"I teach without noise of words, without confusion of opinions, without the arrogance of honour, without the assault of arguments."
De Imitatione Christi, chap. xliii.

"Come what come may,
Time and the hour runs through the roughest day."
Macbeth, Act I. Sc. 3.

Ἄδην δ' ἔχων βοηθὸν ὀυ τρέμω σκιάς.

"Having death for my friend, I tremble not at shadows."
Unknown Greek Author.

MARK RUTHERFORD'S DELIVERANCE.

CHAPTER I.

NEWSPAPERS.

WHEN I had established myself in my new lodgings in
Camden Town, I found I had ten pounds in my pocket,
and again there was no outlook. I examined carefully
every possibility. At last I remembered that a relative
of mine, who held some office in the House of Commons,
added to his income by writing descriptive accounts of
the debates, throwing in by way of supplement any
stray scraps of gossip which he was enabled to collect.
The rules of the House as to the admission of strangers
were not so strict then as they are now, and he assured
me that if I could but secure a commission from a
newspaper, he could pass me into one of the galleries,
and, when there was nothing to be heard worth describing, I could remain in the lobby, where I should
by degrees find many opportunities of picking up
intelligence which would pay. So far, so good; but
how to obtain the commission? I managed to get hold
of a list of all the country papers, and I wrote to nearly

every one, offering my services. I am afraid that I somewhat exaggerated them, for I had two answers, and, after a little correspondence, two engagements. This was an unexpected stroke of luck; but alas! both journals circulated in the same district. I never could get together more stuff than would fill about a column and a half, and consequently I was obliged, with infinite pains, to vary, so that it could not be recognised, the form of what, at bottom, was essentially the same matter. This was work which would have been disagreeable enough, if I had not now ceased in a great measure to demand what was agreeable. In years past I coveted a life, not of mere sensual enjoyment—for that I never cared—but a life which should be filled with activities of the noblest kind, and it was intolerable to me to reflect that all my waking hours were in the main passed in merest drudgery, and that only for a few moments at the beginning or end of the day could it be said that the higher sympathies were really operative. Existence to me was nothing but these few moments, and consequently flitted like a shadow. I was now, however, the better of what was half disease and half something healthy and good. In the first place, I had discovered that my appetite was far larger than my powers. Consumed by a longing for continuous intercourse with the best, I had no ability whatever to maintain it, and I had accepted as a fact, however mysterious it might be, that the human mind is created with the impulses of a seraph and the strength of a man. Furthermore, what was I that I should demand exceptional treatment? Thousands of men and women superior to myself, are condemned, if that is the proper word to use, to almost total absence from themselves. The roar of the world for them is never lulled to rest, nor can silence ever be secured in which the voice of the Divine can be heard.

My letters were written twice a week, and as each contained a column and a half, I had six columns weekly to manufacture. These I was in the habit of writing in the morning, my evenings being spent at the House. At first I was rather interested, but after a while the occupation became tedious beyond measure, and for this reason. In a discussion of any importance about fifty members perhaps would take part, and had made up their minds beforehand to speak. There could not possibly be more than three or four reasons for or against the motion, and as the knowledge that what the intending orator had to urge had been urged a dozen times before on that very night never deterred him from urging it again, the same arguments, diluted, muddled, and mis-presented, recurred with the most wearisome iteration.

The public outside knew nothing or very little of the real House of Commons, and the manner in which time was squandered there, for the reports were all of them much abbreviated. In fact, I doubt whether anybody but the Speaker, and one or two other persons in the same position as myself, really felt with proper intensity what the waste was, and how profound was the vanity of members and the itch for expression; for even the reporters were relieved at stated intervals, and the impression on their minds was not continuous. Another evil result of these attendances at the House was a kind of political scepticism. Over and over again I have seen a Government arraigned for its conduct of foreign affairs. The evidence lay in masses of

correspondence which it would have required some days
to master, and the verdict, after knowing the facts, ought
to have depended upon the application of principles,
each of which admitted a contrary principle for which
much might be pleaded. There were not fifty members
in the House with the leisure or the ability to understand what it was which had actually happened, and
if they had understood it, they would not have had
the wit to see what was the rule which ought to have
decided the case. Yet, whether they understood or
not, they were obliged to vote, and what was worse,
the constituencies also had to vote, and so the gravest
matters were settled in utter ignorance. This has
often been adduced as an argument against an extended
suffrage, but, if it is an argument against anything, it
is an argument against intrusting the aristocracy and
even the House itself with the destinies of the nation ;
for no dock labourer could possibly be more entirely
empty of all reasons for action than the noble lords,
squires, lawyers, and railway directors whom I have
seen troop to the division bell. There is something
deeper than this scepticism, but the scepticism is the
easiest and the most obvious conclusion to an open
mind dealing so closely and practically with politics
as it was my lot to do at this time of my life. Men
must be governed, and when it comes to the question,
by whom ? I, for one, would far sooner in the long
run trust the people at large than I would the few,
who in everything which relates to Government are
as little instructed as the many and more difficult to
move. The very fickleness of the multitude, the theme
of such constant declamation, is so far good that it
proves a susceptibility to impressions to which men

hedged round by impregnable conventionalities cannot yield.[1]

When I was living in the country, the pure sky and the landscape formed a large portion of my existence, so large that much of myself depended on it, and I wondered how men could be worth anything if they could never see the face of nature. For this belief my early training on the "Lyrical Ballads" is answerable. When I came to London the same creed survived, and I was for ever thirsting for intercourse with my ancient friend. Hope, faith, and God seemed impossible amidst the smoke of the streets. It was now very difficult for me, except at rare opportunities, to leave London, and it was necessary for me, therefore, to understand that all that was essential for me was obtainable there, even though I should never see anything more than was to be seen in journeying through the High Street, Camden Town, Tottenham Court Road, the Seven Dials, and Whitehall. I should have been guilty of a simple surrender to despair if I had not forced myself to make this discovery. I cannot help saying, with all my love for the literature of my own day, that it has an evil side to it which none know except the millions of sensitive persons who are condemned to exist in great towns. It might be imagined from much of this literature that true humanity and a belief in God are the offspring of the hills or the ocean; and by implication, if not expressly, the vast multitudes who hardly ever see the hills or the ocean must be without a religion. The long poems which turn altogether upon scenery,

---

[1] This was written many years ago, but is curiously pertinent to the discussions of this year.—EDITOR, 1884.

perhaps in foreign lands, and the passionate devotion to it which they breathe, may perhaps do good in keeping alive in the hearts of men a determination to preserve air, earth, and water from pollution; but speaking from experience as a Londoner, I can testify that they are most depressing, and I would counsel everybody whose position is what mine was to avoid these books and to associate with those which will help him in his own circumstances.

Half of my occupation soon came to an end. One of my editors sent me a petulant note telling me that all I wrote he could easily find out himself, and that he required something more " graphic and personal." I could do no better, or rather I ought to say, no worse than I had been doing. These letters were a great trouble to me. I was always conscious of writing so much of which I was not certain, and so much which was indifferent to me. The unfairness of parties haunted me. But I continued to write, because I saw no other way of getting a living, and surely it is a baser dishonesty to depend upon the charity of friends because some pleasant, clean, ideal employment has not presented itself, than to soil one's hands with a little of the inevitable mud. I don't think I ever felt anything more keenly than I did a sneer from an acquaintance of mine who was in the habit of borrowing money from me. He was a painter, whose pictures were never sold because he never worked hard enough to know how to draw, and it came to my ears indirectly that he had said that " he would rather live the life of a medieval ascetic than condescend to the degradation of scribbling a dozen columns weekly of utter trash on subjects with which he had no concern." At that very moment he owed me five pounds. God knows that I admitted my dozen columns to be utter trash, but it ought to have been forgiven by those who saw that I was struggling to save myself from the streets and to keep a roof over my head. Degraded, however, as I might be, I could not get down to the "graphic and personal," for it meant nothing less than the absolutely false. I therefore contrived to exist on the one letter, which, excepting the mechanical labour of writing a second, took up as much of my time as if I had to write two.

Never, but once or twice at the most, did my labours meet with the slightest recognition beyond payment. Once I remember that I accused a member of a discreditable manœuvre to consume the time of the House, and as he represented a borough in my district, he wrote to the editor denying the charge. The editor without any inquiry—and I believe I was mistaken — instantly congratulated me on having "scored." At another time, when Parliament was not sitting, I ventured, by way of filling up my allotted space, to say a word on behalf of a now utterly forgotten novel. I had a letter from the authoress thanking me, but alas ! the illusion vanished. I was tempted by this one novel to look into others which I found she had written, and I discovered that they were altogether silly. The attraction of the one of which I thought so highly, was due not to any real merit which it possessed, but to something I had put into it. It was dead, but it had served as a wall to re-echo my own voice. Excepting these two occasions, I don't think that one solitary human being ever applauded or condemned one solitary word of which I was the author. All my friends knew where my contributions were to be

found, but I never heard that they looked at them.
They were never worth reading, and yet such complete
silence was rather lonely.   The tradesman who makes
a good coat enjoys the satisfaction of having fitted and
pleased his customer, and a bricklayer, if he be diligent,
is rewarded by knowing that his master understands
his value, but I never knew what it was to receive a
single response.   I wrote for an abstraction; and spoke
to empty space.   I cannot help claiming some pity and
even respect for the class to which I belonged.   I have
heard them called all kinds of hard names, hacks,
drudges, and something even more contemptible, but
the injustice done to them is monstrous.   Their wage
is hardly earned; it is peculiarly precarious, depending
altogether upon their health, and no matter how ill they
may be they must maintain the liveliness of manner
which is necessary to procure acceptance.   I fell in
with one poor fellow whose line was something like my
own.   I became acquainted with him through sitting
side by side with him at the House.   He lived in
lodgings in Goodge Street, and occasionally I walked
with him as far as the corner of Tottenham Court Road,
where I caught the last omnibus northward.   He wrote
like me a " descriptive article " for the country, but he
also wrote every now and then—a dignity to which
I never attained—a "special" for London.   His
" descriptive articles " were more political than mine,
and he was obliged to be violently Tory.   His creed,
however, was such a pure piece of professionalism, that
though I was Radical, and was expected to be so, we
never jarred, and often, as we wandered homewards, we
exchanged notes, and were mutually useful, his observations appearing in my paper, and mine in his, with

proper modifications.   How he used to roar in the
Gazette against the opposite party, and yet I never
heard anything from him myself but what was diffident
and tender.   He had acquired, as an instrument necessary to him, an extraordinarily extravagant style, and
he laid about him with a bludgeon, which inevitably
descended on the heads of all prominent persons if they
happened not to be Conservative, no matter what their
virtues might be.   One peculiarity, however, I noted in
him.   Although he ought every now and then, when
the subject was uppermost, to have flamed out in the
Gazette on behalf of the Church, I never saw a word
from him on that subject.   He drew the line at religion.
He did not mind acting his part in things secular, for
his performances were, I am sure, mostly histrionic, but
there he stopped.   The unreality of his character was a
husk surrounding him, but it did not touch the core.
It was as if he had said to himself, "Political controversy is nothing to me, and, what is more, is so uncertain
that it matters little whether I say yes or no, nor indeed
does it matter if I say yes *and* no, and I must keep my
wife and children from the workhouse; but when it
comes to the relationship of man to God, it is a different
matter."   His altogether outside vehemence and hypocrisy did in fact react upon him, and so far from affecting harmfully what lay deeper, produced a more complete sincerity and transparency extending even to
the finest verbal distinctions.   Over and over again
have I heard him preach to his wife, almost with pathos,
the duty of perfect exactitude in speech in describing
the commonest occurrences.   "Now, my dear, *is* that
so?" was a perpetual remonstrance with him; and he
always insisted upon it that there is no training more

necessary for children than that of teaching them
not merely to speak the truth in the ordinary, vulgar
sense of the term, but to speak it in a much higher
sense, by rigidly compelling, point by point, a correspondence of the words with the fact external or
internal. He never would tolerate in his own children
a mere hackneyed, borrowed expression, but demanded
exact portraiture; and nothing vexed him more than
to hear one of them spoil and make worthless what he
or she had seen, by reporting it in some stale phrase
which had been used by everybody. This refusal to
take the trouble to watch the presentment to the mind
of anything which had been placed before it, and to
reproduce it in its own lines and colours was, as he
said, nothing but falsehood, and he maintained that the
principal reason why people are so uninteresting is not
that they have nothing to say. It is rather that they
will not face the labour of saying in their own tongue
what they have to say, but cover it up and conceal it in
commonplace, so that we get, not what they themselves
behold and what they think, but a hieroglyphic or
symbol invented as the representative of a certain class
of objects or emotions, and as inefficient to represent a
particular object or emotion as x or y to set forth the
relation of Hamlet to Ophelia. He would even exercise
his children in this art of the higher truthfulness, and
would purposely make them give him an account of
something which he had seen and they had seen, check-
ing them the moment he saw a lapse from originality.
Such was the Tory correspondent of the *Gazette*.

I ought to say, by way of apology for him, that in
his day it signified little or nothing whether Tory or
Whig was in power. Politics had not become what

they will one day become, a matter of life or death, dividing men with really private love and hate. What a mockery controversy was in the House! How often I have seen members, who were furious at one another across the floor, quietly shaking hands outside, and inviting one another to dinner! I have heard them say that we ought to congratulate ourselves that parliamentary differences do not in this country breed personal animosities. To me this seemed anything but a subject of congratulation. Men who are totally at variance ought not to be friends, and if Radical and Tory are not totally, but merely superficially at variance, so much the worse for their Radicalism and Toryism.

It is possible, and even probable, that the public fury and the subsequent amity were equally absurd. Most of us have no real loves and no real hatreds. Blessed is love, less blessed is hatred, but thrice accursed is that indifference which is neither one nor the other, the muddy mess which men call friendship.

M'Kay—for that was his name—lived, as I have said, in Goodge Street, where he had unfurnished apartments. I often spent part of the Sunday with him, and I may forestall obvious criticism by saying that I do not pretend for a moment to defend myself from inconsistency in denouncing members of Parliament for their duplicity, M'Kay and myself being also guilty of something very much like it. But there was this difference between us and our parliamentary friends, that we always divested ourselves of all hypocrisy when we were alone. We then dropped the stage costume which members continued to wear in the streets and at the dinner-table, and in which some of them even slept and said their prayers.

London Sundays to persons who are not attached to
any religious community, and have no money to spend,
are rather dreary. We tried several ways of getting
through the morning. If we heard that there was a
preacher with a reputation, we went to hear him. As
a rule, however, we got no good in that way. Once
we came to a chapel where there was a minister supposed to be one of the greatest orators of the day.
We had much difficulty in finding standing room.
Just as we entered we heard him say, " My friends, I
appeal to those of you who are parents. You know
that if you say to a child ' go,' he goeth, and if you
say ' come,' he cometh. So the Lord "—— But at this
point M'Kay, who had children, nudged me to come
out; and out we went. Why does this little scene
remain with me? I can hardly say, but here it stands.
It is remembered, not so much by reason of the
preacher as by reason of the apparent acquiescence
and admiration of the audience, who seemed to be
perfectly willing to take over an experience from their
pastor—if indeed it was really an experience—which
was not their own. Our usual haunts on Sunday were
naturally the parks and Kensington Gardens; but
artificial limited enclosures are apt to become wearisome after a time, and we longed for a little more
freedom if a little less trim. So we would stroll
towards Hampstead or Highgate, the only drawback
to these regions being the squalid, ragged, half town,
half suburb, through which it was necessary to pass.
The skirts of London when the air is filled with north-
easterly soot, grit, and filth, are cheerless, and the least
cheerful part of the scene is the inability of the vast
wandering masses of people to find any way of amusing

themselves. At the corner of one of the fields in
Kentish Town, just about to be devoured, stood a
public-house, and opposite the door was generally
encamped a man who sold nothing but Brazil nuts.
Swarms of people lazily wandered past him, most of
them waiting for the public-house to open. Brazil
nuts on a cold black Sunday morning are not exhilarat-
ing, but the costermonger found many customers who
bought his nuts, and ate them, merely because they
had nothing better to do. We went two or three
times to a freethinking hall, where we were entertained
with demonstrations of the immorality of the patri-
archs and Jewish heroes, and arguments to prove that
the personal existence of the devil was a myth, the
audience breaking out into uproarious laughter at
comical delineations of Noah and Jonah. One morning we found the place completely packed. A " celebrated Christian," as he was described to us, having
heard of the hall, had volunteered to engage in debate
on the claims of the Old Testament to Divine authority.
He turned out to be a preacher whom we knew
quite well. He was introduced by his freethinking
antagonist, who claimed for him a respectful hearing.
The preacher said that before beginning he should like
to " engage in prayer." Accordingly he came to the front
of the platform, lifted up his eyes, told God why he was
there, and besought Him to bless the discussion in the
conversion " of these poor wandering souls, who have
said in their hearts that there is no God, to a saving
faith in Him and in the blood of Christ." I expected
that some resentment would be displayed when the
wandering souls found themselves treated like errant
sheep, but to my surprise they listened with perfect

silence; and when he had said "Amen," there were
great clappings of hands, and cries of "Bravo." They
evidently considered the prayer merely as an elocu-
tionary show-piece. The preacher was much discon-
certed, but he recovered himself, and began his sermon,
for it was nothing more. He enlarged on the fact that
men of the highest eminence had believed in the Old
Testament. Locke and Newton had believed in it,
and did it not prove arrogance in us to doubt when
the "gigantic intellect which had swept the skies, and
had announced the law which bound the universe
together was satisfied?" The witness of the Old
Testament to the New was another argument, but his
main reliance was upon the prophecies. From Adam
to Isaiah there was a continuous prefigurement of
Christ. Christ was the point to which everything
tended; and "now, my friends," he said, "I cannot
sit down without imploring you to turn your eyes on
Him who never yet repelled the sinner, to wash in
that eternal Fountain ever open for the remission of
sins, and to flee from the wrath to come. I believe the
sacred symbol of the cross has not yet lost its efficacy.
For eighteen hundred years, whenever it has been
exhibited to the sons of men, it has been potent to
reclaim and save them. 'I, if I be lifted up,' cried the
Great Sufferer, 'will draw all men unto Me,' and He
has drawn not merely the poor and ignorant but the
philosopher and the sage. Oh, my brethren, think
what will happen if you reject Him. I forbear to
paint your doom. And think again, on the other
hand, of the bliss which awaits you if you receive
Him, of the eternal companionship with the Most
High and with the spirits of just men made perfect."

His hearers again applauded vigorously, and none less
so than their appointed leader, who was to follow on
the other side. He was a little man with small eyes;
his shaven face was dark with a black beard lurking
under the skin, and his nose was slightly turned up.
He was evidently a trained debater who had practised
under railway arches, discussion "forums," and in the
classes promoted by his sect. He began by saying
that he could not compliment his friend who had just
sat down on the inducements which he had offered
them to become Christians. The New Cut was not
a nice place on a wet day, but he had rather
sit at a stall there all day long with his feet on a
basket than lie in the bosom of some of the just
men made perfect portrayed in the Bible. Nor, being
married, should he feel particularly at ease if he had
to leave his wife with David. David certainly ought
to have got beyond all that kind of thing, considering
it must be over 3000 years since he first saw Bath-
sheba; but we are told that the saints are for ever
young in heaven, and this treacherous villain, who
would have been tried by a jury of twelve men and
hung outside Newgate if he had lived in the nineteenth
century, might be dangerous now. He was an amorous
old gentleman up to the very last. (Roars of laughter.)
Nor did the speaker feel particularly anxious to be shut
up with all the bishops, who of course are amongst the
elect, and on their departure from this vale of tears tempered by ten thousand a year, are duly supplied with
wings. Much more followed in the same strain upon
the immorality of the Bible heroes, their cruelty, and
the cruelty of the God who sanctioned it. Then followed
a clever exposition of the inconsistencies of the Old

Testament history, the impossibility of any reference to Jesus therein, and a really earnest protest against the quibbling by which those who believed in the Bible as a revelation sought to reconcile it with science. "Finally," said the speaker, "I am sure we all of us will pass a vote of thanks to our reverend friend for coming to see us, and we cordially invite him to come again. If I might be allowed to offer a suggestion, it would be that he should make himself acquainted with our case before he pays us another visit, and not suppose that we are to be persuaded with the rhetoric which may do very well for the young women of his congregation, but won't go down here." This was fair and just, for the eminent Christian was nothing but an ordinary minister, who, when he was prepared for his profession, had never been allowed to see what are the historical difficulties of Christianity, lest he should be overcome by them. On the other hand, his sceptical opponents were almost devoid of the faculty for appreciating the great remains of antiquity, and would probably have considered the machinery of the Prometheus Bound or of the Iliad a sufficient reason for a sneer. That they should spend their time in picking the Bible to pieces when there was so much positive work for them to do, seemed to me as melancholy as if they had spent themselves upon theology. To waste a Sunday morning in ridiculing such stories as that of Jonah was surely as imbecile as to waste it in proving their verbal veracity.

CHAPTER II.

M'KAY.

IT was foggy and overcast as we walked home to Goodge Street. The churches and chapels were emptying themselves, but the great mass of the population had been " nowhere." I had dinner with M'Kay, and as the day wore on the fog thickened. London on a dark Sunday afternoon, more especially about Goodge Street, is depressing. The inhabitants drag themselves hither and thither in languor and uncertainty. Small mobs loiter at the doors of the gin palaces. Costermongers wander aimlessly, calling " walnuts " with a cry so melancholy that it sounds as the wail of the hopelessly lost may be imagined to sound when their anguish has been deadened by the monotony of a million years.

About two or three o'clock decent working men in their best clothes emerge from the houses in such streets as Nassau Street. It is part of their duty to go out after dinner on Sunday with the wife and children. The husband pushes the perambulator out of the dingy passage, and gazes doubtfully this way and that way, not knowing whither to go, and evidently longing for the Monday, when his work, however disagreeable it may be, will be his plain duty. The wife follows carrying a child, and a boy and girl in unaccustomed apparel walk by her side. They come out into Mor-

timer Street. There are no shops open; the sky over
their heads is mud, the earth is mud under their feet,
the muddy houses stretch in long rows, black, gaunt,
uniform. The little party reach Hyde Park, also
wrapped in impenetrable mud-grey. The man's face
brightens for a moment as he says, "It is time to go
back," and so they return, without the interchange of
a word, unless perhaps they happen to see an omnibus horse fall down on the greasy stones. What is
there worth thought or speech on such an expedition?
Nothing! The tradesman who kept the oil and colour
establishment opposite to us was not to be tempted
outside. It was a little more comfortable than Nassau
Street, and, moreover, he was religious and did not
encourage Sabbath-breaking. He and his family always moved after their mid-day Sabbath repast from
the little back room behind the shop up to what they
called the drawing-room overhead. It was impossible
to avoid seeing them every time we went to the window. The father of the family, after his heavy meal,
invariably sat in the easy-chair with a handkerchief
over his eyes and slept. The children were always at
the windows, pretending to read books, but in reality
watching the people below. At about four o'clock
their papa generally awoke, and demanded a succession
of hymn tunes played on the piano. When the weather
permitted, the lower sash was opened a little, and the
neighbours were indulged with the performance of "Vital
Spark," the father "coming in" now and then with a
bass note or two at the end where he was tolerably
certain of the harmony. At five o'clock a prophecy of
the incoming tea brought us some relief from the contemplation of the landscape or brick-scape. I say

"some relief," for meals at M'Kay's were a little disagreeable. His wife was an honest, good little woman,
but so much attached to him and so dependent on him
that she was his mere echo. She had no opinions
which were not his, and whenever he said anything
which went beyond the ordinary affairs of the house,
she listened with curious effort, and generally responded
by a weakened repetition of M'Kay's own observations.
He perpetually, therefore, had before him an enfeebled
reflection of himself, and this much irritated him, notwithstanding his love for her; for who could help loving a woman who, without the least hesitation, would
have opened her veins at his command, and have given
up every drop of blood in her body for him? Over
and over again I have heard him offer some criticism
on a person or event, and the customary chime of
approval would ensue, provoking him to such a degree
that he would instantly contradict himself with much
bitterness, leaving poor Mrs. M'Kay in much perplexity.
Such a shot as this generally reduced her to timid
silence. As a rule, he always discouraged any topic at
his house which was likely to serve as an occasion for
showing his wife's dependence on him. He designedly
talked about her household affairs, asked her whether
she had mended his clothes and ordered the coals. She
knew that these things were not what was upon his
mind, and she answered him in despairing tones, which
showed how much she felt the obtrusive condescension
to her level. I greatly pitied her, and sometimes, in
fact, my emotion at the sight of her struggles with her
limitations almost overcame me and I was obliged to
get up and go. She was childishly affectionate. If
M'Kay came in and happened to go up to her and kiss

her, her face brightened into the sweetest and happiest smile. I recollect once after he had been unusually annoyed with her he repented just as he was leaving home, and put his lips to her head, holding it in both his hands. I saw her gently take the hand from her forehead and press it to her mouth, the tears falling down her cheek meanwhile. Nothing would ever tempt her to admit anything against her husband. M'Kay was violent and unjust at times. His occupation he hated, and his restless repugnance to it frequently discharged itself indifferently upon everything which came in his way. His children often thought him almost barbarous, but in truth he did not actually see them when he was in one of these moods. What was really present with him, excluding everything else, was the sting of something more than usually repulsive of which they knew nothing. Mrs. M'Kay's answer to her children's remonstrances when they were alone with her always was, " He is so worried," and she invariably dwelt upon their faults which had given him the opportunity for his wrath.

I think M'Kay's treatment of her wholly wrong. I think that he ought not to have imposed himself upon her so imperiously. I think he ought to have striven to ascertain what lay concealed in that modest heart, to have encouraged its expression and development, to have debased himself before her that she might receive courage to rise, and he would have found that she had something which he had not; not *his* something perhaps, but something which would have made his life happier. As it was, he stood upon his own ground above her. If she could reach him, well and good, if not, the helping hand was not proffered,

and she fell back, hopeless. Later on he discovered
his mistake. She became ill very gradually, and
M'Kay began to see in the distance a prospect of
losing her. A frightful pit came in view. He became
aware that he could not do without her. He imagined
what his home would have been with other women
whom he knew, and he confessed that with them he
would have been less contented. He acknowledged
that he had been guilty of a kind of criminal epicurism ;
that he rejected in foolish, fatal, nay, even wicked
indifference, the bread of life upon which he might
have lived and thriven. His whole effort now was to
suppress himself in his wife. He read to her, a thing
he never did before, and when she misunderstood, he
patiently explained ; he took her into his counsels
and asked her opinion ; he abandoned his own opinion for hers, and in the presence of her children
he always deferred to her, and delighted to acknowledge that she knew more than he did, that she
was right and he was wrong. She was now confined to her house, and the end was near, but this was
the most blessed time of her married life. She grew
under the soft rain of his loving care, and opened out,
not, indeed, into an oriental flower, rich in profound
mystery of scent and colour, but into a blossom of the
chalk - down. Altogether concealed and closed she
would have remained if it had not been for this beneficent and heavenly gift poured upon her. He had
just time enough to see what she really *was*, and then
she died. There are some natures that cannot unfold
under pressure or in the presence of unregarding power.
Hers was one. They require a clear space round them,
the removal of everything which may overmaster them,

and constant delicate attention. They require too a recognition of the fact, which M'Kay for a long time did not recognise, that it is folly to force them and to demand of them that they shall be what they cannot be. I stood by the grave this morning of my poor, pale, clinging little friend now for some years at peace, and I thought that the tragedy of Promethean torture or Christ-like crucifixion may indeed be tremendous, but there is a tragedy too in the existence of a soul like hers, conscious of its feebleness and ever striving to overpass it, ever aware that it is an obstacle to the return of the affection of the man whom she loves.

Meals, as I have said, were disagreeable at M'Kay's, and when we wanted to talk we went out of doors. The evening after our visit to the debating hall we moved towards Portland Place, and walked up and down there for an hour or more. M'Kay had a passionate desire to reform the world. The spectacle of the misery of London, and of the distracted swaying hither and thither of the multitudes who inhabit it, tormented him incessantly. He always chafed at it, and he never seemed sure that he had a right to the enjoyment of the simplest pleasures so long as London was before him. What a farce, he would cry, is all this poetry, philosophy, art, and culture, when millions of wretched mortals are doomed to the eternal darkness and crime of the city! Here are the educated classes occupying themselves with exquisite emotions, with speculations upon the Infinite, with addresses to flowers, with the worship of waterfalls and flying clouds, and with the incessant portraiture of a thousand moods and variations of love, while their neighbours lie grovelling in the mire, and never know anything more of

life or its duties than is afforded them by a police
report in a bit of newspaper picked out of the kennel.
We went one evening to hear a great violin-player,
who played such music, and so exquisitely, that the
limits of life were removed.   But we had to walk up
the Haymarket home, between eleven and twelve
o'clock, and the violin-playing became the merest
trifling.   M'Kay had been brought up upon the Bible.
He had before him, not only there, but in the history
of all great religious movements, a record of the improvement of the human race, or of large portions of it,
not merely by gradual civilisation, but by inspiration
spreading itself suddenly.   He could not get it out of
his head that something of this kind is possible again
in our time.   He longed to try for himself in his own
poor way in one of the slums about Drury Lane.   I
sympathised with him, but I asked him what he had
to say.   I remember telling him that I had been into
St. Paul's Cathedral, and that I pictured to myself
the cathedral full, and myself in the pulpit.   I was
excited while imagining the opportunity offered me of
delivering some message to three or four thousand
persons in such a building, but in a minute or two
I discovered that my sermon would be very nearly as
follows: "Dear friends, I know no more than you
know; we had better go home."   I admitted to him
that if he could believe in hell-fire, or if he could proclaim the Second Advent, as Paul did to the Thessalonians, and get people to believe, he might change
their manners, but otherwise he could do nothing but
resort to a much slower process.   With the departure
of a belief in the supernatural departs once and for
ever the chance of regenerating the race except by the

school and by science.[1] However, M'Kay thought he
would try. His earnestness was rather a hindrance
than a help to him, for it prevented his putting certain
important questions to himself, or at any rate it prevented his waiting for distinct answers. He recurred
to the apostles and Bunyan, and was convinced that it
was possible even now to touch depraved men and
women with an idea which should recast their lives.
So it is that the main obstacle to our success is a
success which has preceded us. We instinctively
follow the antecedent form, and consequently we
either pass by, or deny altogether, the life of our own
time, because its expression has changed. We never do
practically believe that the Messiah is not incarnated
twice in the same flesh. He came as Jesus, and we
look for Him as Jesus now, overlooking the manifestation of to-day, and dying, perhaps, without recognising it.

M'Kay had found a room near Parker Street, Drury
Lane, in which he proposed to begin, and that night, as
we trod the pavement of Portland Place, he propounded
his plans to me, I listening without much confidence,
but loth nevertheless to take the office of Time upon
myself, and to disprove what experience would disprove
more effectually. His object was nothing less than
gradually to attract Drury Lane to come and be saved.

The first Sunday I went with him to the room. As
we walked over the Drury Lane gratings of the cellars
a most foul stench came up, and one in particular I

---

[1] Not exactly untrue, but it sounds strangely now when socialism,
nationalisation of the land, and other projects have renewed in men the
hope of regeneration by political processes. The reader will, however,
please remember the date of these memoirs.—EDITOR, 1884.

remember to this day. A man half dressed pushed open a broken window beneath us, just as we passed by, and there issued such a blast of corruption, made up of gases bred by filth, air breathed and rebreathed a hundred times, charged with odours of unnameable personal uncleanness and disease, that I staggered to the gutter with a qualm which I could scarcely conquer. At the doors of the houses stood grimy women with their arms folded and their hair disordered. Grimier boys and girls had tied a rope to broken railings, and were swinging on it. The common door to a score of lodgings stood ever open, and the children swarmed up and down the stairs carrying with them patches of mud every time they came in from the street. The wholesome practice which amongst the decent poor marks off at least one day in the week as a day on which there is to be a change; when there is to be some attempt to procure order and cleanliness; a day to be preceded by soap and water, by shaving, and by as many clean clothes as can be procured, was unknown here. There was no break in the uniformity of squalor; nor was it even possible for any single family to emerge amidst such altogether suppressive surroundings. All self-respect, all effort to do anything more than to satisfy somehow the grossest wants, had departed. The shops were open; most of them exhibiting a most miscellaneous collection of goods, such as bacon cut in slices, fire-wood, a few loaves of bread, and sweetmeats in dirty bottles. Fowls, strange to say, black as the flagstones, walked in and out of these shops, or descended into the dark areas. The undertaker had not put up his shutters. He had drawn down a yellow blind, on which was painted a picture of a suburban cemetery. Two funerals, the loftiest effort of his craft, were depicted approaching the gates. When the gas was alight behind the blind, an effect was produced which was doubtless much admired. He also displayed in his window a model coffin, a work of art. It was about a foot long, varnished, studded with little brass nails, and on the lid was fastened a rustic cross stretching from end to end. The desire to decorate existence in some way or other with more or less care is nearly universal. The most sensual and the meanest almost always manifest an indisposition to be content with mere material satisfaction. I have known selfish, gluttonous, drunken men spend their leisure moments in trimming a bed of scarlet geraniums, and the vulgarest and most commonplace of mortals considers it a necessity to put a picture in the room or an ornament on the mantelpiece. The instinct, even in its lowest forms, is divine. It is the commentary on the text that man shall not live by bread alone. It is evidence of an acknowledged compulsion—of which art is the highest manifestation—to *escape*. In the alleys behind Drury Lane this instinct, the very salt of life, was dead, crushed out utterly, a symptom which seemed to me ominous, and even awful to the last degree. The only house in which it survived was in that of the undertaker, who displayed the willows, the black horses, and the coffin. These may have been nothing more than an advertisement, but from the care with which the cross was elaborated, and the neatness with which it was made to resemble a natural piece of wood, I am inclined to believe that the man felt some pleasure in his work for its own sake, and that he was not utterly submerged. The cross in such dens as these, or, worse

than dens, in such sewers! If it be anything, it is a
symbol of victory, of power to triumph over resistance,
and even death.   Here was nothing but sullen subjugation, the most grovelling slavery, mitigated only by a
tendency to mutiny.   Here was a strength of circumstance to quell and dominate which neither Jesus nor
Paul could have overcome—worse a thousandfold than
Scribes or Pharisees, or any form of persecution.   The
preaching of Jesus would have been powerless here; in
fact, no known stimulus, nothing ever held up before
men to stir the soul to activity, can do anything in the
back streets of great cities so long as they are the cesspools which they are now.

We came to the room.   About a score of M'Kay's
own friends were there, and perhaps half-a-dozen outsiders, attracted by the notice which had been pasted
on a board at the entrance.   M'Kay announced his
errand.   The ignorance and misery of London he said
were intolerable to him.   He could not take any pleasure in life when he thought upon them.   What could
he do? that was the question.   He was not a man of
wealth.   He could not buy up these hovels.   He could
not force an entrance into them and persuade their inhabitants to improve themselves.   He had no talents
wherewith to found a great organisation or create public
opinion.   He had determined, after much thought, to
do what he was now doing.   It was very little, but it
was all he could undertake.   He proposed to keep this
room open as a place to which those who wished might
resort at different times, and find some quietude, instruction, and what fortifying thoughts he could collect
to enable men to endure their almost unendurable
sufferings.   He did not intend to teach theology.   Any-

thing which would be serviceable he would set forth,
but in the main he intended to rely on holding up the
examples of those who were greater than ourselves
and were our redeemers.   He meant to teach Christ in
the proper sense of the word.   Christ now is admired
probably more than He had ever been.   Everybody
agrees to admire Him, but where are the people who
really do what He did?   There is no religion now-a-
days.   Religion is a mere literature.   Cultivated persons
sit in their studies and write overflowingly about Jesus,
or meet at parties and talk about Him; but He is not
of much use to me unless I say to myself, *how is it with
thee?* unless I myself become what He was.   This was
the meaning of Jesus to the Apostle Paul.   Jesus was
in him; he had put on Jesus; that is to say, Jesus
lived in him like a second soul, taking the place of his
own soul and directing him accordingly.   That was
religion, and it is absurd to say that the English nation
at this moment, or any section of it, is religious.   Its
educated classes are inhabited by a hundred minds.
We are in a state of anarchy, each of us with a different
aim and shaping himself according to a different type;
while the uneducated classes are entirely given over
to the "natural man."   He was firmly persuaded that
we need religion, poor and rich alike.   We need some
controlling influence to bind together our scattered
energies.   We do not know what we are doing.   We
read one book one day and another book another day,
but it is idle wandering to right and left; it is not
advancing on a straight road.   It is not possible to
bind ourselves down to a certain defined course, but
still it is an enormous, an incalculable advantage for
us to have some irreversible standard set up in us by

which everything we meet is to be judged. That is
the meaning of the prophecy—whether it will ever be
fulfilled God only knows—that Christ shall judge the
world. All religions have been this. They have said
that in the midst of the infinitely possible—infinitely
possible evil and infinitely possible good too—we become distracted.   A thousand forces good and bad act
upon us. It is necessary, if we are to be men, if we
are to be saved, that we should be rescued from this
tumult, and that our feet should be planted upon a
path. His object, therefore, would be to preach Christ,
as before said, and to introduce into human life His
unifying influence. He would try and get them to see
things with the eyes of Christ, to love with His love,
to judge with His judgment. He believed Christ was
fitted to occupy this place. He deliberately chose
Christ as worthy to be our central, shaping force. He
would try by degrees to prove this; to prove that
Christ's way of dealing with life is the best way, and
so to create a genuinely Christian spirit, which, when
any choice of conduct is presented to us, will prompt
us to ask first of all, *how would Christ have it?* or,
when men and things pass before us, will decide
through Him what we have to say about them. M'Kay
added that he hoped his efforts would not be confined
to talking. He trusted to be able, by means of this
little meeting, gradually to gain admittance for himself
and his friends into the houses of the poor and do some
practical good.   At present he had no organisation and
no plans. He did not believe in organisation and plans
preceding a clear conception of what was to be accomplished.   Such, as nearly as I can now recollect, is an
outline of his discourse.   It was thoroughly character-

istic of him. He always talked in this fashion. He
was for ever insisting on the aimlessness of modern
life, on the powerlessness of its vague activities to
mould men into anything good, to restrain them from
evil or moderate their passions, and he was possessed
by a vision of a new Christianity which was to take
the place of the old and dead theologies. I have reported him in my own language. He strove as much
as he could to make his meaning plain to everybody.
Just before he finished, three or four out of the half-
a-dozen outsiders who were present whistled with all
their might and ran down the stairs shouting to one
another. As we went out they had collected about the
door, and amused themselves by pushing one another
against us, and kicking an old kettle behind us and
amongst us all the way up the street, so that we were
covered with splashes. Mrs. M‘Kay went with us,
and when we reached home, she tried to say something
about what she had heard. The cloud came over her
husband's face at once; he remained silent for a minute,
and getting up and going to the window, observed that
it ought to be cleaned, and that he could hardly see
the opposite house. The poor woman looked distressed,
and I was just about to come to her rescue by continuing what she had been saying, when she rose, not
in anger, but in trouble, and went upstairs.

CHAPTER III.

MISS LEROY.

DURING the great French war there were many French prisoners in my native town. They led a strange isolated life, for they knew nothing of our language, nor, in those days, did three people in the town understand theirs. The common soldiers amused themselves by making little trifles and selling them. I have now before me a box of coloured straw with the date 1799 on the bottom, which was bought by my grandfather. One of these prisoners was an officer named Leroy. Why he did not go back to France I never heard, but I know that before I was born he was living near our house on a small income; that he tried to teach French, and that he had as his companion a handsome daughter who grew up speaking English. What she was like when she was young I cannot say, but I have had her described to me over and over again. She had rather darkish brown hair, and she was tall and straight as an arrow. This she was, by the way, even into old age. She surprised, shocked, and attracted all the sober persons in our circle. Her ways were not their ways. She would walk out by herself on a starry night without a single companion, and cause thereby infinite talk, which would have converged to a single focus if it had not happened that she was also in the habit of walking out at four o'clock on a summer's morning, and that in the church porch of a little village not far from us, which was her favourite resting-place, a copy of the *De Imitatione Christi* was found which belonged to her. So the talk was scattered again and its convergence prevented. She used to say doubtful things about love. One of them struck my mother with horror. Miss Leroy told a male person once, and told him to his face, that if she loved him and he loved her, and they agreed to sign one another's foreheads with a cross as a ceremony, it would be as good to her as marriage. This may seem a trifle, but nobody now can imagine what was thought of it at the time it was spoken. My mother repeated it every now and then for fifty years. It may be conjectured how easily any other girls of our acquaintance would have been classified, and justly classified, if they had uttered such barefaced Continental immorality. Miss Leroy's neighbours were remarkably apt at classifying their fellow-creatures. They had a few, a very few holes, into which they dropped their neighbours, and they must go into one or the other. Nothing was more distressing than a specimen which, notwithstanding all the violence which might be used to it, would not fit into a hole, but remained an exception. Some lout, I believe, reckoning on the legitimacy of his generalisation, and having heard of this and other observations accredited to Miss Leroy, ventured to be slightly rude to her. What she said to him was never known, but he was always shy afterwards of mentioning her name, and when he did he was wont to declare that she was "a rum un." She was not particular, I have heard, about personal tidiness, and this I can well believe, for she was certainly not distinguished when I knew her for this virtue. She cared nothing for the linen-closet, the spotless bed-hangings, and the bright poker, which were the true household gods of the respectable women of those days. She would have been instantly set down as "slut," and as having "nasty dirty forrin ways," if a peculiar habit of hers had not unfortunately presented itself, most irritating to her critics, so anxious promptly to gratify their philosophic tendency towards scientific grouping. Mrs. Mobbs, who lived next door to her, averred that she always slept with the window open. Mrs. Mobbs, like everybody else, never opened her window except to "air the room." Mrs. Mobbs' best bedroom was carpeted all over, and contained a great four-post bedstead, hung round with heavy hangings, and protected at the top from draughts by a kind of firmament of white dimity. Mrs. Mobbs stuffed a sack of straw up the chimney of the fireplace, to prevent the fall of the "sutt," as she called it. Mrs. Mobbs, if she had a visitor, gave her a hot supper, and expected her immediately afterwards to go upstairs, draw the window curtains, get into this bed, draw the bed curtains also, and wake up the next morning "bilious." This was the proper thing to do. Miss Leroy's sitting-room was decidedly disorderly; the chairs were dusty; "yer might write yer name on the table," Mrs. Mobbs declared; but, nevertheless, the casement was never closed night nor day; and, moreover, Miss Leroy was believed by the strongest circumstantial evidence to wash herself all over every morning, a habit which Mrs. Mobbs thought "weakening," and somehow connected with ethical impropriety. When Miss Leroy was married, and first as an elderly woman became known to me, she was very inconsequential in her opinions, or at least appeared so to our eyes. She must have been much more so when she was younger. In our town we were all formed upon recognised patterns, and those who possessed any one mark of the pattern, had all. The wine-merchant, for example, who went to church, eminently respectable, Tory, by no means associating with the tradesfolk who displayed their goods in the windows, knowing no "experience," and who had never felt the outpouring of the Spirit, was a specimen of a class like him. Another class was represented by the dissenting iron-monger, deacon, presiding at prayer-meetings, strict Sabbatarian, and believer in eternal punishments; while a third was set forth by "Guffy," whose real name was unknown, who got drunk, unloaded barges, assisted at the municipal elections, and was never once seen inside a place of worship. These patterns had existed amongst us from the dimmest antiquity, and were accepted as part of the eternal order of things; so much so, that the deacon, although he professed to be sure that nobody who had not been converted would escape the fire—and the wine-merchant certainly had not been converted—was very far from admitting to himself that the wine-merchant ought to be converted, or that it would be proper to try and convert him. I doubt, indeed, whether our congregation would have been happy, or would have thought any the better of him, if he had left the church. Such an event, however, could no more come within the reach of our vision than a reversal of the current of our river. It would have broken up our foundations and party-walls, and would have been considered as ominous, and anything but a

subject for thankfulness.   But Miss Leroy was not the
wine-merchant, nor the ironmonger, nor Guffy, and even
now I cannot trace the hidden centre of union from
which sprang so much that was apparently irreconcil-
able.   She was a person whom nobody could have
created in writing a novel, because she was so inconsistent.   As I have said before, she studied Thomas à
Kempis, and her little French Bible was brown with
constant use.   But then she read much fiction in which
there were scenes which would have made our hair
stand on end.   The only thing she constantly abhorred
in books was what was dull and opaque.   Yet, as we
shall see presently, her dislike to dulness, once at least
in her life, notably failed her.   She was not Catholic,
and professed herself Protestant, but such a Protestant-
ism!   She had no sceptical doubts.   She believed implicitly that the Bible was the Word of God, and that
everything in it was true, but her interpretation of it
was of the strangest kind.   Almost all our great doctrines seemed shrunk to nothing in her eyes, while
others, which were nothing to us, were all-important to
her.   The atonement, for instance, I never heard her
mention, but Unitarianism was hateful to her, and
Jesus was her God in every sense of the word.   On the
other hand, she was partly Pagan, for she knew very
little of that consideration for the feeble, and even for
the foolish, which is the glory of Christianity.   She was
rude to foolish people, and she instinctively kept out of
the way of all disease and weakness, so that in this respect she was far below the commonplace tradesman's
wife, who visited the sick, sat up with them, and,
in fact, never seemed so completely in her element as
when she could be with anybody who was ill in bed.

Miss Leroy's father was republican, and so was my grandfather. My grandfather and old Leroy were the only people in our town who refused to illuminate when a victory was gained over the French. Leroy's windows were spared on the ground that he was not a Briton, but the mob endeavoured to show my grandfather the folly of his belief in democracy by smashing every pane of glass in front of his house with stones. This drew him and Leroy together, and the result was, that although Leroy himself never set foot inside any chapel or church, Miss Leroy was often induced to attend our meeting-house in company with a maiden aunt of mine, who rather "took to her." Now comes the for ever mysterious passage in her history. There was amongst the attendants at that meeting-house a young man who was apprentice to a miller. He was a big, soft, quiet, plump-faced, awkward youth, very good, but nothing more. He wore on Sunday a complete suit of light pepper-and-salt clothes, and continued to wear pepper-and-salt on Sunday all his life. He taught in the Sunday-school, and afterwards, as he got older, he was encouraged to open his lips at a prayer-meeting, and to "take the service" in the village chapels on Sunday evening. He was the most singularly placid, even-tempered person I ever knew. I first became acquainted with him when I was a child and he was past middle life. What he was then, I am told, he always was; and I certainly never heard one single violent word escape his lips. His habits, even when young, had a tendency to harden. He went to sleep after his mid-day dinner with the greatest regularity, and he never could keep awake if he sat by a fire after dark. I have seen him, when

kneeling at family worship and praying with his family,
lose himself for an instant and nod his head, to the confusion of all who were around him.   He is dead now,
but he lived to a good old age, which crept upon him
gradually with no pain, and he passed away from this
world to the next in a peaceful doze.   He never read
anything, for the simple reason that whenever he was
not at work or at chapel he slumbered.   To the utter
amazement of everybody, it was announced one fine
day that Miss Leroy and he—George Butts—were to
be married.   They were about the last people in the
world, who, it was thought, could be brought together.
My mother was stunned, and never completely recovered.
I have seen her, forty years after George Butts' wedding-
day, lift up her hands, and have heard her call out with
emotion, as fresh as if the event were of yesterday,
"What made that girl have George I can *not* think—
but there!"   What she meant by the last two words
we could not comprehend.   Many of her acquaintances
interpreted them to mean that she knew more than she
dared communicate, but I think they were mistaken.
I am quite certain if she had known anything she
must have told it, and, in the next place, the phrase
"but there" was not uncommon amongst women in
our town, and was supposed to mark the consciousness
of a prudently restrained ability to give an explanation
of mysterious phenomena in human relationships.   For
my own part, I am just as much in the dark as my
mother.   My father, who was a shrewd man, was
always puzzled, and could not read the riddle.   He
used to say that he never thought George could have
"made up" to any young woman, and it was quite clear
that Miss Leroy did not either then or afterwards dis-

play any violent affection for him. I have heard her
criticise and patronise him as a "good soul," but incapable, as indeed he was, of all sympathy with her.
After marriage she went her way and he his. She
got up early, as she was wont to do, and took her
Bible into the fields while he was snoring. She would
then very likely suffer from a terrible headache during
the rest of the day, and lie down for hours, letting
the house manage itself as best it could. What made
her selection of George more obscure was that she
was much admired by many young fellows, some of
whom were certainly more akin to her than he was;
and I have heard from one or two reports of encouraging words, and even something more than words, which
she had vouchsafed to them. A solution is impossible.
The affinities, repulsions, reasons in a nature like that
of Miss Leroy's are so secret and so subtle, working
towards such incalculable and not-to-be-predicted results, that to attempt to make a major and minor pre-
miss and an inevitable conclusion out of them would
be useless. One thing was clear, that by marrying
George she gained great freedom. If she had married
anybody closer to her, she might have jarred with him;
there might have been collision and wreck as complete
as if they had been entirely opposed; for she was not
the kind of person to accomodate herself to others even
in the matter of small differences. But George's road
through space lay entirely apart from hers, and there
was not the slightest chance of interference. She was
under the protection of a husband; she could do things
that, as an unmarried woman, especially in a foreign
land, she could not do, and the compensatory sacrifice
to her was small. This is really the only attempt at

elucidation I can give.   She went regularly all her life
to chapel with George, but even when he became
deacon, and "supplied" the villages round, she never
would join the church as a member.   She never agreed
with the minister, and he never could make anything
out of her.   They did not quarrel, but she thought
nothing of his sermons, and he was perplexed and
uncomfortable in the presence of a nondescript who
did not respond to any dogmatic statement of the
articles of religion, and who yet could not be put
aside as "one of those in the gallery"—that is to say,
as one of the ordinary unconverted, for she used to
quote hymns with amazing fervour, and she quoted
them to him with a freedom and a certain superiority
which he might have expected from an aged brother
minister, but certainly not from one of his own congregation.   He was a preacher of the Gospel, it was true;
and it was his duty, a duty on which he insisted, to
be "instant in season and out of season" in saying
spiritual things to his flock; but then they were things
proper, decent, conventional, uttered with gravity at
suitable times—such as were customary amongst all
the ministers of the denomination.   It was not pleasant
to be outbid in his own department, especially by one
who was not a communicant, and to be obliged, when
he went on a pastoral visit to a house in which Mrs.
Butts happened to be, to sit still and hear her, regard-
less of the minister's presence, conclude a short mystical
monologue with Cowper's verse—

> " Exults our rising soul,
>   Disburdened of her load,
> And swells unutterably full
>   Of glory and of God."

This was *not* pleasant to our minister, nor was it pleasant to the minister's wife. But George Butts held a responsible position in our community, and the minister's wife held also a responsible position, so that she taxed all her ingenuity to let her friends understand at tea-parties what she thought of Mrs. Butts without saying anything which could be the ground of formal remonstrance. Thus did Mrs. Butts live among us, as an Arabian bird with its peculiar habits, cries, and plumage might live in one of our barnyards with the ordinary barn-door fowls.

I was never happier when I was a boy than when I was with Mrs. Butts at the mill, which George had inherited. There was a grand freedom in her house. The front door leading into the garden was always open. There was no precise separation between the house and the mill. The business and the dwelling-place were mixed up together, and covered with flour. Mr. Butts was in the habit of walking out of his mill into the living-room every now and then, and never dreamed when one o'clock came that it was necessary for him to change his floury coat before he had his dinner. His cap he also often retained, and in any weather, not extraordinarily cold, he sat in his shirt-sleeves. The garden was large and half-wild. A man from the mill, if work was slack, gave a day to it now and then, but it was not trimmed and raked and combed like the other gardens in the town. It was full of gooseberry trees, and I was permitted to eat the gooseberries without stint. The mill-life, too, was inexpressibly attractive—the dark chamber with the great, green, dripping wheel in it, so awfully mysterious as the central life of the whole structure;

the machinery connected with the wheel—I knew
not how; the hole where the roach lay by the side
of the mill-tail in the eddy; the haunts of the water-
rats which we used to hunt with Spot, the black and
tan terrier, and the still more exciting sport with
the ferrets—all this drew me down the lane perpetually. I liked, and even loved Mrs. Butts, too, for her
own sake. Her kindness to me was unlimited, and she
was never overcome with the fear of "spoiling me,"
which seemed the constant dread of most of my
hostesses. I never lost my love for her. It grew as
I grew, despite my mother's scarcely suppressed
hostility to her, and when I heard she was ill, and
was likely to die, I went to be with her. She was
eighty years old then. I sat by her bedside with her
hand in mine. I was there when she passed away,
and—but I have no mind and no power to say any
more, for all the memories of her affection and of the
sunny days by the water come over me and prevent
the calmness necessary for a chronicle. She with all
her faults and eccentricities will always have in my
heart a little chapel with an ever-burning light. She
was one of the very very few whom I have ever seen
who knew how to love a child.

Mrs. Butts and George had one son who was named
Clement. He was exactly my own age, and naturally
we were constant companions. We went to the same
school. He never distinguished himself at his books,
but he was chief among us. He had a versatile talent
for almost every accomplishment in which we delighted, but he was not supreme in any one of them.
There were better cricketers, better football players,
better hands at setting a night-line, better swimmers

than Clem, but he could do something, and do it
well, in all these departments. He generally took
up a thing with much eagerness for a time, and then
let it drop. He was foremost in introducing new
games and new fashions, which he permitted to
flourish for a time, and then superseded. As he
grew up he displayed a taste for drawing and
music. He was soon able to copy little paintings of
flowers, or even little country scenes, and to play a
piece of no very great difficulty with tolerable effect.
But as he never was taught by a master, and never
practised elementary exercises and studies, he was
deficient in accuracy. When the question came what
was to be done with him after he left school, his
father naturally wished him to go into the mill. Clem,
however, set his face steadily against this project,
and his mother, who was a believer in his genius,
supported him. He actually wanted to go to the
University, a thing unheard of in those days amongst
our people; but this was not possible, and after
dangling about for some time at home, he obtained
the post of usher in a school, an occupation which he
considered more congenial and intellectual than that of
grinding flour. Strange to say, although he knew less
than any of his colleagues, he succeeded better than
any of them. He managed to impress a sense of his
own importance upon everybody, including the head-
master. He slid into a position of superiority above
three or four colleagues who would have shamed him at
an examination, and who uttered many a curse because
they saw themselves surpassed and put in the shade
by a stranger, who, they were confident, could hardly
construct a hexameter. He never quarrelled with them

nor did he grossly patronise them, but he always let them know that he considered himself above them. His reading was desultory; in fact, everything he did was desultory. He was not selfish in the ordinary sense of the word. Rather was he distinguished by a large and liberal open-handedness; but he was liberal also to himself to a remarkable degree, dressing himself expensively, and spending a good deal of money in luxuries. He was specially fond of insisting on his half French origin, made a great deal of his mother, was silent as to his father, and always signed himself C. Leroy Butts, although I don't believe the second Christian name was given him in baptism. Notwithstanding his generosity he was egotistical and hollow at heart. He knew nothing of friendship in the best sense of the word, but had a multitude of acquaintances, whom he invariably sought amongst those who were better off than himself. He was popular with them, for no man knew better than he how to get up an entertainment, or to make a success of an evening party. He had not been at his school for two years before he conceived the notion of setting up for himself. He had not a penny, but he borrowed easily what was wanted from somebody he knew, and in a twelvemonth more he had a dozen pupils. He took care to get the ablest subordinates he could find, and he succeeded in passing a boy for an open scholarship at Oxford, against two competitors prepared by the very man whom he had formerly served. After this he prospered greatly, and would have prospered still more, if his love of show and extravagance had not increased with his income. His talents were sometimes taxed when people who came to place their sons with him supposed

ignorantly that his origin and attainments were what
might be expected from his position; and poor Chalmers,
a Glasgow M.A., who still taught, for £80 a year, the
third class in the establishment in which Butts began
life, had some bitter stories on that subject. Chalmers
was a perfect scholar, but he was not agreeable. He
had black finger-nails, and wore dirty collars. Having
a lively remembrance of his friend's "general acquaintance" with Latin prosody, Chalmers' opinion of Providence was much modified when he discovered what
Providence was doing for Butts. Clem took to the
Church when he started for himself. It would have
been madness in him to remain a Dissenter. But in
private, if it suited his purpose, he could always be
airily sceptical, and he had a superficial acquaintance,
second-hand, with a multitude of books, many of them of
an infidel turn. I once rebuked him for his hypocrisy,
and his defence was that religious disputes were indifferent to him, and that at any rate a man associates
with gentlemen if he is a churchman. Cultivation
and manners he thought to be of more importance than
Calvinism. I believe that he partly meant what he
said. He went to church because the school would
have failed if he had gone to chapel; but he was sufficiently keen-sighted and clever to be beyond the petty
quarrels of the sects, and a song well sung was of
much greater moment to him than an essay on pædo-
baptism. It was all very well of Chalmers to revile
him for his shallowness. He was shallow, and yet he
possessed in some mysterious way a talent which I
greatly coveted, and which in this world is inestimably
precious—the talent of making people give way before
him—a capacity of self-impression. Chalmers could

never have commanded anybody. He had no power whatever, even when he was right, to put his will against the wills of others, but yielded first this way and then the other. Clem, on the contrary, without any difficulty or any effort, could conquer all opposition, and smilingly force everybody to do his bidding.

Clem had a peculiar theory with regard to his own rights and those of the class to which he considered that he belonged. He always held implicitly and sometimes explicitly that gifted people live under a kind of dispensation of grace; the law existing solely for dull souls. What in a clown is a crime punishable by the laws of the land might in a man of genius be a necessary development, or at any rate an excusable offence. He had nothing to say for the servant-girl who had sinned with the shopman, but if artist or poet were to carry off another man's wife, it might not be wrong.

He believed, and acted upon the belief, that the inferior ought to render perpetual incense to the superior, and that the superior should receive it as a matter of course. When his father was ill he never waited on him or sat up a single night with him. If duty was disagreeable to him Clem paid homage to it afar off, but pleaded exemption. He admitted that waiting on the sick is obligatory on people who are fitted for it, and is very charming. Nothing was more beautiful to him than tender, filial care spending itself for a beloved object. But it was not his vocation. His nerves were more finely ordered than those of mankind generally, and the sight of disease and suffering distressed him too much. Everything was surrendered to him in the houses of his friends. If any inconvenience was to be

endured, he was the first person to be protected from
it, and he accepted the greatest sacrifices, with a graceful acknowledgment, it is true, but with no repulse.
To what better purpose could the best wine be put
than in cherishing his imagination. It was simple
waste to allow it to be poured out upon the earth, and
to give it to a fool was no better. After he succeeded
so well in the world, Clem, to a great extent, deserted
me, although I was his oldest friend and the friend of
his childhood. I heard that he visited a good many
rich persons, that he made much of them, and they
made much of him. He kept up a kind of acquaintance
with me, not by writing to me, but by the very cheap
mode of sending me a newspaper now and then with a
marked paragraph in it announcing the exploits of his
school at a cricket-match, or occasionally with a report
of a lecture which he had delivered. He was a decent
orator, and from motives of business if from no other,
he not unfrequently spoke in public. One or two of
these lectures wounded me a good deal. There was
one in particular on *As You Like It*, in which he held
up to admiration the fidelity which is so remarkable in
Shakespeare, and lamented that in these days it was so
rare to find anything of the kind. He thought that we
were becoming more indifferent to one another. He
maintained, however, that man should be everything
to man, and he then enlarged on the duty of really
cultivating affection, of its superiority to books, and on
the pleasure and profit of self-denial. I do not mean to
accuse Clem of downright hypocrisy. I have known
many persons come up from the country and go into
raptures over a playhouse sun and moon who have
never bestowed a glance or a thought on the real sun

and moon to be seen from their own doors; and we are
all aware it by no means follows because we are moved
to our very depths by the spectacle of unrecognised,
uncomplaining endurance in a novel, that therefore we
can step over the road to waste an hour or a sixpence
upon the unrecognised, uncomplaining endurance of
the poor lone woman left a widow in the little villa
there.   I was annoyed with myself because Clem's
abandonment of me so much affected me.   I wished I
could cut the rope and carelessly cast him adrift as he
had cast me adrift, but I could not.   I never could
make out and cannot make out what was the secret of
his influence over me; why I was unable to say, " If
you do not care for me I do not care for you."   I
longed sometimes for complete rupture, so that we
might know exactly where we were, but it never came.
Gradually our intercourse grew thinner and thinner,
until at last I heard that he had been spending a
fortnight with some semi-aristocratic acquaintance
within five miles of me, and during the whole of that
time he never came near me.   I met him in a railway
station soon afterwards, when he came up to me
effusive and apparently affectionate.   " It was a real
grief to me, my dear fellow," he said, " that I could not
call on you last month, but the truth was I was so
driven : they would make me go here and go there,
and I kept putting off my visit to you till it was too
late."   Fortunately my train was just starting, or I
don't know what might have happened.   I said not a
word; shook hands with him; got into the carriage;
he waved his hat to me, and I pretended not to see
him, but I did see him, and saw him turn round immediately to some well-dressed officer-like gentleman with

whom he walked laughing down the platform. The rest of that day was black to me. I cared for nothing. I passed away from the thought of Clem, and dwelt upon the conviction which had long possessed me that I was *insignificant*, that there was *nothing much in me*, and it was this which destroyed my peace. We may reconcile ourselves to poverty and suffering, but few of us can endure the conviction that there is *nothing in us*, and that consequently we cannot expect anybody to gravitate towards us with any forceful impulse. It is a bitter experience. And yet there is consolation. The universe is infinite. In the presence of its celestial magnitudes who is there who is really great or small, and what is the difference between you and me, my work and yours? I sought refuge in the idea of GOD, the God of a starry night with its incomprehensible distances; and I was at peace, content to be the meanest worm of all the millions that crawl on the earth.

CHAPTER IV.

A NECESSARY DEVELOPMENT.

THE few friends who have read the first part of my
autobiography may perhaps remember that in my
younger days I had engaged myself to a girl named
Ellen, from whom afterwards I parted. After some
two or three years she was left an orphan, and came
into the possession of a small property, over which
unfortunately she had complete power. She was
attractive and well-educated, and I heard long after
I had broken with her, and had ceased to have
intercourse with Butts, that the two were married.
He of course, living so near her, had known her
well, and he found her money useful. How they
agreed I knew not save by report, but I was told
that after the first child was born, the only child
they ever had, Butts grew indifferent to her, and
that she, to use my friend's expression, "went off,"
by which I suppose he meant that she faded. There
happened in those days to live near Butts a small
squire, married, but with no family. He was a
lethargic creature, about five-and-thirty years old,
farming eight hundred acres of his own land. He did
not, however, belong to the farming class. He had
been to Harrow, was on the magistrates' bench, and
associated with the small aristocracy of the country

round. He was like every other squire whom I remember in my native county, and I can remember scores of them. He read no books and tolerated the usual conventional breaches of the moral law, but was an intense worshipper of respectability, and hated a scandal. On one point he differed from his neighbours. He was a Whig and they were all Tories. I have said he read no books, and this, on the whole, is true, but nevertheless he did know something about the history of the early part of the century, and he was rather fond at political gatherings of making some allusion to Mr. Fox. His father had sat in the House of Commons when Fox was there, and had sternly opposed the French war. I don't suppose that anybody not actually *in it*—no Londoner certainly—can understand the rigidity of the bonds which restricted county society when I was young, and for aught I know may restrict it now. There was with us one huge and dark exception to the general uniformity. The earl had broken loose, had ruined his estate, had defied decorum and openly lived with strange women at home and in Paris, but this black background did but set off the otherwise universal adhesion to the Church and to authorised manners, an adhesion tempered and rendered tolerable by port wine. It must not, however, be supposed that human nature was different from the human nature of to-day or a thousand years ago. There were then, even as there were a thousand years ago, and are to-day, small, secret doors, connected with mysterious staircases, by which access was gained to freedom; and men and women, inmates of castles with walls a yard thick, and impenetrable portcullises, sought those doors and descended those stairs night and day.

But nobody knew, or if we did know, the silence was profound. The broad-shouldered, yellow-haired Whig squire, had a wife who was the opposite of him. She came from a distant part of the country, and had been educated in France. She was small, with black hair, and yet with blue eyes. She spoke French perfectly, was devoted to music, read French books, and, although she was a constant attendant at church, and gave no opportunity whatever for the slightest suspicion, the matrons of the circle in which she moved were never quite happy about her. This was due partly to her knowledge of French, and partly to her having no children. Anything more about her I do not know. She was beyond us, and although I have seen her often enough I never spoke to her. Butts, however, managed to become a visitor at the squire's house. Fancy *my* going to the squire's! But Butts did, was accepted there, and even dined there with a parson, and two or three half-pay officers. The squire never called on Butts. That was an understood thing, nor did Mrs. Butts accompany her husband. That also was an understood thing. It was strange that Butts could tolerate and even court such a relationship. Most men would scorn with the scorn of a personal insult an invitation to a house from which their wives were expressly excluded. The squire's lady and Clem became great friends. She discovered that his mother was a Frenchwoman, and this was a bond between them. She discovered also that Clem was artistic, that he was devotedly fond of music, that he could draw a little, paint a little, and she believed in the divine right of talent wherever it might be found to assert a claim of equality with those who were better born.

The women in the country-side were shy of her; for the men she could not possibly care, and no doubt she must at times have got rather weary of her heavy husband with his one outlook towards the universal in the person of George James Fox, and the Whig policy of 1802. I am under some disadvantage in telling this part of my story, because I was far away from home, and only knew afterwards at second hand what the course of events had been; but I learned them from one who was intimately concerned, and I do not think I can be mistaken on any essential point. I imagine that by this time Mrs. Butts must have become changed into what she was in later years. She had grown older since she and I had parted; she had seen trouble; her child had been born, and although she was not exactly estranged from Clem, for neither he nor she would have admitted any coolness, she had learned that she was nothing specially to him. I have often noticed what an imperceptible touch, what a slight shifting in the balance of opposing forces, will alter the character. I have observed a woman, for example, essentially the same at twenty and thirty—who is there who is not always essentially the same?—and yet, what was a defect at twenty, has become transformed and transfigured into a benignant virtue at thirty; translating the whole nature from the human to the divine. Some slight depression has been wrought here, and some slight lift has been given there, and beauty and order have miraculously emerged from what was chaotic. The same thing may continually be noticed in the hereditary transmission of qualities. The redeeming virtue of the father palpably present in the son becomes his curse, through a faint diminution of the strength of the check which caused that virtue to be the father's salvation. The propensity, too, which is a man's evil genius, and leads him to madness and utter ruin, gives vivid reality to all his words and thoughts, and becomes all his strength, if by divine assistance it can just be subdued and prevented from rising in victorious insurrection. But this is a digression, useful, however, in its way, because it will explain Mrs. Butts when we come a little nearer to her in the future.

For a time Clem's visits to the squire's house always took place when the squire was at home, but an amateur concert was to be arranged in which Clem was to take part together with the squire's lady. Clem consequently was obliged to go to the Hall for the purpose of practising, and so it came to pass that he was there at unusual hours and when the master was afield. These morning and afternoon calls did not cease when the concert was over. Clem's wife did not know anything about them, and, if she noticed his frequent absence, she was met with an excuse. Perhaps the worst, or almost the worst effect of relationships which we do not like to acknowledge, is the secrecy and equivocation which they beget. From the very first moment when the intimacy between the squire's wife and Clem began to be anything more than harmless, he was compelled to shuffle and to become contemptible. At the same time I believe he defended himself against himself with the weapons which were ever ready when self rose against self because of some wrong-doing. He was not as other men. It was absurd to class what he did with what an ordinary person might do, although externally his actions and those of the ordinary person might resemble one another. I cannot trace the steps

by which the two sinners drew nearer and nearer
together, for the simple reason that this is an autobiography, and not a novel. I do not know what the
development was, nor did anybody except the persons
concerned. Neither do I know what was the mental
history of Mrs. Butts during this unhappy period. She
seldom talked about it afterwards. I do, however,
happen to recollect hearing her once say that her
greatest trouble was the cessation, from some unknown
cause, of Clem's attempts—they were never many—
to interest and amuse her. It is easy to understand
how this should be. If a man is guilty of any defec-
tion from himself, of anything of which he is ashamed,
everything which is better becomes a farce to him.
After he has been betrayed by some passion, how can
he pretend to the perfect enjoyment of what is pure?
The moment he feels any disposition to rise, he is
stricken through as if with an arrow, and he drops.
Not until weeks, months, and even years have elapsed,
does he feel justified in surrendering himself to a noble
emotion. I have heard of persons who have been able
to ascend easily and instantaneously from the mud to
the upper air, and descend as easily; but to me at
least they are incomprehensible. Clem, less than most
men, suffered permanently, or indeed in any way from
remorse, because he was so shielded by his peculiar
philosophy; but I can quite believe that when he got
into the habit of calling at the Hall at mid-day, his
behaviour to his wife changed.

One day in December the squire had gone out with
the hounds. Clem, going on from bad to worse, had
now reached the point of planning to be at the Hall
when the squire was not at home. On that particular

afternoon Clem was there.   It was about half-past
four o'clock, and the master was not expected till six.
There had been some music, the lady accompanying,
and Clem singing.   It was over, and Clem, sitting
down beside her at the piano, and pointing out with
his right hand some passage which had troubled him,
had placed his left arm on her shoulder, and round her
neck, she not resisting.   He always swore afterwards
that never till then had such a familiarity as this been
permitted, and I believe that he did not tell a lie.   But
what was there in that familiarity?   The worst was
already there, and it was through a mere accident that
it never showed itself.   The accident was this.   The
squire, for some unknown reason, had returned earlier
than usual, and dismounting in the stable-yard, had
walked round the garden on the turf which came close
to the windows of the ground-floor.   Passing the
drawing-room window, and looking in by the edge of
the drawn-down blind, he saw his wife and Clem just
at the moment described.   He slipped round to the
door, took off his boots so that he might not be heard,
and as there was a large screen inside the room he was
able to enter it unobserved.   Clem caught sight of
him just as he emerged from behind the screen, and
started up instantly in great confusion, the lady, with
greater presence of mind, remaining perfectly still.
Without a word the squire strode up to Clem, struck
out at him, caught him just over the temple, and felled
him instantaneously.   He lay for some time senseless,
and what passed between husband and wife I cannot
say.   After about ten minutes, perhaps, Clem came to
himself; there was nobody to be seen; and he managed
to get up and crawl home.   He told his wife he had

met with an accident; that he would go to bed, and
that she should know all about it when he was better.
His forehead was dressed, and to bed he went. That
night Mrs. Butts had a letter. It ran as follows:—

"MADAM,—It may at first sight seem a harsh thing
for me to write and tell you what I have to say, but I
can assure you I do not mean to be anything but kind
to you, and I think it will be better, for reasons which
I will afterwards explain, that I should communicate
with you rather than with your husband. For some
time past I have suspected that he was too fond of my
wife, and last night I caught him with his arms round
her neck. In a moment of not unjustifiable anger I
knocked him down. I have not the honour of knowing
you personally, but from what I have heard of you I
am sure that he has not the slightest reason for playing
with other women. A man who will do what he has
done will be very likely to conceal from you the true
cause of his disaster, and if you know the cause you
may perhaps be able to reclaim him. If he has any
sense of honour left in him, and of what is due to you,
he will seek your pardon for his baseness, and you will
have a hold on him afterwards which you would not
have if you were in ignorance of what has happened.
For him I do not care a straw, but for you I feel
deeply, and I believe that my frankness with you,
although it may cause you much suffering now, will
save you more hereafter. I have only one condition
to make. Mr. Butts must leave this place, and never
let me see his face again. He has ruined my peace.
Nothing will be published through me, for, as far as I
can prevent it, I will have no public exposure. If

Mr. Butts were to remain here it would be dangerous for us to meet, and probably everything, by some chance, would become common property.—Believe me to be, Madam, with many assurances of respect, truly yours,
                                   ———

I cannot distinguish the precise proportion of cruelty in this letter. Did the writer designedly torture Butts by telling his wife, or did he really think that she would in the end be happier because Butts would not have a secret reserved from her,—a temptation to lying —and because with this secret in her possession, he might perhaps be restrained in future? Nobody knows. All we know is that there are very few human actions of which it can be said that this or that taken by itself produced them. With our inborn tendency to abstract, to separate mentally the concrete into factors which do not exist separately, we are always disposed to assign causes which are too simple, and which, in fact, have no being *in rerum natura*. Nothing in nature is propelled or impeded by one force acting alone. There is no such thing, save in the brain of the mathematician. I see no reason why even motives diametrically opposite should not unite in one resulting deed, and think it very probable that the squire was both cruel and merciful to the same person in the letter; influenced by exactly conflicting passions, whose conflict ended *so*.

As to the squire and his wife, they lived together just as before. I do not think, that, excepting the four persons concerned, anybody ever heard a syllable about the affair, save myself a long while afterwards. Clem, however, packed up and left the town, after selling his business. He had a reputation for restlessness; and his departure, although it was sudden, was no surprise. He betook himself to Australia, his wife going with him. I heard that they had gone, and heard also that he was tired of school-keeping in England, and had determined to try his fortune in another part of the world. Our friendship had dwindled to nothing, and I thought no more about him. Mrs. Butts never uttered one word of reproach to her husband. I cannot say that she loved him as she could have loved, but she had accepted him, and she said to herself that as perhaps it was through her lack of sympathy with him that he had strayed, it was her duty more and more to draw him to herself. She had a divine disposition, not infrequent amongst women, to seek in herself the reason for any wrong which was done to her. That almost instinctive tendency in men, to excuse, to transfer blame to others, to be angry with somebody else when they suffer from the consequences of their own misdeeds, in her did not exist.

During almost the whole of her married life, before this affair between the squire and Clem, Mrs. Butts had had much trouble, although her trouble was, perhaps, rather the absence of joy than the presence of any poignant grief. She was much by herself. She had never been a great reader, but in her frequent solitude she was forced to do something in order to obtain relief, and she naturally turned to the Bible. It would be foolish to say that the Bible alone was to be credited with the support she received. It may only have been the occasion for a revelation of the strength that was in her. Reading, however, under such circumstances, is likely to be peculiarly profitable. It is never so profitable as when it is undertaken in order that a positive need may be satisfied or an inquiry answered. She discovered in the Bible much that persons to whom it is a mere literature would never find. The water of life was not merely admirable to the eye; she drank it, and knew what a property it possessed for quenching thirst. No doubt the thought of a heaven hereafter was especially consolatory. She was able to endure, and even to be happy because the vision of lengthening sorrow was bounded by a better world beyond. "A very poor, barbarous gospel," thinks the philosopher who rests on his Marcus Antoninus and Epictetus. I do not mean to say, that in the shape in which she believed this doctrine, it was not poor and barbarous, but yet we all of us, whatever our creed may be, must lay hold at times for salvation upon something like it. Those who have been plunged up to the very lips in affliction know its necessity. To such as these it is idle work for the prosperous and the comfortable to preach satisfaction with the life that now is. There are seasons when it is our sole resource to recollect that in a few short years we shall be at rest. While upon this subject I may say, too, that some injustice has been done to the Christian creed of immortality as an influence in determining men's conduct. Paul preached the imminent advent of Christ and besought his disciples, therefore, to watch, and we ask ourselves what is the moral value to us of such an admonition. But surely if we are to have any reasons for being virtuous, this is as good as any other. It is just as respectable to believe that we ought to abstain from iniquity because Christ is at hand, and we expect to meet Him, as to abstain from it because by our abstention we shall be healthier or more prosperous. Paul had a dream—an absurd dream let us call it—of an immediate millennium, and of the return of his Master surrounded with divine splendour, judging mankind and adjusting the balance between good and evil. It was a baseless dream, and the enlightened may call it ridiculous. It is anything but that, it is the very opposite of that. Putting aside its temporary mode of expression, it is the hope and the prophecy of all noble hearts, a sign of their inability to concur in the present condition of things.

Going back to Clem's wife; she laid hold, as I have said, upon heaven. The thought wrought in her something more than forgetfulness of pain or the expectation of counterpoising bliss. We can understand what this something was, for although we know no such heaven as hers, a new temper is imparted to us, a new spirit breathed into us; I was about to say a new hope bestowed upon us, when we consider that we live surrounded by the soundless depths in which the stars repose. Such a consideration has a direct practical effect upon us, and so had the future upon the mind of Mrs. Butts. "Why dost thou judge thy brother," says Paul, "for we shall all stand before the judgment-seat of God." Paul does not mean that God will punish him and that we may rest satisfied that our enemy will be turned into hell fire. Rather does he mean, what we, too, feel, that, reflecting on the great idea of God, and upon all that it involves, our animosities are softened, and our heat against our brother is cooled.

One or two reflections may perhaps be permitted here on this passage in Mrs. Butts, history.

The fidelity of Clem's wife to him, if not entirely due to the New Testament, was in a great measure traceable to it. She had learned from the Epistle to the Corinthians that charity beareth all things, believeth all things, hopeth all things, endureth all things; and she interpreted this to mean, not merely charity to those whom she loved by nature, but charity to those with whom she was not in sympathy, and who even wronged her. Christianity no doubt does teach such a charity as this, a love which is to be independent of mere personal likes and dislikes, a love of the human in man. The, natural man, the man of this century, uncontrolled by Christianity, considers himself a model of what is virtuous and heroic if he really loves his friends, and he permits all kinds of savage antipathies to those of his fellow creatures with whom he is not in harmony. Jesus on the other hand asks with His usual perfect simplicity, "If ye love them which love you, what reward have ye? Do not even the publicans the same?" It would be a great step in advance for most of us to love anybody, and the publicans of the time of Jesus must have been a much more Christian set than most Christians of the present day; but that we should love those who do not love us is a height never scaled now, except by a few of the elect in whom Christ still survives. In the gospel of Luke, also, Mrs. Butts read that she was to hope for nothing again from her love, and that she was to be merciful, as her Father in heaven is merciful. That is really the expression of the *idea* in morality, and incalculable is the blessing that our great religious teacher should have been bold enough to teach the idea, and not any limitation of it. He always taught it, the inward born, the heavenly law towards which everything strives. He always trusted it; He did not deal in exceptions; He relied on it

to the uttermost, never despairing. This has always
seemed to me to be the real meaning of the word faith.
It is permanent confidence in the idea, a confidence
never to be broken down by apparent failure, or by
examples by which ordinary people prove that quali-
fication is necessary.   It was precisely because Jesus
taught the idea, and nothing below it, that He had
such authority over a soul like my friend's, and the
effect produced by Him could not have been produced
by anybody nearer to ordinary humanity.

It must be admitted, too, that the Calvinism of those
days had a powerful influence in enabling men and
women to endure, although I object to giving the name
of Calvin to a philosophy which is a necessity in all
ages.   "Are not two sparrows sold for a farthing? and
one of them shall not fall on the ground without your
Father." This is the last word which can be said.
Nothing can go beyond it, and at times it is the only
ground which we feel does not shake under our feet.
All life is summed up, and due account is taken of it,
according to its degree.   Mrs. Butts' Calvinism, however, hardly took the usual dogmatic form. She was
too simple to penetrate the depths of metaphysical
theology, and she never would have dared to set down
any of her fellow creatures as irrevocably lost. She
adapted the Calvinistic creed to something which suited
her. For example, she fully understood what St. Paul
means when he tells the Thessalonians that *because*
they were called, *therefore* they were to stand fast. She
thought with Paul that being called; having a duty
plainly laid upon her; being bidden as if by a general
to do something, she *ought* to stand fast; and she stood
fast, supported against all pressure by the consciousness

of fulfilling the special orders of One who was her superior. There is no doubt that this dogma of a personal calling is a great consolation, and is a great truth. Looking at the masses of humanity, driven this way and that way, the Christian teaching is apt to be forgotten that for each individual soul there is a vocation as real as if that soul were alone upon the planet. Yet it is a fact. We are blinded to it and can hardly believe it, because of the impotency of our little intellects to conceive a destiny which shall take care of every atom of life on the globe: we are compelled to think that in such vast crowds of people as we behold, individuals must elude the eye of the Maker, and be swept into forgetfulness. But the truth of truths is that the mind of the universe is not our mind, or at any rate controlled by our limitations.

This has been a long digression which I did not intend; but I could not help it. I was anxious to show how Mrs. Butts met her trouble through her religion. The apostle says that "*they drank of that spiritual Rock which followed them, and that Rock was Christ.*" That was true of her. The way through the desert was not annihilated; the path remained stony and sore to the feet, but it was accompanied to the end by a sweet stream to which she could turn aside, and from which she could obtain refreshment and strength.

Just about the time that we began our meetings near Drury Lane, I heard that Clem was dead; that he had died abroad. I knew nothing more; I thought about him and his wife perhaps for a day, but I had parted from both long ago, and I went on with my work.

CHAPTER V.

WHAT IT ALL CAME TO.

For two years or thereabouts, M'Kay and myself continued our labours in the Drury Lane neighbourhood. There is a proverb that it is the first step which is the most difficult in the achievement of any object, and the proverb has been altered by ascribing the main part of the difficulty to the last step. Neither the first nor the last has been the difficult step with me, but rather what lies between. The first is usually helped by the excitement and the promise of new beginnings, and the last by the prospect of triumph; but the intermediate path is unassisted by enthusiasm, and it is here we are so likely to faint. M'Kay nevertheless persevered, supporting me, who otherwise might have been tempted to despair, and at the end of the two years we were still at our posts. We had, however, learned something. We had learned that we could not make the slightest impression on Drury Lane proper. Now and then an idler, or sometimes a dozen, lounged in, but what was said was strange to them; they were out of their own world as completely as if they were in another planet, and all our efforts to reach them by simplicity of statement and by talking about things which we supposed would interest them utterly failed. I did not know, till I came in actual contact with them, how far away the

classes which lie at the bottom of great cities are from
those above them ; how completely they are inaccessible
to motives which act upon ordinary human beings, and
how deeply they are sunk beyond ray of sun or stars,
immersed in the selfishness naturally begotten of their
incessant struggle for existence and the incessant war-
fare with society.   It was an awful thought to me, ever
present on those Sundays, and haunting me at other
times, that men, women, and children were living
in such brutish degradation, and that as they died
others would take their place.   Our civilisation seemed
nothing but a thin film or crust lying over a volcanic
pit, and I often wondered whether some day the pit
would not break up through it and destroy us all.
Great towns are answerable for the creation and main-
tenance of the masses of dark, impenetrable, subter-
ranean blackguardism, with which we became acquainted.
The filthy gloom of the sky, the dirt of the street, the
absence of fresh air, the herding of the poor into huge
districts which cannot be opened up by those who would
do good, are tremendous agencies of corruption which
are active at such a rate that it is appalling to reflect
what our future will be if the accumulation of population be not checked.   To stand face to face with the
insoluble is not pleasant.   A man will do anything
rather than confess it is beyond him.   He will create
pleasant fictions, and fancy a possible escape here and
there, but this problem of Drury Lane was round and
hard like a ball of adamant.   The only thing I could do
was faintly, and I was about to say stupidly, hope—
for I had no rational, tangible grounds for hoping—that
some force of which we are not now aware might some
day develop itself which will be able to resist and

remove the pressure which sweeps and crushes into a hell, sealed from the upper air, millions of human souls every year in one quarter of the globe alone.

M'Kay's dreams therefore were not realised, and yet it would be a mistake to say that they ended in nothing. It often happens that a grand attempt, although it may fail—miserably fail—is fruitful in the end and leaves a result, not the hoped for result it is true, but one which would never have been attained without it. A youth strives after the impossible, and he is apt to break his heart because he has never even touched it, but nevertheless his whole life is the sweeter for the striving; and the archer who aims at a mark a hundred yards away will send his arrow further than he who sets his bow and his arm for fifty yards. So it was with M'Kay. He did not convert Drury Lane, but he saved two or three. One man whom we came to know was a labourer in Somerset House, a kind of coal porter employed in carrying coals into the offices there from the cellars below, and in other menial duties. He had about fifteen or sixteen shillings a week, and as the coals must necessarily be in the different rooms before ten o'clock in the morning, he began work early, and was obliged to live within an easy distance of the Strand. This man had originally been a small tradesman in a country town. He was honest, but he never could or never would push his trade in any way. He was fond of all kinds of little mechanical contrivings, disliked his shop, and ought to have been a carpenter or cabinet-maker—not as a master but as a journeyman, for he had no ability whatever to control men or direct large operations. He was married, and a sense of duty to his wife—he fortunately had no children—induced him to stand or sit behind his counter with regularity, but people would not come to buy of him, because he never seemed to consider their buying as any favour conferred on him; and thus he became gradually displaced by his more energetic or more obsequious rivals.   In the end he was obliged to put up his shutters.   Unhappily for him, he had never been a very ardent attendant at any of the places of religious worship in the town, and he had therefore no organisation to help him.   Not being master of any craft, he was in a pitiable plight, and was slowly sinking, when he applied to the solicitor of the political party for which he had always voted to assist him.   The solicitor applied to the member, and the member, much regretting the difficulty of obtaining places for grown-up men, and explaining the pressure upon the Treasury, wrote to say that the only post at his disposal was that of labourer.   He would have liked to offer a messengership, but the Treasury had hundreds of applications from great people who wished to dispose of favourite footmen whose services they no longer required.   Our friend Taylor had by this time been brought very low, or he would have held out for something better, but there was nothing to be done. He was starving, and he therefore accepted; came to London; got a room, one room only, near Clare Market, and began his new duties.   He was able to pick up a shilling or two more weekly by going on errands for the clerks during his slack time in the day, so that altogether on the average he made up about eighteen shillings.   Wandering about the Clare Market region on Sunday he found us out, came in, and remained constant.   Naturally, as we had so few adherents, we gradually knew these few very intimately, and Taylor would often spend a holiday or part of the Sunday with us. He was not eminent for anything in particular, and an educated man, selecting as his friends those only who stand for something, would not have taken the slightest notice of him. He had read nothing particular, and thought nothing particular—he was indeed one of the masses—but in this respect different, that he had not the tendency to association, aggregation, or clanship which belong to the masses generally. He was different, of course, in all his ways from his neighbours born and bred to Clare Market and its alleys. Although commonplace, he had demands made upon him for an endurance by no means commonplace, and he had sorrows which were as exquisite as those of his betters. He did not much resent his poverty. To that I think he would have submitted, and in fact he did submit to it cheerfully. What rankled in him was the brutal disregard of him at the office. He was a servant of servants. The messengers, who themselves were exposed to all the petty tyrannies of the clerks, and dared not reply, were Taylor's masters, and sought a compensation for their own serfdom by making his ten times worse. The head messenger, who had been a butler, swore at him, and if Taylor had "answered" he would have been reported. He had never been a person of much importance, but at least he had been independent, and it was a new experience for him to feel that he was a thing fit for nothing but to be cuffed and cursed. Upon this point he used to get eloquent—as eloquent as he could be, for he had small power of expression, and he would describe to me the despair which came over him down in those dark vaults at the prospect of life continuing after this fashion, and with not the

minutest gleam of light even at the very end.   Nobody
ever cared to know the most ordinary facts about him.
Nobody inquired whether he was married or single ;
nobody troubled himself when he was ill.   If he was
away, his pay was stopped ; and when he returned
to work nobody asked if he was better.   Who can
wonder that at first, when he was an utter stranger
in a strange land, he was overcome by the situation,
and that the world was to him a dungeon worse than
that of Chillon ?   Who can wonder that he was becoming reckless ?   A little more of such a life would have
transformed him into a brute.   He had not the ability
to become revolutionary, or it would have made him a
conspirator.   Suffering of any kind is hard to bear, but
the suffering which especially damages character is that
which is caused by the neglect or oppression of man.
At any rate it was so in Taylor's case.   I believe that
he would have been patient under any inevitable ordi-
nance of nature, but he could not lie still under contempt, the knowledge that to those about him he was
of less consequence than the mud under their feet.   He
was timid and, after his failure as a shopkeeper, and
the near approach to the workhouse, he dreaded above
everything being again cast adrift.   Strange conflict
arose in him, for the insults to which he was exposed
drove him almost to madness ; and yet the dread of
dismissal in a moment checked him when he was about
to "fire up," as he called it, and reduced him to a silence
which was torture.   Once he was ordered to bring some
coals for the messenger's lobby.   The man who gave
him the order, finding that he was a long time bringing
them, went to the top of the stairs, and bawled after
him with an oath to make haste.   The reason of the

delay was that Taylor had two loads to bring up—one for somebody else. When he got to the top of the steps, the messenger with another oath took the coals, and saying that he "would teach him to skulk there again," kicked the other coal-scuttle down to the bottom. Taylor himself told me this; and yet, although he would have rejoiced if the man had dropped down dead, and would willingly have shot him, he was dumb. The check operated in an instant. He saw himself without a penny, and in the streets. He went down into the cellar, and raged and wept for an hour. Had he been a workman, he would probably have throttled his enemy, or tried to do it, or what is more likely, his enemy would not have dared to treat him in such fashion, but he was powerless, and once losing his situation he would have sunk down into the gutter, whence he would have been swept by the parish into the indiscriminate heap of London pauperism, and carted away to the Union, a conclusion which was worse to him than being hung.

Another of our friends was a waiter in one of the public-houses and chop-houses combined, of which there are so many in the Strand. He lived in a wretched alley which ran from St. Clement's Church to Boswell Court—I have forgotten its name—a dark crowded passage. He was a man of about sixty—invariably called John, without the addition of any surname. I knew him long before we opened our room, for I was in the habit of frequently visiting the chop-house in which he served. His hours were incredible. He began at nine o'clock in the morning with sweeping the dining-room, cleaning the tables and the gas globes, and at twelve business commenced

with early luncheons. Not till three-quarters of an
hour after midnight could he leave, for the house was
much used by persons who supped there after the
theatres. During almost the whole of this time he
was on his legs, and very often he was unable to find
two minutes in the day in which to get his dinner.
Sundays, however, were free. John was not a head
waiter, but merely a subordinate, and I never knew
why at his time of life he had not risen to a better
position. He used to say that "things had been
against him," and I had no right to seek for further
explanations. He was married, and had had three
children, of whom one only was living—a boy of ten
years old, whom he hoped to get into the public-house
as a potboy for a beginning. Like Taylor, the world
had well-nigh overpowered John entirely—crushed him
out of all shape, so that what he was originally, or
might have been, it was almost impossible to tell.
There was no particular character left in him. He
may once have been this or that, but every angle now
was knocked off, as it is knocked off from the rounded
pebbles which for ages have been dragged up and down
the beach by the waves. For a lifetime he had been
exposed to all sorts of whims and caprices, generally
speaking of the most unreasonable kind, and he had
become so trained to take everything without remonstrance or murmuring that every cross in his life came
to him as a chop alleged by an irritated customer to
be raw or done to a cinder. Poor wretch! he had one
trouble, however, which he could not accept with such
equanimity, or rather with such indifference. His wife
was a drunkard. This was an awful trial to him. The
worst consequence was that his boy knew that his

mother got drunk. The neighbours kindly enough
volunteered to look after the little man when he was
not at school, and they waylaid him and gave him
dinner when his mother was intoxicated; but frequently he was the first when he returned to find
out that there was nothing for him to eat, and many
a time he got up at night as late as twelve o'clock,
crawled downstairs, and went off to his father to tell
him that "she was very bad, and he could not go to
sleep." The father, then, had to keep his son in the
Strand till it was time to close, take him back, and
manage in the best way he could. Over and over
again was he obliged to sit by this wretched woman's
bedside till breakfast time, and then had to go to work
as usual. Let anybody who has seen a case of this
kind say whether the State ought not to provide for
the relief of such men as John, and whether he ought
not to have been able to send his wife away to some
institution where she might have been tended and
restrained from destroying, not merely herself, but her
husband and her child. John hardly bore up under
this sorrow. A man may endure much, provided he
knows that he will be well supported when his day's
toil is over; but if the help for which he looks fails,
he falls. Oh those weary days in that dark back
dining-room, from which not a square inch of sky was
visible! weary days haunted by a fear that while he
was there unknown mischief was being done! weary
days, whose close nevertheless he dreaded! Beaten
down, baffled, disappointed, if we are in tolerable health
we can contrive to live on some almost impossible
chance, some most distant flicker of hope. It is
astonishing how minute a crack in the heavy uniform

cloud will relieve us; but when with all our searching
we can see nothing, then at last we sink. Such was
John's case when I first came to know him. He
attracted me rather, and bit by bit he confided his
story to me. He found out that I might be trusted,
and that I could sympathise, and he told me what
he had never told to anybody before. I was curious
to discover whether religion had done anything for
him, and I put the question to him in an indirect
way. His answer was that "some on 'em say there's
a better world where everything will be put right, but
somehow it seemed too good to be true." That was
his reason for disbelief, and heaven had not the slightest
effect on him. He found out the room, and was one
of our most constant friends.

Another friend was of a totally different type. His
name was Cardinal. He was a Yorkshireman, broad-
shouldered, ruddy in the face, short-necked, inclined
apparently to apoplexy, and certainly to passion. He
was a commercial traveller in the cloth trade, and as he
had the southern counties for his district, London was
his home when he was not upon his journeys. His
wife was a curious contrast to him. She was dark-
haired, pinched-up, thin-lipped, and always seemed as
if she suffered from some chronic pain or gnawing—
not sufficient to make her ill, but sufficient to make
her miserable. They had no children. Cardinal in
early life had been a member of an orthodox Dissenting
congregation, but he had fallen away. He had nobody
to guide him, and the position into which he fell was
peculiar. He never busied himself about religion or
philosophy; indeed he had had no training which would
have led him to take an interest in abstract questions,

but he read all kinds of romances and poetry without
any order and upon no system. He had no dis-
criminating faculty, and mixed up together the most
heterogeneous mass of trumpery novels, French translations, and the best English authors, provided only
they were unworldly or sentimental. Neither did he
know how far to take what he read and use it in
his daily life. He often selected some fantastical
motive which he had found set forth as operative in
one of his heroes, and he brought it into his business, much to the astonishment of his masters and
customers. For this reason he was not stable. He
changed employers two or three times; and, so far as
I could make out, his ground of objection to each of
the firms whom he left might have been a ground of
dislike in a girl to a suitor, but certainly nothing more.
During the intervals of his engagements, unless he was
pressed for money, he did nothing—not from laziness,
but because he had got a notion in his head that his
mind wanted rest and reinvigoration. His habit then
was to consume the whole day—day after day—in
reading or in walking out by himself. It may easily
be supposed that with a temperament like his, and with
nobody near him to take him by the hand, he made
great mistakes. His wife and he cared nothing for one
another, but she was jealous to the last degree. I never
saw such jealousy. It was strange that, although she
almost hated him, she watched him with feline sharp-
ness and patience, and would even have killed any
woman whom she knew had won his affection. He, on
the other hand, openly avowed that marriage without
love was nothing, and flaunted without the least modi-
fication the most ideal theories as to the relation

between man and woman. Not that he ever went actually wrong. His boyish education, his natural purity, and a fear never wholly suppressed, restrained him. He exasperated people by his impracticability, and it must be acknowledged that it is very irritating in a difficult complexity demanding the gravest considera-tion—the balancing of this against that—to hear a man suddenly propose some naked principle with which everybody is acquainted, and decide by it solely. I came to know him through M'Kay, who had known him for years; but M'Kay at last broke out against him, and called him a stupid fool when he threw up a handsome salary and refused to serve any longer under a house which had always treated him well, because they, moving with the times, had determined to offer their customers a cheaper description of goods, which Cardinal thought was dishonest. M'Kay said, and said truly, that many poor persons would buy these goods who could buy nothing else, and that Cardinal, before yielding to such scruples, ought to satisfy himself that, by yielding, he would not become a burden upon others less fanciful. This was just what happened. Cardinal could get no work again for a long time, and had to borrow money. I was sorry; but for my part, this and other eccentricities did not disturb my con-fidence in him. He was an honest, affectionate soul, and his peculiarities were a necessary result of the total chaos of a time without any moral guidance. With no church, no philosophy, no religion, the wonder is that anybody on whom use and wont relax their hold should ever do anything more than blindly rove hither and thither, arriving at nothing. Cardinal was adrift, like thousands and hundreds of thousands of others, and amidst the storm and pitchy darkness of the night, thousands and hundreds of thousands of voices offer us pilotage. It spoke well for him that he did nothing worse than take a few useless phantoms on board which did him no harm, and that he held fast to his own instinct for truth and goodness. I never let myself be annoyed by what he produced to me from his books. All that I discarded. Underneath all that was a solid worth which I loved, and which was mostly not vocal. What was vocal in him was, I am bound to say, not of much value.

About the time when our room opened, Mrs. Cardinal had become almost insupportable to her husband. Poor woman; I always pitied her; she was alone sometimes for a fortnight at a stretch; she read nothing; there was no child to occupy her thoughts; she knew that her husband lived in a world into which she never entered, and she had nothing to do but to brood over imaginary infidelities. She was literally possessed, and who shall be hard upon her? Nobody cared for her; everybody with whom her husband associated disliked her, and she knew perfectly well they never asked her to their houses except for his sake. Cardinal vowed at last he would endure her no longer, and that they must separate. He was induced one Sunday morning, when his resolution was strong within him, and he was just about to give effect to it, to come with us. The quiet seemed to soothe him, and he went home with me afterwards. He was not slow to disclose to me his miserable condition, and his resolve to change it. I do not know now what I said, but it appeared to me that he ought not to change it, and that change would be for him most perilous. I thought that with a little care life

might become at least bearable with his wife; that by
treating her not so much as if she were criminal, but as
if she were diseased, hatred might pass into pity, and
pity into merciful tenderness to her, and that they
might dwell together upon terms not harder than those
upon which many persons who have made mistakes in
youth agree to remain with each other; terms which,
after much consideration, they adjudge it better to
accept than to break loose, and bring upon themselves
and those connected with them all that open rupture
involves. The difficulty was to get Cardinal to give up
his theory of what two abstract human beings should
do between whom no love exists. It seemed to him
something like atheism to forsake his clearly-discerned,
simple rule for a course which was dictated by no easily-
grasped higher law, and it was very difficult to persuade
him that there is anything of equal authority in a law
less rigid in its outline. However, he went home. I
called on him some time afterwards, and saw that a
peace, or at any rate a truce, was proclaimed, which
lasted up to the day of his death. M'Kay and I agreed
to make as much of Mrs. Cardinal as we could, and
yielding to urgent invitation, she came to the room.
This wonderfully helped to heal her. She began to
feel that she was not overlooked, put on one side, or
despised, and the bonds which bound her constricted
lips into bitterness were loosened.

Another friend, and the last whom I shall name
was a young man named Clark. He was lame, and
had been so from childhood. His father was a tradesman, working hard from early morning till late at
night, and burdened with a number of children. The
boy Richard, shut out from the companionship of his

fellows, had a great love of books. When he left school
his father did not know what to do with him—in fact
there was only one occupation open to him, and that
was clerical work of one kind or another. At last he
got a place in a house in Fleet Street, which did a large
business in those days in sending newspapers into the
country. His whole occupation all day long was to
write addresses, and for this he received twenty-five
shillings a week, his hours being from nine o'clock till
seven. The office in which he sat was crowded, and
in order to squeeze the staff into the smallest space,
rent being dear, a gallery had been run round the wall
about four feet from the ceiling. This was provided
with desks and gas lamps, and up there Clark sat,
artificial light being necessary four days out of five.
He came straight from the town in which his father
lived to Fleet Street, and once settled in it there
seemed no chance of change for the better. He knew
what his father's struggles were; he could not go back
to him, and he had not the energy to attempt to lift
himself. It is very doubtful too whether he could
have succeeded in achieving any improvement, whatever his energy might have been. He had got lodgings
in Newcastle Street, and to these he returned in the
evening, remaining there alone with his little library,
and seldom moving out of doors. He was unhealthy
constitutionally, and his habits contributed to make
him more so. Everything which he saw which was
good seemed only to sharpen the contrast between
himself and his lot, and his reading was a curse to
him rather than a blessing. I sometimes wished that
he had never inherited any love whatever for what is
usually considered to be the Best, and that he had

been endowed with an organisation coarse and commonplace, like that of his colleagues. If he went into company which suited him, or read anything which interested him, it seemed as if the ten hours of the gallery in Fleet Street had been made thereby only the more insupportable, and his habitual mood was one of despondency, so that his fellow clerks who knew his tastes not unnaturally asked what was the use of them if they only made him wretched; and they were more than ever convinced that in their amusements lay true happiness. Habit, which is the saviour of most of us, the opiate which dulls the otherwise unbearable miseries of life, only served to make Clark more sensitive. The monotony of that perpetual address-copying was terrible. He has told me with a kind of shame what an effect it had upon him—that sometimes for days he would feed upon the prospect of the most childish trifle because it would break in some slight degree the uniformity of his toil. For example, he would sometimes change from quill to steel pens and back again, and he found himself actually looking forward with a kind of joy—merely because of the variation—to the day on which he had fixed to go back to the quill after using steel. He would determine, two or three days beforehand, to get up earlier, and to walk to Fleet Street by way of Great Queen Street and Lincoln's Inn Fields, and upon this he would subsist till the day came. He could make no longer excursions because of his lameness. All this may sound very much like simple silliness to most people, but those who have not been bound to a wheel do not know what thoughts come into the head of the strongest man who is extended on it. Clark sat side by side in his gallery with other young men of rather a degraded type, and the confinement bred in them a filthy grossness with which they tormented him. They excited in him loathsome images, from which he could not free himself either by day or night. He was peculiarly weak in his inability to cast off impressions, or to get rid of mental pictures when once formed, and his distress at being haunted by these hateful, disgusting thoughts was pitiable. They were in fact almost more than thoughts, they were transportations out of himself—real visions. It would have been his salvation if he could have been a carpenter or a bricklayer, in country air, but this could not be.

Clark had no power to think connectedly to a conclusion. When an idea came into his head, he dwelt upon it incessantly, and no correction of the false path upon which it set him was possible, because he avoided society. Work over, he was so sick of people that he went back to himself. So it came to pass that when brought into company, what he believed and cherished was frequently found to be open to obvious objection, and was often nothing better than nonsense which was rudely, and as he himself was forced to admit, justly overthrown. He ought to have been surrounded with intelligent friends, who would have enabled him to see continually the other side, and who would have prevented his long and useless wanderings. Like many other persons, too, whom I have known—just in proportion to his lack of penetrative power was his tendency to occupy himself with difficult questions. By a cruel destiny he was impelled to dabble in matters for which he was totally unfitted. He never could go beyond his author a single step, and he lost himself in endless mazes.   If he could but have been persuaded to content himself with sweet presentations of wholesome happy existence, with stories and with history, how much better it would have been for him !   He had had no proper training whatever for anything more, he was ignorant of the exact meaning of the proper terminology of science, and an unlucky day it was for him when he picked up on a bookstall some very early translation of some German book on philosophy.   One reason, as may be conjectured, for his mistakes was his education in dissenting Calvinism, a religion which is entirely metaphysical, and encourages, unhappily, in everybody a taste for tremendous problems.   So long as Calvinism is unshaken, the mischief is often not obvious, because a ready solution taken on trust is provided ; but when doubts arise, the evil results become apparent, and the poor helpless victim, totally at a loss, is torn first in this direction and then in the other, and cannot let these questions alone.   He has been taught to believe they are connected with salvation, and he is compelled still to busy himself with them, rather than with simple external piety.

CHAPTER VI.

DRURY LANE THEOLOGY.

SUCH were some of our disciples. I do not think that
church or chapel would have done them much good.
Preachers are like unskilled doctors with the same
pill and draught for every complaint. They do not
know where the fatal spot lies on lung or heart or
nerve which robs us of life. If any of these persons
just described had gone to church or chapel they
would have heard discourses on the usual set topics,
none of which would have concerned them. Their
trouble was not the forgiveness of sins, the fallacies
of Arianism, the personality of the Holy Ghost, or
the doctrine of the Eucharist. They all *wanted* something distinctly. They had great gaping needs which
they longed to satisfy, intensely practical and special.
Some of these necessities no words could in any way
meet. It was obvious, for instance, that Clark must
at once be taken away from his gallery and his copying
if he was to live—at least in sanity. He had fortunately learned shorthand, and M'Kay got him employment on a newspaper. His knowledge of his art was
by no means perfect at first, but he was sent to attend
meetings where *verbatim* reports were not necessary,
and he quickly advanced. Taylor, too, we tried to
remove, and we succeeded in attaching him to a large

club as an out-of-doors porter. The poor man was now at least in the open air, and freed from insolent tyranny. This, however, was help such as anybody might have given. The question of most importance is, What gospel had we to give? Why, in short, did we meet on the Sunday? What was our justification? In the first place, there was the simple quietude. The retreat from the streets and from miserable cares into a place where there was peace and room for reflection was something. It is all very well for cultivated persons with libraries to scoff at religious services. To the poor the cathedral or the church might be an immense benefit, if only for the reason that they present a barrier to worldly noise, and are a distinct invitation by architecture and symbolic decoration to meditation on something beyond the business which presses on them during the week. Poor people frequently cannot read for want of a place in which to read. Moreover, they require to be provoked by a stronger stimulus than that of a book. They willingly hear a man talk if he has anything to say, when they would not care to look at what he said if it were printed. But to come more closely to the point. Our main object was to create in our hearers contentment with their lot, and even some joy in it. That was our religion; that was the central thought of all we said and did, giving shape and tendency to everything. We admitted nothing which did not help us in that direction, and everything which did help us. Our attempts, to any one who had not the key, may have seemed vague and desultory. We might by a stranger have been accused of feeble wandering, of idle dabbling, now in this subject and now in that, but after a while

he would have found that though we were weak
creatures, with no pretence to special knowledge in
any subject, we at least knew what we meant, and
tried to accomplish it.   For my own part, I was happy
when I had struck that path.   I felt as if somehow,
after many errors, I had once more gained a road, a
religion in fact, and one which essentially was not
new but old, the religion of the Reconciliation, the
reconciliation of man with God; differing from the
current creed in so far as I did not lay stress upon
sin as the cause of estrangement, but yet agreeing with
it in making it my duty of duties to suppress revolt,
and to submit calmly and sometimes cheerfully to the
Creator.   This surely, under a thousand disguises, has
been the meaning of all the forms of worship which
we have seen in the world.   Pain and death are nothing new, and men have been driven into perplexed
scepticism and even insurrection by them, ever since
men came into being.   Always, however, have the
majority, the vast majority of the race, felt instinctively
that in this scepticism and insurrection they could not
abide, and they have struggled more or less blindly
after explanation; determined not to desist till they
had found it, and reaching a result embodied in
a multitude of shapes irrational and absurd to the
superficial scoffer, but of profound interest to the
thoughtful.   I may observe, in passing, that this is
a reason why all great religions should be treated
with respect, and in a certain sense preserved.   It is
nothing less than a wicked waste of accumulated
human strivings to sneer them out of existence.
They will be found, every one of them, to have incarnated certain vital doctrines which it has cost

centuries of toil and devotion properly to appreciate. Especially is this true of the Catholic faith, and if it were worth while, it might be shown how it is nothing less than a divine casket of precious reme- dies, and if it is to be brutally broken, it will take ages to rediscover and restore them. Of one thing I am certain, that their rediscovery and restoration will be necessary. I cannot too earnestly insist upon the need of our holding, each man for himself, by some faith which shall anchor him. It must not be taken up by chance. We must fight for it, for only so will it become *our* faith. The halt in indifference or in hostility is easy enough and seductive enough. The half-hearted thinks that when he has attained that stage he has completed the term of human wisdom. I say go on: do not stay there; do not take it for granted that there is nothing beyond; incessantly attempt an advance, and at last a light, dim it may be, will arise. It will not be a completed system, perfect in all points, an answer to all our questions, but at least it will give ground for hope.

We had to face the trials of our friends, and we had to face death. I do not say for an instant that we had any effectual reply to these great arguments against us. We never so much as sought for one, knowing how all men had sought and failed. But we were able to say there is some compensation, that there is another side, and this is all that man can say. No theory of the world is possible. The storm, the rain slowly rotting the harvest, children sickening in cellars are obvious; but equally obvious are an evening in June, the delight of men and women in one another, in music, and in the exercise of thought. There can surely be no question that the sum of satisfaction is increasing, not merely in the gross but for each human being, as the earth from which we sprang is being worked out of the race, and a higher type is being developed. I may observe, too, that although it is usually supposed, it is erroneously supposed, that it is pure doubt which disturbs or depresses us. Simple suspense is in fact very rare, for there are few persons so constituted as to be able to remain in it. It is dogmatism under the cloak of doubt which pulls us down. It is the dogmatism of death, for example, which we have to avoid. The open grave is dogmatic, and we say *that man has gone*, but this is as much a transgression of the limits of certitude as if we were to say *he is an angel in bliss*. The proper attitude, the attitude enjoined by the severest exercise of the reason is, *I do not know ;* and in this there is an element of hope, now rising and now falling, but always sufficient to prevent that blank despair which we must feel if we consider it as settled that when we lie down under the grass there is an absolute end.

The provision in nature of infinity ever present to us is an immense help. No man can look up to the stars at night and reflect upon what lies behind them without feeling that the tyranny of the senses is loosened, and the tyranny, too, of the conclusions of his logic. The beyond and the beyond, let us turn it over as we may, let us consider it as a child considers it, or by the light of the newest philosophy, is a constant, visible warning not to make our minds the measure of the universe. Underneath the stars what dreams, what conjectures arise, shadowy enough, it is true; but one thing we cannot help believing as irresistibly as if by geometrical deduction—that the sphere of that understanding of ours, whose function it seems to be to imprison us, is limited.

Going through a churchyard one afternoon I noticed that nearly all the people who were buried there, if the inscriptions on the tombstones might be taken to represent the thoughts of the departed when they were alive, had been intent solely on their own personal salvation. The question with them all seemed to have been, shall *I* go to heaven. Considering the tremendous difference between heaven and hell in the popular imagination, it was very natural that these poor creatures should be anxious above everything to know whether they would be in hell or heaven for ever. Surely, however, this is not the highest frame of mind, nor is it one to be encouraged. I would rather do all I can to get out of it, and to draw others out of it too. Our aim ought not so much to be the salvation of this poor petty self, but of that in me which alone makes it worth while to save me; of that alone which I hope will be saved, immortal truth. The very centre of the existence of the ordinary chapel-goer and church-goer needs to be shifted from self to what is outside self, and yet is truly self, and the sole truth of self. If the truth lives, *we* live, and if it dies, we are dead. Our theology stands in need of a reformation greater than that of Luther's. It may be said that the attempt to replace the care for self in us by a care for the universal is ridiculous. Man cannot rise to that height. I do not believe it. I believe we can rise to it. Every ordinary unselfish act is a proof of the capacity to rise to it; and the mother's denial of all care for her own happiness, if she can but make her child happy, is a sublime anticipation. It may be called an instinct, but in the course of time it will be possible to develop a wider instinct in us, so that our love for the truth shall be even maternally passionate and self-forgetting.

After all our searching it was difficult to find anything which, in the case of a man like John the waiter, for example, could be of any service to him. At his age efficient help was beyond us, and in his case the problem presented itself in its simple nakedness. What comfort is there discoverable for the wretched which is not based upon illusion? We could not tell him that all he endured was right and proper. But even to him we were able to offer something. We did all we could to soothe him. On the Sunday, at least, he was able to find some relief from his labours, and he entered into a different region. He came to see us in the afternoon and evening occasionally, and brought his boy. Father and son were pulled up out of the vault, brought into the daylight, and led into an open expanse. We tried above everything to interest them, even in the smallest degree, in what is universal and impersonal, feeling that in that direction lies healing. We explained to the child as well as we could some morsels of science, and in explaining to him we explained to the father as well. When the anguish begotten by some outbreak on the part of the wife more violent than usual became almost too much to bear, we did our best to counsel, and as a last consolation we could point to Death, divine Death, and repose. It was but for a few more years at the utmost, and then must come a rest which no sorrow could invade.

" Having death as an ally, I do not tremble at shadows," is an immortal quotation from some unknown Greek author. Providence, too, by no miracle, came to our relief. The wife died, as it was foreseen she must, and that weight being removed, some elasticity and recoil developed itself. John's one thought now was for his child, and by means of the child the father passed out of himself, and connected himself with the future. The child did in fact teach the father exactly what we tried to teach, and taught it with a power of conviction which never could have been produced by any mere appeals to the reason. The father felt that he was battered, useless, and a failure, but that in the boy there were unknown possibilities, and that he might in after life say that it was to this battered, useless failure of a father he owed his success. There was nothing now that he would not do to help Tom's education, and we joyfully aided as best we could. So, partly I believe by us, but far more by nature herself, John's salvation was wrought out at least in a measure; discord by the intervention of another note resolved itself into a kind of harmony, and even through the skylight in the Strand a glimpse of the azure was obtained.

I hope my readers, if I should ever have any, will remember that what I wish to do is to give some account of the manner in which we sought to be of service to the small and very humble circle of persons whom we had collected about us. I have preserved no record of anything; I am merely putting down what now comes into my mind—the two or three articles, not thirty-nine, nor, alas! a third of that number—which we were able to hold. I recollect one

or two more which perhaps are worth preservation.
In my younger days the aim of theologians was the
justification of the ways of God to man. They could
not succeed. They succeeded no better than ourselves
in satisfying the intellect with a system. Nor does
the Christian religion profess any such satisfaction.
It teaches rather the great doctrine of a Remedy, of
a Mediator; and therein it is profoundly true. It is
unphilosophical in the sense that it offers no explanation
from a single principle, and leaves the ultimate mystery
as dark as before, but it is in accordance with our in-
tuitions. Everywhere in nature we see exaction of
penalties down to the uttermost farthing, but following after this we discern forgiveness, obliterating and
restorative. Both tendencies exist. Nature is Rhada-
manthine, and more so, for she visits the sins of the
fathers upon the children; but there is in her also an
infinite Pity, healing all wounds, softening all calamities,
ever hastening to alleviate and repair. Christianity in
strange historical fashion is an expression of nature, a
projection of her into a biography and a creed.

We endeavoured to follow Christianity in the depth
of its distinction between right and wrong. Herein
this religion is of priceless value. Philosophy proclaims the unity of our nature. To philosophy every
passion is as natural as every act of saintlike negation,
and one of the usual effects of thinking or philo-
sophising is to bring together all that is apparently
contrary in man, and to show how it proceeds really
from one centre. But Christianity had not to propound
a theory of man; it had to redeem the world. It laid
awful stress on the duality in us, and the stress laid on
that duality is the world's salvation. The words right

and wrong are not felt now as they were felt by Paul. They shade off one into the other. Nevertheless, if mankind is not to be lost, the ancient antagonism must be maintained. The shallowest of mortals is able now to laugh at the notion of a personal devil. No doubt there is no such thing existent; but the horror at evil which could find no other expression than in the creation of a devil is no subject for laughter, and if it do not in some shape or other survive, the race itself will not survive. No religion, so far as I know, has dwelt like Christianity with such profound earnestness on the bisection of man—on the distinction within him, vital to the very last degree, between the higher and the lower, heaven and hell. What utter folly is it because of an antique vesture to condemn as effete what the vesture clothes! Its doctrine and its sacred story are fixtures in concrete form of precious thoughts purchased by blood and tears.

I fancy I see the sneer of theologians and critics at our efforts. The theologians will mock us because we had nothing better to say. I can only reply that we did our best. We said all we knew, and we would most thankfully have said more, had we been sure that it must be true. I would remind, too, those of our judges who think that we were such wretched mortals, blind leaders of the blind, that there have been long ages during which men never pretended to understand more than we professed to understand. To say nothing of the Jews, whose meagre system would certainly not have been thought either satisfying or orthodox by modern Christians, the Greeks and Romans lived in no clearer light than that which shines on me. The critics, too, will condemn because of our weakness; but this defect I at once concede. The severest critic could not possibly be so severe as I am upon myself. I *know* my failings. He, probably, would miss many of them. But, again I urge that men are not to be debarred by reason of weakness from doing what little good may lie within reach of their hands. Had we attempted to save scholars and thinkers we should have deserved the ridicule with which no doubt we shall be visited. We aspired to save nobody. We knew no salvation ourselves. We ventured humbly to bring a feeble ray of light into the dwellings of two or three poor men and women; and if Prometheus, fettered to his rock, dwelt with pride on the blind hopes which he had caused to visit mortals, the hopes which " stopped the continual anticipation of their destiny," we perhaps may be pardoned if at times we thought that what we were doing was not altogether vanity.

CHAPTER VII.

QUI DEDIT IN MARI VIAM.

FROM time to time I received a newspaper from my
native town, and one morning, looking over the advertisements, I caught sight of one which arrested me.
It was as follows:—

"A Widow Lady desires a situation as Daily Governess to
little children. Address E. B., care of Mrs. George Andrews,
Fancy Bazaar, High Street."

Mrs. George Andrews was a cousin of Ellen Butts,
and that this was her advertisement I had not the
slightest doubt.   Suddenly, without being able to give
the least reason for it, an unconquerable desire to see
her arose within me.   I could not understand it.   I recollected that memorable resolution after Miss Arbour's
story years ago.   How true that counsel of Miss
Arbour's was! and yet it had the defect of most
counsel.   It was but a principle; whether it suited
this particular case was the one important point on
which Miss Arbour was no authority.   What *was* it
which prompted this inexplicable emotion?   A thousand things rushed through my head without reason or
order.   I begin to believe that a first love never dies.
A boy falls in love at eighteen or nineteen.   The
attachment comes to nothing.   It is broken off for a

multitude of reasons, and he sees its absurdity. He
marries afterwards some other woman whom he even
adores, and he has children for whom he spends his
life; yet in an obscure corner of his soul he preserves
everlastingly the cherished picture of the girl who first
was dear to him. She, too, marries. In process of
time she is fifty years old, and he is fifty-two. He has
not seen her for thirty years or more, but he continually
turns aside into the little oratory, to gaze upon the face
as it last appeared to him when he left her at her gate
and saw her no more. He inquires now and then
timidly about her whenever he gets the chance. And
once in his life he goes down to the town where she
lives, solely in order to get a sight of her without her
knowing anything about it. He does not succeed, and
he comes back and tells his wife, from whom he never
conceals any secrets, that he has been away on business.
I did not for a moment confess that my love for Ellen
had returned. I knew who she was and what she was,
and what had led to our separation; but nevertheless, all
this obstinately remained in the background, and all the
passages of love between us, all our kisses, and above
everything, her tears at that parting in her father's
house, thrust themselves upon me. It was a mystery
to me. What should have induced that utterly unexpected resurrection of what I believed to be dead
and buried, is beyond my comprehension. However,
the fact remains. I did not to myself admit that this
was love, but it *was* love, and that it should have shot
up with such swift vitality merely because I had happened to see those initials was miraculous. I pretended
to myself that I should like once more to see Mrs.
Butts—perhaps she might be in want and I could help

her. I shrank from writing to her or from making
myself known to her, and at last I hit upon the ex-
pedient of answering her advertisement in a feigned
name, and requesting her to call at the King's Arms
hotel upon a gentleman who wished to engage a widow
lady to teach his children. To prevent any previous
inquiries on her part, I said that my name was
Williams, that I lived in the country at some little
distance from the town, but that I should be there
on business on the day named. I took up my quarters
at the King's Arms the night before. It seemed very
strange to be in an inn in the place in which I was
born. I retired early to my bedroom and looked out
in the clear moonlight over the river. The landscape
seemed haunted by ghosts of my former self. At one
particular point, so well known, I stood fishing. At
another, equally well known, where the water was
dangerously deep, I was examining the ice; and round
the corner was the boathouse where we kept the little
craft in which I had voyaged so many hundreds of
miles on excursions upwards beyond where the navi-
gation ends, or, still more fascinating, down to where
the water widens and sails are to be seen, and there is
a foretaste of the distant sea. It is no pleasure to me
to revisit scenes in which earlier days have been passed.
I detest the sentimental melancholy which steals over
me; the sense of the lapse of time, and the reflection
that so many whom I knew are dead. I would always,
if possible, spend my holiday in some new scene, fresh
to me, and full of new interest. I slept but little, and
when the morning came, instead of carrying out my
purpose of wandering through the streets, I was so sick
of the mood by which I had been helplessly overcome,

that I sat at a distance from the window in the coffee-room, and read diligently last week's *Bell's Weekly Messenger*. My reading, however, was nothing. I do not suppose I comprehended the simplest paragraph. My thoughts were away, and I watched the clock slowly turning towards the hour when Ellen was to call. I foresaw that I should not be able to speak to her at the inn. If I have anything particular to say to anybody, I can always say it so much better out of doors. I dreaded the confinement of the room, and the necessity for looking into her face. Under the sky, and in motion, I should be more at liberty. At last eleven struck from the church in the square, and five minutes afterwards the waiter entered to announce Mrs. Butts. I was therefore right, and she was "E. B." I was sure that I should not be recognised. Since I saw her last I had grown a beard, my hair had got a little grey, and she was always a little short-sighted. She came in, and as she entered she put away over her bonnet her thick black veil. Not ten seconds passed before she was seated on the opposite side of the table to that on which I was sitting, but I re-read in her during those ten seconds the whole history of years. I cannot say that externally she looked worn or broken. I had imagined that I should see her undone with her great troubles, but to some extent, and yet not alto-gether, I was mistaken. The cheek-bones were more prominent than of old, and her dark-brown hair drawn tightly over her forehead increased the clear paleness of the face ; the just perceptible tint of colour which I recollect being now altogether withdrawn. But she was not haggard, and evidently not vanquished. There was even a gaiety on her face, perhaps a trifle enforced,

and although the darkness of sorrow gleamed behind
it, the sorrow did not seem to be ultimate, but to be in
front of a final background, if not of joy, at least of
resignation. Her ancient levity of manner had vanished,
or at most had left nothing but a trace. I thought I
detected it here and there in a line about the mouth,
and perhaps in her walk. There was a reminiscence of
it too in her clothes. Notwithstanding poverty and
distress, the old neatness—that particular care which
used to charm me so when I was little more than a
child, was there still. I was always susceptible to
this virtue, and delicate hands and feet, with delicate
care bestowed thereon, were more attractive to me
than slovenly beauty. I noticed that the gloves,
though mended, fitted with the same precision, and
that her dress was unwrinkled and perfectly graceful.
Whatever she might have had to endure, it had not
destroyed that self-centred satisfaction which makes
life tolerable.

I was impelled at once to say that I had to beg her
pardon for asking her there. Unfortunately I was
obliged to go over to Cowston, a village which was
about three miles from the town. Perhaps she would
not mind walking part of the way with me through
the meadows, and then we could talk with more
freedom, as I should not feel pressed for time. To
this arrangement she at once agreed, and dropping her
thick veil over her face, we went out. In a few
minutes we were clear of the houses, and I began the
conversation.

"Have you been in the habit of teaching?"

"No. The necessity for taking to it has only lately
arisen."

" What can you teach ? "

" Not much beyond what children of ten or eleven years old are expected to know; but I could take charge of them entirely."

" Have you any children of your own ? "

" One."

" Could you take a situation as resident teacher if you have a child ? "

" I must get something to do, and if I can make no arrangement by which my child can live with me, I shall try and place her with a friend. I may be able to hear of some appointment as a daily governess."

" I should have thought that in your native town you would have been easily able to find employment —you must be well known ? "

There was a pause, and after a moment or so she said :—

" We were well known once, but we went abroad and lost all our money. My husband died abroad. When I returned, I found that there was very little which my friends could do for me. I am not accomplished, and there are crowds of young women who are more capable than I am. Moreover, I saw that I was becoming a burden, and people called on me rather as a matter of duty than for any other reason. You don't know how soon all but the very best insensibly neglect very poor relatives if they are not gifted or attractive. I do not wonder at being made to feel this, nor do I blame anybody. My little girl is a cripple, my rooms are dull, and I have nothing in me with which to amuse or entertain visitors. Pardon my going into this detail. It was necessary to say something in order to explain my position."

"May I ask what salary you will require if you live in the house?"

"Five-and-thirty pounds a year, but I might take less if I were asked to do so."

"Are you a member of the Church of England?"

"No."

"To what religious body do you belong?"

"I am an Independent, but I would go to Church if my employers wished it."

"I thought the Independents objected to go to Church."

"They do; but I should not object, if I could hear anything at the Church which would help me."

"I am rather surprised at your indifference."

"I was once more particular, but I have seen much suffering, and some things which were important to me are not so now, and others which were not important have become so."

I then made up a little story. My sister and I lived together. We were about to take up our abode at Cowston, but were as yet strangers to it. I was left a widower with two little children whom my sister could not educate, as she could not spare the time. She would naturally have selected the governess herself, but she was at some distance. She would like to see Mrs. Butts before engaging her finally, but she thought that as this advertisement presented itself, I might make some preliminary inquiries. Perhaps, however, now that Mrs. Butts knew the facts, she would object to living in the house. I put it in this way, feeling sure that she would catch my meaning.

"I am afraid that this situation will not suit me. I could not go backwards and forwards so far every day."

" I understand you perfectly, and feared that this would be your decision. But if you hesitate, I can give you the best of references. I had not thought of that before. References of course will be required by you as well as by me."

I put my hand in my pocket for my pocket-book, but I could not find it. We had now reached a part of our road familiar enough to both of us. Along that very path Ellen and I had walked years ago. Under those very trees, on that very seat had we sat, and she and I were there again. All the old confidences, confessions, tendernesses, rushed upon me. What is there which is more potent than the recollection of past love to move us to love, and knit love with closest bonds? Can we ever cease to love the souls who have once shared all that we know and feel? Can we ever be indifferent to those who have our secrets, and whose secrets we hold? As I looked at her, I remembered what she knew about me, and what I knew about her, and this simple thought so overmastered me, that I could hold out no longer. I said to her that if she would like to rest for one moment, I might be able to find my papers. We sat down together, and she drew up her veil to read the address which I was about to give her. She glanced at me, as I thought, with a strange expression of excited interrogation, and something swiftly passed across her face, which warned me that I had not a moment to lose. I took out one of my own cards, handed it to her, and said, " Here is a reference which perhaps you may know." She bent over it, turned to me, fixed her eyes intently and directly on mine for one moment, and then I thought she would have fallen. My arm was around her in an instant, her head was on my shoulder, and my many wanderings were over. It was broad, high, sunny noon, the most solitary hour of the daylight in those fields. We were roused by the distant sound of the town clock striking twelve; we rose and went on together to Cowston by the river bank, returning late in the evening.

CHAPTER VIII.

FLAGELLUM NON APPROQUINABIT TABERNACULO TUO.

I SUPPOSE that the reason why in novels the story ends
with a marriage is partly that the excitement of the
tale ceases then, and partly also because of a theory
that marriage is an epoch, determining the career of
life after it. The epoch once announced, nothing more
need be explained; everything else follows as a matter of
course. These notes of mine are autobiographical, and
not a romance. I have never known much about
epochs. I have had one or two, one specially when I
first began to read and think; but after that, if I
have changed, it has been slowly and imperceptibly.
My life, therefore, is totally unfitted to be the basis
of fiction. My return to Ellen, and our subsequent
marriage, were only partially an epoch. A change had
come, but it was one which had long been preparing.
Ellen's experiences had altered her position, and mine
too was altered. She had been driven into religion by
trouble, and knowing nothing of criticism or philosophy,
retained the old forms for her religious feeling. But
the very quickness of her emotion caused her to
welcome all new and living modes of expressing it. It
is only when feeling has ceased to accompany a creed
that it becomes fixed, and verbal departures from it are

counted heresy. I too cared less for argument, and it even gave me pleasure to talk in her dialect, so familiar to me, but for so many years unused.

It was now necessary for me to add to my income. I had nothing upon which to depend save my newspaper, which was obviously insufficient. At last, I succeeded in obtaining some clerical employment. For no other work was I fit, for my training had not been special in any one direction. My hours were long, from ten in the morning till seven in the evening, and as I was three miles distant from the office, I was really away from home for eleven hours every day, excepting on Sundays. I began to calculate that my life consisted of nothing but the brief spaces allowed to me for rest, and these brief spaces I could not enjoy because I dwelt upon their brevity. There was some excuse for me. Never could there be any duty incumbent upon man much more inhuman and devoid of interest than my own. How often I thought about my friend Clark, and his experiences became mine. The whole day I did nothing but write, and what I wrote called forth no single faculty of the mind. Nobody who has not tried such an occupation can possibly forecast the strange habits, humours, fancies, and diseases which after a time it breeds. I was shut up in a room half below the ground. In this room were three other men besides myself, two of them between fifty and sixty, and one about three or four-and-twenty. All four of us kept books or copied letters from ten to seven, with an interval of three-quarters of an hour for dinner. In all three of these men, as in the case of Clark's companions, there had been developed, partly I suppose by the circumstance of enforced idleness of brain, the most loath-

some tendency to obscenity.   This was the one subject
which was common ground, and upon which they
could talk.   It was fostered too by a passion for beer,
which was supplied by the publican across the way,
who was perpetually travelling to and fro with cans.
My horror when I first found out into what society I
was thrust was unspeakable.   There was a clock within
a hundred yards of my window which struck the hours
and quarters.   How I watched that clock!   My spirits
rose or fell with each division of the day.   From ten to
twelve there was nothing but gloom.   By half-past
twelve I began to discern dinner time, and the prospect
was brighter.   After dinner there was nothing to be
done but doggedly to endure until five, and at five I
was able to see over the distance from five to seven.
My disgust at my companions, however, came to be
mixed with pity.   I found none of them cruel, and I
received many little kindnesses from them.   I discovered that their trade was largely answerable for the
impurity of thought and speech which so shocked me.
Its monotony compelled some countervailing stimulus,
and as they had never been educated to care for anything in particular, they found the necessary relief in
sensuality.   At first they "chaffed" and worried me a
good deal because of my silence, but at last they began
to think I was "religious," and then they ceased to
torment me.   I rather encouraged them in the belief
that I had a right to exemption from their conversation,
and I passed, I believe, for a Plymouth brother.   The
only thing which they could not comprehend was that
I made no attempt to convert them.

The whole establishment was under the rule of a
deputy-manager, who was the terror of the place.   He

was tall, thin, and suffered occasionally from spitting of
blood, brought on no doubt from excitement.   He was
the strangest mixture of exactitude and passion.   He
had complete mastery over every detail of the business,
and he never blundered.   All his work was thorough,
down to the very bottom, and he had the most into-
lerant hatred of everything which was loose and in-
accurate.   He never passed a day without flaming out
into oaths and curses against his subordinates, and they
could not say in his wildest fury that his ravings were
beside the mark.   He was wrong in his treatment of
men—utterly wrong—but his facts were always correct.
I never saw anybody hated as he was, and the hatred
against him was the more intense because nobody could
convict him of a mistake.   He seemed to enjoy a storm,
and knew nothing whatever of the constraints which
with ordinary men prevent abusive and brutal language
to those around them.   Some of his clerks suffered
greatly from him, and he almost broke down two or
three from the constant nervous strain upon them produced by fear of his explosions.   For my own part,
although I came in for a full share of his temper, I at
once made up my mind as soon as I discovered what he
was, not to open my lips to him except under compulsion.
My one object now was to get a living.   I wished also
to avoid the self-mortification which must ensue from
altercation.   I dreaded, as I have always dreaded
beyond what I can tell, the chaos and wreck which,
with me, follows subjugation by anger, and I held to my
resolve under all provocation.   It was very difficult,
but how many times I have blessed myself for adhesion to it.   Instead of going home undone with excitement, and trembling with fear of dismissal, I have

walked out of my dungeon having had to bite my lips till the blood came, but still conqueror, and with peace of mind.

Another stratagem of defence which I adopted at the office was never to betray to a soul anything about myself. Nobody knew anything about me, whether I was married or single, where I lived, or what I thought upon a single subject of any importance. I cut off my office life in this way from my life at home so completely that I was two selves, and my true self was not stained by contact with my other self. It was a comfort to me to think the moment the clock struck seven that my second self died, and that my first self suffered nothing by having anything to do with it. I was not the person who sat at the desk downstairs and endured the abominable talk of his colleagues and the ignominy of serving such a chief. I knew nothing about him. I was a citizen walking London streets; I had my opinions upon human beings and books; I was on equal terms with my friends; I was Ellen's husband; I was, in short, a man. By this serupulous isolation, I preserved myself, and the clerk was not debarred from the domain of freedom. It is very terrible to think that the labour by which men are to live should be of this order. The ideal of labour is that it should be something in which we can take an interest and even a pride. Immense masses of it in London are the merest slavery, and it is as mechanical as the daily journey of the omnibus horse. There is no possibility of relieving it, and all the ordinary copybook advice of moralists and poets as to the temper in which we should earn our bread is childish nonsense. If a man is a painter, or a physician, or a barrister, or even a tradesman, well

and good. The maxims of authors may be of some
service to him, and he may be able to exemplify them;
but if he is a copying clerk they are an insult, and he
can do nothing but arch his back to bear his burden
and find some compensation elsewhere. True it is, that
beneficent Nature here, as always, is helpful. Habit,
after a while, mitigated much of the bitterness of
destiny. The hard points of the flint became smoothed
and worn away by perpetual tramping over them, so
that they no longer wounded with their original sharp-
ness; and the sole of the foot was in time provided
with a merciful callosity. Then, too, there was developed an appetite which was voracious for all that
was best. Who shall tell the revulsion on reaching
home, which I should never have known had I lived
a life of idleness. Ellen was fond of hearing me read,
and with a little care I was able to select what would
bear reading—dramas, for example. She liked the
reading for the reading's sake, and she liked to know
that what I thought was communicated to her; that
she was not excluded from the sphere in which I lived.
Of the office she never heard a word, and I never would
tell her anything about it; but there was scarcely a
single book in my possession which could be read aloud,
that we did not go through together in this way. I
don't prescribe this kind of life to everybody. Some
of my best friends, I know, would find it intolerable,
but it suited us. Philosophy and religion I did not
touch. It was necessary to choose themes with varying
human interest, such as the best works of fiction, a play,
or a poem; and these perhaps, on the whole, did me
more good at that time than speculation. Oh, how
many times have I left my office humiliated by some

silently endured outbreak on the part of my master, more galling because I could not put it aside as altogether gratuitous; and in less than an hour it was two miles away, and I was myself again. If a man wants to know what the potency of love is, he must be a menial; he must be despised. Those who are prosperous and courted cannot understand its power. Let him come home after he has suffered what is far worse than hatred—the contempt of a superior, who knows that he can afford to be contemptuous, seeing that he can replace his slave at a moment's notice. Let him be trained by his tyrant to dwell upon the thought that he belongs to the vast crowd of people in London who are unimportant; almost useless; to whom it is a charity to offer employment; who are conscious of possessing no gift which makes them of any value to anybody, and he will then comprehend the divine efficacy of the affection of that woman to whom he is dear. God's mercy be praised ever more for it! I cannot write poetry, but if I could, no theme would tempt me like that of love to such a person as I was— not love, as I say again, to the hero, but love to the Helot. Over and over again, when I have thought about it, I have felt my poor heart swell with a kind of uncontrollable fervour. I have often, too, said to myself that this love is no delusion. If we were to set it down as nothing more than a merciful cheat on the part of the Creator, however pleasant it might be, it would lose its charm. If I were to think that my wife's devotion to me is nothing more than the simple expression of a necessity to love somebody, that there is nothing in me which justifies such devotion, I should be miserable. Rather, I take it, is the love of woman to man a revelation of the relationship in which God stands to him—of what *ought* to be, in fact.   In the love of a woman to the man who is of no account God has provided us with a true testimony of what is in His own heart.   I often felt this when looking at myself and at Ellen.   "What is there in me?" I have said, "is she not the victim of some self-created deception?" and I was wretched till I considered that in her I saw the Divine Nature itself, and that her passion was a stream straight from the Highest.   The love of woman is, in other words, a living witness never failing of an actuality in God which otherwise we should never know.   This led me on to connect it with Christianity; but I am getting incoherent and must stop.

My employment now was so incessant, for it was still necessary that I should write for my newspaper— although my visits to the House of Commons had per- force ceased—that I had no time for any schemes or dreams such as those which had tormented me when I had more leisure.   In one respect this was a blessing. Destiny now had prescribed for me.   I was no longer agitated by ignorance of what I ought to do.   My present duty was obviously to get my own living, and having got that, I could do little besides save continue the Sundays with M'Kay.

We were almost entirely alone.   We had no means of making any friends.   We had no money, and no gifts of any kind.   We were neither of us witty nor attrac- tive, but I have often wondered, nevertheless, what it was which prevented us from obtaining acquaintance with persons who thronged to houses in which I could see nothing worth a twopenny omnibus fare.   Certain it is, that we went out of our way sometimes to induce people to call upon us whom we thought we should like; but, if they came once or twice, they invariably dropped off, and we saw no more of them. This behaviour was so universal that, without the least affectation, I acknowledge there must be something repellent in me, but what it is I cannot tell. That Ellen was the cause of the general aversion, it is impossible to believe. The only theory I have is, that partly owing to a constant sense of fatigue, due to imperfect health, and partly to chafing irritation at mere gossip, although I had no power to think of anything better, or say anything better myself, I was avoided both by the commonplace and those who had talent. Commonplace persons avoided me because I did not chatter, and persons of talent because I stood for nothing. "There was nothing in me." We met at M'Kay's two gentlemen whom we thought we might invite to our house. One of them was an antiquarian. He had discovered in an excavation in London some Roman remains. This had led him on to the study of the position and boundaries of the Roman city. He had become an authority upon this subject, and had lectured upon it. He came; but as we were utterly ignorant, and could not, with all our efforts, manifest any sympathy which he valued at the worth of a pin, he soon departed, and departed for ever The second was a student of Elizabethan literature, and I rashly concluded at once that he must be most delightful. He likewise came. I showed him my few poor books, which he condemned, and I found that such observations as I could make he considered as mere twaddle. I knew nothing, or next to nothing, about the editions or the curiosities, or the proposed emendations of obscure passages, and he, too, departed

abruptly.   I began to think after he had gone that my
study of Shakespeare was mere dilettantism, but I afterwards came to the conclusion that if a man wishes to
spoil himself for Shakespeare, the best thing he can do
is to turn Shakespearian critic.

My worst enemy at this time was ill health, and it
was more distressing than it otherwise would have been,
because I had such responsibilities upon me.   When I
lived alone I knew that if anything should happen to
me it would be of no particular consequence, but now
whenever I felt sick I was anxious on account of Ellen.
What would become of her—this was the thought which
kept me awake night after night when the terrors of
depression were upon me, as they often were.   But
still, terrors with growing years had lost their ancient
strength.   My brain and nerves were quiet compared
with what they were in times gone by, and I had
gradually learned the blessed lesson which is taught by
familiarity with sorrow, that the greater part of what
is dreadful in it lies in the imagination.   The true
Gorgon head is seldom seen in reality.   That it exists
I do not doubt, but it is not so commonly visible as we
think.   Again, as we get older we find that all life is
given us on conditions of uncertainty, and yet we walk
courageously on.   The labourer marries and has children,
when there is nothing but his own strength between
him and ruin.   A million chances are encountered every
day, and any one of the million accidents which might
happen would cripple him or kill him, and put into the
workhouse those who depend upon him.   Yet he treads
his path undisturbed.   Life to all of us is a narrow
plank placed across a gulf, which yawns on either side,
and if we were perpetually looking down into it we

should fall. So at last, the possibility of disaster ceased to affright me. I had been brought off safely so many times when destruction seemed imminent, that I grew hardened, and lay down quietly at night, although the whim of a madman might to-morrow cast me on the pavement. Frequently, as I have said, I could not do this, but I strove to do it, and was able to do it when in health.

I tried to think about nothing which expressed whatever in the world may be insoluble or simply tragic. A great change is just beginning to come over us in this respect. So many books I find are written which aim merely at new presentation of the hopeless. The contradictions of fate, the darkness of death, the fleeting of man over this brief stage of existence, whence we know not, and whither we know not, are favourite subjects with writers who seem to think that they are profound, because they can propose questions which cannot be answered. There is really more strength of mind required for resolving the commonest difficulty than is necessary for the production of poems on these topics. The characteristic of so much that is said and written now is melancholy; and it is melancholy, not because of any deeper acquaintance with the secrets of man than that which was possessed by our forefathers, but because it is easy to be melancholy, and the time lacks strength.

As I am now setting down, without much order or connection, the lessons which I had to learn, I may perhaps be excused if I add one or two others. I can say of them all, that they are not book lessons. They have been taught me by my own experience, and as a rule I have always found that in my own most special perplexities I got but little help from books or other persons. I had to find out for myself what was for me the proper way of dealing with them.

My love for Ellen was great, but I discovered that even such love as this could not be left to itself. It wanted perpetual cherishing.   The lamp, if it was to burn brightly, required daily trimming, for people become estranged and indifferent, not so much by open quarrel or serious difference, as by the intervention of trifles which need but the smallest, although continuous effort for their removal. The true wisdom is to waste no time over them, but to eject them at once.   Love, too, requires that the two persons who love one another shall constantly present to one another what is best in them, and to accomplish this, deliberate purpose, and even struggle, are necessary.   If through relapse into idleness we do not attempt to bring soul and heart into active communion day by day, what wonder if this once exalted relationship become vulgar and mean ?

I was much overworked. It was not the work itself which was such a trial, but the time it consumed. At best, I had but a clear space of an hour, or an hour and a half at home, and to slave merely for this seemed such a mockery ! Day after day sped swiftly by, made up of nothing but this infernal drudgery, and I said to myself—Is this life ? But I made up my mind that *never would I give myself tongue.* I clapped a muzzle on my mouth. Had I followed my own natural bent, I should have become expressive about what I had to endure, but I found that expression reacts on him who expresses and intensifies what is expressed. If we break out into rhetoric over a toothache, the pangs are not the easier, but the worse to be borne.

I naturally contracted a habit of looking forward from the present moment to one beyond. The whole week seemed to exist for the Sunday. On Monday morning I began counting the hours till Sunday should arrive. The consequence was, that when it came, it was not enjoyed properly, and I wasted it in noting the swiftness of its flight. Oh, how absurd is man! If we were to reckon up all the moments which we really enjoy for their own sake, how few should we find them to be! The greatest part, far the greatest part, of our lives is spent in dreaming over the morrow, and when it comes, it, too, is consumed in the anticipation of a brighter morrow, and so the cheat is prolonged, even to the grave. This tendency, unconquerable though it may appear to be, can to a great extent at any rate, be overcome by strenuous discipline. I tried to blind myself to the future, and many and many a time, as I walked along that dreary New Road or Old St. Pancras Road, have I striven to compel myself not to look at the image of Hampstead Heath or Regent's Park, as yet six days in front of me, but to get what I could out of what was then with me.

The instinct which leads us perpetually to compare what we are with what we might be is no doubt of enormous value, and is the spring which prompts all action, but, like every instinct, it is the source of greatest danger. I remember the day and the very spot on which it flashed into me, like a sudden burst of the sun's rays, that I had no right to this or that— to so much happiness, or even so much virtue. What title-deeds could I show for such a right? Straightway it seemed as if the centre of a whole system of dissatisfaction were removed, and as if the system collapsed. God, creating from His infinite resources a whole infinitude of beings, had created me with a definite position on the scale, and that position only could I claim. Cease the trick of contrast. If I can by any means get myself to consider myself alone without reference to others, discontent will vanish. I walk this Old St. Pancras Road on foot—another rides. Keep out of view him who rides and all persons riding, and I shall not complain that I tramp in the wet. So also when I think how small and weak I am.

How foolish it is to try and cure by argument what time will cure so completely and so gently if left to itself. As I get older, the anxiety to prove myself right if I quarrel dies out. I hold my tongue and time vindicates me, if it is possible to vindicate me, or convicts me if I am wrong. Many and many a debate too which I have had with myself alone has been settled in the same way. The question has been put aside and has lost its importance. The ancient Church thought, and seriously enough, no doubt, that all the vital interests of humanity were bound up with the controversies upon the Divine nature; but the centuries have rolled on, and who cares for those controversies now. The problems of death and immortality once upon a time haunted me so that I could hardly sleep for thinking about them. I cannot tell how, but so it is, that at the present moment, when I am years nearer the end, they trouble me but very little. If I could but bury and let rot things which torment me and come to no settlement—if I could always do this —what a blessing it would be.

CHAPTER IX.

HOLIDAYS.

I HAVE said that Ellen had a child by her first husband.
Marie, for that was her name, was now ten years old.
She was like neither her mother nor father, and yet
was *shot* as it were with strange gleams which reminded me of her paternal grandmother for a moment,
and then disappeared.   She had rather coarse dark
hair, small black eyes, round face, and features somewhat blunt or blurred, the nose in particular being so.
She had a tendency to be stout.   For books she did
not care, and it was with the greatest difficulty we
taught her to read.   She was not orderly or careful
about her person, and in this respect was a sore disappointment—not that she was positively careless,
but she took no pride in dress, nor in keeping her
room and her wardrobe neat.   She was fond of bright
colours, which was another trial to Ellen, who disliked
any approach to gaudiness.   She was not by any means
a fool, and she had a peculiarly swift mode of expressing herself upon persons and things.   A stranger looking at her would perhaps have adjudged her inclined
to sensuousness, and dull.   She was neither one nor
the other.   She ate little, although she was fond of
sweets.   Her rather heavy face, with no clearly cut

outline in it, was not the typical face for passion; but she was capable of passion to an extraordinary degree, and what is more remarkable, it was not explosive passion, or rather it was not passion which she suffered to explode. I remember once when she was a little mite she was asked out somewhere to tea. She was dressed and ready, but it began to rain fast, and she was told she could not go. She besought, but it was in vain. We could not afford cabs, and there was no omnibus. Marie, finding all her entreaties were use-less, quietly walked out of the room; and after some little time her mother, calling her and finding she did not come, went to look for her. She had gone into the back-yard, and was sitting there in the rain by the side of the water-butt. She was soaked, and her best clothes were spoiled. I must confess that I did not take very kindly to her. I was irritated at her slow-ness in learning; it was, in fact, painful to be obliged to teach her. I thought that perhaps she might have some undeveloped taste for music, but she showed none, and our attempts to get her to sing ordinary melodies were a failure. She was more or less of a locked cabinet to me. I tried her with the two or three keys which I had, but finding that none of them fitted, I took no more pains about her.

One Sunday we determined upon a holiday. It was a bold adventure for us, but we had made up our minds. There was an excursion train to Hastings, and accord-ingly Ellen, Marie, and myself were at London Bridge Station early in the morning. It was a lovely summer's day in mid-July. The journey down was uncomfortable enough in consequence of the heat and dust, but we heeded neither one nor the other in the hope of seeing

the sea. We reached Hastings at about eleven o'clock,
and strolled westwards towards Bexhill. Our pleasure
was exquisite. Who can tell, save the imprisoned
Londoner, the joy of walking on the clean sea-sand!
What a delight that was, to say nothing of the beauty
of the scenery! To be free of the litter and filth of a
London suburb, of its broken hedges, its brickbats, its
torn advertisements, its worn and trampled grass in
fields half given over to the speculative builder: in
place of this, to tread the immaculate shore over which
breathed a wind not charged with soot; to replace the
dull, shrouding obscurity of the smoke by a distance so
distinct that the masts of the ships whose hulls were
buried below the horizon were visible—all this was
perfect bliss. It was not very poetic bliss, perhaps;
but nevertheless it is a fact that the cleanness of the
sea and the sea air was as attractive to us as any of the
sea attributes. We had a wonderful time. Only in
the country is it possible to note the change of morning
into mid-day, of mid-day into afternoon, and of afternoon into evening; and it is only in the country, therefore, that a day seems stretched out into its proper
length. We had brought all our food with us, and sat
upon the shore in the shadow of a piece of the cliff.
A row of heavy white clouds lay along the horizon
almost unchangeable and immovable, with their sum-
mit-lines and the part of the mass just below them
steeped in sunlight. The level opaline water differed
only from a floor by a scarcely perceptible heaving
motion, which broke into the faintest of ripples at our
feet. So still was the great ocean, so quietly did everything lie in it, that the wavelets which licked the beach
were as pure and bright as if they were a part of the

mid-ocean depths. About a mile from us, at one o'clock, a long row of porpoises appeared, showing themselves in graceful curves for half-an-hour or so, till they went out farther to sea off Fairlight. Some fishing-boats were becalmed just in front of us. Their shadows slept, or almost slept, upon the water, a gentle quivering alone showing that it was not complete sleep, or if sleep, that it was sleep with dreams. The intensity of the sunlight sharpened the outlines of every little piece of rock, and of the pebbles, in a manner which seemed supernatural to us Londoners. In London we get the heat of the sun, but not his light, and the separation of individual parts into such vivid isolation was so surprising that even Marie noticed it, and said it " all seemed as if she were looking through a glass." It was perfect—perfect in its beauty—and perfect because, from the sun in the heavens down to the fly with burnished wings on the hot rock, there was nothing out of harmony. Everything breathed one spirit. Marie played near us ; Ellen and I sat still, doing nothing. We wanted nothing, we had nothing to achieve ; there were no curiosities to be seen, there was no particular place to be reached, no " plan of operations," and London was forgotten for the time. It lay behind us in the north-west, and the cliff was at the back of us shutting out all thought of it. No reminiscences and no anticipations disturbed us ; the present was sufficient, and occupied us totally.

I should like, if I could, to write an essay upon the art of enjoying a holiday. It is sad to think how few people know how to enjoy one, although they are so precious. We do not sufficiently consider that enjoyment of every kind is an art carefully to be learnt, and specially the art of making the most of a brief space set apart for pleasure. It is foolish, for example, if a man, city bred, has but twelve hours before him, to spend more of it in eating and drinking than is necessary. Eating and drinking produce stupidity, at least in some degree, which may just as well be reserved for town. It is foolish also to load the twelve hours with a task—so much to be done. The sick person may perhaps want exercise, but to the tolerably healthy the best of all recreation is the freedom from fetters even when they are self-imposed.

Our train homewards was due at Bexhill a little after seven. By five o'clock a change gradual but swift was observed. The clouds which had charmed us all through the morning and afternoon were in reality thunder-clouds, which woke up like a surprised army under perfect discipline, and moved magnificently towards us. Already afar off we heard the softened echoing roll of the thunder. Every now and then we saw a sharp thrust of lightning down into the water, and shuddered when we thought that perhaps underneath that stab there might be a ship with living men. The battle at first was at such a distance that we watched it with intense and solemn delight. As yet not a breath of air stirred, but presently, over in the south-east, a dark ruffled patch appeared on the horizon, and we agreed that it was time to go. The indistinguishable continuous growl now became articulated into distinct crashes. I had miscalculated the distance to the station, and before we got there the rain, skirmishing in advance, was upon us. We took shelter in a cottage for a moment in order that Ellen might get a glass of water —bad-looking stuff it was, but she was very thirsty— and put on her cloak. We then started again on our way. We reached the station at about half-past six, before the thunder was overhead, but not before Ellen had got wet, despite all my efforts to protect her. She was also very hot from hurrying, and yet there was nothing to be done but to sit in a kind of covered shed till the train came up. The thunder and lightning were, however, so tremendous, that we thought of nothing else. When they were at their worst, the lightning looked like the upset of a cauldron of white glowing metal—with such strength, breadth, and volume did it descend. Just as the train arrived, the roar began to abate, and in about half-an-hour it had passed over to the north, leaving behind the rain, cold and continuous, which fell all round us from a dark, heavy, grey sky. The carriage in which we were was a third-class, with seats arranged parallel to the sides. It was crowded, and we were obliged to sit in the middle, exposed to the draught which the tobacco smoke made necessary. Some of the company were noisy, and before we got to Red Hill became noisier, as the brandy-flasks which had been well filled at Hastings began to work. Many were drenched, and this was an excuse for much of the drinking; although for that matter, any excuse or none is generally sufficient. At Red Hill we were stopped by other trains, and before we came to Croydon we were an hour late. We had now become intolerably weary. The songs were disgusting, and some of the women who were with the men had also been drinking, and behaved in a manner which it was not pleasant that Ellen and Marie should see. The carriage was lighted fortunately by one dim lamp only which hung in the middle, and I succeeded at last in getting seats at the further end, where there was a knot of more decent persons who had huddled up there away from the others. All the glory of the morning was forgotten. Instead of three happy, exalted creatures, we were three dejected, shivering mortals, half poisoned with foul air and the smell of spirits. We crawled up to London Bridge at the slowest pace, and, finally, the railway company discharged us on the platform at ten minutes past eleven. Not a place in any omnibus could be secured, and we therefore walked for a mile or so till I saw a cab, which—unheard-of expense for me—I engaged, and we were landed at our own house exactly at half-past twelve. The first thing to be done was to get Marie to bed. She was instantly asleep, and was none the worse for her journey. With Ellen the case was different. She could not sleep, and the next morning was feverish. She insisted that it was nothing more than a bad cold, and would on no account permit me even to give her any medicine. She would get up presently, and she and Marie could get on well enough together. But when I reached home on Monday evening, Ellen was worse, and was still in bed. I sent at once for the doctor, who would give no opinion for a day or two, but meanwhile directed that she was to remain where she was, and take nothing but the lightest food. Tuesday night passed, and the fever still increased. I had become very anxious, but I dared not stay with her, for I knew not what might happen if I were absent from my work. I was obliged to try and think of somebody who would come and help us. Our friend Taylor, who once was the coal-porter at Somerset House, came into my mind. He, as I have said when talking about him, was married, but had no children. To him accordingly I went. I never shall forget the alacrity with which he prompted his wife to go, and with which she consented. I was shut up in my own sufferings, but I remember a flash of joy that all our efforts in our room had not been in vain. I was delighted that I had secured assistance, but I do believe the uppermost thought was delight that we had been able to develop gratitude and affection. Mrs. Taylor was an "ordinary woman." She was about fifty, rather stout, and entirely uneducated. But when she took charge at our house, all her best qualities found expression. It is true enough, *omnium consensu capax imperii nisi imperasset*, but it is equally true that under the pressure of trial and responsibility we are often stronger than when there is no pressure. Many a man will acknowledge that in difficulty he has surprised himself by a resource and coolness which he never suspected before. Mrs. Taylor I always thought to be rather weak and untrustworthy, but I found that when *weight* was placed upon her, she was steady as a rock, a systematic and a perfect manager.

There was no doubt in a very short time as to the nature of the disease. It was typhoid fever, the cause probably being the impure water drunk as we were coming home. I have no mind to describe what Ellen suffered. Suffice it to say, that her treatment was soon reduced to watching her every minute night and day, and administering small quantities of milk. Her prostration and emaciation were excessive, and without the most constant attention she might at any moment have slipped out of our hands. I was like a man shipwrecked and alone in a polar country, whose existence depends upon one spark of fire, which he tries to cherish, left glimmering in a handful of ashes. Oh

those days, prolonged to weeks, during which that
dreadful struggle lasted—days swallowed up with one
sole, intense, hungry desire that her life might be
spared!—days filled with a forecast of the blackness
and despair before me if she should depart. I tried to
obtain release from the office. The answer was that
nobody could of course prevent my being away, but
that it was not usual for a clerk to be absent merely
because his wife was not well. The brute added with
a sneer that a wife was "a luxury" which he should
have thought I could hardly afford. We divided
between us, however, at home the twenty-four hours
during which we stood sentinels against death, and
occasionally we were relieved by one or two friends. I
went on duty from about eight in the evening till one
in the morning, and was then relieved by Mrs. Taylor,
who remained till ten or eleven. She then went to
bed, and was replaced by little Marie. What a change
came over that child! I was amazed at her. All at
once she seemed to have found what she was born to
do. The key had been discovered, which unlocked and
revealed what there was in her, of which hitherto I
had been altogether unaware. Although she was so
little, she became a perfect nurse. Her levity disappeared; she was grave as a matron, moved about as
if shod in felt, never forgot a single direction, and gave
proper and womanly answers to strangers who called.
Faculties unsuspected grew almost to full height in
a single day. Never did she relax during the whole
of that dreadful time, or show the slightest sign of
discontent. She sat by her mother's side, intent,
vigilant; and she had her little dinner prepared and
taken up into the sickroom by Mrs. Taylor before she

went to bed. I remember once going to her cot in the
night, as she lay asleep, and almost breaking my heart
over her with remorse and thankfulness—remorse, that
I, with blundering stupidity, had judged her so superficially; and thankfulness, that it had pleased God to
present to me so much of His own divinest grace.
Fool that I was, not to be aware that messages from
Him are not to be read through the envelope in which
they are enclosed. I never should have believed, if it
had not been for Marie, that any grown-up man
could so love a child. Such love, I should have
said, was only possible between man and woman,
or, perhaps, between man and man. But now I
doubt whether a love of that particular kind could
be felt towards any grown-up human being, love so
pure, so imperious, so awful. My love to Marie was
love of God Himself as He is—an unrestrained adoration of an efflux from Him, adoration transfigured into
love, because the revelation had clothed itself with a
child's form. It was, as I say, the love of God as He
is. It was not necessary, as it so often is necessary,
to qualify, to subtract, to consider the other side, to
deplore the obscurity or the earthly contamination
with which the Word is delivered to us. This was the
Word itself, without even consciousness on the part of
the instrument selected for its vocalisation. I may
appear extravagant, but I can only put down what
I felt and still feel. I appeal, moreover, to Jesus
Himself for justification. I had seen the kingdom
of God through a little child. I, in fact, have done
nothing more than beat out over a page in my
own words what passed through His mind when He
called a little child and set him in the midst of His dis-

ciples. How I see the meaning of those words now!
and so it is that a text will be with us for half a
lifetime, recognised as great and good, but not penetrated till the experience comes round to us in which
it was born.

Six weeks passed before the faint blue point of light
which flickered on the wick began to turn white and
show some strength. At last, however, day by day,
we marked a slight accession of vitality which increased with change of diet. Every evening when I
came home I was gladdened by the tidings which
showed advance, and Ellen, I believe, was as much
pleased to see how others rejoiced over her recovery
as she was pleased for her own sake. She, too, was
one of those creatures who always generously admit
improvement. For my own part, I have often noticed
that when I have been ill, and have been getting
better, I have refused to acknowledge it, and that
it has been an effort to me to say that things were
not at their worst. She, however, had none of this
niggardly baseness, and always, if only for the sake
of her friends, took the cheerful side. Mrs. Taylor now
left us. She left us a friend whose friendship will
last, I hope, as long as life lasts. She had seen all
our troubles and our poverty: we knew that she knew
all about us: she had helped us with the most precious
help—what more was there necessary to knit her to
us?—and it is worth noting that the assistance which
she rendered, and her noble self-sacrifice, so far from
putting us, in her opinion, in her debt, only seemed to
her a reason why she should be more deeply attached
to us.

It was late in the autumn before Ellen had thoroughly

recovered, but at last we said that she was as strong as
she was before, and we determined to celebrate our
deliverance by one more holiday before the cold
weather came. It was again Sunday—a perfectly still,
warm, autumnal day, with a high barometer and the
gentlest of airs from the west. The morning in London
was foggy, so much so that we doubted at first whether
we should go; but my long experience of London fog
told me that we should escape from it with that wind
if we got to the chalk downs away out by Letherhead
and Guildford. We took the early train to a point at
the base of the hills, and wound our way up into the
woods at the top. We were beyond the smoke, which
rested like a low black cloud over the city in the north-
east, reaching a third of the way up to the zenith.
The beech had changed colour, and glowed with
reddish-brown fire. We sat down on a floor made of
the leaves of last year. At midday the stillness was
profound, broken only by the softest of whispers
descending from the great trees which spread over us
their protecting arms. Every now and then it died
down almost to nothing, and then slowly swelled and
died again, as if the gods of the place were engaged
in divine and harmonious talk. By moving a little
towards the external edge of our canopy we beheld
the plain all spread out before us, bounded by the
heights of Sussex and Hampshire. It was veiled with
the most tender blue, and above it was spread a sky
which was white on the horizon and deepened by
degrees into azure over our heads. The exhilaration of
the air satisfied Marie, although she had no playmate,
and there was nothing special with which she could
amuse herself. She wandered about looking for flowers

and ferns, and was content. We were all completely
happy. We strained our eyes to see the furthest point
before us, and we tried to find it on the map we had
brought with us. The season of the year, which is
usually supposed to make men pensive, had no such
effect upon us. Everything in the future, even the
winter in London, was painted by Hope, and the death
of the summer brought no sadness. Rather did summer
dying in such fashion fill our hearts with repose, and
even more than repose—with actual joy.

Here ends the autobiography. A month after this
last holiday my friend was dead and buried. He
had unsuspected disease of the heart, and one day
his master, of whom we have heard something, was
more than usually violent. Mark, as his custom
was, was silent, but evidently greatly excited. His
tyrant left the room; and in a few minutes afterwards Mark was seen to turn white and fall forward
in his chair. It was all over! His body was taken
to a hospital and thence sent home. The next morning his salary up to the day of his death came in an
envelope to his widow, without a single word from
his employers save a request for acknowledgment. Towards midday, his office coat, and a book found in
his drawer, arrived in a brown paper parcel, carriage
unpaid.

On looking over his papers, I found the sketch of
his life and a mass of odds and ends, some apparently
written for publication. Many of these had evidently

been in envelopes, and had most likely, therefore, been offered to editors or publishers, but all, I am sure, had been refused.   I add one or two by way of appendix, and hope they will be thought worth saving.

R. S.

NOTES ON THE BOOK OF JOB.

———

HERE is a book which has for its subject not this or that remote question which touches us only in idle or careless moods: it is a book which deals directly with one of the deepest problems which have occupied the mind of man.

We are a long way towards understanding anything under our consideration when we have properly laid it open, even without comment. Job is a wealthy and blameless man in whom God takes pride, and when Satan presents himself before God, God asks him whether he has considered Job. God thinks Job something worth consideration. Satan stands for the sceptic. He sneers at Job's virtue. Job is well paid for his piety. It is easy for a pious man to be good, but if his prosperity departs he will curse; his creed is the product of his circumstances. God, who is Job's Maker, is, on the other hand, a believer. He stands by Job, puts a stake on him, and authorises Satan to try him. Job loses all his children and his property, and he knows not what is intended by the loss. He is ignorant of what has passed between God and Satan; the secret transactions of the high heavens are unrevealed to him, but nevertheless he is steadfast. What he

loses was not his, and in the depths of his sorrow he
blesses the name of the Lord. Satan again presents
himself before God, and God justly claims the victory
—"he holdeth fast his integrity." Satan replies that
Job as yet has not known the worst, and that sickness
is the test of all tests. With health a man may
endure anything, but if that fail, it will be seen what
becomes of his religion. God is still confident, and
Job is smitten with sore boils from head to foot. The
torment cannot be surpassed, for not only is it extreme
taken by itself, but it is aggravated by the contrast
with his former condition. Death of course presents
itself to him as the welcome end, and he thinks of
suicide, suggested to him by his wife. If he could
have but a word of explanation he could bear all with
patience. But no word comes; the sky gives no sign.
Separation from those he has loved, loathsome disease
infecting him up to his very brain, are terrible, but the
real agony is the silence, the ignorance of the why and
the wherefore, the sphinx-like imperturbability which
meets his prayers. Nevertheless he sins not. "What!
we have received good at the hand of God, and shall
we not receive evil?" God had been gracious to him;
he recollects all the benefits bestowed on him, and he
refuses to turn upon Him because of present reverses.
He submits; he is unable to explain, but still he
submits.

His three friends forsake him not, but visit him.
When they see him afar off they rend their mantles,
sprinkle dust upon their heads, and coming near to
him, say nothing for seven days and seven nights, for
they see that his grief is very great. The consolation
offered by these three men to Job has passed into a

proverb; but who that knows what most modern consolation is can prevent a prayer that Job's comforters may be his? They do not call upon him for an hour, and invent excuses for the departure which they so anxiously await; they do not write notes to him and go about their business as if nothing had happened; they do not inflict on him meaningless commonplaces. They honour him by remaining with him, and by their mute homage, and when they speak to him, although they are mistaken, they offer him the best that they have been able to think. Eliphaz the Temanite, Bildad the Shuhite, and Zophar the Naamathite, sitting in the dust with Job, not daring to intrude upon him, are for ever an example of what man once was and ought to be to man.

After a while, Job "opened his mouth and cursed his day," in words which are so vital that they are an everlasting formula for all those of the sons of men whose only hope is their last sleep. There the wicked cease from troubling, and there the weary be at rest. There the prisoners rest together; they hear not the voice of the oppressor. The small and great are there, and the servant is free from his master. One touch, that in the twenty-fifth verse of the third chapter, is so intense, that it must be the record of a very vivid experience. "For the thing which I greatly feared is come upon me, and that which I was afraid of is come unto me," or more correctly, "For I fear a fear; it meets me; and what I shudder at comes to me." The object of the dread which haunts us does not generally become real to us, but to Job the horror of all his worst dreams had become actual.

Job's three friends begin their reply, and Eliphaz

is the first. He asserts generally the just rule of
God, and the connection between doing good and
prosperity on the one hand, and between evil doing
and adversity on the other, ending with an amplifi-
cation of the text that the man is happy whom God
correcteth, for by chastisement are we redeemed.
Nothing that Eliphaz says is commonplace, although it
has no direct bearing on Job's case. If he had been a
fool he would never have been dear to Job, nor would
he have been one of the three amongst all Job's acquaintances who came to him from afar. We must
remember, too, that in a simple, honest society righteousness and temporal prosperity, sin and poverty, may
be more immediately conjoined than they are with
ourselves, and that Eliphaz may have felt that much
that he said was true, although to us it is mere
talk. Eliphaz is partly a rhetorician, and, like all
persons with that gift, he is frequently carried off his
feet and ceases to touch the firm earth. His famous
vision in the night, which caused the hair of his flesh
to stand up, is an exaggeration, and does nothing but
declare what might as well have been declared without
it, that man is not just in the eyes of perfect purity.
On the other hand, his eloquence assists him to golden
sayings which will never be forgotten. Such, for
example, are the verses: "Thou shalt be hid from the
scourge of the tongue; neither shalt thou be afraid
of destruction when it cometh. At destruction and
famine thou shalt laugh; neither shalt thou be afraid
of the beast of the earth. For thou shalt be in league
with the stones of the field, and the beasts of the field
shall be at peace with thee." The main moments of
the oration of Eliphaz are these. Rest upon thy piety;

no one who is innocent has perished. In the eyes of God the purest is impure; His angels He charges with folly. The fool may take root, but suddenly his habitation is cursed. Commit your cause unto God who doeth great things and unsearchable, and think yourself happy in His correction. Doing this He will deliver you; you shall come to a good old age and die in peace.

It will be seen that there is here no direct imputation of crime against Job. Eliphaz holds generally nevertheless to the belief that crime is followed by punishment. A certain want of connection and pertinence is observable in him. A man who is made up of what he hears or reads always lacks unity and directness. Confronted by any difficulty or by any event which calls upon him, he answers, not by an operation of his intellect on what is immediately before him, but by detached remarks which he has collected, and which are never a fused homogeneous whole. In conversation he is the same, and will first propound one irrelevant principle and then another—the one, however, not leading to the other, and sometimes contradicting it. The transition from Eliphaz to Job in this respect is very remarkable. The sixth and seventh chapters are molten from end to end, and run in one burning stream. He complains that Eliphaz is beside the mark. "How forcible are right words! but what doth your arguing reprove?" Eliphaz is like the torrent which the caravans expected, but, when they came to it, it had been consumed out of its place, and they were ashamed. Barren sand was all that was offered instead of the living water. Everything which can be said by a sick man against life is in these chapters.

The whole of a vast subsequent literature is summed up here, and he who has once read it may fairly ask never to be troubled with anything more on that side. Death to Job is as the shadow for which he looks as an hireling looks for the reward of his work. He calls upon God to remember that his life is wind; that as a cloud is consumed and vanisheth away, so he that goeth down to the grave shall come up no more; and therefore he prays for consideration. What is man, too, that the Almighty should set Himself against him? "Supposing I have sinned, what can I do unto Thee? Why set me up as a mark against Thee? Why dost Thou not pardon my transgression?" There is nothing in all poetry more sublime than this: it was a complete answer to Eliphaz, and is a complete answer to all those who suppose that God, after the fashion of a man, proposes to punish man deliberately for his trivial misdeeds, and to punish him, too, not that he may be cured, but because the dignity of the Maker has received an affront.

Bildad, unaffected by what he has heard, referring to it in no way whatever, reiterates the old tale. It is the testimony of the fathers. We are but of yesterday, and know nothing. Age after age has declared that although the wicked may be green before the sun, and his branch shoot forth in his garden, he will be destroyed, and God will not cast away a perfect man. The confidence of Bildad and his friends upon this point is very remarkable. It must have been based upon something. Such a creed did not grow up without some root; and it is equally curious if it was the result of a philosophy, a felt impossibility to consider God as unjust, or if it was an induction from observed facts. If it was due to a philosophy, it at least bears testi-

mony to the authority of the *ought* in the minds of
these men and the depth of the distinction between
justice and injustice; injustice being so hateful to them,
that in spite of everything which seems to prove the
contrary, they were unable to ascribe it to God. If it
was an induction from the facts—an induction which,
as I have before observed, might in those times be
perfectly valid—then it is no less remarkable that such
a theocracy should ever have existed.

Job makes no direct answer. "How shall I contend
with Him? I cannot answer one of his thousand questions!" The conception of God in Job's mind has
greatly enlarged, and he dwells upon his incomprehensibility. He is the maker of Arcturus, Orion, and
the Pleiades, of that which is farthest from us. "He
goeth by me, and I see Him not; He passeth on also,
but I perceive Him not." He is for ever before me
and about me; what He does I see perpetually, but I
know Him not. How can I plead with such a being?
"If I had called, and He had answered me, yet I would
not believe that He had hearkened unto my voice."
One thing Job knows. "He destroyeth the perfect and
the wicked . . . the earth is given into the hand of the
wicked; He covereth the faces of the judges thereof;
if not, who is it?" What is the use of debating with
Him? "For He is not a man, as I am, that I should
answer Him, and we should come together in judgment. Neither is there any daysman betwixt us that
might lay his hand upon us both," or as the Vulgate
says, "*Non est qui utrumque valeat arguere, et ponere
manum suam in ambobus*"—a saying which has in it
a grandeur as of some mountain summit "holding dark
communion with the cloud." Nevertheless can God

carelessly cast aside the work of His hands?—so much
care apparently has been bestowed upon it.   "Hast
Thou not poured me out as milk, and curdled me like
cheese ?   Thou hast clothed me with skin and flesh,
and hast fenced me with bones and sinews.   Thou hast
granted me life and favour, and Thy visitation hath preserved my spirit.   And these things hast Thou hid in
Thy heart: I know that this is with Thee," *i.e.*, was intended by Thee.   This book in a sense is terribly
modern, for this is a question which is continually but
resultlessly asked by us all.   A woman of seven-and-
twenty died the other day.   She was German, and had
been in England five or six years.   She had applied
herself with such diligence to learning English, that
she spoke it without the least perceptible accent.   She
knew French just as well, and her general training,
the result of years of most strenuous work, was most
accurate.   She was handsome, and had been married
to an English husband two years.   One child was born,
and her friends rejoiced at the chances it would have
with a German mother in England.   It was a preter-
naturally bright child, and it was destroyed—a year
old.   Three months before its death the mother began
to show signs of consumption, and now she has gone.
As I stood by her grave, the thought came into my
mind—His hands had made and fashioned her: why
then did He kill her ?   Why was all this carefully,
drop-by-drop collected store, precious beyond calcula-
tion, emptied on the ground ?   I know not.   I cannot
answer him one of a thousand !

The example of Job protects us from the charge of
blasphemy in not suppressing our doubts.   Nothing
can be more daring than his interrogations.   There is

no impiety whatever in them, nor are they recognised
as impious in the final chapters of the book.   The
question is put to us directly by him—it is no creation of ours—and shall we be thought irreverent because we hear it?

Zophar now ventures to express in plain words what
before had been merely a hint.   "God exacteth of thee
less," says he, "than thy iniquity deserveth."   What
was observed to be true of Eliphaz is true of Zophar.
He is made up of disjointed propositions accumulated
from time to time, and now inappropriately vented on
Job.   For example: "Thou hast said, my doctrine is
pure, and I am clean in Thine eyes.   But oh that God
would speak, and open His lips against thee; and that
He would show thee the secrets of wisdom, that they
are double to that which is (double thine own—*et quod
multiplex esset lex ejus:* Vulg.); know therefore that
God exacteth of thee less than thine iniquity deserveth.
Canst thou by searching find out God? canst thou find
out the Almighty unto perfection?   It is high as heaven;
what canst thou do? deeper than hell; what canst thou
know?"   All this about the incomprehensibility of God
is true and great, but what has it to do with the preceding assertion of Job's sin?   It is something gathered,
something Zophar had been told, and something he has
had the wit to feel and admire, but it is not Zophar
himself.

Job holds fast to the evidence of his own eyes.   "I
have understanding as well as you; I am not inferior
to you."   Zophar had appealed to antiquity.   Job appeals
to the beasts, "and they shall teach thee; and the fowls
of the air, and they shall tell thee."   Of all that happens
God is the cause.   "With Him is strength and wisdom:

the deceived and the deceiver are His." It is curious
to see what the image of this book becomes after it has
passed through the refracting glass of orthodoxy. In
the heading to the twelfth chapter we are told, as a
summary of the seventh and following verses, that Job
acknowledgeth the general doctrine of God's omnipotency,
and so the texts, "the deceived and the deceiver are
His," "He removeth away the speech of the trusty"
(*i.e.* of the confident), "and taketh away the understanding of the aged. He taketh away the heart of the
chief of the people of the earth, and causeth them to
wander in a wilderness where there is no way. They
grope in the dark without light, and He maketh them
to stagger like a drunken man"—words tremendous
and dangerous—are smothered up under the decent
formula of *the general doctrine of God's omnipotency*.
It is in fact a very particular doctrine, and not by any
means the harmless platitude of the theologians. The
difference is great between the preacher in gown and
bands acknowledging the general doctrine of God's
omnipotency, and Job, who is forced to break away
from the faith of his church, sacred through the testimony of ages of miracle and prophecy—Job, who feels
the ground shake under him as he is compelled to admit
that He whom he worshipped holds both cheat and
victim in His hand, smites the eloquent with paralytic
stammerings, turns the old man into a melancholy
childish driveller, and causes nations to swerve aside
over precipices, under the guidance of leaders whom He
has blinded. Job is the type of those great thinkers
who cannot compromise; who cannot say *but yet;* who
faithfully follow their intellect to its very last results,
and admit all its conclusions. They are better to a

man so constituted than living in a fool's paradise, however paradisiacal it may be. "For," translating the twelfth verse of the thirteenth chapter into intelligibility by the help of the German Version, "your sayings are sayings of ashes; your ramparts are ramparts of mud"—mere mud before the attack thinks Job, although the fool may dwell behind them in placid content, believing them to be granite.

Job renews his desire to speak with God. He renews also his request for death; and yet death, the passing of life like a shadow, is to him most pathetic, although the pathos in his case had never been sharpened by the loss of a hope in immortality. "His sons came to honour, and he knoweth it not; and they are brought low, but he perceiveth it not of them. But *his* flesh upon him shall have pain, and *his* soul within him shall mourn." He is shut out from all sympathy with the joys and the sorrows of the children whom he has so much loved. He lies cold and dead, when they are exulting in love, in marriage, in well-deserved gratulations from their fellows. He is cold and dead, when they are in complicated difficulty or distress from which he could save them!

The three friends, having each said what they had to say, and Job having answered, begin again, Eliphaz taking the lead as before. His position is unaltered. How should it be altered? It is not possible for a man committed, as Eliphaz and his companions are committed, to alter, whatever the facts may be, and the same argument returns with little variation. Eliphaz condemns Job because his talk can do no good. Always has this been urged against those who, with no thought of consequences, cannot but utter that which is in them;

and it is held to be especially pertinent against the man who, like Job, challenges the constitution under which he lives, and "has no remedy to propose." It is incredible to Eliphaz that there should be anything in Job's case which had not been anticipated. "Art thou the first man that was born? Hast thou heard the secret of God?" This was supposed to be conclusive in Job's day, and has been thought to be conclusive ever since.

Although there must necessarily be a certain monotony in the continuous counter-statements of Job, there is not a single dead repetition. For example, in this second answer to Eliphaz, Job, after the retort that he, too, "could heap up words" if he pleased, adds, "my purposes are broken off, even the thoughts of my heart." Happy is the man, no matter what his lot may be otherwise, who sees some tolerable realisation of the design he has set before him in his youth or in his earlier manhood. Many there are who, through no fault of theirs, know nothing but mischance and defeat. Either sudden calamity overturns in tumbling ruins all that they had painfully toiled to build, and success for ever afterwards is irrecoverable; or, what is most frequent, each day brings its own special hindrance, in the shape of ill-health, failure of power, or poverty, and a fatal net is woven over the limbs preventing all activity. The youth with his dreams wakes up some morning, and finds himself fifty years old with not one solitary achievement, with nothing properly learned, with nothing properly done, with an existence consumed in mean, miserable, squalid cares, and his goal henceforth is the grave in which to hide himself ashamed.

Bildad's second response travels over the old ground. "The light of the wicked shall be put out, and the spark of his fire shall not shine," &c., &c., and Job reiterates that all this is nothing but clatter. "Know now that God hath overthrown me, and hath compassed me with His net. Behold, I cry out of wrong, but I am not heard: I cry aloud, but there is no judgment. He hath fenced up my way that I cannot pass, and He hath set darkness in my paths." Into the much disputed question of the meaning of the famous verses at the end of the 19th chapter, which have been so generally supposed to refer to the resurrection, I cannot enter. I do not know what they mean, and it is a pity that commentators, where there is no certain light, cannot say there is none, but feel themselves compelled to give an interpretation. I will only go so far as to admit that if there be any allusion to future life here, much of what goes before and comes after is obscured. We are at a loss to know why Job should have dwelt upon the finality of death if he had immortality before him. It is inconsistent with the thought that he was about to go "whence he should not return," and it destroys the parallel between the flower, which revives at the scent of water, and man who "giveth up the ghost, and where is he?"—man who "lieth down and riseth not: till the heavens be no more they shall not awake nor be raised out of their sleep." It is curious, too, that Job's friends do not allude to the doctrine, as one would think they would certainly do, at least after having seen Job's reliance upon it. Zophar's speech in the 20th chapter does not refer to it. He contents himself with the affirmation that in *this* life the avenger of the wicked will appear: "The increase of his house shall depart—shall flow away in the day of his wrath. *This* is the portion of a wicked man from God, and the heritage appointed unto him by God."

As the action of the poem proceeds, Job becomes more and more direct. "Mark me," says he in the 21st chapter, "and be astonished, and lay your hand upon your mouth. Even when I reflect I am afraid, and trembling taketh hold on my flesh. Wherefore do the wicked live, become old, yea, are mighty in power?" They openly defy God. They say, "What is the Almighty that we should serve Him?" and yet "their bull gendereth, and faileth not, their cow calveth, and slippeth not her calf." His friends, in order to avoid the significance of what is obvious, had explained it away by the assumption that iniquity is laid up for the children of the wicked. "His own eyes," replies Job, "ought to see his destruction, and he himself ought to drink of the wrath of the Almighty. For what care hath he in his house after him, when the number of his months is cut off in the midst?" Good and evil "lie down alike in the dust, and the worms do cover them." The closing verses of the chapter must be given as they stand: "Behold, I know your thoughts, and the devices that ye wrongfully imagine against me. For ye say, where is the house of the prince? and where the tent of the dwellings of the wicked? Have ye not asked them that go by the way, and do ye not know their tokens (*i.e.*, do ye not know what travellers will tell you), that the wicked is spared at the day of destruction: they are led away at the day of wrath? who shall declare his way to his face? and who shall repay him what he hath done? He is brought to the grave, and over his tomb is watch kept. The clods of the valley are sweet unto him, and every man draws after him, and innumerable before him. How, then, comfort ye me in vain! Your answers are but falsehood." Once more Job takes his stand on actual eyesight. He relies, too, on the testimony of those who have travelled. He prays his friends to turn away from tradition, from the idle and dead ecclesiastical reiteration of what had long since ceased to be true, and to look abroad over the world, to hear what those have to say who have been outside the narrow valleys of Uz. Job demands of his opponents that they should come out into the open universe. If they will but lift up their eyes across the horizon which hitherto has hemmed them in, what enlargement will not thereby be given to them! Herein lies the whole contention of the philosophers against the preachers. The philosophers ask nothing more than that the conception of God should be wide enough to cover *what we see;* that it shall not be arbitrarily framed to serve certain ends; that it shall be inclusive of everything which is discovered beyond Uz and its tabernacles; and if the conclusions we desire cannot be drawn from that conception, so much the worse for them.

Inexpressibly touching is the last verse but one. It is a revelation of the inmost heart striving to be at peace with death. Not one grain of comfort is sought outside, and it is this which makes it so precious. There is not even a hint of a hope. All is drawn from within, and is solid and real. To this we can come when religion, dreams, metaphysics, all fail. The clods of the valley shall be sweet even to us. Why should we complain, why should we be in mortal fear! We do but go the path which the poorest, the weakest, the most timid have all trodden; which the poorest, the weakest, the most timid for millions of years will still tread. Every man draws after us, and innumerable have drawn thither before us. None who have passed have ever rebelled or repented, nor shall we. Job, in building on rest, and on community, has struck the adamant which cannot be shaken.

So strong is the superstition of the friends that Eliphaz now advances to a creation of crimes which Job *must* have committed. It is more easy to believe him to be a sinner than that their creed can be shaken. "Thou hast taken," says Eliphaz, "a pledge from thy brother for nought, and stripped the naked of their clothing. Thou hast not given water to the weary to drink, and thou hast withholden bread from the hungry. But as for the mighty man, he had the earth; and the honourable man dwelt in it. Thou hast sent widows away empty, and the arms of the fatherless have been broken. Therefore snares are round about thee, and sudden fear troubleth thee." There was no shadow of truth in the accusation. Job seems, on the contrary, to have been remarkable for the virtues which were the very opposite of these sins. It is worth while to notice how our measure of wrong has altered. To Eliphaz, wrong, when he wishes specially to name it, is a class of actions, not one of which is to us accounted an offence, except by certain sentimental persons. A man now-a-days may be a good Christian and a good citizen, and do every one of these deeds which in Job's time were so peculiarly reprehensible, and which are taken, as we shall see afterwards, with Job's full consent, as the very type of misdoing. Eliphaz, as before observed,

is the church.   But what a world that must have been,
when the church's anathemas were reserved for him
who exacted pledges from his brother, who neglected
the famishing, and who paid undue respect to the great.
Job's answer is an indignant denial of the charge.   It
is not worth an answer, and again he implores God to
speak to him.   "Behold, I go forward, but He is not
there; and backward, but I cannot perceive Him; on
the right hand where He doth work, but I cannot behold Him: He hideth Himself on the right hand, that
I cannot see Him."   Job adds to the last repetition
however, of his complaint something which is new—
that He is irreversible.   He is "in one mind:" more
probably the Unexampled, the Unique—"and who can
turn Him?" and he proceeds in the next verse to a
still plainer exposition.   "He performeth the thing
that is appointed for me: and many such things are
with Him.   Therefore am I troubled at His presence:
when I consider I am afraid of Him.   For God maketh
my heart soft, and the Almighty troubleth me."   The
temptation is great, when we find anything approaching modern learning in an ancient book, to suppose
that we have got hold of an anticipation of it, but we
cannot conclude from this passage that Job's belief in
the impossibility of altering the divine decree is our
belief in the uniformity of nature.   Nevertheless Job's
dejection, because no man can turn Him, and the fear
at His presence, because He performeth the thing appointed, are the dejection and the fear of our nineteenth century as certainly as they were those of the
seventh century B.C.

In the twenty-fourth chapter Job turns aside from
the charge brought by Zophar against him, and points

to what cannot be disputed, the success of the wandering savage tribes, which must have made such a figure
in the domestic history of the time. They, says Job,
go on their desperate way unrebuked, and die as the
others die. "Drought and heat consume the snow
waters; so doth the grave those which have sinned."
These are they who "are wet with the showers of the
mountains, and embrace the rock for want of a shelter."

The controversy has now been fully developed.
Bildad mumbles in half-a-dozen weak words, what is
nothing to the point, that man in God's sight must be
unclean. His short monologue sounds rather as a meditation meant for himself, the only refuge he could find
from the difficulty which pressed upon him. Zophar,
who ought to have spoken again, is silent. The victory
remains with Job, and he sums up his case.

First of all, he competes as it were with Bildad
in his account of the Almighty. It is as if Job
said—I also know Him and what He is. "Hast thou
plentifully declared the thing as it is?" and then he
describes God as hanging the earth upon nothing, as
the Maker of the constellations, and yet these are but
the very fringe of His doings; "what a mere whisper
of Him do we hear; but the thunder of His power who
shall understand?" He holds fast too, by his integrity.
Nothing that his friends have urged will convince him
against his own clear conscience. He remains to them
in an utterly unconverted and even horribly profane
state of mind—"My heart is not ashamed for one of
my days." He casts up his accounts, and refuses to
allow any sin, actual or imputed, open or secret. The
rest of the 27th chapter is a mystery which is insoluble.
It stands in Job's name, but it is an admission of

everything which he had before denied. "This is the portion of a wicked man with God, and the heritage of oppressors, which they shall receive of the Almighty. If his children be multiplied, it is for the sword; and his offspring shall not be satisfied with bread." In the 21st chapter Job had urged on this very point, "Let his *own* eyes" the eyes of the wrong-doer himself— "see his destruction." Again in the 21st chapter, "Their seed is established in their sight with them, and their offspring before their eyes." In the 27th chapter "terrors take hold on him as waters, a tempest stealeth him away in the night." In the 21st chapter "their houses are safe from fear . . . they spend their days in wealth, and in a moment go down to the grave. Therefore they say unto God, Depart from us." Whether in the 27th chapter there is a remnant of a speech by Zophar, from whom one is due, or whether it is an interpolation devised to save Job's orthodoxy, I have no means of determining, but that it is unintelligible is certain, and the only thing to be done with it is to pass it by. The 28th chapter is not free from difficulty, and both the 27th and 28th are rendered doubly suspicious by the commencement of the 29th. "Moreover, Job continued his parable and said," the sequel being a reversion to the old pang so authentic and so familiar. "Oh that I were as in months past." But the 28th chapter is so exquisite, that even if it does not help the development of the poem, or is inharmonious with it, it cannot be neglected. It is a passionate personification of Wisdom, and the desire for her is almost sensuous in its intensity. "It cannot be gotten for gold, neither shall silver be weighed for the price thereof. It cannot be valued with the

gold of Ophir, with the precious onyx, or the sapphire."
This is the wisdom by which the world was framed;
by which the winds and waters were measured "when
He made a decree for the rain, and a way for the lightning of the thunder." This very same wisdom it is
which is the fear of the Lord. "Unto man he said,
Behold, the fear of the Lord, that is wisdom; and to
depart from evil is understanding." It is wisdom in
both cases—the same wisdom. It is not going beyond
the text to say that this is what it teaches. What we
call morality is no separate science. It is the science
by which a decree was made for the rain and a way for
the lightning of the thunder. These immortal words
should not be narrowed down to the poverty-stricken
conclusion that the sum-total of all wisdom is con-
formity to half-a-dozen plain rules, and that the divine
ambition of man is to be limited within the bounds
of departing from evil. Rather do we discover in
these words the essential unity of fearing the Lord
and wisdom. To be wise is to fear Him. Wisdom,
the wisdom searched out by Him in His creation of
the universe, when it is brought down to man, is
morality. Whatever we may think of the date of this
portion of the book, there is no question as to the
three following chapters. Job protests, not merely his
innocence, but his active righteousness, and remembers
his past prosperity. He dwells upon the time when
he laughed away his friends' trouble, and they were
not able to darken the cheerfulness of his countenance.
Immovable he was when fear was abroad, and the
hearts of men were shaken. "I chose out their way,
and sat chief, and dwelt as a king in the army, as one
that comforteth the mourners." The humanities of

these chapters reveal the best side of the Semitic race. They are the burden of the prophets—of Micah, who invokes God's vengeance on those who "covet fields, and take them by violence, and houses, and take them away: so they oppress a man and his house, even a man and his heritage;" and they are the soul of the Revolution, which will one day make foolish the modern quarrels over forms of government. Job goes down to the very root of the matter. "Did not He that made me in the womb make him? and did not one fashion us in the womb? If I have withheld the poor from their desire, or have caused the eyes of the widow to fail; or have eaten my morsel myself alone, and the fatherless hath not eaten thereof (for from my youth he was brought up with me, as with a father, and I have guided her from my mother's womb); if I have seen any perish for want of clothing, or any poor without covering; if his loins have not blessed me, and if he were not warmed with the fleece of my sheep; if I have lifted up my hand against the fatherless, when I saw my help in the gate: then let mine arm fall from my shoulder-blade, and mine arm be broken from the bone." Again, let it be laid to heart that the obligations, the breach of which was a "terror" to him, are not one of them legal obligations, and not one of them moral obligations in the modern sense of the word. The races to whom we owe the Bible were cruel in war; they were revengeful; their veins were filled with blood hot with lust; they knew no art, nor grace, nor dialectic, such as Greece knew, but one service they at least have rendered to the world. They have preserved in their prophets and poets this eternal verity—*He that made me in the womb made him*

—and have proclaimed with divine fury a divine wrath
upon all those who may be seduced into forgetfulness
of it.   In discernment of the real breadth and depth of
social duty, nothing has gone beyond the book of Job.
Much of it ought to be engraved upon brass and set
upon pillars throughout the land, as a perpetual re-
minder of the truth as between man and man.   In
one of the shires of this country stands, or used to
stand, a tablet with a mark on it twenty or thirty feet
above the level of the river which runs beneath, and
on the tablet it is recorded, incredible almost to all
present inhabitants, that on a certain day years ago the
water in a great flood reached that mark.   So with the
book of Job.   It is a monument testifying, although
its testimony is now hardly believable, that this was a
rich man's notion of duty; and more extraordinary still,
that this was his religion.

   As to Elihu's speech I have nothing to say.   Whether
there is sufficient philological evidence against it I am
unable to determine, but the evidence supplied by the
instinct of the ordinary reader is sufficient.   Setting
apart that it is entirely unnecessary in the progress of
the poem, and that it is tame and flat compared with
the other portion of it, the omission of Elihu in the
prologue and the epilogue is almost decisive.

   "Then the Lord answered Job out of the whirlwind."
He makes no reference whatever to what had passed
in heaven.   It would have been easy, one would think,
to have cleared up all Job's doubts by telling him at
once that his trials were ordained to establish his
steadfastness and confound the Accuser.   But no; He
does not, and cannot allude to that act of the drama
which had been enacted unseen.   The very first words

of the Almighty are the key to the whole of what follows. "Where wast thou when I laid the foundations of the earth? declare if thou hast understanding?
Who hath laid the measures thereof, if thou knowest?
or who hath stretched out the line upon it? Whereupon are the foundations thereof fastened? or who
laid the corner-stone thereof: when the morning stars
sang together, and all the sons of God shouted for
joy?" The appeal is in no sense whatever to the
bare omnipotence of God. He is omnipotent, but not
upon His omnipotence does He rely in His divine
argument with Job. Listen, for example, to such
passages as these: "Who hath divided a watercourse
for the overflowing of waters, or a way for the lightning of thunder; *to cause it to rain on the earth, where
no man is;* on the wilderness, wherein there is no
man; to satisfy the desolate and waste ground, and to
cause the bud of the tender herb to spring forth?"
Still more noteworthy, there is the ostrich, "which
leaveth her eggs in the earth and warmeth them in the
dust, and forgetteth that the foot may crush them, or
that the wild beast may break them. She is hardened
against her young ones as though they were not hers;
her labour is in vain without fear; because God hath
deprived her of wisdom, neither hath He imparted to
her understanding." There are also the hawk and the
eagle: "Doth the hawk fly by thy wisdom and stretch
her wings towards the south? Doth the eagle mount
up at thy command, and make his nest on high? He
dwelleth and abideth upon the rock, upon the crag of the
rock, and the strong place. From thence he seeketh his
prey, and his eyes behold afar off. His young ones also
suck up blood: and where the slain are, there is he."

The Almighty pauses. "Moreover the Lord answered Job and said, "Shall he who censures God contend with Him? He that reproveth God, let Him answer it." Job humiliates himself: "Behold, too insignificant am I; what shall I answer Thee? I will lay mine hand upon my mouth." Jehovah again speaks from the storm: "Gird up thy loins now like a man: I will demand of thee, and declare thou unto Me. Wilt thou also disannul My right? wilt thou condemn Me, that thou mayest be righteous? Hast thou an arm like God? or canst thou thunder with a voice like Him? Deck thyself now with majesty and excellency, and array thyself with glory and beauty! Cast abroad the rage of thy wrath: and behold every one that is proud, and abase him! look on every one that is proud, and bring him low, and tread down the wicked in their place! Hide them in the dust together, and bind their faces in secret! Then will I also confess unto thee that thine own right hand can save thee?" The description of behemoth and the leviathan follows.

There are two observations plain enough but most important to be made upon the Divine oration. One is, that God vouchsafes to Job no revelation in order to solve the mystery with which he was oppressed. There is no promise of immortality, nothing but an injunction to open the eyes and look abroad over the universe. Whatever help is to be obtained is to be had, not through an oracle, but by the exercise of Job's own thought.

In the next place, there is no trace of any admission on the part of Jehovah that the well-meant theories of the friends are correct. On the contrary, His wrath is kindled against them. Jehovah does not admit for a moment that He has established any unvarying connection between righteousness and prosperity, sin and adversity.

What then is God's meaning? It behoves us to keep close to the text in our interpretation of it. We have not to ascertain what we might imagine or wish Him to say. We have to find out what He did say. Most scrupulously are we to avoid foisting upon Him any idea of our own. It is much easier to impose a meaning upon the Bible, written in an age so unlike our own, than to extract *the* meaning from it. God reminds us of His wisdom, of the mystery of things, and that man is not the measure of His creation. The world is immense, constructed on no plan or theory which the intellect of man can grasp. It is *transcendent* everywhere. This is the burden of every verse, and is the secret, if there be one, of the poem. Sufficient or insufficient, there is nothing more. Job is to hold fast to the law within; that is his candle which is to light his path: but God is infinite. Job, if he is not satisfied, submits. Henceforth he will be mute—"once have I spoken, but I will not answer: yea twice; but I will proceed no further." "I have uttered that I understood not; things too wonderful for me, which I knew not." All his thinkings seemed like hearsay. This then was the real God. "Now mine eye seeth Thee."

It is impossible to neglect the epilogue in which Job is restored to his prosperity. If we do neglect it, we may perhaps turn the book into something more accordant with our own notions, but the book itself we have not got. There is nothing really inconsistent in it. The Almighty has explained Himself, and the explanation stands, but there is no reason why Job should be left in such utter misery. The anguish which completely envelops the sufferer does break and yield with time, and often disappears. On the other hand, we have no right to demand happiness, and we are not told that Job's happiness returned to him because he demanded it. It is utterly to mistake the purpose of the last chapter to suppose that in it lies the meaning of all that has gone before, and that it teaches us that we have only to wait and God will reward us. God is great, we know not His ways. He takes from us all we have, but yet, if we possess our souls in patience, we *may* pass the valley of the shadow and come out in sunlight again. We may or we may not. If we had before us a statement of a nineteenth-century philosophy, there would undoubtedly have been no epilogue; but the book is not a philosophy, but a record of an experience.

What more have we to say now than God said from the whirlwind over 2500 years ago? We have passed through much since that memorable day. We have had new religions which have overspread the world, and yet the sum total of all that we can add is but small. Scientific discovery—astronomy for example— contributes something. The earth is no longer the centre of the starry system, and with the disappearance of that belief much more has disappeared. Man has not become of less importance, but it is seen that all things do not converge to him. We have learned too more intimately God's infinity. It is this which caused Job to put his hand on his mouth—the truth that even the dry clod and the desert grass are dear to Him though no man is near them. Why should they not be? Why should I say that dew falling on a thorn in a desert is wasted, but falling on my flower shows proper economy? Furthermore, if resources are inexhaustible, there can be no waste. It might be waste if *I* were to lavish time and treasure on building up the blue succory perfect in its azure, which springs by the wayside, to be smothered by the chalk dust and to be destroyed in its pride by a chance cut from a boy's stick, but it is no waste to God. In this way the lesson which the whirlwind taught us has been expanded and intensified. We return to it anew after all the creeds, and we say that they are but the hearing of Him, and that this is *seeing* Him.

PRINCIPLES.

———

I HAVE often reproached myself that principles have done so little for me. It is not that I have not got any. I have been for years familiar with all the wisest and noblest principles which are to be found in philosophical and religious books from the time of Moses downwards. Nor is it a failing of mine that I have not the courage or strength to apply principles. I am weak as other men are, and liable to yield to temptation; but this is not my main difficulty; my trouble is that I never know how to apply my principles. Take a case: It is true that every man ought to be satisfied with the limitations of his own nature. He ought not to repine that he cannot write poems or carve statues. The principle is of some service when the question is of poems or statues; but I should be equally helped without it, for the most uncultivated of mortals is not so foolish as to be melancholy because he cannot fly. At other times, when I most need assistance, and call upon this principle to aid me, I am all adrift. I am placed in such a position, for example, that it is my duty to exercise control over somebody below me. I ought to tell him that he is going wrong and put him right, but I feel that I cannot, and that he is too strong for me. This may be mere conquerable cowardice, or it may be that in this direction I am as limited as I am in relation to poems or statues. I do not know. When I have done what I think I can do, am I to sit down contented and say I can do no more, or am I to listen to a voice which for ever prompts me and whispers, "*All* you can do you have not done"?

During the major portion of my life I am the victim of antagonisms, and each opposing force seems able to plead equal justification. This, however, is the system on which the world is built. It is a mistake to expect a principle to be anything else than abstract. An act is concrete, and that means that it is something in which oppositions find their solution and lie in repose. This, it will be said, leaves us just where we were and gives us no assistance. It is a just criticism. Man is man because he possesses the proud prerogative of actualising the abstract. He is not its fool. In each deed he does he has to be aware of two poles, and say, "Between them, doing justice to both, I fix this deed *so*." Instead of two poles there may be a dozen or more, not exactly poles, but divergent or opposite pulls. The richer the nature is, the more there will be of them; the stronger the nature, the more perfect will be the harmony in which they will all meet in external life.

To know principles, although at first it seems as if the consciousness of them is of no service to us, is really an enormous benefit. The more we have, if we have only the gift to manage them, the more real and less shadowy shall we be. Let it ever be remembered that the reality of an act or of a man is in exact pro-

portion to the number of principles which lie in that
man or act, and that the single abstract is unreality,
unsubstantiality, uselessness. Let us not be cast down
at our difficulties. Let us rejoice rather at the exalted,
the divine task that is imposed on us. Man is the
very top of the creation, the express image of the
Creator, because at every moment of his life he resolves
abstracts into realities.

The curse of every truth is that a counterfeit of it
always waits on it, and is its greatest enemy. What
is this which I have said but the mere commonplace
that we must never go too far, and that compromise is
the rule of life? But between my doctrine and this
commonplace there is a great difference. The commonplace teaches that no principle is ultimately efficacious;
that it is to be trusted to a certain arbitrary point, and
beyond that it somehow ceases to be valid. The truth,
on the other hand, is that *every* principle is efficacious
up to the uttermost, and that faith in it is never to be
abandoned. The compromise comes of imbecility or
impotence, and is essentially contrary to the concrete
reconciliation of abstracts.

It is difficult to separate morals from wisdom, and
in fact no clear line of demarcation is possible; but
perhaps we may say that in morals a single clear
principle is more distinctly supreme than in wisdom.
Morality is the region of the abstract. It is mercifully
provided that that which is of the most importance to
us in the conduct of life should be under the dominion
of the abstract, and therefore be plain to everybody.
There is no wit necessary in order to discover what we
ought to do when the question is one of telling a lie or
speaking the truth. This seems to me as valid a dis-

tinction between morality and wisdom as any I know.
The abstractness of the moral law gives it a certain
sublimity and ideality which is very remarkable.

Perpetual undying faith in principles is of the utmost importance. I sometimes think it is the very
Alpha and Omega of life. Belief in principles is
the only intelligible interpretation I have ever been
able to attach to the word faith. A man with faith in
principles, even if they be not first-rate, is sure to
succeed. The man who has no faith in them is sure
to fail. Nothing finer after all can be said of faith
than that which is said in the epistle to the Hebrews,
and no finer example can be given of it than that of
Noah there given. Noah was warned of God that
destruction would visit the impious race by which he
was surrounded. He quietly set to work to build his
ark. There is no record that it was built by miracle,
and he must have been a long time about it. Glorious
days of unclouded sunshine with no hint of rain, weeks
perhaps of drought, must have passed over his head as
he sat and wrought at this wondrous stucture. Imagine
the scoffs of the irreverent Canaanites, the jeers of the
mob which passed by or peeped over fences; imagine
the suggestions of lunacy! Worse and worse, imagine
what was said and done when, seven days before the
rain, though not a drop had fallen, the pious man with
all his family, and with that wonderful troop of animals,
entered the ark, *and the Lord shut him in.* But God
had spoken to him : he had heard a divine word, and
in that word he believed, despite the absence of a single
fleck of vapour in the sky. What a time, though, it
must have been for him during those seven days!
Would it come true? Would he have to walk out again

down those planks with the clean beasts and unclean
beasts after him, amidst the inextinguishable laughter
of all his pagan, God-denying neighbours ? But in a
week he heard the first growl of the tempest. He was
justified, God was justified; and for evermore Noah
stands as a divine type of what we call faith. This is
really it. What we have once *heard*, really heard in
our best moments, by that let us abide. There are
multitudes of moments in which intelligent conviction
in the truth of principles disappears, and we are able
to do nothing more than fall back on mere dogged
determinate resolution to go on; not to give up what
we have once found to be true. This power of dogged
determinate resolution, which acts independently of
enthusiasm, is a precious possession. A principle
cannot for ever appear to us in its pristine splendour.
Not only are we tempted to forsake it by other and
counter attractions, but it gets wearisome to us because
it is a principle. It becomes a fetter, we think. Then
it is that faith comes into operation. We hold fast,
and by-and-by a third state follows the second, and
we emerge into confidence again. One would like to
have a record of all that passed through the soul of
Ulysses when he was rowed past the Sirens. In what
intellectually subtle forms did not the desire to stay
clothe itself to that intellectually subtle soul ? But
he had bound himself beforehand, and he reached
Ithaca and Penelope at last. I remember once having
determined after much deliberation that I ought to
undertake a certain task which would occupy me for
years. It was one which I could at any moment
relinquish. After six months I began to flag, and my
greatest hindrance was, not the confessed desire for

rest, but all kinds of the most fascinating principles or
pseudo principles, which flattered what was best and
not what was worst in me. I was narrowing my intellect, preventing the proper enjoyment of life, neglecting
the sunshine, &c. &c. But I thought to myself, " Now
the serpent was more subtile than any beast of the
field," and that his temptation specially was that "your
eyes shall be opened, and ye shall be as gods." I was
enabled to persevere, oftentimes through no other motive
than that aforesaid divine doggedness, and presently I
was rewarded.

As an instance of the necessity of reconciling principles, the experience of advancing years may be taken.
A man must for ever keep himself open to the reception
of new light. As he gets older, he will find that the
tendency grows to admit nothing into his mind which
does not corroborate something he has already believed,
and that the new truth acquired is very limited. If
he wishes to keep himself young he must use his
utmost efforts to maintain his susceptibility. He must
not converse solely with himself and turn over and over
again the thoughts of the past. He must not in reading
a book dwell upon those passages only which are a
reflection of his own mind. This is true, but it is also
true that he must put certain principles beyond debate.
Life is too short to admit of the perpetual discussion
and re-discussion of what is fundamental and has been
settled after bestowing on it all the care of which we
are capable. If, by reason of patient and long-continued
experiment, we have found out, for example, that a
certain regimen is good for us, we should be foolish, at
the bidding of even a scientific man, to begin experi-
menting again. We must simply say that this matter

is once for all at rest, whether rightly or wrongly, and that our days here are but threescore years and ten. Neither can we afford to make quite certain between opposing principles. The demand for certainty is a sign of weakness, and if we persist in it, induces paralysis. The successful man is he who when he sees that no further certainty is attainable, promptly decides on the most probable side, as if he were completely sure it was right. If we come to a parting of roads, and this one goes slightly east and the other a little west, then, if we believe that our town lies westward, we are bound, supposing we have no other guide, instantaneously to take the western road, although we know that the tracks thereabouts twist in every direction, and that the one to the west may bend southwards and bring us back to the point from which we started.

It is an old theory that our action depends on wisdom. We do what we see to be good. If we really see it to be good, we must do it. There is no doubt that a certain dimness of vision accompanies temptation. We do not discern in its real splendour the virtue which, properly discerned, would fascinate and compel us. But, nevertheless, the part which pure resolution has to play is very great. It is, as Burns says, the stalk of carle hemp in us. A man must continually put his back to the wall, just as in pain the hero determines through sheer force of will to endure. Inflexibility, Will, the power of holding fast to a principle, is a primary faculty, not altogether to be resolved into insight, although of course it is easy enough to argue the identity of everything in man, and to prove that will is science, or love, or a superior capacity of definition, or anything else. We often fail through a lamentable trick of reopening negotiations with what we have determined to abandon. Severed once and for good reason, let it remain once and for all severed.

Principles are more useful to us in time of danger when they are presented to us incarnated in living men. We should ask ourselves, how would Paul or Jesus have acted in this case. That question will often settle a difficulty when the appeal to abstract principles would only bewilder us through the difficulty of selection. Furthermore, the reference to men rather than to abstractions puts us in good company : we are conscious of society and of fellowship : we see the faces of the heroes looking on us and encouraging us. Plutarch in his essay—*How a man may perceive his own proceeding and going forward in virtue* (Holland's translation)— says, " Hereupon also it followeth by good consequence that they who have once received so deep an impression in their hearts take this course with themselves, that when they begin any enterprise or enter into the administration of government, or when any sinister accident is presented to them, they set before their eyes the examples of those, who either presently are or heretofore have been worthy persons, discoursing in this manner : What is it that Plato would have done in this case ? What would Epaminondas have said to this ? How would Lycurgus or Agesilaus have behaved themselves herein ? After this sort (I say) will they labour to frame, compose, reform, and adorn their manners, as it were, before a mirror or looking-glass, to wit, in correcting any unseemly speech that they have let fall, or repressing any passion that hath risen in them. They that have learned the names of the demi-gods called *Idæi Dactyli* know how to use them as counter charms, or preservatives against sudden frights, pronouncing the same one after another readily and ceremoniously; but the remembrance and thinking upon great and worthy men represented suddenly unto those who are in the way of perfection, and taking hold of them in all passions and complexions which shall encounter them, holdeth them up, and keepeth them upright that they cannot fall." This we know is the secret of the Christian religion. It is based upon a Person, and the whole drift of Paul's epistles is specially this—to turn Christ into a second conscience. More particularly for simple people easily led away, but, indeed, for all people, the importance, the overwhelming importance of maintaining a personal basis for religion, cannot be overstated. I only speak my own experience : I am not talking theology or philosophy. I *know* what I am saying, and can point out the times and places when I should have fallen if I had been able to rely for guidance upon nothing better than a commandment or a deduction. But the pure, calm, heroic image of Jesus confronted me, and I succeeded. I had no doubt as to what *He* would have done, and through Him I did not doubt what I ought to do.

A MYSTERIOUS PORTRAIT.

I REMEMBER some years ago that I went to spend a Christmas with an old friend who was a bachelor. He might, perhaps, have been verging on sixty at the time of my visit. On his study wall hung the portrait— merely the face—of a singularly lovely woman. I did not like to ask any questions about it. There was no family likeness to him, and we always thought that early in life he had been disappointed. But one day, seeing that I could hardly keep my eyes off it, he said to me, "I have had that picture for many years, although you have never seen it before. If you like, I will tell you its history." He then told me the following story.

"In the year 1817, I was beginning life, and struggling to get a living. I had just started in business. I was alone, without much capital, and my whole energies were utterly absorbed in my adventure. In those days the master, instead of employing a commercial traveller, often used to travel himself, and one evening I had to start for the North to see some customers. I chose to go by night in order to save time, and as it was bitterly cold and I was weakly in the chest, I determined to take a place inside the coach. We left St. Martin's-le-

Grand at about half-past eight, and I was the sole inside passenger. I could not sleep, but fell into a kind of doze, which was not sufficiently deep to prevent my rousing myself at every inn where we changed horses. Nobody intruded upon me, and I continued in the same drowsy, half-waking, half-slumbering condition till we came to the last stage before reaching Eaton Socon. I was then thoroughly awake, and continued awake until after the coach started. But presently I fell sound asleep for, perhaps, half-an-hour, and woke suddenly. To my great surprise I found a lady with me. How she came there I could not conjecture. I was positive that she did not get in when the coach last stopped. She sat at the opposite corner, so that I could see her well, and a more exquisite face I thought I had never beheld. It was not quite English—rather pale, earnest, and abstracted, and with a certain intentness about the eyes which denoted a mind accustomed to dwell upon ideal objects. I was not particularly shy with women, and perhaps if she had been any ordinary, pretty girl I might have struck up a conversation with her. But I was dumb, for I hardly dared to intrude. It would have been necessary to begin by some commonplaces, and somehow my lips refused the utterance of commonplaces. Nor was this strange. If I had happened to find myself opposite the great Lord Byron in a coach I certainly should not have thrust myself upon him, and how should I dare to thrust myself upon a person who seemed as great and grand as he, although I did not know her name? So I remained perfectly still, only venturing by the light of the moon to watch her through my half-shut eyes. Just before we got to Eaton, although I was never more thoroughly or even excitedly awake in my life, I must have lost consciousness for a minute. I came to myself when the coach was pulling up at an inn. I looked round instantly, and my companion was gone. I jumped out on pretence of getting something to eat and drink, and hastily asked the guard where the lady who had just got out was put into the coach. He said they had never stopped since they had last changed horses, and that I must have been dreaming. He knew nothing about the lady, and he looked at me suspiciously, as if he thought I was drunk. I for my part was perfectly confident that I had not been deluded by an apparition of my own brain. I had never suffered from ghost-like visitations of any kind, and my thoughts, owing to my preoccupation with business, had not run upon women in any way whatever. More convincing still, I had noticed that the lady wore a light blue neckerchief; and when I went back into the coach I found that she had left it behind her. I took it up, and I have it to this day. You may imagine how my mind dwelt upon that night. I got to Newcastle, did what I had to do, came back again, and made a point this time of sleeping at Eaton Socon in order to make inquiries. Everybody recollected the arrival of the down coach by which I travelled, and everybody was perfectly sure that no lady was in it. I produced the scarf, and asked whether anybody who lived near had been observed to wear it. Eaton is a little village, and all the people in it were as well known as if they belonged to one family, but nobody recognised it. It was certainly not English. I thought about the affair for months, partly because I was smitten with my visitor, and partly because I was half afraid my brain had been a little upset by worry.

However, in time, the impression faded. Meanwhile I began to get on in the world, and after some three or four years my intense application was rewarded by riches. In seven or eight years I had become wealthy, and I began to think about settling myself in life. I had made the acquaintance of influential people in London, and more particularly of a certain baronet whom I had met in France while taking a holiday. Although I was in business I came of good family, and our acquaintance grew into something more. He had two or three daughters, to each of whom he was able to give a good marriage portion, and I became engaged to one of them. I don't know that there was much enthusiasm about our courtship. She was a very pleasant, good-looking girl, and although I can acquit myself of all mercenary motives in proposing to her, I cannot say that the highest motives were operative. I was as thousands of others are. I had got weary of loneliness; I wanted a home. I cast about me to see who amongst all the women I knew would best make me a wife. I selected this one, and perhaps the thought of her money may have been a trifle determinatory. I was not overmastered by a passion which I could not resist, nor was I coldly indifferent. If I had married her we should probably have lived a life of customary married comfort, and even of happiness; the same level, and perhaps slightly grey life which is lived by the ordinary English husband and wife. Things had gone so far that it was settled we were to be married in the spring of 1826, and I had begun to look out for a house, and make purchases in anticipation of house-keeping. In 1825 I had to go to Bristol. I shall never forget to the day of my death one morning in that city.

I had had my breakfast, and was going out to see the head of one of the largest firms in the city, with whom I had an appointment. I met him in the street, and I noted before he spoke that there was something the matter. I soon found out what it was. The panic of 1825 had begun; three great houses in London had failed, and brought him down. He was a ruined man, and so was I. I managed to stagger back to the hotel, and found letters there confirming all he had said. For some two or three days I was utterly prostrate, and could not summon sufficient strength to leave Bristol. One of the first things I did when I came to myself was to write to the baronet, telling him what had happened, that I was altogether penniless, and that in honour I felt bound to release his daughter from her engagement. I had a sympathising letter from him in return, saying that he was greatly afflicted at my misfortune, that his daughter was nearly broken-hearted, but that she had come to the conclusion that perhaps it would be best to accept my very kind offer. Much as she loved me, she felt that her health was far from strong, and although he had always meant to endow her generously on her marriage, her fortune alone would not enable her to procure those luxuries which, for her delicate constitution, alas! were necessaries. But the main reason with her was that she was sure that, with my independence, I should be unhappy if I felt that my wife's property was my support. His letter was long, but although much wrapped up, this was the gist of it. I went back to London, sold every stick I had, and tried to get a situation as clerk in some house, doing the business in which I had been engaged. I failed, for the distress was great, and I

was reduced nearly to my last sovereign when I determined to go down to Newcastle, and try the friend
there whom I had not seen since 1817. It was once
more winter, and, although I was so poor, I was obliged
to ride inside the coach again, for I was much troubled
with my ancient enemy—the weakness in the chest.
The incidents of my former visit I had nearly forgotten
till we came near to Eaton Socon, and then they returned to me.   But now it was a dull January day,
with a bitter thaw, and my fellow passengers were a
Lincolnshire squire, with his red-faced wife, who never
spoke a syllable to me, and by reason of their isolation
seemed to make the thaw all the more bitter, the fen
levels all the more dismally flat, and the sky all the
more leaden.   At last we came to Newcastle.   During
the latter part of the journey I was alone, my Lincolnshire squire and his lady having left me on the road.
It was about seven o'clock in the evening when we
arrived; a miserable night, with the snow just melting
under foot, and the town was wrapped in smoke and
fog.   I was so depressed that I hardly cared what
became of me, and when I stepped out of the coach
wished that I had been content to lie down and die in
London.   I could not put up at the coaching hotel, as
it was too expensive, but walked on to one which was
cheaper.   I almost lost my way, and had wandered
down a narrow street, which at every step became
more and more squalid, and at last ended opposite a
factory gate.   Hard by was a wretched marine store
shop, in the window of which were old iron, old tea-
pots, a few old Bibles, and other miscellaneous effects.
I stepped in to ask for directions to the Cross Keys.
Coming out, whom should I see crossing the road, as if

to meet me, but the very lady who rode with me in the coach to Eaton some nine years ago. There was no mistaking her. She seemed scarcely a day older. The face was as lovely and as inspired as ever. I was almost beside myself. I leaned against the railing of the shop, and the light from the window shone full on her. She came straight towards me on to the pavement; looked at me, and turned up the street. I followed her till we got to the end, determined not to lose sight of her; and we reached an open, broad thoroughfare. She stopped at a bookseller's, and went in. I was not more than two minutes after her; but when I entered she was not there. A shopman was at the counter, and I asked him whether a lady, my sister, had not just left the shop. No lady, he said, had been there for half-an-hour. I went back to the marine store shop. The footsteps were still there which I saw her make as she crossed. I knelt down, tracing them with my fingers to make sure I was not deceived by my eyes, and was more than ever confounded. At last I got to my inn, and went to bed a prey to the strangest thoughts. In the morning I was a little better. The stagnant blood had been stirred by the encounter of the night before, and though I was much agitated, and uncertain whether my brain was actually sound or not, I was sufficiently self-possessed and sensible to call upon my friend and explain my errand. He did what he could to help me, and I became his clerk in Newcastle. For a time I was completely broken, but gradually I began to recover my health and spirits a little. I had little or no responsibility, and nothing to absorb me after office hours. As a relief and an occupation, I tried to take up with a science, and chose geology.

On Sundays I used to make long rambling excursions, and for a while I was pleased with my new toy. But by degrees it became less and less interesting. I suppose I had no real love for it. Furthermore, I had no opportunities for expression. My sorrow had secluded me. I demanded more from those around me than I had any right to expect. As a rule, we all of us demand from the world more than we are justified in demanding, especially if we suffer; and because the world is not so constituted that it can respond to us as eagerly and as sympathetically as we respond to ourselves, we become morose. So it was with me. People were sorry for me; but I knew that my trouble did not disturb them deeply, that when they left me, their faces, which were forcibly contracted while in my presence, instantly expanded into their ordinary self-satisfaction, and that if I were to die I should be forgotten a week after the funeral. I therefore recoiled from men, and frequently, with criminal carelessness and prodigality, rejected many an offer of kindness, not because I did not need it, but because I wanted too much of it. My science, as I have said, was a failure. I cannot tell how it may be with some exceptionally heroic natures, but with me expression in some form or other, if the thing which should be expressed is to live, is an absolute necessity. I cannot read unless I have somebody to whom I can speak about my reading, and I lose almost all power of thinking if thought after thought remains with me. Expression is as indispensable to me as expiration of breath. Inspiration of the air is a necessity, but continued inspiration of air without expiration of the same is an impossibility. The geology was neglected, and at first I thought it was because it was geology, and I tried something else. For some months I fancied I had found a solace in chemistry. With my savings I purchased some apparatus, and began to be proficient. But the charm faded from this also; the apparatus was put aside, and the sight of it lying disused only made my dissatisfaction and melancholy the more profound. Amidst all my loneliness, I had never felt the least inclination to any baser pleasures, nor had I ever seen a woman for whom I felt even the most transient passion. My spectral friend—if spectre she was—dominated my existence, and seemed to prevent not only all licentiousness, but all pleasure, except of the most superficial kind, in other types of beauty. This need be no surprise to anybody. I have known cases in which the face of a singularly lovely woman, seen only for a few moments in the street, has haunted a man all through his life, and deeply affected it. In time I was advanced in my position as clerk, and would have married, but I had not the least inclination thereto. I did not believe in the actual reality of my vision, and had no hope of ever meeting in the flesh the apparition of the coach and the dingy street; I felt sure that there was some mistake, something wrong with me—the probabilities were all in favour of my being deceived; but still the dream possessed me, and every woman who for a moment appealed to me was tried by that standard and found wanting.

After some years had passed, during which I had scarcely been out of Newcastle, I took a holiday, and went up to London. It was about July. I was now a man on the wrong side of fifty, shy, reserved, with a reputation for constitutional melancholy, a shadowy creature, of whom nobody took much notice and who was noticed by nobody. While in London I went to see the pictures at the Academy. The place was thronged, and I was tired; I just looked about me, and was on the point of coming out wearied, when in a side room where there were crayon drawings, I caught sight of one of a face. I was amazed beyond measure. It was the face which had been my companion for so many years. There could be no mistake about it; even the necker-chief was tied as I remembered it so well, the very counterpart of the treasure I still preserved so sacredly at home. I was almost overcome with a faintness, with a creeping sensation all over the head, as if something were giving way, and with a shock of giddiness. I went and got a catalogue, found out the name of the artist, and saw that the picture had merely the name of 'Stella' affixed to it. It might be a portrait, or it might not. After gazing myself almost blind at it, I went out and instantly posted to the artist's house. He was at home. He seemed a poor man, and was evidently surprised at any inquiry after his picture so late in the season. I asked him who sat for it. 'Nobody,' he said; 'it was a mere fancy sketch. There might be a reminiscence in it of a girl I knew in France years ago; but she is long since dead, and I don't think that anybody who knew her would recognise a likeness in it. In fact, I am sure they would not.' The price of the drawing was not much, although it was a good deal for me. I said instantly I would have it, and managed to get the money together by scraping up all my savings out of the savings bank. That is the very picture which you now see before you. I do not pretend to explain every-thing which I have told you. I have long since given up the attempt, and I suppose it must be said that I have suffered from some passing disorder of the brain, although that theory is not sound at all points, and there are circumstances inconsistent with it."

The next morning my friend went to his office, after an early breakfast. His hours were long, and I was obliged to leave Newcastle before his return. So I bade him good-bye before he left home. I never saw him again. Two years afterwards I was shocked to see an announcement in the *Times* of his death. Knowing his lonely way of life, I went down to Newcastle to gather what I could about his illness and last moments. He had caught cold, and died of congestion of the lungs. His landlady said that he had made a will, and that what little property had remained after paying his funeral expenses had been made over to a hospital. I was anxious to know where the picture was. She could not tell me. It had disappeared just before his death, and nobody knew what had become of it.

THE END.